Spirit

OR

The Princess of Bois Dormant

GWYNETH JONES

Spirit © 2008 Gwyneth Jones
All rights reserved

First published in Great Britain in 2008 by Gollancz
An imprint of the Orion Publishing Group
Orion House, 5 Upper St Martin's Lane, London WC2H 9EA
An Hachette Livre UK Company

A CIP catalogue record for this book is available
from the British Library

ISBN 978 0 575 07472 9 (Cased)
ISBN 978 0 575 07473 6 (Trade Paperback)

1 3 5 7 9 10 8 6 4 2

Typeset by Input Data Systems Ltd,
Bridgwater, Somerset

Printed in Great Britain by
CPI Mackays, Chatham ME5 8TD

The Orion Publishing Group's policy is to use papers that are
natural, renewable and recyclable products and made
from wood grown in sustainable forests. The logging and
manufacturing processes are expected to conform to the
environmental regulations of the country of origin.

www.orionbooks.co.uk

for Richard Gwilliam
a prince among digerati

PART ONE

I

The tent held a camp bed, with a single olive blanket folded on it. Daylight streamed through clear bands in the grey-green walls; the slick floor bore the imprint of muddy, booted feet. A stack of unopened camp-furniture packs stood to one side, bearing General Yu's indigo seal. A small girl, ten or eleven years old, sat on the bed where the soldiers had left her, looking around her vaguely; listening to the tramp and bustle of a great military camp. Through the clear bands she could glimpse rocky slopes and distant crags that seemed familiar in a general way, but she didn't know where she was.

The tent door was opened, and a troop of different soldiers appeared. They stood to attention as a woman with stars on the shoulders of her uniform came in. This was Lady Nef, the wife of the General: someone of considerable rank in her own right. The captive, obeying instinct, quickly got down, knelt on the floor and pressed her forehead to the groundsheet. Lady Nef was a tall woman, dark-haired and still beautiful in middle age. She knelt and raised the girl up, so that she could see her face.

The woman and the child looked at each other.

'Your name is Gwibiwr?'

'It is Gwibiwr. But I am called Bibi.'

'I offer you a choice,' said Lady Nef, in Bibi's own language. 'You may join my husband's household, and become his concubine. That's the way of the world, we can't fight it. You will be kindly treated, as long as you are still a child. After that, it's a competitive life, but a decent career for you, with the opportunity of gaining status. If you bear my husband a child, especially a child with desirable traits, even better.'

Lady Nef paused for a response. She was not sure if the girl was taking in anything that was said to her.

'Or you may join my household. You will become a servant, and always remain so. The work will be hard, but I promise you neither my husband nor any other man will touch you.'

'I will be your servant,' said Bibi.

II

The rebels had used the White Rock caves as a refuge from time immemorial, the core families sometimes retreating there for decades to sit out a prolonged police action. They believed they were invincible in their mountain fastness. They were not: it was just that digging them out had never been worth the trouble, the loss of life; the inevitable human rights violations. Then one day, in the tumultuous years of the Young Emperor, General Yu arrived. He offered surrender terms. The rebels, who had lost all sight of the bigger picture, proudly refused: so the General moved in and destroyed them, by the book. His soldiers used no bombing raids and only commensurate weaponry. They relied on discipline, superior intelligence and an overwhelming force of numbers. Resistance burned fiercely as a straw fire, but in a few weeks it was all over. The caves were penetrated, and almost every man, woman and child was either killed in action or put to death.

The little girl, Gwibiwr, was believed to have been the daughter of one of the chieftains. She'd survived because she'd been found hiding in a tunnel, still alive, after the ceasefire order. General Yu's soldiers had had no qualms about the massacre. Far from home, faced with the bewildering, confident ferocity of these savages, they'd become convinced that the rebels had a terrible secret weapon, and deserved no mercy. But they'd been shocked at themselves afterwards, and incapable of killing a child in cold blood. Perhaps their superiors felt the same – and so a life was spared.

Lady Nef's servants had reproduced, as best they could, in the south-west quadrant of the camp, the same order and calm that the Lady expected at home. The bare-earth alleys and squares were swept and raked. The household troops, barracked separately from the domestic staff now that the action was over, had a spruce parade ground for their daily drill; the admin tents were hives of brisk activity.

Corralled satellite dishes shone, their great silver faces turned up to the sky; the sleek, mettlesome armoured cars were groomed and exercised every morning.

The servants' own quarters were set on three sides of a military-issue *potager*, a flourishing vegetable garden that had been brought to the mountains dehydrated and flat-packed, and would leave the same way. The fourth side was a passage-tent, flanked by fish tanks and poultry houses, leading to Lady Nef's own domain. The little girl, Gwibiwr, was brought to this small world, where she was given a place to sleep, a quilt and a headrest; two uniforms, underclothes and shoes. She cried when they took her battered and bloodstained native clothes away from her, but otherwise showed no marked signs of distress.

The servants had been told to give her a chance to settle in, and then find her some light duties. In effect this meant that she was left completely alone. After a few days the team leader of the junior domestics, Ogul Merdov, realised that the little girl was neither eating nor sleeping. At this point Gwibiwr was offered trauma removal, which she refused, in emphatic dumb-show.

No one knew what to do. None of the servants spoke the child's language, and though she seemed to understand English she didn't speak. They offered her the veil, because the rebels had been Trad-itionalists (ironically, this was also the General's own party). She showed no interest. Soon she stopped responding to anything. She lay curled on her mat, dark eyes wide open and seeming to grow larger by the hour, eating away at her small, pale face. During the day she whimpered a little. At night she'd cry out, loudly and painfully, at random intervals, as if somebody was hitting her. It got everyone down. On the seventh day Rohan Aswad, a sergeant from Orange Company, one of the soldiers who'd brought Bibi out of the caves, remembered the orphan and came to see what had happened to her. He was horrified to find the child sunk in a coma, and more than half-dead.

'You must send for Lady Nef,' he told Ogul.

Ogul was amazed. 'For *the Lady*? For this native? But why?'

'Because she's the only person who can call a lost soul back.'

The caves were squalid, warm and crowded. There were too many children; their noise got on top of Bibi and stopped her from thinking. Whenever she could she escaped up the choke-tunnel, a ventilation shaft that a child could use as a secret passage. She was in the mouth of the shaft, clinging like a bat, looking out on a vista of crag and scree and rock. The morning sun bathed her bare face, and flashed on the silvery granite that gave the refuge its name. To her left and below she had a perfect view of the Ledge and the teenage boy on look-out, hugging his rifle. He didn't know she was there, which gave Bibi great satisfaction. The older boys thought they were so wonderful, just because they had guns—

She had no sense of danger, although she knew there was trouble going on. The men would deal with it. She saw a handful of dots high in the sky, coming up the Rift, and thought it was the swifts. It was a moment she waited for every year: always afraid that her shrilling, dashing, daredevil friends wouldn't return to brighten this prison. 'Oh, Grandpapa,' she whispered, joy bursting through every vein. Her grandfather, who had only one arm and was nearly blind, loved the swifts too. 'The swifts! They're back!'

She saw the boy below scramble to his feet. His jaw fell slack, as if he was struggling to believe something forbidden by nature.

Bibi remembered nothing between. It was as if she scrabbled and fell down the choke-tunnel straight into the last hour: when the men were back, although not Bibi's father, and the fighting was in the caves. She lay curled up, a burning tremor that never reached her outer flesh running through her, thrown again and again from that moment of light to the sight of her mother, niqab askew, lying in a trail of blood; to the deafening gunfire and her little brother's screams. She could not move; time didn't pass. She was terrified that she was losing her mind, but unable to save herself.

Someone brought a light. Faces swam dimly between her and the dreadful images, something wrong with one of them. Maybe it was a dead person, come to fetch her to hell. She heard voices, distantly.

'We can't rescue her from the mental injury that will ruin her young life, if not drive her insane,' said one of them. 'We can tear her screaming from her dead mother, we can force her to watch as her grandfather, her brothers, sisters, die in a welter of blood, but we can't violate her rights—'

'Is that what happened?'

'Of course. I imagine she is watching the replay now.'

'War is ugly: he does his best,' murmured the second speaker, a voice Bibi felt she recognised. 'Clear the room. Francois, you too.'

Alone with the General's wife, Bibi struggled respectfully to sit up, frightened by how weak and dazed she felt. She was dying, and what if she died, and still it didn't stop——?

'You have refused trauma treatment, now why is that?'

'If I take that medicine I'll go to hell.'

'You don't care about that,' said Lady Nef. 'Tell the truth.'

Bibi looked into the Lady's eyes, impressed. The truth was that she was frightened to go to hell, but she'd often been told she'd end up there. Love and grief, loyalty and honour were much stronger bonds.

'I *can't*,' she whispered. 'I can't leave them. They would be all alone.'

'I see.' Lady Nef was silent for a moment. 'You love your family?'

'Yes.'

'Do you want them to live in your mind the way they are now? To hold them imprisoned in horror? You know that things of the mind are real.'

This was technically heresy, but Bibi's people believed it.

'No! I don't want them to suffer.'

'Well then. Will you let us drain the poison of those memories?'

The child shook her head. The dark eyes that were eating her face grew even larger. Perhaps she was hoping for the decision to be taken out of her hands, but she would not consent. Lady Nef saw the creature struggling to be born, rising from the obdurate matrix of suffering, and was moved by a sense of kinship.

'Then you will have to take the hard way out of the place you are in,' she said. 'You must forbid the hateful images to possess you. You'll have to take control of your own mind, Bibi. We all have the ability to do that, without any outside aid, but few have the need or the courage to achieve the task. One must have a compelling reason.' The General's wife took the little girl's hands. 'Believe me, this is the greatest secret I know. Rule your own mind, and you may rule the world. Far more important, *you will be happy*, no matter what comes. And happiness is all that matters, in the end.'

Lady Nef's words were simple, but they went straight to Bibi's heart. The grip of the Lady's hands seemed to be drawing her out of a black, fanged pit that had almost swallowed her. In her light-headed state she thought something genuinely supernatural was happening: a belief that would never quite leave her. Later, when she heard that Lady Nef was destined to become one of the Emperor's immortals, she was not surprised.

The General's wife had someone bring a cup of warm milk, which

Bibi drank; then she fell asleep. The next morning she asked for the clothes that had been taken from her. Unfortunately they'd been destroyed, but the girl was not dismayed by this news. She was seen searching around the vegetable garden (she was not allowed to leave the servants' square), making a small collection of pebbles. Gwibiwr named these fragments of her native land after the family members she had lost, dug a little grave and buried them lovingly.

She had taken Lady Nef's advice to heart. She would rule herself.

III

When the time came for them all to return to the Great House in Kirgiziya, her fellow servants feared for Bibi. How would the little savage cope with that journey, or with the final loss of her homeland? But the girl showed no regrets, and accepted the suborbital journey as if she'd always travelled that way. She was installed in the girls' dorm, Juniper Square.

One afternoon Col Ben Phu and Drez Doyle – two private soldiers from Orange Company who'd befriended her in Cymru along with Sergeant Aswad – arrived. Bibi was glad to see them. The servants who'd been together on campaign had been dispersed. The only familiar face in Juniper was Ogul Merdov, proud possessor of a family name (although she had no actual family living), and she had no time for the 'savage'. Col and Drez took Bibi off with them, ignoring the protests of Serenity, the Han woman who was warden of the girls' dorm: through squares and gardens, over bridges, past many handsome buildings to a guardhouse in the perimeter wall. Sergeant Aswad looked the other way while they smuggled her up to the walkway.

The ancient *di* underfoot glowed indigo and stirred with movement, as if the stone were made of millions of little living snakes. A glittering disturbance in the air (which Bibi had thought was a natural feature of the sky in Kirgiziya) came down to meet the battlements. She realised for the first time that the Great House was enclosed: she was living inside a huge transparent tent. Col lifted the little girl by the armpits and sat her on the parapet. She wiped a hand across the shimmer, like someone clearing condensation from a windowpane. 'That's a *boundary*,' she said. 'That stuff. It's made of microbes or something, and it's tech the Aleutians gave us, it's around every city too. It doesn't seem like much, but it's going to keep you *indoors*, for ever. Now look. See what's outside your world.'

Bibi saw the golden-green plain, the silver streams, the birchwoods, the distant ragged line of rust-red mountains. Col kept a tight hold, her muscular arm a band of warm steel across Bibi's chest, and pointed around.

'That's our market town, where we spend our pay. It's grey-area, you'll never go there. The white flame is the Plasma Plant, you can see it in daylight because it's hot as a star. Far away over that way, where you can't see it, is Baykonur in Khazakh. That's where you came in. It's where the suborbitals take off, and you can get the shuttle to the Elevator.'

'Keep hold of her,' warned Drez. 'She might be desperate.'

Bibi nodded, wondering if there would be swifts here.

The brief window closed by itself. Drez took her from Col and set her on the pavement again. The soldiers glanced to and fro. They weren't afraid of the ever-present surveillance. The Great House AI was forbearing: it wouldn't turn you in for nothing much. But sentries could be officious.

'Now listen,' said Col. 'Orange Company's been assigned to the Lady's service. The old man wants to keep us lot close to his chest, on account of services rendered: that's a good thing for you, because we're your friends.'

'You'll *never* get out,' said Drez, earnestly. 'That's what you got to understand, Bibi. Say you got out, where are you going to go? The town belongs to the Great House. You'd just be brought back, and you'd be in dead trouble.'

'Don't *ever, ever* try it,' growled Col. 'Promise us. No matter how bad things get. We'll be looking out for you, Drez, me an' the Sarge. If someone's picking on you, you come to us. We'll sort them out.'

'Don't fight it, kid,' insisted Drez. 'You were born free, but you're going to live inside, you'll never be free again. *Believe* that.'

Col was a muscular, sturdy, sallow-skinned woman with a cropped skull and a lot of tattoos. Drez Doyle had grey eyes, very bright in his dark face, darker freckles just visible across his cheeks and nose, and a topknot of reddish-black ringlets, which only appeared on feast-days: on duty he kept them stuck down under a little round skullcap. They always looked cheerful and confident: Col especially had a swagger that pleased Bibi. 'The Sarge' was a different character; he had a long chin, solemn eyes, a hooked nose: he could have been one of Bibi's uncles.

Bibi's heart still held, sealed off and almost harmless, the poison memories. She'd first seen these three faces distorted in battle. Drez and Col and Sergeant Aswad had been among the soldiers who had killed her mother, her sisters, her little brother, her grandfather. It was Col Ben Phu who had dragged her from the choke-tunnel. Yet they were now her best friends, and truly wished her well. She accepted the paradox with a child's resignation.

'It's all right. I promise I won't try to escape.'

'That's a good girl' said Drez.

The soldiers hugged her, their arms hard and greasy, their warm skin smelling of sweat and anise, and took her back to the guardroom – where Sergeant Aswad gravely offered her a sweet, and told her that she didn't have to be a servant. When she was old enough, she should apply to be a soldier.

It was close to two years before Bibi saw Lady Nef again, in person. It was the fifth month, Yang Calendar; or Maytime, as Bibi the child would have known it. The House was preparing for Lady Nef's yearly exodus to the mountains, and for the Summer Lists, the prelude to that great adventure. Even Juniper Square had been rife with speculation and competition. On the day of the Lists all juniors who were not eligible were released, after schoolroom and drill, for a half-holiday. Bibi went with her friends to the water garden on East Avenue, where they'd have a good chance of seeing the Family go by. They'd just been issued with their summer uniforms, which made a delicious change because the weather was already very warm.

The youngest children ran around chasing the doves, between huge glazed pots of pomegranate and peach in bloom. Bibi was with some older girls from Juniper, clustered along the rim of one of the water basins. Team-leader Ogul had taken off her slippers and was bathing her bare feet. Bibi's friends, Honesty and Nightingale, the Han Chinese who slept on either side of her, had brought their work with them. The Han were never idle. Honesty had her embroidery; Nightingale, a promising student, had extra coding homework on a tablet. Bibi lay on her stomach and stared into the water, where the stems of the pink lotus flowers took on unlikely angles.

'You'll never be eligible, Bibi,' said Honesty. 'Someone with your background couldn't get the security clearance. That's very sad.'

Bibi didn't think so. She'd liked *seeing* the mountains, when Col and Drez had smuggled her up to the top of the Wall. She had a sense, deeper than memory, that all proper horizons should have that ragged trim, like a brushstroke seeping upward into the pale fibre of the sky. But she never wanted to be among them again.

'I don't mind.' She leaned down, perilously, to feel the cool breath of the water on her face. 'I like the heat. It makes coolness sweeter.'

'What are you doing? You're going to fall in, you baby.'

'No I'm not ... I'm looking for tadpoles.'

Honesty bit her thread, and selected another shade of peach for the fruit she was stitching. 'Maybe she wants to eat them. She's such a savage.'

'Town people eat grasshoppers,' said Nightingale. 'Cook's assistant Chu told me. You can buy strings of them, fried. So why not tadpoles?'

Nobody answered her, because the Family had been spotted. The children abandoned their games of chase mid-flight; the teenagers stood to attention. Lady Nef, familiar to them as a distant figure in uniform on the Assembly Hall screens, was far more beautiful and awe-inspiring in the flesh. In a green and white gown over green trousers, she strolled down the central walk, talking to her secretary, Francois the Aleutian (never far from her side), surrounded by her son, her daughters, her two sons-in-law, her two brothers-in-law and General Yu's middle-aged sisters, the formidable Ladies Yu. Young hands swept up in salute, in a complex wave that rippled through the flowery grove. A steward, hurrying ahead of the Family, darted about correcting the over-enthusiastic, who'd fallen to their knees and started banging their heads on the ground.

'Up! Up! No bottoms in the air! Behave naturally!'

Bibi was not one of those offenders – but she was transfixed. She had suddenly remembered the stark military tent, the horror from which she'd been rescued. The pit opened again in all its fanged despair, and the sunlight and flowers, the affection of her friends, seemed like ropes of liquid gold flowing from the Lady's hands, drawing her up into safety. In that moment, she fully realised, for the first time, what she owed her mistress. Reverence and gratitude pierced her through—

I live only to serve you, she vowed, in her passionate heart.

The steward smacked her on the back of the head. 'SALUTE, stupid girl! "Behave naturally" does not mean showing the Family no respect!'

At the next New Year Honours Bibi was promoted to Grade Seven with a Commendation, and told she could prepare for her career assessment.

She was still a minor apprentice in the myriad tasks of the Household, but it was an important step up. The service squares of the Great House were full of people who would reach Grade Seven just before they retired; or who would never have a chance of attaining that first rung on the ladder of success.

Inevitably, Honesty told her she had probably reached her plateau.

After Evening Dance she was given the honour of taking Juniper Square's treasures, the silver-chased Salt-Horn and the brass Pepper Mill, to the scullery to be replenished. She took her time on the return, not from laziness but from a sense of ceremony. It was February, by her old calendar. Above the Perimeter Walkway, where the soldiers had once taken her, the boundary of the House's microclimate met the freezing air in a cascade of heat-exchange diamonds. Along the corridors of Juniper, landscape screens showed the gold-green plain lost in snow; the Plasma Plant flaring blue in frosty night; a cluster of tiny stars that marked the grey-area town. *There's the world I will never see*, thought Bibi, as she passed. *I shall live and die within these walls, and why not?*

The Dining Hall was empty and already chill: Autonomous Systems had shifted the warmth elsewhere. She carried the Salt and Pepper to the lacquered stand under the Imperial Shrine, set down the Peacock Tray and reverently replaced the Salt – a wild-cattle horn in a silver cradle, hundreds of years old – on its proper shelf. The Pepper Mill had been made in Istanbul, before the Aleutian Invasion; it had a band of acanthus leaves chased around its fat belly. Bibi never thought about her childhood, but at moments like this perhaps she felt a link with the White Rock, a world left behind by time. The Great House was old, too. It had stood, here in Kirgiziya, almost as long as Bibi's people had been rebels. She set the treasures down, each exactly on its accustomed spot, stood back and bowed three times to the cartouche that held a portrait of the First Emperor: forever young, forever beautiful. Below Li Xifeng, in diptych, were portraits of the shadowy Second Emperor, who had never attained immortality; and of the Third Emperor, whose present status was unclear. Maybe he'd retired, maybe he'd abdicated.

The World State had been a Republic since the Aleutians left, but veneration of the Emperors was not a crime: it was encouraged. They represented the proud past. Followers of the 'Young Emperor', the leader Lady Nef and General Yu served, were on more delicate ground. The Young Emperor's campaigns were making the tattered unity of the World State a fact rather than a pious fiction – but if the Republican

Government accepted him as Head of State (as it seemed they might), then what about the Third Emperor? Where did *he* fit in, if the Empire was restored? This was a question that worried Bibi sometimes, when she heard the older servants gossiping. She didn't want to think that Lady Nef was *disloyal*, and besides, she knew what happens to rebels – always, in the end.

Below the portraits was a row of eight much smaller tablets, inscribed in scarlet. One day, one of those names might be Lady Nef's, and then she'd live for ever. Some people in the Great House 'didn't believe in' Imperial Immortality – a scepticism Bibi found puzzling. She'd been told, when she arrived here, that Lady Nef was a Senior. The lady she'd taken to be about thirty-five years old, in Cymru, was closer to a hundred and forty. She had been a young woman when the Aleutians left. If *that* sort of thing was possible (and nobody seemed to doubt it), actual immortality didn't sound like much of a stretch to the child of White Rock.

The disbelievers said that the rank was simply a trap. Immortals-designate could hold no public or private office: Lady Nef had been sidelined, prevented from rising, by jealousy and spite. She should be on Speranza, holding high office in the Hegemony, instead of trailing around after the Young Emperor. And if she was out there she'd be looking after the interests of the Blue Planet (as Earth was known in the Diaspora) – instead of letting aliens run the show, the way the Republicans did.

Others said that Lady Nef's marriage had been her big mistake. Married for love, and disappointed, she stuck by her handsome, phil-andering soldier out of the kindness of her heart, forever rescuing him from his mediocre plots. It was a shame.

Buonarotti, Speranza, Blue Planet, 'the Hegemony' were empty words to Bibi, but she felt that everyone was wrong. *Immortal-designate* was exactly the rank her mistress should hold, and the life she'd chosen, on campaign and in Kirgiz, was the best life possible. Great souls don't lust for power. They serve and guide, they are not the slaves of ambition.

'Those others don't *know*,' murmured Bibi. 'But I do.'

In the spring the General came to visit, after a busy winter season politicking in the city. He was feeling slighted because Lady Nef had declined to play his hostess in Baykonur, but their relationship remained on its usual calm and affectionate terms. He filled his wing of the Great

House with friends and useful contacts – all of them either men, or else Reformers of the masculine or the undecided gender. Wives were not invited; the few female servants in the party were elderly. His needs were accommodated, but he never brought women to Kirgiz: it was a point of honour.

There were hunting expeditions, there were banquets. There were concerts, archery meets, a soccer tournament. The General declared that he would dine at each of the Squares in turn, as a compliment to his wife's household – which caused a flurry of excitement. A Topaz Square chef was hospitalised, vomiting blood, from pure anxiety. The Cypress vs Juniper tournament match was abandoned after a general fight broke out over a slighting remark about a *sauce glacé* . . . Only Lady Nef and her secretary had any inkling of what was behind this tour, and stood ready to intervene.

General Yu had never once asked after the survivor of White Rock, or shown a hint of interest in her progress. But he could be stubborn, and he could be devious when he felt he'd been outmanoeuvred. Bibi was about thirteen years old: her body had begun to change. Since this was a liberal household, without a menstrual hormone mix in the air, she would not 'see blood' – but by many standards she was a nubile young woman.

On the night that the General and his friends honoured Juniper Square the juniors were sent to bed early, with strict instructions to stay out of sight. Bibi was woken very late in the evening by the warden of the girls' dorm, the snappish Han woman inappropriately named Serenity.

'You're to get dressed and go to the Dining Hall.'

'But why? I thought we were supposed to stay in our dorms.'

'How should I know? I was told I was going to get reinforcements, knowing what you girls are like. Instead I have two soldiers from the General at my gates, asking for *you* in particular. Get dressed quickly. You'd better go and see what he wants.'

'I don't want to go.'

'It's not for me to refuse him,' snapped Serenity. 'This is what comes of being a foreigner. You must have brought it on yourself. Hurry up.'

When Bibi reached the Hall the General was alone. He dismissed her escort and suggested that she join him for a nightcap, a cup of warm wine for a chilly spring evening. His intentions could not have been more plain. Bibi had never seen the General in the flesh before. She kept her eyes lowered, and hardly saw him now: a glimpse of a broad chest, thick curling hair and beard, light-coloured little eyes glinting cheerily from a craggy face. She'd expected him to be better looking, but she didn't care. She was terrified.

'No thank you, please, sir. I don't drink wine.'

'Come and sit by me, in any case.'

Bibi didn't have the slightest right to refuse him. She didn't have a weapon either. She scanned the tablecloth for a knife, but then had a better idea. Much better. One can't hope to stab a General and get away with it.

'Yes, sir, I'm coming.'

She walked carefully, with timid glances and small steps, to one of the Dining Room's carved pillars. She'd almost reached it when General Yu burst out laughing and leapt to his feet. He pounced like a tiger, but Bibi was faster. She shot up into the polished foliage, leaving one of her slippers and a fragment of trouser hem in his grip.

'You little monkey!' roared the General. 'Do you think I can't climb!'

Bibi had swarmed up to the cross-beams. It was dark up there, and she was afraid of spiders. In the corners of the great room the roof timbers came down like mighty basket-weave. If she could squeeze between them into the air cavity, he wouldn't be able to follow. Would he? She closed her eyes, and prayed for the House AI to *do something*, give the General an electric shock, save her, somehow—

The double doors of the Hall opened. A slim figure entered, his curious face – glimmering, pale-skinned, dark at the centre – alight with amusement.

'General!' exclaimed the Aleutian. 'Are you admiring our carvings?'

'They're very fine,' growled the General, backing off from the pillar.

'But we can't have this!' Francois advanced, and slipped his arm into the crook of General Yu's handsomely clad elbow. 'You're all alone. Come along to my humble abode, I have some of your friends there, wondering where you are—'

Bibi spent the night on her roof-beam. She crawled down at dawn, frozen stiff and covered with dust. Of course everyone knew what had happened. Some of her fellow servants believed she'd preserved her virtue by her antics (and thought this was hilarious). Most thought she couldn't have done – the General always got his way. Nobody had much sympathy.

'You could take the veil,' suggested Ogul. 'It isn't forbidden in Kirgiz, it just means you can't ever be a citizen. But with you, noble born, well—'

Less forthright than Honesty, who would have explained exactly *why* Bibi needn't worry, the team leader shook her head with a smile of syrupy pity. She laid the dark folds of her suggestion on Bibi's mat and crept away, with dainty, girlish steps.

Bibi drew up her knees to her chin, and brooded.

The term 'noble born' grated. It was what the other girls called her when they really wanted to be annoying. *The chieftain's daughter*, that was another: favoured by people like Ogul, who hated Bibi for no reason … Bibi had been brought up five hundred years in the past, but she'd never been stupid and she was no longer ignorant. She knew that she'd been karyotyped, at White Rock, when they let her live. She didn't remember anything about it, but she'd seen the results on her personal record. She owed her life not only to mercy, but to an accident of the genes. Bibi was rather pretty for her caste, a dangerous fate; worse still, she was a high-functioning natural XX. She could be expected to conceive and bear children without intervention. That wasn't why the General wanted her: he was just a habitual girl-chaser. But it was surely why he'd *remembered* her. It was also, Bibi reasoned, without rancour, probably why she'd been offered an alternative to concubinage by the General's principal wife. Even Lady Nef was only human.

The veil would not protect her honour. On the contrary, it would make her *more* vulnerable, *more* of an outsider, in this modern, liberal Traditionalist household, where nobody else covered up.

She decided she'd better watch out for Ogul.

'I must not be afraid,' she muttered. 'I must rule myself.'

It was Evening Dance time. Serenity would soon be along to shoo her out of the dorm. But that was all right, as she had few choices to ponder. The next day she enrolled herself for army cadet class.

Francois the Aleutian took a close interest in the Great House cadets. He often visited them, in Cypress Drill-Hall, the only hall in the Great House adapted for immersion gaming – a vice the cadets were obliged to practise in preparation for their field training. When Francois arrived, however, everything digital had to be cut off. Aleutians despised 'non-living' technology. Sometimes he took them for drill, and he was a *demon*. Other times he'd dismiss their teacher, a retired Khazakh sergeant major called Sohrab Sepuldevry, and lecture them on the great battles.

The cadets sat in rows on the slick floor, eyes front. Most of them were boys. There were plenty of female private soldiers, like Col Ben Phu, recruited from the dregs of society, but few respectable girls chose a career in the armed forces. The Aleutian paced up and down, in his favourite costume, tailored for a bygone age of the Earth: a grey cutaway coat, a white shirt with a soft neckcloth, pale brown pantaloons, sleek and flexible as skin. His clawed, thick-knuckled Aleutian hands were clasped in the small of his back; his lumpy hip-joints rolled, giving him a gait somewhere between the sway of a dancing girl and a duck's waddle.

Some cadets were terrified of the alien. Others thought Francois was a joke. They copied his mannerisms, and laughed 'behind his back'. Bibi thought both parties were idiots. The important thing was that the Aleutian was Lady Nef's eyes and ears – *obviously*.

'Now then. Cast your minds back to the Gender Wars.'

Francois had a hole lined with stiff dark hairs where his nose should be, and a cleft lip, but he had the phenomenal Aleutian talent for languages (they were either like that, or they didn't speak at all). He spoke Khazakh with the Khazakhs, Kyrgyz with the Kyrgyz, Russian with the Rus, Common Tongue with the favoured few under his tuition, Putonghua and English with everyone – and Ancient French when he wanted to confuse people (at least, he said it was Ancient French). But you could not be completely sure, with an Aleutian. They had strange powers. He could be lecturing them by telepathy, and only *pretending* to speak. The teenagers stared, trying to keep their minds perfectly blank—

'Let us consider the last battle of all, the small affair that turned out to be the *coup de grâce* ... Here are our enemies, securing their position, having conceded a ceasefire. Communications lost – satellites were ephemera in those wars, as you'll recall, always getting shot down by the rail guns. All they're thinking of is this chance to lick their wounds and fight another day. When *suddenly*, without warning—' The Aleutian turned to admire the coloured arrows, contour lines and cross-hatching proliferating across the smartboard. He wasn't fanatical about his anti-tech rules. He spun around, nosehole flaring: 'Fate throws a knife at you, with deadly aim. How are you going to catch it, children?'

The cadets had no idea what Francois was talking about. The Gender Wars had decided the fate of Old Earth and created the world they lived in, but he might as well have asked them to visualise the War of the Spanish Succession. He prowled, staring into stolid faces, and pounced on the girl with the passionate eyes, the only pupil for whom his stories were real.

'Ah, Bibi! I perceive that you have something to say. Forget your natural loyalties, *you* are the Reformer General. Or Speaker for the Tactical Committee, since they eschewed hierarchical rank at that time. *Bon, dis-moi?*'

'By the blade, sir. I would catch General Connelly's knife by the blade.'

'Hm! That is in fact what happened: the Reformers stood and fought, and died to a person. The purpose of the exercise, however, is to suggest a *better* course of action. Explain yourself. Please stand up.'

Bibi stood, trembling, hot colour risen in her face. 'When fate throws a deadly knife at you, sometimes you deserve it,' she explained. 'The way my people in Cymru deserved it. You must c-correct your ideas or ... or if it's too late you must not flinch from the consequence. If you don't deserve it, you still shouldn't flinch. A terrible misfortune that you don't deserve is tragic, and we ought to embrace tragedy.'

'Why?'

'F-for honour? Because tragedy is beautiful?'

'Self preserve me ever from having the *honour* to serve in your army, child. I asked you to tell me what the Reformers *should* have done. Was there a means of retreat? How about a dignified surrender?'

'B-but they knew they were done for, sir. Hardly anyone survived being taken prisoner by the Traditionalists, we didn't believe in—'

'Are you *arguing* with me? Your ancestry, Bibi, is Pakistani and Welsh. On both counts you are thin-skinned, hot-tempered, oversensitive and absurdly intolerant of any slight. If you really want to be a soldier you had better learn to control those traits.'

'Yes, sir.'

'You may sit down.'

Until this incident Bibi had felt safe. She didn't *want* to join the army, but she'd put herself out of the General's reach. After the Aleutian's cruel comments she was frightened again. What she'd said was simply true, but that only made things worse. How can you correct your errors if you don't know what you did wrong?

'It'll be all right,' said Nightingale, whose talent for cryptography made her an exception to the rule about female cadet entry. At her career assessment she'd been advised to prepare for military college. 'He picks on people when he likes them. I've noticed that.'

But when the end-of-term Lists went up, Bibi's fears were confirmed. Against her name she saw the dreaded words *recommended for reappraisal.*

The Young Emperor's conquests had come to a halt for a while, and Orange Company was still serving Lady Nef. Bibi turned to her friends in the guardroom. Col and Drez hadn't wanted her to join the army, but they'd known it was for the best, after the General Yu incident. The old man wouldn't rape a soldier, but he was a persistent bugger once he'd noticed a housemaid. And Bibi wasn't the kind to take it lying down, so to speak.

'Talk to him,' suggested Drez. 'He's all right, for an alien. Ask him how you can improve. You ask for help, he has to help. It's in the book.'

'Nah, you don't want to do that,' advised Col. 'You're not supposed to know *he's* made the decision, are you? An' don't ask Sepuldevry either. Forget the book, it's bad luck thinking like that. Don't attract attention, that was your wrong move. Keep your head down, score average at everything for a bit.'

'I didn't attract attention. He *noticed* me, I don't know why. I can't talk to him. I'd say the wrong things again, I know I would.'

Bibi was afraid of the Aleutian. He could read minds.

Both soldiers looked gloomy.

'They *don't* forget,' mused Drez, with uneasy respect. 'Not the noseless. They can pull up things that happened hundreds of years ago.'

The Aleutians had made First Contact, and gone on to rule most of Earth for three hundred years. Since their Departure, and the development of the Buonarotti Device, there'd been other, peaceable alien visitors. But the noseless, ironically, were the ones who'd earned a kind of affection, a place in human folklore. Col scowled at him. 'Yeah, but their heads get so stuffed they lose half the files for what they did yesterday. Don't f— don't worry the kid.'

Bibi decided to write Francois a letter. She composed her plea with care, copied it out on calligraphy paper in snatched moments of privacy, and kept it inside her tunic until she had a chance to deliver it.

Dear Sir ... Dear Mr Francois the Aleutian ... Your Excellency ...

She had settled on 'Dear Sir'.

From my earliest childhood I have been deeply interested in the art of war.

Conscious of the great debt I owe, it is my dearest wish to serve my Benefactors courageously on the field of battle, as a private soldier. If I should be judged unfit for that proud duty, then I would love to exercise my mind in a technical or clerical corps . . .

A few days before the new term began, she was sent to the Men's Side with a housekeeping trolley. This wouldn't have happened before the roof-beam incident, but now it didn't matter what she said: in Serenity's eyes, she'd become one of those young women – still under the Lady Nef's protection – who could be sent into the danger zone; who tolerated or welcomed male advances. Bibi had found out the Aleutian's address. She added it to the trolley's itinerary and followed it to Porphyry, one of the Greater Squares immediately flanking the Inner House. His door, in a hallway clad in magnificent purple-veined natural stone, opened to the trolley's *ping*, which proved the secretary was not around. It trundled over the threshold. Bibi was scared, but at any moment a gentleman might come by and see her here alone: she steeled herself and darted after.

The light was dim. The trolley bustled about, deeper within. There were no doors leading off the entrance hall, only doorways. She saw the furnishings of a study, took the plunge – and hit an invisible, clinging barrier. She blundered through it and stood brushing at herself, startled and disgusted: gossamer shreds clung to her skin, her nostrils, her mouth. She'd known that the glimmer over the Aleutian's face and hands was quarantine film – which he had to wear, for their protection, when he was in human company. She hadn't known that it could be used the opposite way!

The barrier had re-formed behind her. She could see it now that she knew it was there. The air in here was fuzzy, full of particles of alien life. What would it do to her? Would it eat her from the inside? Would it wrap her up like a fly in a spider's web and call for Francois to deal with the intruder?

Too late to worry about that now, thought Bibi.

The study was furnished with fine antiques. She took out her letter, meaning to place it on the leather-covered desk: but second thoughts are often best. Maybe a handwritten letter from an inferior was an insult. Or maybe she'd been too grovelling. She decided she'd better read it again, and was just unfolding it when she heard footsteps. She stuffed the paper back into her tunic and dived into a screened and curtained alcove.

Francois arrived, with Lady Nef.

He dropped into his usual chair behind the desk: loosened the ribbon that tied the slick, black kelp-strands of his hair, slipped off the built-up shoes that he believed gave him a human style of walking and set the nubs of his heel-spurs, ankles crossed, on a priceless, antique flatscreen.

One day that will crack, thought Nef, placidly. Like the House AIs she had designed, she was forbearing: tolerant of the little rubs of the world that are best left undisturbed. She took her own accustomed place, and they began to review – unrecorded, as was their habit in here – an accumulation of routine files: gossiping comfortably as they worked, about the General, about Baykonur society and other current topics.

'He shouldn't allow himself to be patronised by women,' declared Francois. 'It's the grave mistake I made when I was a statesman in Europe, long ago. It arouses the resentment of rivals who are incapable of charming the ladies; and they will punish you, vindictively. *Et plus*, these women of Traditional society, brilliant hostesses, barred from using their talents for their own advancement, are a weapon that will turn in the hand. They may not mean to, but they will surely do you harm—'

Aleutians, whose reproductive system made reincarnation a matter of fact, had once believed they could be reborn as humans. It was nonsense, but the romantic legend persisted. Nef wasn't sure what Francois actually *believed*, but he treasured his cultivated 'memories' of past lives on Earth. He liked to tell the cadets that he'd seen battlefields where the cavalry charged on horseback, and 'commensurate weaponry' meant cold steel—

'Talent is a debatable term. And may I remind you, women have equal rights in the World State, Francois.'

'Equal and separate development, of course. But Traditionalist concubines, dear Nef, are a little more separate than equal!'

All last winter General Yu had been buzzing around the Principal Concubine of State Councillor Scolari. She was a dazzling beauty; her friends called her Pepper Lily, her enemies 'Scolari's favourite weapon'. She was trouble, and Yu *wouldn't* believe it—

But they had come to the Cadet Lists.

'You've decided you can't make a soldier out of the White Rock child?'

The Aleutian pursed his nasal, the dark expressive cavity that made his face so fascinating to Nef. 'Poor Bibi. I'm afraid she has flat feet.'

'She does not. Speak frankly, please.'

'Very well ... She might make a good officer, *if* by chance she survived long enough to grasp that the object of the exercise, contrary to popular belief, is to *stay alive*, and that low casualties are as much a measure of victory as the capture of the enemy's guns. She is intelligent, active, and she has common sense, which is above rubies.' He shook his head. 'I cannot, in all conscience, recommend her as a private soldier. She wouldn't last a day as cannon fodder: and as we know, the current "Peace" is not going to last.'

Lady Nef set down her tablet, frowning. 'This is unfortunate.'

'Yes.'

Nef had offered Bibi a place in her household because she knew what forced concubinage would mean to a daughter of White Rock. The rebels called their fortresses 'virgins' ... Now she found she had made a promise she couldn't keep, which rankled: and there was no use blaming the General. She imagined a chunky yellow-eyed tomcat, staring at her in amazement over the body of a mangled songbird.

What? What the hell did I do wrong???

The idea was funny, and disquieting. The General would try again, and again. If Bibi stayed in domestic service she would never be safe—

'There are three soldiers in Orange Company who are planning to bust the child out of here,' remarked Francois. 'They've arranged to establish her in a brothel in town, where, if she has to work on her back, she can at least earn her freedom in a few years—'

Lady Nef didn't enquire into the source of his information. Francois's methods were inscrutable, but he was rarely wrong.

'Some kind of outcaste, grey-area freedom. Poor girl.'

'Bibi would never taste the dubious privilege. If the good soldiers' plan succeeds she'll kill herself, as a matter of course – after trying very hard to kill the first man who violates her.'

They were both silent, thinking of the yellow-eyed tomcat.

'A nasty little scandal could arise,' said Nef.

'Because we saved her life.' The Aleutian reached inside his shirt, brought out a tiny red squirming bolus from his throat-glands, and offered it. Nef accepted the intimacy, although she could only swallow; her body couldn't read the freight of biochemical information in his 'wandering cells'.

'Our good deed is being punished.'

'Good deeds usually are. One does not calculate when moved by compassion, and so one blunders. Perhaps I should offer her my protection. I could marry her.'

Nef laughed. 'That won't do! You are an alien — it would be illegal for her to enter such a *mésalliance*. No, I've been thinking it over, and I have a better solution. I'm going to make her a candidate for citizenship.'

The Aleutian's chair dropped to the floor. '*Parbleu!* Can you do that?'

'Certainly I can. She has recanted: she's no longer a rebel, so there's no primary obstacle. I'll tell Yu, he'll understand he has to give up the pursuit. I may have to add a sweetener, but I'll think of something.'

The Aleutian gazed at her in silent admiration. 'Could you make *me* a candidate?'

'No!'

They moved on to other issues: the Peace that could not last, the Republican Government's frustrating indecision, the influence of Speranza ...

Years ago, more than a lifetime ago for unaugmented humanity, these two and their ally, General Yu, had become disillusioned with the Republic and aligned themselves with the man of the hour. They still believed that the Young Emperor offered the best future for the World State: but the uncertainty dragged on, and they must be prepared for an unfavourable outcome. General Yu had been indiscreet, last winter.

'We'll have to make sure Yu has left no "paper trail",' said Francois, softly. 'If we should find ourselves on the losing side, one day, then, well ... I hate going to jail for things I didn't even agree to do.'

'*You* wouldn't go to jail. You'd be repatriated.'

'A worse fate! The Big Pebble is so dull just now. No, I take it back: jail would be sweet, if you and I could share some corner of the common cell.'

Lady Nef and the Aleutian went into another room. Bibi stayed in her alcove, staring at an ancient, bulbous screen on a pedestal (or maybe it was alien, not ancient). It was blank at present. On the table under the pedestal were scattered tablets, sticks, scrolls, bubble packs of ephemer, and stranger objects: thin disks of shining material, with holes in the middle. Maybe large ancient coins? She had a feeling she was in Francois's private chapel. The spirituality of the Great House was material, a love of right action, a reverence for ceremony: but Bibi knew about belief in the supernatural. What did Aleutians worship? She couldn't imagine Francois at prayer. At last the trolley tracked her down. She climbed inside it and left the secretary's rooms hidden in the folds of his dirty washing.

She spent the next hours, and days, in a state of controlled terror. When nothing happened, she knew that the House AI had protected her. It understood that she hadn't been eavesdropping on purpose.

It didn't occur to her until long afterwards that the House AI had been barred from those rooms.

She'd understood nothing of that elliptical, adult conversation, except for the part that applied to herself. When she felt safe she began to realise her good fortune, the dazzling future that opened before her. General Yu would not rape her. She would not have to kill him, or kill herself. (It gave her a shudder to know that Francois had been right. She had been near to death.) She was going to be a candidate-citizen of the Republic.

She had not the slightest doubt that this would happen.

Some nights later, as she lay under her quilt, flanked by the quiet breathing of Honesty and Nightingale, she realised something else. Lady Nef and her secretary were lovers. Whatever that meant, when the Aleutian wasn't a man ... She hadn't seen them touch, but she'd heard their softened voices, she'd heard them move and sigh: she couldn't be mistaken. It was a shock. But Bibi's natural pragmatism asserted itself. She quickly saw that the affair was discreet, tolerated, had been going on for a long time; and that she ought to accept it the way everybody else did.

If anything, her reverence for Lady Nef was increased. She decided that she'd have done the same herself, if her fate had been different. If Bibi (as was fairly likely) had been married off to some horrible old man, or some stupid boy for whom she felt nothing, she'd have respected her husband in every way. Obeyed him, kept his house, given him children; accepted his faults. And she'd have taken a lover – if she'd had the chance, if she'd been sure she wouldn't be punished. Why not?

But it was the end of her friendship with the soldiers. The thought that they'd planned to *sell her to a brothel* (for this was what Bibi had heard, though the truth was rather different) filled her with horror beyond reason. When Col and Drez next came to Juniper she wouldn't see them. She couldn't stand to look at them or speak to them, ever again.

IV

Bibi returned from college in Hanoi travelling alone: a newly qualified Social Practice Officer, sober and contained in her long grey uniform coat, lucky to have secured a window seat in the packed third-class cabin of the suborbital. The cabin was too warm. She looked down, through canyon rifts in a continent of sunset cloud, at the steppes of Khazakh and the winding river, darkening in twilight, and wondered how she'd felt the first time. She didn't have a single memory of the journey from Cymru.

She was coming home, but not to Kirgiz, or the Great House. Lady Nef's life had changed; she and the General needed to live in the city now. The vessel reached its allotted mooring and was made safe. Bibi put on her grey uniform cap with the yellow piping; the third-class passengers collected possessions and shuffled, row by row, to the drop capsules.

She had no luggage except her cabin-bag. In the arrivals hall she said goodbye to her friends of the long flight and set off across the concourse, keeping tight hold of its pull-bar, for reassurance on both sides – and listening for her own name (as everybody listens) in the clamour of earbead traffic that the great hall handled so precisely. Of course it didn't come. In the queue for the shimmer of the Citizens' Gate – neurochemical identity check made visible – she trembled (as maybe everybody trembles). It did not reject her. She passed from the soothing-yet-invigorating moodscape of travel security into a different air ...

From Krainiy Interchange she took a bus into the city centre: resisting the temptation to press her nose against another window, trying hard to look as if she did this all the time. *Baykonur.* One of the greatest cities of Earth. Gateway to the Elevator; to Speranza; to the stars. She wondered if there was a market, somewhere in this huge, black and glittering maze, where you could buy strings of fried grasshoppers—

The Town House was absurdly small in area compared to the Great House, but the entrance tested her nerves. She was glad it was late and dark, and there was nobody about to see her uncertainty. Guidelines, woken by her arrival, led her to a gate in the foyer – where an AI voice gently asked her to state her business. 'I'm Bibi,' she explained, confused. From the shadows on the other side a figure emerged. It was Ogul Merdov, in a clerical blue and red uniform: on concierge-assistant duty.

'What are *you* doing here? You're late and you're not supposed to use this way. Go back to the street, take the RT and change trains to the dedicated link at the last interchange, like you were supposed to. There's a proper gate to the service hall, and it's *downstairs*, what were you thinking!'

'I'm sorry, AI,' said Bibi, with a slight bow to the empty air. 'I came by bus, I didn't read the instructions properly. I'll remember in future.'

'Make sure you do. Welcome home, Bibi.'

The gate opened. Ogul sniffed and stomped away. Bibi found a bank of service elevators and reached her rooms – *rooms!* – on the eighteenth floor without any trouble. She was on an outside corridor, and that was nice. Her bag bumped at her shoulder. 'Calm down,' murmured Bibi, keenly satisfied at the thought of having *rooms*; wishing she hadn't been insolent to Ogul. Never make enemies. Enemies will 'make' you, no need to help them out—

The outer room of her pair held an empty desk, empty shelves and an array of thrilling office gadgets including a hotplate scanner for 3D mail. The inner room held a bed, a dressing table with a stool, a clothes closet and an armchair. The floor was utilitarian grey ceramic, like the walls. Above the bed hung an artscreen: it showed a girl in a blue dress sitting on a clifftop, the wind stirring her hair, arms wrapped around her knees, gazing out at a wide blue vista of sea and sky. The title appeared along the base as the screen detected Bibi's attention: *The Thoughts of Youth*.

She sat on the bed, drinking in her domain. A door that she'd assumed led to another closet opened: a young woman stood there with an armful of fresh towels. She wore the blue-green tunic and trousers of a Juniper domestic; she had a rosy face, level brows, black hair cut in thick bangs and round 'Aleutian' eyes, showing hardly any white.

Bibi stared, thunderstruck.

'The picture's a gateway,' said Honesty, the girl who'd slept by Bibi's side in Juniper dorm, suddenly grown up. 'You have your own access

28

to the datasphere. There's *hundreds* of menus, and live shows from all over the world. You can change the image any time you like.'

'Honesty! Oh, are we sharing these rooms? That's wonderful!'

'Not exactly sharing. I'm your maid.'

Bibi didn't know what to say. They'd all been foundlings in Juniper dorm (except for Ogul with that prized family name); though nobody else had had a past as lurid as Bibi's. She had loved Honesty dearly, not heard from her for six years: now the gulf between Grade Seven and Grade Five was immense, and what was Bibi doing on the wrong side of it?

Honesty grinned, unabashed. 'I was wrong when I said you'd reached your plateau, wasn't I, Savage?' She set the towels on the dressing table and jumped onto Bibi's bed. 'I sleep next door, through your bathroom. I have a bed-with-legs like this, too. I don't like it. I can't sleep!'

'We had beds with legs in college,' said Bibi. 'You get used to it.'

Simultaneously, they burst into giggles. 'Give me your iface, mistress,' ordered Honesty. 'I'll show you how to use the gateway. It's terrific.'

Bibi had to wear dress uniform the next day, for her secondment interview. The formal kit, which had been waiting in her closet, was like her ordinary uniform – but made of finer cloth, with more piping at the cuffs and around the collar. She was immensely proud of it. Gwibiwr of White Rock had grown rather tall, with a good slim figure. The severe tailoring suited her: but she was hard to satisfy. She examined herself from all angles, put on her cap and took it off again; she bit her lips, she unpinned her hair—

'Let me do that,' said Honesty, and Bibi consented to sit in front of the mirror, but remained on edge, shivering like a nervous machine.

'I'll be late.'

'You won't.' Honesty wound up the thick black braid, looked into her mistress's eyes in the glass and smiled maliciously. '*Is* there someone, Bibi?'

'Of course not. What are you talking about?'

'I'm talking about the *someone*-shaped hole in everything you told me last night about how wonderful college was. You've met someone, oh Virgin of the Roof-Beam, and you're expecting to meet the same *someone* here in Baykonur, lucky you. Is it a boy or a girl? Or are you not sure yet?'

'It's a friend,' said Bibi, nettled and blushing. 'I have a friend.'

A boy, thought Honesty. This was a step forward, at least. As far as you could tell, with someone so ridiculously pure, Bibi didn't have the slightest sexual interest in girls, never mind the undecided ... But she detected an intriguing hesitation. A boy, but not a boy, now what could that imply? He'd better be a suitable suitor.

'There. Fit for the New Year Review. Fit to catch a prince, and lead him home helpless as a kitten. Get going, Officer Bibi!'

The secondment interview went well, Bibi thought. Her supervisor was Han, like Honesty. Her name was Verity Tan, she preferred the 'Western' style, and she preferred to be addressed by her given name. She had assigned Bibi to a ward of the lower city that had pockets of extreme and vicious poverty: which would be a challenge to a new graduate. 'Don't expect your clients to behave like training bots,' she said. 'Treat them with respect, but don't be fooled, never turn your back on them. Do you understand me?'

'I think so,' said Bibi. 'Er, Verity.'

Bibi's rebel background wasn't an issue. Baykonur was awash with difficult pasts just now. High-ranking officials were humbled; 'bad elements', blacklisted for years, suddenly in office. But some disputes never go out of style. Verity was a Reformer, and Citizen-Candidate Bibi was a protégé of the great Traditionalist, still-mighty Lady Nef. Through the chemical ambience (friendly efficiency) that Verity chose for her office space, Bibi detected edgier emotion. She stood to salute at the end of the interview, knowing something was coming—

'I have a question for you, Bibi,' said Verity, level-eyed. 'You should know the answer. What is the difference between a rebel and a Reformer?'

'Rebels are just attention-seekers,' answered Bibi. 'Their aim is self-aggrandisement through destructive tactics; they are parasites on the system, offering no genuine opposition. Reformers are sincere. They believe they can change the world, for the good of others, and will always work for that end, even at great cost to themselves.'

Her supervisor didn't smile but she nodded, looking mollified. 'You may go. Think about getting a soc'. It would be a great help to you.'

Bibi sped away, full of energy, scorning the elevator tubes, flying down the abyssal, plunging stairwells: mentally completing her response to Verity Tan's test question, adding the conclusion she'd tactfully withheld.

And therefore rebels, who can easily be paid off, are harmless or even useful to the State: although sometimes they have to be destroyed, as you'd rid a dog of fleas. Whereas Reformers are truly dangerous fanatics, high-minded enemies of order, reason and humanity—

Bibi had no qualms about dilemmas of this kind. Everybody says your superiors will appreciate candour, but they won't. Everybody says you should never lie in Self-Criticism, and everybody does it ... except lunatics and geniuses. Everybody says they joined Social Care out of compassion and respect for human rights – and everybody's just trying to get ahead. But that doesn't mean you don't do a decent job.

The familiar slogans, the ingrained shabbiness of the décor greeted her with affection. This secondment was something she had to get through, an obstacle on the way to her real career in Lady Nef's service. But she would play fair. She meant to do well by Verity Tan, and for those tricky clients—

Since she didn't have an eye-socket gadget, she had to return to her assigned cubicle to download the client files from the ephemer Verity had given her. She hoped she *wouldn't* have to get a soc'. She hated the idea of poking anything into the back of her eye. At least, since she was a Traditionalist, nobody would ask her to have a surgical implant. And off again, racing when the coast was clear, speed-marching past the DON'T RUN ON MOVING BAND signs when it was not. She got lost, she found her way again several times over, and at last reached Dragon Terrace, oldest and most beautiful of the bridges that linked Social Practice and Social Knowledge, across Luna Boulevard. Smiling giants performing helpful actions flanked the great arch. Bibi looked up. She could not read the inscription above the breathtaking statues – 'carved' by First Empire nanotech, four hundred years ago, but she knew the text. It had dominated her life for six years.

The Good of Others Is All We Know of Heaven—

She was late. On the lower level, where brilliant marble dragons, bringing good fortune, leapt out of the chasm and grinned along the waist-high parapet, the lunch tables were empty. There were no tourists strolling under the tailored, citified trees, because it wasn't an Open Day. A young man, in a uniform almost the same as her own, stood alone, looking out at the Boulevard, the streaming walkways, the bulky cabs nosing the crowds, the occasional splendour of a private Semi-AI car.

A dangerous fanatic, an enemy of humanity?

She felt that she always wanted to be late. To run, to fly, breathless, and find him waiting to catch her safe in his arms. Every day of her life. The lower level of Dragon Terrace was where they'd met in the virtual version of the Two Palaces, on the college system. It was their special place. It was the same, and fearfully different, to be here with him in the flesh.

'Mahmood?'

The young man was no taller than Bibi, but more stocky and muscular. He had a brown, oval face, hazel eyes and dark curly hair that he tried in vain to straighten, worn long and tied back. He cultivated (a recent development) a small, crisp moustache. They shook hands with awkward gravity and radiant grins.

'You look very well,' said Mahmood.

'So do you. Hello, Enemy—'

'Hello, Savage—'

They looked around them and sighed in satisfaction. The Palace of Social Practice faced the Palace of Social Knowledge across Baykonur's central thoroughfare, one of the most spectacular views in this city of architectural spectacle, and here they were, together.

'I'm sorry I'm late. I got lost. Real Practice is such a treasure hunt—'

'So is Real Knowledge, I get lost all the time. You should come over and visit, see my hutch.'

She blushed, and shook her head. The Palaces were identical in design, and nearly identical in function; particularly in the work assigned to junior officers. But in Traditionalist dogma 'knowledge' of the social good was assumed to be men's business, and 'practice' was assumed to be women's. Crossing the Bridge, therefore, meant going over to the Men's Side. Six years of virtual co-education had not dented Bibi's prejudices, although she knew that many of Mahmood's superiors were either women or undecided; and vice versa. He changed the subject.

'How did your secondment interview go?'

'Very well, although she's a Reformer. Luckily I had no trouble spotting that she's feminine.' Bibi grinned. 'She doesn't wear a moustache.'

Mahmood touched his masculine adornment tenderly. 'You have no respect ... It won't do you any harm that you belong to Lady Nef's House?'

'Of course not! Lady Nef is an immortal-designate.'

'Mm.'

At White Rock, Bibi's knowledge of world history had been gleaned from her grandfather's stories – and the old warrior had made no distinction between outright fiction, ancient newscasts and his own memories. She'd been very surprised to learn, at school in the Great House, that the island nation of Japan was a real place that still existed, having survived the cataclysm that destroyed half its land mass at the end of the Christian Era. Whereas some of her most revered historical figures were actually fictional characters ... Mahmood had attempted to continue her education in the real facts of life. But though she *listened* to him, because she was interested in knowing the Reformer version, there were issues on which she wouldn't budge. Immortality was one of them. They smiled, and let it go.

They never quarrelled. The gulf between them, which neither could forget, had sweetened and strengthened their friendship: it made squabbling over trifles an absurd waste of time.

Mahmood wanted to ask her a hundred things. He wanted to take her hand again, to feel the touch of her skin. He was acutely conscious of what this meeting implied to Bibi. Alone with a man, *in the real*, even in a public place, he knew how much that meant. There would be a crisis, a moment of truth he dreaded: but they didn't have to face it yet.

'Have you eaten?'

'Already,' lied Bibi. She *couldn't* sit down and eat with him.

'So have I,' lied Mahmood. His stomach was tied in knots anyway. 'We're both free this afternoon. How were you planning to spend the time?'

'I think I'll look at my ward, it's not far from here, vertically. I want to walk around down there: get a feel for the conditions.'

Mahmood clasped his hands behind his back, and bowed from the waist. 'May I accompany you?'

'Yes.'

A lot of things had changed, in the six years that Bibi had been away. Formal 'Chinese gowns' no longer fastened on the side, fashionable women wore full skirts over their trousers, slippers were worn instead of riding boots. Military uniforms were rarely seen, except on the backs of destitute ex-soldiers who had no other clothes to wear. The economic fortunes of the 'Young Emperor' cities, including Baykonur, had taken a sharp downturn; the old 'Aleutian' centres of the tropics were on the rise.

The Young Emperor himself, now better known as Prisoner Haku, had finally pushed the Republic too hard. His struggle was now called a failed rebellion, and he, having lost his nerve, had given himself up to the Hegemony. He was living on Speranza, in dignified captivity a long way from home.

Lady Nef and General Yu had escaped without serious damage, so far. The General's assets had been confiscated, but their great properties had been held in his wife's name, and Lady Nef was untouchable. They were under (mild) house arrest in Baykonur, where Lady Nef was busy making friends with old enemies. In a year or two, with some fancy footwork, they should have recovered the lost ground.

Francois the Aleutian had elected to share his mistress's fate, but it was General Yu who escorted her in society and played host at the Town House. Slightly miffed at the relegation, he'd sealed a set of rooms and rarely emerged. Every day or two Bibi would find a note on her iface, inviting her to 'drop by'. She breathed the fuzzy, populated air – which would do her no harm in small doses – and watched the odd creatures that crept around, swarming over the furniture, nuzzling the upholstery, licking at the carpets; while Francois sat in a wide armchair with his joints reversed, and asked innocuous questions about her day.

Do you think Verity Tan has a lover?

Does her Superintendent still wear a side-fastening gown?

Has anybody changed the artscreens in your shabby labyrinth?

Some of the creatures were like single, glistening tentacles; or complex floating things like magnified diatoms. Others were four-limbed, with distinct heads, muzzles, ears and eyes: like naked rats or cats. He grew them from his own cells. Aleutians did this, when they were alone. He'd been barred from growing any followers at Kirgiz, but the city had different laws.

In Aleutia he would never be alone. He belonged to the élite caste known as 'Signifiers', and was always surrounded by a crowd of silent domestics, ministering to his every need. Or so Francois told it—

She wondered how the creatures grew, and did they have a purpose?

She wondered how it felt to have hips and knees that could bend either way, and what did he look like four-footed in his 'running-gait mode'?

She wondered why Lady Nef's secretary needed a junior-grade spy in the Palaces.

'Social Care,' intoned Francois, 'a multifarious organisation, of ancient evolution, has been locked in symbiotic war with the Military for aeons. The armed forces, as always on Earth, are marginally ruled by Traditionalists, the Social marginally controlled by Reformers. These are the perennial *rouge et noir* of Blue Planet society, the roads to greatness: the cloth for subtlety, the sabre and the drum for blind force. *You should have been a soldier, Bibi*—'

Except that I could never have been an officer, she thought. Candidate status had changed her life: but some things were forever out of reach.

'I don't understand "symbiotic war"—'

Francois lifted his shoulders, in the alien equivalent of a superior smile. 'Nor did we: until we met human beings! It's the most bizarre idea I ever met. Where I come from war is not an amiable competitive sport, war is permanent death: there is no compromise, once the weapons are out.'

One of the naked things, somewhere between a rat and an amoeba, crawled into his lap and nuzzled at the open neck of his shirt, seeking the red, mobile cell-colonies that he secreted: like legless, blood-filled lice. Its 'face' had a disquieting resemblance to Francois himself. Bibi averted her eyes and nibbled at a tube of imported snack-paste, which she was attempting to eat.

Aleutian hospitality was hard going.

There was supposed to be a door somewhere in these dusky rooms – Francois preferred a low light – that led, by discreet passageways, straight to Lady Nef's bedroom. Bibi kept thinking about that door, and what it meant, and finally was emboldened to ask a direct question.

'Francois, are we still in trouble? Is Lady Nef going to be all right?'

The Aleutian gave her a sharp look, and laughed: a human trait he had mastered perfectly. 'At last, the child raises her nasal. Bibi, you are so self-absorbed, and so brutishly flexible in your opinions, that one is astonished when one glimpses your passions. Your master and mistress *could* have been in trouble. They might have found themselves on trial for war crimes, in spite of the amnesty, over incidents such as *that massacre at White Rock*—'

Bibi held her breath. *What adults don't understand*, she thought, *is that there's nothing I can do about White Rock. Or the Young Emperor's fall, or Lady Nef being under house arrest. It's not that I don't care.*

It was the same as in the Cypress Drill-Hall. You could wait him out, and he'd stop tormenting you.

Francois sighed. 'The danger has passed ... You see, Bibi, before the Aleutian Departure, the so-called World Government at Xi'an blithely anticipated that the Empire – destroyed by the Gender Wars, may I say, more than by the Aleutian presence – would spontaneously recombine. *En effect*, swayed by the ideals of the "Human Renaissance" – *liberté egalité amitié* – the World State was refounded as a Republic, and the Third Emperor politely encouraged to step down. But the blithe imperialists were right, Bibi. They are always right. *Liberté egalité amitié* soon vanished. The Empire, now calling itself the "Republic", resumed its repressive, corrupt and feudal course: and therefore many of us threw in our lot with a leader we believed would never assume the title of "Emperor", despite his popular nickname—'

Bibi waited patiently for him to get to the point, while keeping an eye on the slug-creature that was crawling up her left boot.

'Our hero lost patience, forced Xi'an to take arms against him, and it all ended at Vijaya. I have no further use for him: one cannot support a leader who goes squealing to the Hegemony in that unsporting way. But Haku's moderately expansionist, forward-thinking *manifesto* remains justly popular. No relaxation of the Enclosures, but hope for the masses ... It's the platform everyone significant supports. *Therefore* the former Young Emperor's allies will return to the tribune, after a decent delay – while your Lady, her General and myself see no difficulty in becoming devout Republicans once more. Read the runes, child. As long as the Third Emperor remains dormant, whether in retirement or in the grave, we have nothing to fear.'

The slug fell to the carpet, covertly dislodged: but Bibi's eyes had started to water. She suppressed a sneeze.

'I try to educate you in your benighted planet's parochial affairs, and I don't know why I waste my time: I discern the liquid of human boredom. Your eyes have glazed over, Bibi.'

'No they haven't, they're just a bit weepy. I was listening ... I have a friend who says I was brought up like an Aleutian, in the Great House. That I'm steeped in subliminal post-colonialism. Having "traditional" sexes, and human servants instead of machines. Not playing immersion games, dancing every evening. He says the Enclosures were an Aleutian idea, too.'

'He's quite right.' Francois could get sarcastic about flattery, but often it appeased him. 'Our legacy, and not a bad one. A Household that dances in step, changes in step. And what the devil would you do with your teeming masses, if the bulk of them didn't belong to the Households of the more fortunate? Mulch them down for cab-feed? *Your* problems, Bibi, at that Palace on Luna Boulevard, would be appalling. Are you catching a cold? Please don't come here when you have a cold. I'm vulnerable to human viral infection. It makes my teeth itch.'

She thought of suggesting that she could use quarantine film, but she didn't dare. She'd rather endure the snuffles, and continue to be of use. She guessed that the questions he asked were not as bland as they seemed. Or else he was reading her mind, picking out things she didn't know she knew. She would have liked to be better trusted: but accepted she was probably safer, and more useful, as an ignorant pawn.

V

General Yu's army had been disbanded, re-enlistment in the People's Army at the Republic's discretion. Nightingale, who'd seen no active service, had come off better than most. She arrived in Baykonur in the tenth month of that year, resplendent in the olive and scarlet of an officer cadet, to take up a place at the illustrious Cadet Reserve Barracks. The friends had a reunion, the day she came to pay her respects to the Family.

Bibi and Nightingale had kept in touch, as best they could. Honesty, who had minimal access, and a Grade Seven indifference to long-distance contact, had a million questions. Did Nightingale really get a medal for her college results? Did she have it with her? Was the so-called Golden Barracks *really* a nest of dazzling luxury? What were her officers like? How many uniforms did she have? What did she get to eat? Did she have influential friends? Did she know how to use a hotplate—?

The only escape from 'the Magnet's' curiosity was to distract her, so they spent a happy half-hour trying to activate Bibi's prize gadget, without success. 'It's all right,' said Bibi. 'Nobody ever sends me 3D mail anyway.'

On the warm rush mats Honesty had finessed from Housekeeping, they sat sipping green tea from the corridor's *distributeur*: all of them thinking of the Great House, the beloved home they'd probably never see again—

'I've been amazingly, fantastically lucky—' confessed Nightingale.

'I heard it was *merit*, not luck,' said Bibi.

'You heard wrong.' Nightingale shook her head: eyes lowered, black lashes lying thick and soft on her glowing cheeks—

'Lady Nef fixed everything for you, of course,' Honesty put it bluntly. '*But* you deserved it, and now we all have dazzling futures ahead. Bibi will be a Social Care Superintendent, Nightingale will be a general. And I'm going to have a million sexy lovers, rise to be a steward and become incredibly rich by skimming the household accounts—'

The Thoughts of Youth looked down, white clouds drifting across the blue. Bibi felt that the girl on the clifftop was not making career plans. She was looking for something far beyond the horizon.

'I don't know why she loves that picture so much,' grumbled Honesty. 'Absolutely all that happens is that the girl's hair gets blown about, and the clouds keep changing, but what's the use in that? I try to get her to explain, but she's still the Savage. She hasn't learned to express herself.'

'It's because you can't see the girl's face,' said Nightingale, wisely.

'Yes I can,' protested Bibi. 'I mean, I can see what her face *means*.'

The other two jeered happily at this typical Savagism.

'You've been spending too much time with that Aleutian, mistress—'

'Oh, is *Francois* here? I never thought. But of course, he must be—'

The Thoughts of Youth vanished. In its place appeared a view of the corridor outside Bibi's door, embellished by the apparation of Ogul Merdov, her sour face framed by a clerical cap.

'Mistress!' exclaimed Honesty. 'I'm having a beautiful dream. Is that the great *Ogul Merdov* at our door?'

'I can hear you, Honesty,' said Ogul, peering officiously around the room; evidently hoping to spot something contraband. It was annoying, but Ogul could look all she liked: she had seniority, and a legitimate errand. 'I'm here to take Miss Officer Nightingale to the Lady. I should put your stuck-up *mistress* on report for delaying her.'

'Caller acknowledged,' said Bibi, belatedly. 'Thank you.'

The artscreen returned. 'I'd better go,' said Nightingale. 'I mustn't keep her Ladyship waiting. And Lady Nef probably has a full diary, too—'

'Look at you,' said Honesty, bracingly. 'Nightingale is beautiful and talented, and her father was a war hero. You were *nothing*, a dirty little refugee, a rebel. Now you're a candidate-citizen. It's unearned privilege, and you're bound to have enemies. Don't let her get to you, just be careful.'

Bibi straightened her tunic, feeling dishevelled and grubby, as always after an Ogul encounter. 'Thank you for your warm support ... Magnet, was there a "someone"-shaped hole in Nightingale's life story? Or was that my imagination?'

'There's a boyfriend,' Honesty nodded. 'A lover, I'm afraid.'

'Isn't that good? I thought regular sex was the answer to everything.'

'Sex is all right. Love, well, that depends on the circumstances.'

Honesty had investigated Mahmood – having extracted his name by sheer bullying – and executed a search that was not within her rights, but it was within Bibi's, so what's the difference? Mahmood Al-Farzi MacBride proved to be very suitable, aside from the trifling problem of his party. A background of modest means and decent mid-grades, in a minor branch of an illustrious Khazakh Reformer clan: just what Bibi needed to offset her irregular status.

She'd also found out that he favoured the Syr Darya Prospect for his morning exercise – and had swiftly set to work convincing Bibi that they ought to do their drill in the open air. It was so much healthier, and perfectly respectable nowadays. Honesty's own sex life was varied, opportunist and uncomplicated, but she knew that slow movers like Bibi and Mahmood needed a *venue*, or they'd never make any progress.

The Syr Darya was one of the North Bank's best-known 'Street-Level' open spaces. Precipitous towers drew back, like a rampart of cliffs, from the gardens and paved promenades beside the river; the glitter of the boundary seemed as far away as an open sky. There were coffee and cake stalls under the trees; half-tame squirrels marauded for scraps, bright-coloured parakeets and gallahs chattered; young men and women of both parties (mostly junior officers from the Palaces) mingled freely after their exercise. Honesty the irresistible had drawn together a noisy breakfast group that gave shelter to the lovers: allowing them to slip away, without Bibi feeling unchaperoned.

They walked by the thick grey snake of the river, in its pen of storm-walls, sipping good coffee in cardboard cups. On the farther bank the Recoveries floated, discreetly veiled in an illusion of distance. In a city the size of Baykonur, the best of Aleutian recycling-tech still left plenty of dirty work to be done.

'The river's like you, Bibi,' said Mahmood. 'It wasn't born under a roof, it comes to our feuds and gripes innocent, bringing strength and freshness—'

'I was brought up in a cave. Do you know, I hardly heard the words "Traditionalist" or "Reformer" when I was a child? My people didn't think like that. It was just an endless war of independence, us and them—'

40

'That means you could change your allegiance. Birth cultures, as we know, are almost impossible to eradicate.'

'Far less malleable than genetic difference,' agreed Bibi (this was Social Care dogma). She stared at the Recoveries, and cleared her throat. 'As a moral being my allegiance is to my Family, not to a political theory I don't even understand. But it's like Social Practice: it's not the theory, it's more that I'm part of the organism. I don't *want* to be a Traditionalist: I just *am* one.'

'Is organic connection more binding than morality?'

'I think so.'

'No wonder they call you the Savage.'

They had stilted conversations: thrilling to each other's physical nearness, testing the deep waters that held them apart.

One morning they emerged from drill to find their favourite stall besieged by Officer Cadets. The breakfast group immediately pulled up, divided into twos and threes and headed off for second choices. Palace officers, known as *yellowjackets* – boring hive-insects of some kind – invariably took second place to the cadets, known as *gallahs* for their impudence and noise. But Bibi immediately had a call on her iface. Nightingale came racing after them, almost overtaking her message.

'Bibi, Honesty! I hoped I'd find you!' She examined the Reformer, half-smiling, half-challenging. 'Excuse me, sir, but are you the wonderful Mahmood? As in *Mahmood says*? As in *I have a friend who knows*—?'

'I'm Mahmood.'

'Don't tease him,' said Honesty: pleased to see Nightingale, but put out at the interruption – Syr Darya was supposed to be for Bibi. 'Why didn't you say you'd be here? We could have missed each other.'

Nightingale blushed, and grabbed her friends' hands. 'I want you to meet someone. Wait, wait there. Excuse me again, Mahmood—'

She returned with another cadet in tow, a young man. 'This is Caspian Konoe-Hosokawa. Konoe, these are my friends from long ago, the Savage and the Magnet. We call her the Magnet because everybody is irresistibly drawn to do what she says. The Savage, well, you'll find out. She's not uncivilised, just unpredictable. And this is Mahmood, whom I've just met—'

Mahmood, Bibi and Honesty were speechless. They knew Konoe-Hosokawa from the society pages. He was a *prince*, even if it was only Japanese royalty. His family was also (more importantly, in Baykonur) staggeringly, *filthy* rich. They were Konoe-Olofact, the scent people. They created moodscapes and ambiences for half the world—

'Call me "Caspian",' suggested the prince, with a dejected smile, like someone who knows he's branded on the forehead. 'It's my "Western" name, not very original, but I prefer it.'

Touched by his woeful tone, Honesty recovered first, frankly offering her hand. 'Pleased to meet you, Caspian. Won't you join us?'

They looked for a table, and saw that one of the most coveted, right by the river, was empty. A big, tall gallah came over and had a quiet word with the prince, while trays of coffee, steamed milk, cold milk, powdered chocolate, pastries, rolls, syrups, yoghurts swiftly arrived: the food-stall staff suddenly as self-effacing, deferential, expert as if they'd been trained in the Great House.

'I'm so sorry about this,' murmured Caspian, slipping his arm around Nightingale's shoulders. 'I know it's an intrusion. It won't happen again.'

They thought he meant the embarrassing profusion of food. Later, comparing notes, they realised they'd been scanned by Konoe's body-guard. Which was against the law, technically: but not something to protest about.

At last the gallahs rose in a chattering, brilliant flock and flew away, carrying Konoe and Nightingale with them.

'Oh dear,' muttered Honesty, shaking her head. 'Not good! Well, that's what happens at cadet school.'

'He may be serious,' protested Bibi. 'She's a born citizen. Why not?'

'I'm sure he's *serious*.' Honesty rolled her eyes. 'From the way he looked at her, the way he behaved, I'm sure he's madly in love. But he wouldn't put his arm around his fiancée like that, out on the street, I can tell you. Poor kid. I always knew that face of hers was a poisoned treasure.'

'Shut up, Honesty. Give him a chance. You don't *know*.'

'Huh. I just hope it doesn't last, and blight her career.'

Mahmood pretended not to hear any of this.

Bibi made a point of walking around her ward: talking to strangers, sharing the air of the dispossessed; feeling that she'd become her child-self again, Bibi in the choke-tunnel, watching the world unseen. She knew that Verity Tan approved, but that wasn't why she did it; or not the whole reason.

Bibi knew the domesticated poor, and their problems. The Great House had supported plenty of 'servants' who – for one reason or another – were incapable of supporting themselves. Their lives were not placid. But down among the roots of the great towers and the Town Houses, in the charcoal darkness of bare-earth alleys, she found a wild kind of poverty that fascinated her. A people who had evaded protection, who had chosen to escape from every safety net, who found order and security intolerable—

At the Great House she'd been Francois's best pupil, in her year group, in the art of the Common Tongue, the Aleutian skill of reading physical language. 'Silent' speech was not telepathy, not in the sense that people imagined it. The Aleutians themselves, with the added dimension of their 'wandering cells', couldn't truly read each others' minds. But Bibi's skill was enough to make her an expert eavesdropper on her clients: their criminal muttering, their cries of anguish, the secrets and fears unknowingly whispered by the lonely—

She saw some strange things. The illegal human whores who plied their trade around the steps of the Monument to Sputnik – wearing digital masks (which was also illegal) to make themselves look like bots. The fortune-tellers and dream-readers on Gagarin: whose licence to practise was the brand on their foreheads that confirmed they'd been scanned, and didn't possess a trace of 'clairvoyance'. The cavernous Church of Self Club, where the half-castes gathered to watch their flickering screens; in turn carefully watched by the police.

She never found the market where you could buy fried grasshoppers.

But one day she walked into a tiny, gloomy square, and saw a pair of ex-soldiers going through a Palaces Ward refuse sack, on the steps of a drinking fountain. They must have lifted it from a Recovery conduit. Bibi wasn't the police, and it wasn't much of a crime. She was about to look the other way when she saw that their uniforms bore traces of General Yu's insignia, and realised that the rag-pickers were Col Ben Phu and Drez Doyle.

A shock of furious panic went through her: as if her former friends were liable to grab her, stuff her in that sack and take her off and sell her on Sputnik. However, she was now a grown-up—

'*Col?* Drez Doyle? Is it you?'

'Funx me!' exclaimed the larger of the two wrecks. 'It's our Bibi!'

Drez had let his ringlets grow; Col Ben Phu had some crudely done new tats. They'd both lost muscle, and looked twenty years older, not seven. She sat down with them on the steps of the fountain, told her story and heard theirs. The breaking of General Yu's army. The way they'd been allowed to re-enlist, and then treated like dirt. The anger and resentment at the loss of their Active Field Bonuses, *nothing* to show for all those campaigns. The disrespect, the fighting and thieving, the dishonourable discharge.

'We'd have been on half-pay, see,' said Col, 'now there's peace, if they'd kept us on the active list. So they fired us, it was cheaper. The order came from above, and that bastard NCO, she saw we were prime targets.'

Drez was more realistic. 'We did wrong, Bibi. Can't deny it. But they pushed us beyond what we could bear.'

Bibi tried to think of something she could do: ex-soldiers were the worst, notoriously impossible to reclaim. But she saw that Col and Drez expected nothing from her, except maybe a casual handout.

'What about Sergeant Aswad? What happened to him?'

They looked at each other.

'Sarge is in the dreamtime,' said Col.

'Oh, shit.'

The soldiers had never heard Bibi use an expletive before. They were pleased, became visibly relaxed. 'It's a bugger,' agreed Drez. '*We* fell on hard times. It was different for the Sarge. He got himself in trouble.'

'Yeah. Just by being loyal to the cause.'

'Is he ... Is the Sarge ever going to get out?'

Drez grimaced.

'That's a maybe,' said Col, darkly. 'Depends. Depends on how the runes fall in the end, know what I mean?'

She did not know, but she remembered that Francois had used the same odd expression—

'There's a billion, *billion* stars with planets out there!' Drez burst out, staring at her wildly. 'Hundreds of thousands of empty worlds, waiting for us. We don't have to live locked up no more, Bibi—'

'Not a billion *billion* ...' Col liked numbers; it annoyed her to hear them abused. She had been the kind of soldier who collects skills. Her skull was full of patches: inactive now, of course, but the shadows remained—

'Yeah, Einstein, well plenty. *We* funxing invented the Buonarotti Device, didn't we? Why aren't we out there, colonising? Because the rich hate the idea of the masses getting their freedom, that's why. *That's* why they destroyed Haku. He was for the Expansion of the Human Race—'

Col scowled. 'Stupid bastard screwed *himself*, Drez.'

'They hounded him till he destroyed himself in despair.'

'I'd better go.' Bibi stood up, digging in her pockets for *cash*, the currency of the poor. 'I'm making you look like informers. Take care of yourselves. I'll be around, this is my ward—'

She walked away, very quickly.

There were no empty worlds. The tiny number of truly habitable planets so far discovered were already thoroughly inhabited, by the other members of the Hegemony. What's more, the Buonarotti Instantaneous Transit was incredibly dangerous. Even on the 'stronger pathways' between the Hegemony Worlds and Speranza you could arrive at your destination inside out, or physically intact but criminally insane. *Even if all went well* you were mentally scarred for life after a few trips. *The diplomats and the spies and the banished criminals can keep it*, thought Bibi—

But there was worse. What would happen to the Enclosures, to *everything*, if people started getting the idea that the Earth was not enough? The freedom of the stars was a pernicious delusion – which the Young Emperor had rejected, whilst unable to prevent some of his followers from using it as a rabble-rouser. Bibi was really scared. She wondered if she should report the sedition to Francois, before she found a police message on her iface, summoning her for interrogation. But she didn't know how to introduce the subject. She wasn't supposed to know what was going on when he summoned her to his rooms for those little chats.

Later, when she'd calmed down, she felt guilty, and knew she'd overreacted. She understood by now that, for a poor girl, a place in a decent brothel is not such a bad thing. Her soldier friends had meant her no harm, long ago. They'd probably have had to provide a 'dowry' out of their hard-earned pay. She spent days looking for Col and Drez, hoping to help them somehow. But she never saw them.

Autumn turned to winter, and the city's climate mildly reflected the bitter cold outside. There'd be no snow indoors, but on the Syr Darya the trees were bare, and there was often a slick of frost on the morning pavement. A festive mood filled the city. For the rich, Baykonur's winter was an endless round of parties, and to an extent everyone joined in. Prince Caspian – who had confounded Honesty by making a persistent effort to befriend Nightingale's friends – took them skating at the Old Airport, on a field flooded and frozen every holiday season by one of

45

his wealthy friends. They ate hot sausage and drank mulled apple wine at the 'Fisherman' food stalls. They sang and danced, at open cabarets where differences of grade were forgotten, under a midnight boundary sparkling with heat-ex diamonds.

The General and Lady Nef had been given permission to take a lodge at Kushan resort for the New Year. Just after the Eastern Christmas (religious *belief* was a minority taste, but Baykonur was omnivorous when it came to festivals), Bibi found her name on the Winter Lists. Torn between joy at the achievement and distress because she had to tell Mahmood, she arranged to meet him – at lunchtime but not for lunch – in their special place. They arrived on the Dragon Terrace almost together: Bibi first, for a change, and Mahmood coming smiling towards her—

'I won't be here for the New Year,' she blurted, as soon as they'd shaken hands. 'I'm on the Winter Lists, I saw my name this morning. I'm going with the Family to Kushan resort.'

'I won't be here either,' confessed Mahmood, keeping hold of her hand, a blush rising. 'Same reason. I've been putting off telling you.'

'I didn't know Reformers had Winter Lists.'

'We don't. But we have rich relations ... I've been invited to the Major Clan's dacha. It's an honour, I have to be there. Can't say no.'

'Oh well,' said Bibi. 'As long as it's the same for both of us.'

They looked into each other's eyes, and quickly looked away. New Year was the time for wedding plans. Neither of them had said a word, not a word, to the other: but they'd been open about their friendship in self-assessment sessions, and in the routine progress reports they filed at home. Each of them knew this, because of hints that had come back to them. Verity had recently remarked to Bibi that life-partnerships across the divide were not at all frowned upon.

It was all inference, but it was everything.

'The dacha's not at Kushan,' said Mahmood, his throat so constricted he could hardly get the words out. 'But it's almost next door – in the forest. We might see each other, up there.'

Bibi nodded. 'I hope so. I must go now.'

She hurried away, offering up silent thanks to Lady Nef. So this was why she was on the Lists! So that she could be with Mahmood, in the winter forest, at New Year. It was inconceivable to Bibi that her mistress had let this happen by accident. Lady Nef knew *everything*—

*

46

The Winter Lists turned out to be a mixed privilege for a Grade Five with no special duties. The Family's personal servants had their share of the fun, but Bibi had no friends with her, and she was too shy to try and find any. She spent her time lurking in her room, or taking dull walks alone: wishing Honesty was with her, or Nightingale. The Kushan snow could have been blown from cannons in a city park, the fairy-lights in the trees destroyed all illusion of wilderness ... She wondered if the 'Lists' had always been like this, the boredom a well-kept secret. Or had it been far different in the old days, in Lady Nef's own winter house, or the General's hunting lodge?

On the sixth night of the New Year there was a party thrown by Lady Nef's son Amal, which became raucous after the General and the ladies retired. Amal, formerly one of his father's staff officers, now a 'Commander' in the People's Army, without hope of a command, had invited a group of entertainers from the Kushan Games of Adult Happiness. They arrived after midnight, a host of drunken revellers in attendance, and the noise intensified.

Amal, who knew he was likely to be grey-haired before he was made a Senior, was sinking into premature middle age, clinging to 'youth' in a way that showed he'd given up on life—

The rooms on Bibi's floor were not soundproofed. At five a.m. she gave up trying to sleep, dressed and took a quilt out onto the balcony that ran around the building. There was a light enclosure, so she wasn't too cold. Giggling partygoers appeared at random, slipping and falling as they crossed the snowy compound, seeking their sleighs and snomobiles. Maybe everyone would be quiet soon—

'Bibi!'

She had dozed off. Was she dreaming? Mahmood stood in the compound looking up, a blurred figure in snowlight dusk.

'Mahmood, are you real? What are you doing here?'

Their hopes had been disappointed. He was 'next door', but they'd barely been able to have a conversation, between Mahmood's social obligations and the low priority of Grade Five messaging.

'I thought I'd never get away, but here I am.' He stooped to tug at the clips of his skis. 'I don't have to be back until brunch. Can you come down?'

'Wait there!'

She ran to her room, pulled on her boots and cap, and flew down the back stairs. In a few moments she was standing beside him.

Mahmood took her hand. 'Let's go for a walk.'

Kushan was wide awake: party-lights spangling the dawn. Snomos were carrying incapable guests to their lodges; horse-drawn sleighs flew jingling along the slick white streets. Someone was playing a piano on an icy terrace all alone, the pianist's hands and the dark shape of the instrument outlined in rosy fire; what extravagance, a personal heat-ex boundary.

'Have you been out of the resort?'

'No,' said Bibi, 'I didn't feel like it, on my own.'

They walked side by side along a forest path. Fresh snow had fallen: soon there were no tracks but their own, and they seemed lost in the wild. The white world bathed them in the scent of frost and pine. At the brink of a slope too steep for trees there was a viewpoint, a half-smothered rustic bench, and the sky opened ahead, starry at the zenith, peachbloomed in the east.

'There's no AI watching over us here,' said Mahmood. 'The satellites don't care. There is no boundary above us. We are adrift and alone.'

Bibi smiled, and shook her head. 'There's never no surveillance.' She reached up to touch his brow with a gloved finger.

'Of course, you're right. The World State watches from within. It will never let us go. *The good of others is all we know of Heaven.*'

'*And all we may ever know,*' Bibi completed the text, beautiful in its ambiguity, looking at him gravely. 'I believe in it. Don't you?'

'Yes ... But you were born a rebel, Bibi. The wild must call to you, on some level. You must want to escape.'

'No, Mahmood. I've seen where that kind of thing leads.'

They were hopeful young social servants, determined to get ahead, sincere in their ideals. Mahmood thought of everything he'd be giving up. The multiple partners natural to his culture, the feminine side of his sexuality: which he might have to suppress, with lifelong medication. He wasn't an undecided, he was male and looked it (although the moustache was cosmetic, the follicles painted on). But he wasn't fully adult: he could still change. It made no difference. Traditionalist marriage was the only way for Bibi. And she would be his for ever; and he loved her with all his heart.

'Listen!' said Bibi. '*Look—!*'

A rhythmic creaking filled the air. A flight of geese swept over them, high in the sky, in a long, ragged V, heading for one of the lakes that were kept ice-free for the resort's hunters. They gazed, heads tipped back, in a kind of ecstasy, piercing and melancholy. Kushan forest was the shrine of their commitment to each other, and to the beauty of the living world.

'*This* is why we must stay Enclosed,' breathed Mahmood. 'For ever.'

'I believe in that, too.'

'Bibi, will you marry me?'

'If our Families approve, I shall be very glad to marry you.'

They faced each other and touched lips, solemnly: it was their first kiss. Mahmood threw his arms around her. 'I'm not man enough for you, Bibi, but I'll try. Heaven knows I'll try.'

Amal's party, in its death throes, was spilling out of every orifice of the lodge when they got back. Fortunately, the drunks were too preoccupied to notice two Grade Fives slipping through the open gates. 'I'll see you to your door,' said Mahmood, proudly protective. He delivered her to her room, with one more tender kiss, and strode on into the main building: he *could not* sneak out of a servants' exit, not now. He felt like a prince as he clattered down the sweeping wooden stairway to the reception hall, through a litter of bottles, glasses, poppers, spilled liquor, discarded wraps, a single high-heeled golden slipper: but he was strung tight, stunned by the life choice he'd just made—

Bodies, human and licensed robotics from Adult Happiness, were sprawled about, some of them disguised by fancy-dress masks. A little striped cat was dragging off a piece of soft cheese, with staggering steps, from the rifled buffet. As Mahmood appeared it gave up the effort, and began being heartily sick into a cadet's pillbox cap. One of the bots lay spread-eagled, tinsel skirts rucked around her waist, on a sofa facing the main entrance. Between her legs a cadet struggled, slim muscular buttocks heaving, to reach his climax. The bot caught Mahmood's eye, ruefully apologetic, and put a finger to her lips. The cadet was Caspian Konoe.

Mahmood walked on by, but he must have let out some kind of sound. He heard a groan. Staggering noises pursued him. 'Mahmood? Mahmood? It *is* Mahmood, isn't it?' Prince Caspian lunged for the support of the concierge desk and swayed there, clutching his breeches. 'It's you. It is you. What t'funx? You here?'

'I came to see Bibi.'

'Oh. She here? Oh, please ... Please don', don' tell Nightingale—'

'Tell her what?' growled Mahmood. 'It's none of my business.'

'You don' unerstan'. You've got to unerstan'. I LOVE her—'

Mahmood boiled with rage. Konoe's features were suffused, ruined by the night's fun, but he could still glimpse the polished, unnatural beauty of the aristocrat. The World State had laws against cosmetic and longevity work on unborn children, which the rich routinely flouted. The prince's 'promotion' to Seniority would be a total formality. He would be beautiful and useless when Mahmood was dead of old age. Not that Mahmood cared. Not that he wanted anything to do with sexbots, either, but all the freedoms he'd never possess came pounding into his head, with all the meagre joys he had just surrendered, and somehow his anger was turned against Bibi, which shamed him and made him even more furious—

'You're right. I *don't* understand. Which of them is it you love so much? Is it Nightingale, or the bot?'

'*Please*,' gasped the prince, shocked sober. 'It would hurt her so much.'

'Of course I won't tell her.'

Outside the lodge gates he realised he'd left his skis under Bibi's window. He couldn't stand to go back and ask for them. It was a long forced march to the MacBride dacha, driven by the poor relation's imperative: he must not offend his hosts.

VI

Pepper Lily stood in line, a step behind her husband, waiting to be introduced to the Special Envoy of the Standing Committee, here in the flesh from Xi'an. Progress was slow; she had plenty of time to observe her hostess. *Not at her best*, thought Pepper, with satisfaction. *The mighty Lady Nef has reached the age where a woman's inner* elderliness *defeats her, no matter how exclusive her treatments, or how carefully she updates her opinions.* The new, softer body shape didn't suit the old warhorse, either.

The dear old lady always smells of the steppes, however carefully she scents her rooms—

If the 'immortal-designate' were raised to glory in a while, would she take her arrogant ageing with her? Pepper, though a staunch Traditionalist, was cynical about the legends of fantastic pre-Aleutian human achievements. She knew for a fact that 'immortal-designate' simply meant that the lady was untouchable, because she knew awful secrets about the Xi'an government. But Nef as a sagging crone, for all eternity: it was a pleasing image—

Councillor Scolari, massive and shamelessly balding, bowed to the Envoy: who bowed in return and graciously exchanged a few words. Old-fashioned in his manners, he barely acknowledged the existence of the other man's concubine. In consolation, Pepper's host and hostess greeted her particularly kindly, which was hard to bear. At least the General had the grace to look uncomfortable. But with Yu, that probably only meant his dress shoes were pinching ...

She abandoned Scolari as soon as possible, breathed deep of the subtle-yet-daring psychoactive mix in the air, and tried hard to enjoy herself. The crowd, instantly replayed for its own entertainment on floating screens, was splendid. The music (at Nef's parties always general, no private sound clubs allowed) blended richly with the scented air. Antique mirrors, a renowned feature of this Town House, gave back

Pepper Lily's sinuous curves with a romantic depth and shimmer. The pepper-red gown, spangled with silver, was a triumph. But Pepper was *not* untouchable, so she had to take care. The free-thinking poets, scientists, artists, who'd been her courtiers when *she* was the hostess here, were dangerous now. People's Army officers, charming even in their civvies, must be avoided. She must chat with dull, unspeakable government officials, while fear and heartache gnawed her breast.

No one to whom she could say, *Lady Nef still smells of the steppes*—

It should have been me, it should have been me ... How cruel and unjust life is. Pepper Lily didn't believe in immortality, but she believed in Seniority. There were no more than ten thousand Commoners who held that rank in the whole of Eurasia, *including China*, and Pepper Lily had been on her way to joining them. General Yu, a Senior himself, would have divorced Nef, taken Pepper as his concubine and raised her to be his Principal Wife: certain to be awarded her husband's longevity status. It had all been taken care of, all settled, and she'd have been out of reach of stupid political changes. It might *still have happened*, if Nef had not come to the city—

By the Feather Fountain, an exquisite First Empire 'water feature without water' from the Great Drought era, she joined a group watching a squeeze-ball match on a floating screen – simply to escape from the torture of grovelling to bores. A crude grip settled on her hip, alcoholic breath at her ear.

'See anything you fancy?'

It was Ehsan Lukoil, one of her husband's associates, a vile man she always tried to avoid. She slipped away from the hand, adroitly: making it seem she only moved so she could turn and smile. 'Caspian plays with style. He's a darling, isn't he? So full of life, so well bred, he hardly seems Japanese at all. What do you think of the latest news from Speranza, Ehsan?'

Ehsan's crude manners didn't trouble Pepper. (She had nothing to fear from him, sexually!) She hated him because of something cold and superior that *watched* – from behind the eyes of the slack buffoon. It woke and stared at her now. *What had she said?* It was just a line, it was just *the sort of question one asks.* For a moment, horrified, she thought that something gossipworthy *had* happened on Speranza, and she didn't know, she had lost her touch—

'I'll discuss current affairs with your master, my beauty. With you, I'd rather discuss Caspian Konoe's gorgeous arse—'

'My *husband*,' she corrected him, still smiling.

She thought of Scolari as her husband: everybody did. When the Principal Wife is an ageing invalid, and the Principal Concubine is a brilliant and dazzling woman of affairs, the 'Concubine's' future is not in doubt—

'Funx that, Pepper. Your game's up. Hang on to what you've got, while you can.' Lukoil took hold of her behind again, and chuckled as he squeezed. 'No arse is as gorgeous as yours, sweetheart!'

The red gown had a deep décolletage and a high waist, above draperies that clung to her shapely legs, and to the round belly that was newly in fashion. She'd worn it as a *funx you* to all the society women (including Nef) who still thought big skirts were the latest idea. No one else at the party wore anything so extreme. The mirrors showed her a desperate woman, trying to use sex to bludgeon her way into Baykonur's most exclusive circles. The world had changed, the Young Emperor days were over, she looked fashionable like a whore ... It was such a lie! Such a lie! She had been the General's *sponsor*, his fiancée in waiting, graciously 'standing in' for a neglectful wife.

How could people forget that?

There is no pain, for a queen of society, like social humiliation compounded by emotional distress. Pepper Lily had not only lost her chance of joining the elect, she had lost General Yu: whom she truly loved. General Yu and his wily 'Simian' features, his abrupt laugh, his energy. His lusty eagerness, so endearing. She had a violent need to rush up to Lady Nef and hiss in her face: *You'll be sorry, I'll make you pay*. But Pepper was tougher than that. She contained herself and became a huntress, choosing her prey with care – in search of information, bedroom talk, the kind of whisper that's hard to trace. Some source more pliable than Ehsan Lukoil, and for Pepper that left a wide field. Maybe she was just a concubine, a crushed butterfly, and nobody cared: but she knew how to make the great Lady Nef suffer.

They shared the same weakness, after all.

VII

Bibi spent her morning online with a casework team, sorting out help for the dependents of an illicit pig farmer – whose disgusting public health hazard of an operation had been closed, and the villain sent to dreamland.

A lot of Social Practice work, she had discovered, came down to handling the fallout after a police action: but everyone knew the score, so relations between police, criminals and social workers were not unpleasant. Crowded pens of pigs, rabbits, cats, rats provided 'real meat' for the lower city's more affluent outcastes, whose self-esteem was important – and supplied organic brain tissue for the living-machine industry. Crackdowns were merely meant to keep things within bounds.

In the afternoon she had to attend a wake at the Settlement House on her patch. A half-caste known as 'Buster' had collapsed and died, in the miserable partition where he was being entertained by an illegal human whore known as 'Looty Loo'. The nuns at the Settlement were allowing Looty – who had been fond of 'her' client – to use one of their meeting rooms for a send-off.

The guests were a sad collection, mostly half-castes themselves, with an admixture of the particular kind of whore who catered to that persecuted community – like 'Looty Loo'. Bibi walked around, trying to look dignified: uneasy about her role, and wishing she knew exactly what her role *was*. Somewhere close by, inside the Settlement House, children ran: pattering and singing down a corridor.

The rich of the Enclosed Cities, rarely naturally fertile, required their offspring to be perfect. The rejects were not culled, they were 'fostered' in the lower city: a cash crop, like those unfortunate pigs. Settlement nuns reclaimed them, and gave them an education. This was illegal, since all the baby-farmers were licensed ... But the Palaces didn't make trouble for the Settlements. Whatever she thought she heard, she didn't have to investigate.

The House stood on a slope of green rooftops earthed over for *potagers*, an enclave of the Lower Levels perched among the towers. Through the window bands, beyond rows of cabbage, she could admire a rare vista: a vast cosmic basket-weave of braided towers, spiral skyways, storied bridges. Aleutian-developed 'bambu', Eurasia's chief building material, shone like gold in the winter sunlight. Baykonur was a toy for an Emperor: an elegant, intricate, inextricable mass of light and shade.

She thought of the little creatures creeping around Francois's rooms, wearing glimpses of the Aleutian's own face.

In Verity's office, afterwards, she was startled, and alarmed, to learn that she'd been involved in a murder inquiry. 'According to the police medical examiner's report, "Buster" died from internal bleeding,' said Verity. 'It seems he'd been beaten up, two or three days before he died in Looty's arms—'

Bibi nodded. 'He'd had some body-mod, er, I mean gene therapy, that went wrong: gave him skin like treebark and impaired his sense of pain. But he had no visible injuries, he probably didn't even know he was in trouble, he'd just been filling up with blood inside. Would that be *murder?*'

'It's not my job to speculate, Bibi. You didn't pick up any further details? These are half-castes, and you are fluent in the "Common Tongue".'

On Verity's deskscreen the certified record of the event was running. Buster's shabby mourners milled about, avoiding each other's eyes.

'I probably wouldn't have understood,' said Bibi, evasively. 'Common Tongue is highly contextual. Even users who've grown up together can have opposite ideas about what's been said in a "Silent" conversation, and those people were strangers to me. Emotions come over better than facts, unless somebody collapses the wave and speaks aloud, and nobody was doing that. Really devout half-castes hardly speak aloud at all—'

'A refuge for endless ambiguity, trust the Aleutians. Can you discern anything more on review? Any comments you can translate for me?'

Bibi shook her head. 'I'm sorry. Half-castes can be silent, in the Silent speech, if you see what I mean, better than most people. Nobody was being very communicative: I suppose they were shocked, after a sudden death.'

Verity gave Bibi one of the level looks that presaged a bombshell. 'A suspicious death may have suspicious connections. If you *had* been able to tell me anything, I would have been obliged to pass it on to another authority.'

'Oh.' *Another authority* generally meant the secret police.

'Yes, it seems the half-castes are up to something again ...' Verity shrugged. 'But since you can tell me nothing, our involvement ends here.'

Bibi nodded, straight-faced.

'Hm. Are you able to read secrets in *my* little facial tics and gestures?'

'Oh no. Not at all. It really doesn't work like that.'

It was the second month. Bibi and Mahmood were engaged. Their Families had approved the match; their karyotypes had been declared compatible by a Traditionalist matchmaker, and acceptable by the Reformer Health Board. She left the office feeling that she'd had a lucky escape, and grateful to Verity for guiding her to the correct answers. You don't have to be an Aleutian to know when your boss is quietly telling you to stay out of trouble ...

Mahmood was waiting in the Palaces' RT concourse. They flew to each other through the crush, practically colliding with Superintendent Natouri, the chief of Bibi's section, as they embraced. 'I'll pretend I didn't see that, Bibi,' remarked Natouri, *almost* smiling, as s/he stepped onto a Horizontal and sailed away. The lovers pushed into a crowded Ascent, laughing and blushing.

'Natouri knows your name!' said Mahmood. 'I'm impressed.'

'It was probably you s/he recognised. So it had to be me, by default, unless you have a string of fiancées.' *Superintendent Natouri is still wearing a side-fastening gown*, thought Bibi, and wondered if this was important. Francois hadn't interrogated her for a while.

Now all they had to do was get through 'Training for a Life Together', the pre-partnership course mandatory for Palace officers. A third of entrants failed, terrifying thought: but every sign was hopeful. *Natouri*, with hir well-known negative views on permanent partners, and either/or sexuality, had seen them hugging in public: and had almost smiled!

They met Honesty at Gagarin. Caspian and Nightingale, it transpired, had arrived early at the rendezvous and were ensconced in one of the most fashionable coffee shops in this very upmarket part of town. Honesty was despatched to fetch them. The SP Officers would be stung for a punishing cover charge if they crossed the threshold: Honesty was safe, as her Grade Seven credit line didn't even register at a place like the Luna B.

'There's a simple solution,' Mahmood remarked, as they waited under the eye of the 'bouncer', a sculpted ancient spaceman with a haughty black faceplate. 'We stop worrying and let him pay for everything. He's absurdly wealthy, we're poor, he likes our company, why not?'

'That won't do, Mahmood. I don't mind freeloading – much – but how can we be *friends* when it's as if he's paying us to chaperone her?'

'Which is, in fact, what's happening.'

'He really loves her.'

'As Honesty would say, I'm sure you're right!'

Mahmood had not told tales about the sexbot, though the rancour of that encounter was still burning inside him somewhere. What good would it do? If Nightingale so much as glanced at the society pages (where her existence was never once acknowledged), she must know Konoe had not given up the vices of his caste. And after all, to be honest, it's something to have a prince in your debt—

Gagarin Circle, far above the 'Gagarin' of the branded fortune-tellers, was one of Baykonur's great set pieces. Public buildings and showcase virtual installations vied in the grandeur of their effects; the spectacular floating globes of the gaming arenas rose above trees and lawns. The Starry Arrow of Police HQ presided over the hub. All vehicle traffic, except for VIP access, was removed to arabesques of skyway that swept around the platter, light-catching rings around a spinning planet. It was a place of State ceremony, designed for mass events. In the winter dusk it felt vast, sad and eerily quiet.

'What's taking her so long?' muttered Bibi.

'She's betrayed us, she's eating cake.'

A semi-AI Limo, gold-skinned with a 'chrome' trim, emerged from the Government Hall underpass. Bibi noticed at once that it was a Family car, though it had no insignia.

'Oh, look. It's General Yu—'

'That's a sign of the times. Your General is on the way up again.'

Suddenly a much more plebeian vehicle, a dark-coloured Cruiser, lunged into view, bursting out of a narrow downchute to the left of the underpass. It slalomed through the police barriers at speed and rammed itself into the Limo's offside wing. There was a small explosion, a burst of smoke and flame. The semi-AI reared up, and fell on its side with a shrieking groan—

The Cruiser disengaged, reversed and sped away.

Nightingale, Honesty and the prince had just emerged from the coffee shop. '*What* was that—?' demanded Konoe, as sirens began to wail.

'General Yu—!' cried Bibi.

She ran and the others followed, infected by her urgency. When they reached the scene, two black-visored motorcycle cops from Government Hall had taken charge. The General and the aide-de-camp with him were uninjured. They were watching their driver, who was testing the wreck of the Limo's forward ganglion. One cop was calling for a disposal unit, while the other intimidated a small crowd, drawn into being by the collision.

'Officer!' Bibi elbowed her way to the front. 'We saw everything! We'll give you a statement! That was *not* an accident!'

'Witness claims a hit-and-run,' intoned the cop, scanning Bibi and finding her to be respectable. 'You could identify the perp, or its driver, Miss Officer?' Sex workers and contact-level law enforcement were the two areas exempted, for humanitarian reasons, from the World State's ban on embodied AIs. The robocops, notoriously, did not challenge the Intelligence barrier—

'Sable Brown Cruiser,' reported Nightingale. 'A cab, but no licence or number visible, it has to be injured and I think it was masked. Oh, and I think the driver was a half-caste—'

General Yu's chauffeur got to his feet and announced that the gold Limo had to be put down. Front ganglion gone, extensive collateral damage, it's like it had a massive stroke. There was a murmur of instant sentiment, from the instant crowd: ah, the noble vehicle, it died protecting its master—

'Poor brute.' The General ran a hand through his vigorous chestnut hair. 'I was fond of that car. See to it.' He didn't seem to recognise Honesty or Bibi. There was no reason why he should – it was a long time since the Virgin of the Roof-Beam. 'Now then, Officer, what do you need from me?'

'A disposal facility is on its way, General: and we have a witness, General, sir. The young lady cadet here says—'

'*All* of us,' broke in Honesty, who didn't want to be involved but couldn't desert Nightingale and Bibi. 'We saw the whole thing.'

'These young people are all willing to testify, sir.'

'And one of them is *me*!' added Caspian, not to be outdone by a domestic.

'And one of them is Caspian Konoe, sir ...' The robocop, having relayed this information, bowed deeply. 'Excuse me, Your Majesty, didn't see you there.'

'You do me too much honour, officer. *Your Royal Highness* is sufficient, thank you.'

'Nonsense,' said General Yu, addressing himself to the prince. 'I'm sorry, Caspian, but I think I'd know. The driver of that cab, probably new to the job, didn't know the city, lost his way in the rings and panicked when he found himself shooting out onto Gagarin. It wasn't an assassination attempt, for Heaven's sake. If you think you saw anything else, well, the light's very confusing, this time of day.' He dusted off his gloved hands. 'Cancel the knackers' cart, Officer, my own people will be here shortly. I'd prefer they took him home. Where's that fresh car?'

Another Limo arrived, from the Hall of Government's pool. The General and his ADC were driven away, the passers-by dispersed. The cop Bibi had accosted took a statement, as his basic programming obliged him to do: but it was obvious that he considered the incident closed.

They went flying, after that, at the micro-gravity arena, where Nightingale had guest passes earned as tournament prizes. Honesty and Mahmood's full-sensorium avatars didn't get past the training simulation. Caspian and Bibi did better (Bibi had beginner's luck; the prince had taken a course and was averagely competent). Nightingale was astonishing. The rest of them retired to the spectators' lounge, and just watched her.

By the time they emerged it was midnight, but they were fired with the energy of the arena's adjuvant mix. It was still winter, still party time. They took the RT out to the cabarets at the Old Airport. The dancing was fast and furious, the crowd ebullient: but Bibi was preoccupied, and she (without knowing it) was the one who held this disparate group together. Soon they left the floor, ordered sausage with hot apple wine, and vodka chasers, and found a good table under the Fisherman's protective arms – a tiny guardian, monstrously overwhelmed by the galaxies of Krainiy Ward, one of the few traces left of what the original Baykonur had been.

When they were with Konoe they invariably found a good table. The process was invisible: no fuss, no ceremony, it just happened.

'At least we have one adept,' began Caspian. 'If ever the Blue Planet's armies are called to battle in outer space, which Heaven forbid—'

'What d'you think was going on?' asked Bibi, chin on hand.

Of course, she meant the accident. If anything remotely concerning General Yu or Lady Nef came up, it was impossible to distract her—

Honesty shrugged. 'One of the perks of being a General and a Senior, that's all. If you're knocked down in the street by a mad cabbie, it gets wiped to save you from embarrassment.'

'We don't know it was wiped. *Was* there an explosion? Or did I imagine that?'

'It could have been just the crash,' said Mahmood, 'setting fire to something in the Limo's innards—'

'There was an explosion.' Nightingale stared ahead of her, checking the footage on her eye soc's working record. 'A small one, hardly dangerous. Unless it misfired, maybe. You weren't capt'ing, Mahmood?'

Mahmood used his eye soc' for work and study: not when he had to pay the tariff himself. 'No, I wasn't ... But I did think the General behaved strangely. Why didn't he kick up more of a fuss? He could have been killed.'

Nightingale grinned. 'Maybe he's kicking up a fuss right now, at a dignified level. He just didn't want to waste his time with the robocops.'

'He probably has gambling debts.' Honesty chopped her sausage, and scooped mustard. 'That was his bookie, giving him a heavy hint.'

Caspian Konoe frowned, and moved his chair back—

Bibi's expression had become speculative, and determined. 'Genius? Could you use your skills to find out what happened to my statement?'

Nightingale had been 'the Genius' when Bibi was the Savage and Honesty was the Magnet, back in Juniper Square. 'No skill involved, dear Savage. It should be on the public incident sheet by now.' She communed with her soc'. 'Vehicle collision, Gagarin and HoG, 17.07.39. Oh, it's not there. It must be down as a civil recovery. No, it's not there—'

'Told you,' smirked Honesty. 'Wiped out of history.'

'Maybe you got the time wrong?'

'Well, that's the time of the collision on my soc' and it's telling the right time now.' Nightingale blinked, returning to the material world. 'That's me cleaned out. I'm not going to poke around in secured police data for you.'

'*But* you captured it all on your soc'. You thought the Cruiser was disguised — could you strip the mask out? Could you trace its licence? And you said something about the driver, the driver was a *half-caste*—?'

Honesty rolled her eyes. 'What's the use in that? Nightingale's soc' isn't evidence, Bibi.' Eye-socket records rated poorly as legal testimony: they could be faked, they could be contaminated by the brain, they were regularly torn apart by defence or prosecution—

'We're not in court,' Mahmood pointed out. 'We're just curious.'

'Let me see.' Nightingale's gloved fingertips moved swiftly, under the tabletop. Her lips parted in a dreamy little smile; it was her coding face. 'Hm, well. The Cruiser *was* masked, but not deeply. I can recover the licence plate and put it through the city for you ... Oooh, now, this is funny!'

'What's funny?' demanded Honesty.

'The cab that viciously attacked General Yu's Limo belongs to a company that's listed as one of the holdings of August Councillor Scolari—'

Honesty choked, and had to be thumped between the shoulders. Mahmood took a second or two to get the joke, and snorted in delighted disbelief. Everyone knew about General Yu and the concubine. The whole city, if not the whole World State, had callously enjoyed Pepper Lily's fall — and the General's discomfiture at her poor-taste attempts to win him back. Even Bibi grinned, although she hated scandal—

Konoe finished his chaser and stood up, a proprietorial hand on Nightingale's shoulder. 'You're getting chilled, sweetheart. Let's have another whirl, and leave Honesty to keep the yellowjackets out of trouble. She's a sensible girl.' He signalled for the waiter to bring another round.

Nightingale rose to her feet, smiling: Mahmood caught the briefest of glances, just enough for the *accept* gesture to pass between them.

Two beefy individuals, rather old for cadet uniform, left a nearby table and followed the handsome couple. Nightingale, after that one glance, didn't look back. The prince turned, before he vanished into the crowd, to give the friends his odd, dejected smile.

Nobody spoke until the waiter had come and gone.

The only cloud on the glory of Bibi's future was the fear, amounting to certainty, that her beautiful, brilliant friend was doomed to cruel unhappiness. A prince could be 'madly in love' and get over it in a day or two. Nightingale had a different kind of heart. 'Oh, I hope they don't go for the temporary marriage. That really *would* blight her career.'

'He won't do it,' said Honesty. 'No fear. Not even for a weekend. Why should he? He's got what he wants, and very nice, for as long as he wants her. What a hateful trap she's fallen into, poor girl. Oh, it's *rotten* luck for one of us to be born looking like a princess. It only ends one way.'

Mahmood had never accepted a soc' download from a beautiful girl before. He felt mysteriously shaken: it was as if she'd touched him, intimately, somewhere he couldn't quite locate. He cleared his throat.

'Konoe was right to take himself off. The bodyguards and the society pages are no account, they clip us out and dump us. But he's bound to have a police trace on him, he's a foreigner after all – and that's something else. Nightingale too, by now, poor kid. D'you want to hear what I've got?'

Potentially, theoretically, the least flick of an eyelash in the darkest alley could be recovered from the city's surveillance. Without 'probable cause' the vast majority of Baykonur's inhabitants – mere residents, Palace officers, household servants or citizens of the Empire – could rely on being ignored. They could say what they liked, where they liked; and they did. The girls nodded eagerly, grabbed their second chasers and knocked them back.

What did he mean by smiling at us like that? wondered Bibi. *As if he knows something we don't, as if we're children in his eyes—*

'Well, I've got the whole incident, and the company search, and it looks as if the driver *was* a half-caste. The Cruiser was masked, but he wasn't.'

'Why a half-caste? That's so random—'

'No it isn't, Bibi,' said Mahmood, glad to air his knowledge. 'It's a historical fact that the Aleutians have super-powers over biotech. That's how they conquered us, I mean, apart from us conquering ourselves by starting the Gender Wars. Half-castes can have strange abilities too. I don't know how it adds up, but you'll find them working at every racing stable in the world. You see, it would have been very hard for any normal driver to force that cab to attack a semi-AI. I mean, if it wasn't an accident—'

Bibi and Honesty knew nothing whatever about cars.

'Go on,' said Bibi, feeling a prickle of adrenalin.

'Er ... That's about all, really.'

But *'about all'* was thrilling enough. A half-caste, with something like occult powers, using a masked vehicle for an attack on General Yu's Limo—

'I don't believe it's anything to do with Pepper Lily,' said Honesty. 'In her master's own car? That's ridiculous. She can't be *that* stupid.'

Mahmood had lost interest in the famous concubine. 'Where are we going with this? Are we taking it to the police?'

'I'm not sure—' said Bibi.

The young women looked at each other, frowning, and Mahmood realised, with a twinge of envy, that for them this was personal. It was all about honour: that absurd, Traditionalist obsession. Bibi and Honesty had to protect the Family's name, to shield General Yu from unpleasantness. They were idiots, and yet he wished he felt so close to his Clan Superiors—

'There might be something going on that Lady Nef needs to know about,' muttered Honesty. 'Should we report to her, mistress?'

'Not *yet*,' said Bibi, slowly. 'First we should investigate.'

'How?'

'Well, coincidentally, my supervisor asked me, just today, if I'd noticed anything suspicious going on in the half-caste community—'

This was not precisely true, but near enough.

'Am I allowed to come in on this? Or is it Traditionalists only?'

Honesty whispered audibly into Bibi's ear. 'We should have him along. Reformers, they're all crazy, enemies of the State. When we get caught and dressed down, we can blame him for everything—'

'I agree. If we have to mix with lowlifes, he'll be good cover.'

VIII

Bibi returned to the Settlement House, to ask if she could be put in touch with Looty Loo – or with his sponsor, a cab driver named Aqeel. The nun who received her, in the small office they called their 'parlour', didn't give her a warm welcome. The woman's bare head was cropped and grey, her uniform nondescript: the only flourish a gold bar fastened to the breast, inscribed *Liberté, Egalité, Amitié* ... Bibi remembered that this had once been Lady Nef's creed, and felt a little guilty. But she wasn't going to cause the Settlement any trouble—

'You're the Common Tongue expert, aren't you?'

'Not really,' said Bibi, taken aback.

'I thought you were,' said the nun, dryly. 'We were told that an SP Officer with experience in reading half-castes would attend Buster's wake, and you turned up. Well, whatever you say: I'm sure the Palaces know what they're doing ... Looty and Aqeel's registered domiciles are in the police file. I don't know what more I can do for you.'

'You see, I'd rather meet them informally, somewhere neutral. This isn't a police matter. It's just that Looty Loo seemed very distressed.'

'Buster was one of her regulars, they were close. They don't have much, people like Looty. Losing a friend hits hard, and pointless harassment does not make the loss easier to bear.'

'I was brought up in a Great House,' Bibi answered, with dignity, 'as a foundling. As far as I'm concerned, my patch is my Household, and Looty Loo is family, as if we were in service together. I want to offer what help I can. We have bereavement treatment, or maybe he'd just like to talk?'

'You're the one who walks everywhere. And you have no eye-socket gadget. Isn't that awkward, in your work?'

'I don't like the idea,' explained Bibi. 'My i's good enough for me.'

The nun *almost* smiled. The Sisters of the Human Renaissance liked

64

non-compliance, and independence of mind; especially in a young woman.

'Why don't you try the Church of Self? Looty can often be found there. And I've heard that cab drivers frequent the canteens in that neighbourhood, Aqeel could be among them ... You might find it better not to go in uniform.'

'Thank you very much.'

'Just one more thing. Don't call Looty "he". She doesn't like it.'

The raw freshness of the vegetable gardens reminded Bibi of Kirgiz and tempted her to linger: but it wouldn't be tactful to hang around, where she had been identified as an informer. *Thanks for nothing,* she thought. It wasn't news that a whore who specialised in half-castes might be found working around the Church of Self ... Still, it was an idea. *The Common Tongue expert* – she would have to get rid of that reputation; she hoped she could trust Verity Tan to help her. Who had ordered the SP to send a 'Common Tongue' expert to the wake? And why had the nuns allowed their House (full of illicit children) to be used for a suspicious gathering in the first place? Were they cooperating – like the SP – to protect themselves?

The nun had been on her guard, but the words Bibi had 'heard in her head' as she quit the office had been very clear: *If you are as innocent as you seem, child, then stay out of this. Run away, get away—* She had no idea what was going on, but she knew she was brushing against the fringes of something big and dangerous. All the more reason to find out what was behind that Limo incident.

IX

The Xi'an Government's Baykonur Residence was an old Town House on Arbat, metaphorically and physically far away from the majestic shopfront of Gagarin – a snub that wasn't lost on the locals. Leaders of fashion affected to find Arbat receptions tedious, cheapskate affairs. They were having to change their tune this time, however. The problems that made wealthy stockbrokers irritable at breakfast were trickling down into real life. The Gateway City urgently needed to win favours from Central Government: which was exactly Nef's mission, when she arrived for a private interview with His Excellency. But Xue was an old friend, old sparring partner, so they came to the point gradually.

He was waiting for her when she was shown to his rooms: still slim as a blade, his hair still black, though sadly thinning, his lined, aquiline features as vivid as they had ever been.

'You don't change, Snow.'

The Envoy passed a rueful palm over his depleted crown. 'Nor do you, Beauty, and *I* can say that without flattery—'

'My mirror can't. But thank you.'

The cast of their features betrayed a shared ancestry in the north-east of Africa, though Xue's complexion was darker. Their approach to ageing belonged to the generation of the Departure, when those few who'd earned the right to an extended lifespan disdained cosmetic 'youthfulness'. Neither of them liked the backlash that they had lived to see: the fervid, furtive pursuit of perfect babies, the cruel shedding of substandard offspring. But that's the price you pay for becoming a Senior. You don't just outlive your own drama, you live to see the effects of your treasured ideals on the next generation, and the next—

Xue kissed her hands and led her into the room; they settled on two throne-like chairs that were more comfortable than they looked. The

Arbat House ran cold – a self-defeating austerity in the Upper City's self-generated heat, but symbolically important. The Envoy wore a round silk cap and a long, padded, crimson Chinese gown over his trousers, fastened with frogging down the centre. Nef had dressed warmly, anticipating the chill: but she hadn't anticipated the front fastening. Yarrow stalks tumble. The dice roll to a standstill. Click follows clack as the gears engage—

'Tell me all about you,' he ordered, expansively. 'And all about me, too, of course.'

Nef folded her hands. 'Well. I'm worried about my son—'

'He'll find himself.'

'Maybe, maybe not. Talent often skips a generation, and I'm afraid Yu has left Amal too much to his own devices. I'm very happy that my daughters are both settled, *and* that neither of them chose an ambitious husband, it's so refreshing—'

'Nothing about Beauty herself.'

'I'm saving my conversation for our social meetings, and telling you the things that would cause an awkward silence. There are no hopes of grandchildren, which I very much regret: but I accept my fate, and shall not leave the narrow path that the people tread without any choice.'

The collapse of (natural) human fertility would right itself, soon: all scientific opinion was agreed on that. Soon, but not yet.

Xue was childless himself. He inclined his head, smiling sadly. 'And what about me?'

'You're a boring old skinflint.'

'Excellent!'

'No one would cross a walkway to get invited to this house.'

'That's the way I like it.'

'But they find they love you anyway. Dazzling society beauties are plotting as we speak to draw you out, and shower you with attentions.'

'Sounds expensive ... Is one of the dazzlers Scolari's concubine?'

'I'm afraid so. I hope she succeeds in pleasing you. She's so angry with the General, it's getting on my nerves.'

'Well, well.' The Envoy grinned. 'Does she always dress like that?'

'Except when she wears less.'

One of the awkward silences descended. A Dutch clock, older than First Contact, sang out from the mantel above a fine enamelled stove: *Ting! Ting! Ting!* The Envoy pressed the ball of his right thumb to his lips, where his smile had stalled in regret. He felt that this woman,

67

whom he'd known since the world was young, had been putting her affairs in order, auditing her soul.

'Are you *sure* that you want this post for him?'

'I'm certain. My "Swimmer" and I need a new direction.'

'Lest he sink beneath the waves?'

'We need to grow. I look forward to my old age, Snow. I fully intend to end my days peacefully in the Great House, in Kirgiz. But that doesn't mean I want to spend the second half of my career waiting for the holidays to start.'

'Have you thought of adopting? Grandchildren, I mean.'

Nef laughed. 'Old friend, I am *not* looking for a diplomatic commission for my husband because I have no babies to play with! I'm surrounded by young people, many of whom are dear to me, and I have followed their careers with great pleasure.'

'Ah, the past tense.' He sighed. 'It's yours. His, I mean, of course.'

Nef had known this the moment she walked into the room.

'Thank you.'

'You could leave in about six weeks. Is that far too soon?'

'It's *very* soon—' said Nef, doubtfully.

He raised his hands to forestall her. 'It's immaterial – if you need six months, a year, you can have it. You'll want to talk it all over with Yu and Francois, anyway. Oh, I assume Francois will be travelling with you?'

'Of course.'

Another silence. Xue Pao reached to the carved table that stood by his chair, and ran a wooden wand around the rim of a small bronze bowl. A singing tone welled up, a simple, complex lotos flower of sound—

'We shouldn't talk about it, but I believe you really met her, once: the Mother Queen of the West ... What did she say to you?'

Lady Nef looked at the Tibetan bowl, admiring the deep lustre of its inner surface. 'She said that anyone who desires immortality is unfit for it, and the promise is better if it's never kept. She said that I hold an empty title, Snow, but it would be useful for mystification.'

The doors of the room opened. A very pretty maid appeared, with a tray of wine and cakes. She was a robot, which told her role in the Envoy's life, and another old friend. She set the tray down, and bowed—

'Let's have some wine,' exclaimed Xue. 'Let's enjoy the meagre refreshments those skinflints in Xi'an allow me to provide, and the three of us can talk about old times.'

And try forget, he added, to himself, *that I shall never see you again.*

Lady Nef took her wine cup from Sea-Rose's porcelain-perfect hands, and prepared to be good company for at least another hour or so: while deep inside, the Nef of the awkward silences allowed herself a mental pose of trembling, exhausted relief. *So that's done,* she thought. *That's settled.*

Next, to tackle the new mess that had been uncovered, blessedly and quite fortuitously, by Pepper Lily's idiotic malice.

Six weeks was not too soon. It was hardly soon enough.

X

The Church of Self was called a 'club' because, strictly speaking, half-castes had no right of religious assembly. The Republic did not *persecute* the living fossils of an alien regime, but it didn't encourage them. It stood, a big domed cube of rusty brown with vaulted extensions on each of the four faces, on one of the most dismal squares in Bibi's patch. Bedraggled shrubs struggled around it; a Recovery conduit shuddered overhead – almost grazing the dome, almost blocking the distant light from above. On the steps and forecourt the lowest of human whores plied their trade. In the canteens round about the cab drivers – some of them half-castes, most of them police informers, pimps, receivers of stolen goods – closed shady deals.

The building had been destroyed several times, but there was supposed to have been a 'Church of Self' on the site for hundreds of years, almost from the birth of this strange sect. Most of the half-castes in Baykonur lived close by, many of them in great poverty – which didn't prevent their 'normal' human neighbours from regarding them as sinister criminals, always the first to be suspected in any kind of trouble.

Mahmood and Honesty surveyed the grimy monument uneasily. 'What's our story again?' wondered Mahmood.

'We're yellowjackets, partners looking for an elusive client,' said Bibi. 'What could be more ordinary?' The nun had advised Bibi to leave her uniform at home, but that would have been a big mistake. In plain clothes, even Bibi would have become a threatening stranger around here.

'What about me?' Honesty had never been down so far before. She preferred not to know about places like this. 'What's *my* cover?'

'You're our chaperone, of course. Come on, let's go.'

They moved around the square, politely accosting the illegal sex-workers – presenting as women, but actually male: for some reason this was the arrangement that half-castes preferred. Bibi and Honesty kept making the 'he' mistake, they couldn't help it. Mahmood never did. None of the whores admitted to knowing Looty, or recognising 'her' mugshot. But that meant nothing. It was still daylight up above: maybe it was too early. Bibi decided they should check inside the Church itself.

Honesty didn't like the idea. 'Won't the critters mind?'

'Not at all. I've often been inside.'

'But why would he, er, she be in a church?'

'Well, it's where her customers are. And it's dark, should they be shy.'

'Eech.'

Bibi was stung by her friends' reaction to her favourite monstrosity. 'It's an interesting, historical place. You ought to see it once. We'll do the same as out here, show the image, try to make contact. It's better if we split up, so we don't look too intrusive. If you get a response, and it's "Silent", you can fetch me. Oh, but remember, don't speak aloud unless they speak to you first.'

The rotting metal doors hadn't been opened for a long time. Bibi lifted the latch on a postern of recovered plastic, which itself looked very old. In the dark space they entered she covered her face, briefly. Mahmood and Honesty copied the gesture. A sign appeared in the air, triggered by their arrival: big silver Roman capitals admonishing SILENCE.

'They've never met our Francois,' muttered Honesty.

Bibi set her finger across her lips. Honesty rolled her eyes and grinned.

The body of the church, so cave-like it seemed excavated rather than built, was divided by two rows of thick, rugged columns. Mahmood pointed at the floor, mugging, *Meet back here?* The young women nodded: Mahmood took the left aisle, Honesty took the right.

Bibi walked into the dark, using the brightness of her iface as a torch. There were no windows. No provision for lighting, no light except the glimmer of the screens. Every column was a shrine. Most were open, displaying place-holder footage from the lives of half-caste martyrs and heroes. Some were occupied. Hunched bodies stirred as she approached: mutilated human faces turned, blotted black in the centre. Saw the familiar yellowjacket and resumed their worship, indifferent.

Bibi had once spent a terrifying half-hour trapped in an Aleutian's character shrine. She hadn't known what it was, at the time (or she'd have been even more scared). She was better informed now. Aleutian children, physically reincarnated, were set to study the records of their former lives, waiting for the *moment of recognition* – when they awoke, remembered, became themselves again. There were 'priests' who helped people to make more records, every life, to add to the store. Character study for Aleutians was as necessary as learning to walk; mystical if you wanted it to be.

The Self is God.

But what did the half-castes believe? A hundred years after the aliens had left, why did human beings still mutilate themselves, still choose to become outcasts? Nobody outside the community really understood. They had no *real* records of their own past lives, of course. They crouched, indifferently, in front of newsreels, famous fiction, ancient CCTV archives from before the Enclosures – as if only the act of gazing mattered. As if any face in the teeming human past might become a pathway to True Self. Bibi thought of the flowery courtyards of the Great House, the forest of Kushan, wild geese in a dawn sky. The fried grasshoppers she had never found, all the fascinating and disturbing sights of the lower city.

Loyalty, honour, obligation—

Mahmood realised that someone was following him, and the hairs rose on the back of his neck. A monster that had once been human was creeping up on him in the dark. The shrines on either side were empty, screens buzzing grey, maybe out of service. He stepped into one, and the light of his iface caught a wriggle of movement. A string of tiny human limbs had been hung above the screen, a little leg kicking, a miniature hand fumbling the air. Broken toys, nothing more: but what did it mean? He heard the beastlike footfalls, and spun around to find it right behind him: peering, with altered eyes that showed no whites at all, through a tangle of lank seaweed hair. It was ridiculous to be afraid. *Don't be the first to speak*, he remembered. He pointed at the doll's body parts, mugging puzzlement.

What does it mean?

'You're a part,' said the half-caste, in a voice as thin and rusty as if it hadn't been used for centuries. 'I'm apart. We're ghosts, see. Layers of ghosts, all touching, all throughout space. I'm Top Layer, I'm an illusion.'

'Top Layer' wore ragged overalls the colour of mud, open to the waist over a bare, ropy-muscled chest about the same hue; so you could see he'd had his nipples removed. His nasal wound, rough-edged and mucus-crusted, made a skull of the ravaged face: the upper lip was crudely split, drawn back from naked, yellowed baboon fangs. Half-castes rejected human gender. They were neither male, female nor undecided, but this one *felt* masculine to the Reformer. It, he, raised a crooked paw, palm outwards, in front of his face.

'Talk to the hand.'

Mahmood relaxed. Stupid indeed to be afraid. 'So, um, Top Layer. Who were you? Have you ever been anyone famous?'

He knew that in the old days they always used to believe they'd been famous in previous incarnations: Elvis, Mahatma Gandhi, Braemar Wilson. Superman or Fiorinda, fact or fiction, they didn't care.

The half-caste chuckled. 'Who are *you*? And what are you doing here?'

He, it, took a step backwards and immediately vanished. Instinctively Mahmood gave chase. He hurried up and down, blundering into echoey, interconnecting side chapels – getting thoroughly bewildered, while trying to stay respectful in a place of worship. There was no sign of his quarry.

Bibi and Honesty were waiting at the back of the church. 'One of them spoke to me!' he hissed, far too loud. 'But then he *vanished*!'

The silver letters sprang out again, indignant.

SILENCE!

Bibi took his arm, and pointed to the postern. Outside on the steps he described the encounter. 'I didn't get to, *Do you know Looty Loo*, didn't have a chance. But he followed me, *spoke* to me, inside the Church of Self, right after we'd been asking for her outside. That's got to mean something—'

'Let's find a canteen full of shifty cab drivers,' suggested Bibi, after a pause for thought. 'And regroup.'

There were a couple of soup kitchen *distributeurs* nearby, where the food and drink were free, and unadulterated. But if you really couldn't stand living on the city's welfare, you could come to a place like The Aleutia, on the corner of Church of Self Square, and get yourself poisoned instead. Nobody looked up when the yellowjackets and their maid walked into the canteen. Maybe the stark white lighting (sure sign of a recent brush with the police) hurt people's eyes. The investigators chose food from the moving band, paid in *cash* and took their pasteboard trays to a niche between roof supports; where they could watch both doorways. Honesty wrinkled her nose at a caterpillar roll, grey flecked with an oozy ochre yellow. 'What's *in* this, d'you think?'

'About seven per cent poor-quality insect protein,' Mahmood offered, promptly. 'Ninety-two per cent water, air and sterilised human excrement. Plus approved flavourings, vitamins and trace elements. Social Knowledge did a survey.' He tucked in.

The Han girl pushed her plate away, and watched with respect. 'Look at him, he has no fear. He's a *real* Social Warrior.'

'Killed shit won't hurt you, as long as you don't eat it too often—'

'Let me tell you what happened at the Settlement,' said Bibi, stirring her bowl of green noodles and scummy broth. The smell was oddly authentic, detergent and sour kasha, like Francois's food parcels—

'When you went back there?'

'No, the first time. It was a ... a kind of murder inquiry, disguised as a wake. The friends and contacts of the deceased had come along, maybe they were scared to stay away, and Looty Loo was asking them if they knew anything. But they wouldn't talk.'

Mahmood uncapped his beer and peered down the neck of the bottle. One hundred per cent insect protein in there, in the shape of a long-dead fly. '*Could* they speak? Aren't there some who literally can't?'

'There used to be half-castes who had their tongues cut out, or even had their speech centres fried. But they must all be dead by now. No, I mean they weren't talking at all. I realise now they were too frightened.'

'Of course they were scared,' said Honesty. 'Anything to do with the police—'

Mahmood set down his fork. '*Wait* a moment. I thought you told Verity Tan you couldn't understand a word?'

'I did,' said Bibi. 'She as good as ordered me to say that. When she told me she'd have had to pass on any information to "another authority", I was very glad I'd got the message—'

'The Starry Arrow,' murmured Honesty. 'Oooh.'

Not all of Baykonur's police were good-natured bulky toys.

'You have to let me explain. I told Verity the truth: I told her I'd nothing much to add to the transcript. But when I went back, and the nun said, "You're the Common Tongue expert," I realised that any of the guests at the wake could have known of me as the SP officer who "speaks a bit of Common Tongue" and that changes the context. Often, even if people are spilling their guts, you only understand a Silent conversation *afterwards*, when you have context—'

'Unless you're a real Aleutian,' put in Honesty.

'Well, yes, I suppose. So now I can tell you, I did "hear" a few fragments. There was *something big*, and *a sick friend, far away* – that could have been Buster, being dead. And Looty Loo was into something frightening. I suppose that could have meant trying to find out how his friend got killed—'

Honesty jumped in. 'What's all this got to do with the General?'

'Nothing.' Mahmood ate another mouthful of caterpillar roll; it wasn't too bad. 'It's an excuse to hang around half-castes, and ask questions.'

'Nothing,' agreed Bibi, quickly. 'I *hope*, but—'

'Oh, if there's trouble, he's in it,' growled Honesty. 'I can *smell* him, getting into something rank as this shit roll—'

These are murky waters, thought Mahmood. 'Look,' he began, 'can we recap? Someone tried to run the General down, Pepper Lily seems implicated. Or else Scolari himself. Everyone knows the wily old brute uses his trophy mistress to ensnare fools like Yu, but maybe the mad way she's been behaving has got even him jealous—'

Bibi and Honesty recoiled, deeply affronted. Pepper Lily was a leader of society. Concubine was a legal status, a respectable career, although not one they'd have chosen. *Mistress* meant something completely different. They felt that both Pepper and their lady were insulted by this insensitive Reformer language—

'What did I say? I'm sorry, whatever it was. Look, how about trying the racing stables? Maybe the Church of Self idea is a false trail, the wrong way forward—' He stopped, his mouth dropping open.

'What's the matter?' asked Bibi. 'Are you feeling sick?'

'Don't look now,' breathed Mahmood, electrified, 'but Top Layer just sneaked in by the side door, behind you two. He's sitting with someone, looks like a rendezvous. *I think it's the driver of the Cruiser.*'

'You're kidding!' yelped Honesty, and put her hand over her mouth.

Mahmood pulled up the collision footage, aligned the best headshot, on Nightingale's capture of the accident, with the profile across the room, and blinked again. 'It's him: no question. *Don't* look round, Honesty—'

'I'm not!'

Bibi's dark eyes were black with excitement. 'Can "Top Layer" see us? Has he seen *you*?'

'I don't think so. He's keeping his head down, I don't think he likes the white light. Oh … he's given the driver something. Now he's leaving—'

'We should follow him,' hissed Honesty. 'Find out what he's up to.'

'Except he's already spotted me, and warned me off. Here's an idea. I'll get another beer and tag the driver. We can follow *him*. Better than trying to question him in here.'

'Sure you can do it without the client knowing?' asked Bibi, briskly.

'Sure.'

Mahmood strolled to the counter and strolled back, making a slight detour to pass the table where the half-caste cab driver sat huddled, in an oversized greatcoat, staring into a beaker of broth. He didn't look inhuman, this one. He looked like a tired little man whose creased, defeated face had been in a knife fight; or who'd been punished, long ago, for some squalid, shameful crime.

He sat down again, giving Bibi a wink. Honesty was scandalised and impressed. 'You two carry *tags* around with you? What for?'

'You'd be surprised.' Bibi grinned. 'Caseworkers often have to chase people. Our clients need help, but they don't always want it—'

'It was a required course at college: location and pursuit.'

The tired little man with no nose kept them waiting for another five minutes. At last he crumpled his beaker, stuffed it in the recovery slot and shuffled out of The Aleutia. Mahmood and Bibi consulted the tracking function on their ifaces—

'Got him,' murmured Mahmood.

'Me too. Give him another minute, and let's go.'

It was dusk by now up above, almost full dark in this shadowy realm. Glims of light showed the whores' pitches around the Church of Self; furtive couples drifted across the square, melted into the shrubbery, slipped out of the Church or into it. The tired little man, however, had not lingered. He was out of sight already. Bibi paused for thought. She and Mahmood had signed themselves out for an afternoon of home study. No one would be looking for them. No one would be looking for Honesty, either. But still—

'You ought to go home, Honesty.'

'*Why?*'

'Because we're yellowjackets, invisible, but you look like what you are, incredibly out of place. It was all right in daylight, but—'

'My tunic has a grey lining. I'll turn it inside out.' The Magnet pulled

76

her tunic over her head, revealing a very pretty and low-cut chemise, and neatly reversed it.

'We'd better hurry,' said Mahmood, blushing (she hadn't given him a chance to look away), 'or we'll lose him.'

There were no moving walkways, no escalators, no elevators in the lower city. Maintenance had proved too difficult. The natives tended to view transport mechanisms as handy weapons for murder or intimidation. A nest of alleys, broken paving and mud: footpath-width, but clearly used by determined vehicles. A small market of open booths, in pools of dim light, selling live rats and rabbits, old clothes, toys, broken curios: all the random oddments that only *cash* would buy. In a way it was an ideal Baykonur they traversed, a minimum-energy, closed-cycle city where everyone was out on the street, keeping an eye on everyone else. But nobody challenged the Social Care Officers and their maid (the reversed tunic didn't disguise Honesty much). Yellowjackets on some charitable errand were a familiar sight, the only invaders from above who were accepted; even welcome—

At last the trace came to a standstill. They peered round a corner: the driver stood at the entrance to a gated yard. A thundering high-speed stream of lights passed overhead, shedding blackness in its wake – and the little man was gone. They approached the gate, cautiously.

Honesty recoiled. 'Gaggh. What's that *smell*?'

The lower city had powerful, gamey and challenging perfumes. This one surpassed the lot: silage and rotting flesh, with a soupçon of foul gas.

'It's a breaker's yard,' said Mahmood, who'd been spooling through the Palace Ward directory on his soc'. 'Or it was, fairly recently. Smells like the kind of dump where they pretend to recycle, and really they patch up the crashes with bits of animal tissue, put them back on the road—'

'The *Cruiser*!' exclaimed Bibi. 'The hit-and-run car. It was injured, they had to hide it somewhere! I bet he's come here with a killcard, so the police can't question it! I bet that's what "Top Layer" was fixing up!'

Semi-AI vehicles were expensive, few and strictly regulated, cradle to cradle: the World State feared their emergent consciousness. The ubiquitous Cruisers, Sedans, Coupes, Jazzes were, ironically, much more difficult to render inert. The General's Limo had a CNS that could be burned out at a keystroke, leaving nothing but inanimate carbon, ceramic and crystal. A cab was grown from Aleutian cell culture. Its limited sentience, working memory, might be recovered to some extent from a handful of bodywork.

The breaker's yard was contained in an envelope of hygienic membrane, which didn't contain the stink but made it impossible for them to get inside except through the gate: which was guarded by a stun-beam box with a faded *Danger of Death* warning. Mahmood and Bibi considered their options. They couldn't contemplate backing off now.

'I'll switch off my eye soc',' said Mahmood, carefully. 'I can't afford to record every living minute.'

'Good idea. Can you get us in? The air of neglect may be deceptive.'

'I'll see what I can do.' Mahmood walked up and down in the dark, found a sweet-spot and used his iface to call the night desk at Social Knowledge.

'What's he doing?' whispered Honesty.

'Getting an override key to the stun-beam. We can usually do that, without special authority, if the security's private and low grade.'

'So you can *burglarize*, as well as tag people! I think I'll change my career plan.'

'There's not a lot of money in social work,' Bibi warned her.

They passed safely through, into a fog of stench. Mahmood restored the beam. Faint, raw methane flares lit a graveyard of dead and dying cars: bodywork collapsed into bags of leathery skin, coloured hide defaulted to grey; great patient, suffering, lidless eyes that watched them go by.

'Disgusting,' muttered Mahmood. 'Fuse the parts from different brutes, patch up the operating systems with blobs of brain from feral cats, which will wake up in agony and go mad when the idiot who bought the melange is trapped inside—'

'Coming to a shiny-looking Scolari dealership near you,' agreed Honesty. 'It's horrible what happens in this city.'

Bibi shrugged. In the Great House, too, the grotesque, and even the wicked side of life had not been stifled. Baykonur was just bigger. The Palace officers took a grip on their stun batons. Honesty walked between them. They spotted the little half-caste near the back: on his knees, half-in and half-out of a hulk that might once have been a Sable Brown Cruiser.

They crouched as near as they dared, between two elephantine corpses. They could hear the little man talking to the dying cab, in a

78

crooning singsong: *Hush, hush, there's my good lass, you lie quiet, soon be better now* ...

'What if we play innocent?' hissed Mahmood. 'Walk up and ask him what he's up to? If the car's worth killing, that proves it knows something. We stop him from destroying the evidence. He runs for it, we report this place to the police, they do the rest—'

'Oh, hm, the police—?' Bibi felt there was a breakdown in communication. She and Honesty wanted to report to Lady Nef.

Honesty grabbed Bibi's arm. '*Look!*'

They were no longer alone. Black shadows, moving fast, had appeared from nowhere and were flowing through the yard: bodymasks, bent double, noiseless, glimpsed as they crossed between rows. The half-caste looked over his shoulder, jumped up and ran for the perimeter. A stab of white, a penetrating acid smell. The little man's silhouette squeezed through the tear he'd made; the shadows followed him and were suddenly gone: the whole drama vanished. Bibi raced to the Cruiser. The driver's door hung open. The dashboard casing had started to liquefy, the killcard itself a spreading stain, inextricably mingled with the machine's tissue, leaching all life from it—

'*Damn!* Too late, it's gone.'

'Forensics can probably still prove it was the hit-and-run car.'

'But we need to know *why* he got attacked.'

'Let's get away from here,' suggested Honesty. 'I don't want to meet those, those black ninjas. I wonder who they were—'

They left the way they had come in. The RT way, far above, was quiet; it was very dark. No sign of any ninjas, but as they crossed the alley, heading back to the lighted streets, Bibi stumbled over a yielding obstacle.

It was the tired little cabbie. He lay with one arm across his face, in a spreading, sticky puddle that gleamed black as she turned up her iface. She squatted, coat tucked out of the way of the blood, and felt for a pulse.

'I think they've killed him—'

The half-caste stirred and gripped her wrist.

'*Yellowjackets ... Real?*'

'Yes. Who are you? Who were those masked people?'

'*Tell him. Tell him I succeeded! Ah. Long live the Republic!*'

The cabbie smiled, pride and life went out of his eyes, a shudder passed over his mutilated face. 'I've still got the trace,' cried Mahmood, his voice breaking with bewilderment and shock. 'I still have the trace!'

Then they saw, as if painted on the dark, a white face with a blot at the centre, looking back at them from along the alley: an expression of implacable, sly malevolence. A half-caste, *another* half-caste, holding a light under his face, the cabbie's greatcoat bundled under his arm—

'After him!' cried Mahmood.

The face vanished. When they reached the spot they found an open door, at the foot of a lightless, precipitous flight of steps. They pelted upwards and along a level passage, in the greenish glow of *perpetual illumination*, the city's oldest lighting system. Long-dead indoor trees, espaliered along broken mirrored walls, reflected their iface lights in white dashes as they ran. Withered tendrils reached from overhead. Bibi guessed they'd joined a *traverse*, one of the old secret ways to cross the city, from one great Town House to another: used now only by the underworld. Another flight of steps, plunging down, flung them out into a tiny brilliant square full of lights, tables, white linen. The diners, well dressed in a certain style, were on their feet, several with guns in their hands, blocking the pursuit—

'Let us pass, let us pass—'

'We're not the police, we're the SP, that person's a client—!'

'He needs help!'

'Oh, it's Bibi.' A heavy-jowled toad of a man with a red face and a gold chain flicked the guns aside. 'Let her go. Bibi's all right.'

'Thank you, *thank you*, Nazrat—'

A squirm of ragged children, huddled together for the night. An open footbridge crossing the smell of grass and water; by and gone. A roofless hangar where a crowd of people danced in silence, each in a separate trance of music. They never lost the trace, it seemed they *couldn't* lose it, but they couldn't catch the fugitive—

'D'you know where we are, Bibi?'

Mahmood's breath was close in the utter dark.

'I've a feeling we're back on my patch. And I've lost the trace—'

'Me too ... I think we may actually be underground.'

'Let's have some light. Can't do any harm if we've lost him.'

Breathless, they held up their ifaces and peered around, murmuring in amazement at what they saw.

'What a lot of *bones*. Are they human bones?'

'Looks like it, Honesty.' Bibi let her frail white glow rest on a stack of black-eyed skulls, all lacking the lower jaw.

'Hence the expression—' Mahmood had spotted a plaque with incised Roman lettering '—*Ossuary*. That means a human boneyard.'

'In what language?' demanded Honesty. 'You're making that up.'

'We might be under the Church of Self,' said Bibi. 'It's the only place I can think of where there are big structures under the original ground level. And they used to preserve their dead, like, like dried meat. They thought it was what Aleutians do.'

'Eech. But how did we get in? And how are we going to get out?'

There were tombs among the bones. Mouldering stone boxes, carved and lettered, stood around on the dank earth floor: one, two, five or six, more: vanishing into the dark. *That's not right*, thought Bibi. *Half-castes don't do that ...* Puzzled, obscurely *attracted*, she approached one and touched it. The stone was not stone: it was a mask. Holding up her i in one hand, she ran the other palm over the outline of a glassy-smooth, man-sized sarcophagus.

'Mahmood? Come here.'

Mahmood made the same bewildering discovery. 'What *are* these things? What are they doing here? Any ideas?'

The context that she'd been lacking descended on Bibi like a falling banner. She could not understand the hit-and-run, but she knew why the nuns at the Settlement had been scared, why Buster had died, why the police were on the alert, maybe why the half-castes had been complicit—

Her world fell apart.

She had no future.

The ossuary was suddenly flooded with light. The ninjas' bodymasks looked like black paper cut-outs against the yellowed bones and clay-coloured earth walls. They stood aside, in two rows, like a troop of soldiers making way for their officers. The men, if they were men, who came forward were also in black, but wore vivid fancy-dress head-masks: a dragon, a demon, a white tiger, a glaring eagle with two eyes in front. She didn't know the others, but she was horrified to know she *recognised* the dragon, all gold and crimson feelers – by the presence she had been trained to read, as a student of the Silence. By the way he stood, by the set of his shoulders—

The half-caste who'd led them into the trap was there too: malicious, satisfied.

'You won't get anything out of this,' said Bibi to that person. 'They don't care about your people. They're just *using* you, whatever they've promised—'

'You must die,' boomed the white tiger, pompous even through the distortion on his voice. 'Your young bodies will be found, victims of bitter underclass discontent, how sad, how shocking, what a proof of our cause. But you don't have to suffer.'

'Surrender quietly,' warned the eagle, his vocal identity equally mangled. 'Dupes of an evil regime. Or it will be slow and ugly—'

'The tombs are Buonarotti couches!' shouted Bibi. 'They're *expecting* someone! RUN for it, get out if you can. Long live the Republic—!'

She launched herself at the tiger, using her stun baton like a club: saw Mahmood crash through the cordon of black masks, Honesty dropping and rolling, then lost sight of both. She was grabbed, smacked around the head, punched in the mouth, her arms dragged behind her back. She pulled up her feet, kicking out high, and flung her weight backwards. Her assailant went down. Bibi landed free but was immediately crushed, percussive toecap blows raining on her ribs, her belly. She was dragged to her feet again; she fought so that something cold slicing across her throat missed its target but got her shoulder: and then something *else*, an animal, a monster, came like a whirlwind on clawed feet. It tore her away from the knife, threw her aside and leapt back into the fray.

Fool! Get the hell out of here!

—couldn't tell if the monster had spoken aloud, or if the snarled, inhuman order was in her mind.

XI

There was an item of 3D mail waiting when Bibi finally got to her rooms. It must have arrived after she'd gone out to work, the day before. She made the *accept* gesture with her left hand, and watched a small dark blue envelope materialise. It was from Caspian Konoe. She picked it up, transferred it awkwardly to her right hand, which was held against the opposite shoulder by the sling the First Aid room had applied, and tipped the contents out onto her palm. No letter. Just a paper flower, acrid-scented, storm-cloud blue striated with bruise-maroon ... So that was a warning: Caspian wouldn't lie with scent or colour.

Maybe something horrible had happened to Nightingale.

Bibi didn't like psychoactive media; she didn't even like taking the adjuvants in a games arena. But she tossed the wafer into her mouth and went through into the bedroom.

All in a blank daze.

Someone was speaking to her, in a low, rapid voice ... *Throughout all history, China, like Japan, has striven to keep the military away from power. Even the First Emperor disarmed her Generals as soon as she had established her reign. That's why our battles are fought with frail flesh, not invincible robotics. It isn't just to keep the underclass numbers down!*

Caspian was sitting beside her, in his scarlet and olive uniform: intensely earnest, trying to get her to understand something.

*General Yu is involved in something that has been discovered and is about to explode, destroying all who touch it. I know what loyalty means to you, but don't let him drag you down with him, stay out of this, **please**, Bibi—*

The room in her mind, ephemeral construct where the message could not be intercepted, and outside of which the message did not exist, became her room in the external world again. Caspian had gone. Her gashed

83

shoulder was hurting, her ribs ached, her bruised face felt twice its size. She wondered if Nightingale had helped him with the encryption.

Too late. Old news. And what now?

In another part of the house, in a drawing room clad in the grand, austere style of the First Empire – modestly refurbished for house arrest – her fate was being decided: among other topics of discussion. General Yu, a little out of place in his wife's suite, a little dishevelled, his uniform tunic open over a white shirt that wasn't fresh, restlessly occupied a wide armchair. He grasped the boot propped on his right knee by the ankle, and rocked to and fro.

'I looked up and there your girl was. *Unbelievable* bad luck ... Pepper's smart idea, you see, was that the Limo would be impounded for CNS disposal, they'd find the contraband and I would be disgraced. She really is the *stupidest* little tart alive—'

'Please don't insult her,' said Lady Nef. 'You embarrass me.'

The General looked at his wife: and grimaced, ruefully. 'All right. I'm sorry, point taken, I won't mention her name.'

When she had realised, a year or two into their marriage, that Yu would always be unfaithful, Nef had chosen concubines for him: as was her right, in the archaic, resurrected terms of their culture. When he'd persisted in finding other women, whose principal attraction was that Nef had *not* chosen them, she'd withdrawn from their sexual relation-ship – and allowed him to discover, over time, without a murmur of confrontation, that the breach was permanent. And Yu had accepted her decision, without a murmur.

Every young Traditionalist woman who marries for love thinks she'll have the man to herself, and every one of them is disappointed. But time forges stronger bonds than jealousy, passion or affection, or even mutual respect. Time and a common cause, and the habit of perils shared.

The contraband had been hidden in the head of the young man posing as General Yu's ADC. Francois and Nef had believed that their ally was free and clear of involvement in the doomed conspiracy. Of course, being Yu, he had not warned them about this 'last favour' that Scolari had extracted, until he'd run into trouble—

'*Unbelievable* bad luck,' muttered the General again.

His wife and her secretary exchanged a wry glance. On the contrary, Pepper's hit-and-run had been a piece of unbelievable *good* luck. They had gone to work immediately: repairing the damage in bold strokes, quietly chasing loose ends. The Limo had been disposed of, with impeccable certification. The cab driver recruited by Pepper had been traced, along with his vehicle, and had turned out to be a loyal patriot of the Republic. (The fact that this driver had worked for a company traceable to Scolari's holdings seemed to have been pure coincidence. Or else proof that Pepper really *was* the stupidest tart alive ...) Francois had convinced the trusting soul that he, Francois, was a Xi'an Government agent. Pepper Lily was the enemy, and General Yu was a good guy. The injured cab must wiped with a killcard, in case it held memories that might be useful to the forces of evil.

But General Yu had not mentioned Bibi.

Francois, ironically looking the neatest and most rested of the three, rubbed a clawed fist against the rim of his nasal. 'What about the fellow who led our young friends to the crypt? I believe it was our old friend Looty Loo, masked. He turns up too often, which strikes me as dangerous: what do you know of him?'

'Only that you should have killed the bastard.'

'I disagree. I felt more disposed to break up that charming party, without further casualties or revelations ... What about his real name?'

'His *real name*!' Yu writhed around to face the speaker, glaring. 'You know as well as I do, that's a meaningless question! James Bond. Genghis Khan. All right? Are you satisfied?'

'There is a great deal of difference between *James Bond* and *Genghis Khan*. If you could settle on one of those, it would tell me much.'

'For God's sake! What's *your* name, *Francois*?'

'Oh, I'm Top Layer. I'm an illusion.' Francois groaned and stretched: he wasn't used to running gait, all his muscles seemed in spasm this morning. 'Ah, what a coil. If I had spoken to Bibi in the Church she would have known me at once, obeyed me implicitly and never gone near that accursed place again. Instead, wary of discovery, I cunningly accosted the Reformer boy, made sure he was in the dark, and calmly proceeded to my rendezvous – right over the young people's nasals, completely unaware that I had aroused the suspicions of a trio of detectives. And then I quit the scene. *My Self*, if I had not become uneasy, and decided to retrace my steps ...'

He reached a hand to the General, palm open in contrition. 'Forgive my *amertume*, I am responsible for the death of someone who trusted me: it's never easy, though he died very well. It's been a long night.'

The General grunted acknowledgement, and folded his arms across his chest. 'The vital thing is to save Amal. Not that he's guilty of anything beyond flirting with dangerous ideas, but one has to worry.'

'Amal won't be touched,' said Nef. 'That is taken care of.'

'Hm. And Bibi, exactly what does she know?'

They turned to the screen in a First Empire frame on the wall, which was at present a window into Bibi's pair. The girl sat on her bed, her right arm supported by a sling, her uniform coat over her shoulders, grey skirts spread on the coverlet. The cut on her shoulder had been deep, but not dangerous. The bruises on her face stood out painfully dark against her dazed pallor ... They felt no compunction at invading the child's privacy like this. They were her Gods, she knew they were always watching.

'Too much,' said Francois. 'Certainly enough to put her in danger.'

'What did she say to you?'

'Very little, she's a wise child.'

'She will have to come with us,' said Lady Nef. 'Honesty too.'

'What about the Reformer boy?' wondered the General, shifty-eyed.

Nef had never been *convinced* by Mahmood Al-Farzi as a suitor. He was a decent, fairly intelligent young man, the fact that he was infertile was no obstacle, but she could not believe he was the one to conquer the fortress. She couldn't see him as an equal match for that passionate, secret soul. She had discounted these feelings, she always hated to let one of her protégées go: it hadn't occurred to her to withhold her consent. And now? A very long engagement, at best.

'Mahmood is safe. His clan will protect him, if need be.'

There was a silence, not so much awkward as complicit. These rooms did not have diplomatic immunity. Frankness was advisable, so that the Town House record, should it be taken in evidence, would not seem incomplete. But there were questions that must not be asked: or answered. The General stood, cleared his throat and tugged at his rumpled tunic. 'Well, I think I'll leave you. I'll be in my study. I have to ... to sort out a few things.'

Francois and Nef continued to gaze at Bibi – who had slipped down to kneel on the floor, the beloved uniform coat still huddled around her – as if she were some soothing, anodyne form of entertainment. She tugged on an empty sleeve, wiped tears from her cheeks with a yellow-piped cuff and laid her head on her good arm, on the green bedspread. *The Thoughts of Youth*, sky and sea, seemed to hold her rapt attention—

'I knew she would adore that picture,' murmured the Aleutian.

Lady Nef watched him, watching the black-eyed girl; and smiled. She was old enough to have learned how to love and be wise – in Francois's case, at least. And now, the flurry of that last-minute panic over, she realised how profoundly glad she would be to leave Baykonur, this city of false glitter and frantic hearts: with all its conspiracies, its vicious, petty plots, its scandals and betrayals. Her life in Kirgiz had meant something to her, but never this place. A new beginning is a blessed thing. She wondered what Yu would be doing in his study. Staring into space? Destroying evidence? Planning further idiocy? But she would not spy on him: she never opened that window. The yellow-eyed tomcat had been straight with her, in his own way. The conspiracy, well ... The three of them had always been inveterate gamblers. He had not understood the odds, this time: that was all.

'Shall we go on monitoring his calls?' asked Francois, softly.

'Yes. But let him know we're doing it.'

XII

Honesty scratched on the bathroom door, crept into Bibi's room and sat on the end of the bed. She was wearing a clean uniform, the only mark of their adventure a glistening strip of fresh skin over a cut on one cheek; but she looked utterly unlike herself: shrinking, timid, desolate-eyed.

'How did you know they were Buonarotti couches?'

Bibi got up from the floor and sat back against the bedhead, rubbing the heel of her left hand across her brow. She'd been given a painkiller, but her head still throbbed. 'We did a course at college, in second year. It was part of The Welfare of the Insane: because criminal insanity can be triggered by a Buonarotti Transit. We got a tour of a virtual Transit Lounge. You could lie down in a couch. I didn't, but ... It was *very* spooky, not something to forget.'

'You're amazing, what a memory.'

'It's because I don't stick gadgets behind my eye. Partly it was that, and partly it was putting things together. Remember I said, the Common Tongue sometimes only comes clear afterwards—?'

Don't talk about Him, don't even think ...

Mahmood and Honesty had found the tunnel they'd come in by unguarded, and escaped while Bibi was taking on the army. They'd called the police, and immediately, scarily, they'd been picked up by a pair of gracile robots disguised in plainclothes: taken to the nearest station, and told that the affair of the Church of Self was in police hands, no cause for alarm ... They'd been terrified for Bibi, unable to convince the bots that their friend was in desperate danger; they'd had to submit to being escorted to their homes. You can't talk to robocops, can't get past them unless you have the right keyword. But then Bibi had been safe back at the Town House: getting debriefed by Lady Nef's secretary.

'How did you escape, Bibi? What happened?'

'I don't think I should talk about it.'

'We were meddling where we shouldn't. *Why* did we? And now there's no way back.' Honesty, the all-powerful Magnet, began to cry. 'Bibi, I don't want to know anything you're not supposed to tell me, but have we done something really terrible? Will the Family be struck by scandal?'

'The Family will be all right. Nothing will happen to them.'

Because Lady Nef is an immortal-designate, she thought, her head aching fit to burst with all the things she knew and guessed. *And maybe because Superintendent Natouri is still wearing a side-fastening gown—*

Honesty trembled and trembled. 'But, but we'll be interrogated.'

'No, we won't. It's taken care of.'

'But we must be! And they'll take our minds apart!'

Bibi looked up at *The Thoughts of Youth*. 'Francois told me something I *am* allowed to tell you. It'll be announced in a few days. Lady Nef has secured a Diplomatic Commission for the General. From the Hegemony.'

Honesty stared at her friend, her tears stopped, mouth open.

'Yes,' said Bibi. 'Yes.'

XIII

Mahmood, Bibi and Honesty came to their Starry Arrow appointment in dress uniform, with scraped clean, shining faces. The bruises were gone, but Bibi's arm was still strapped up. The General, Lady Nef and Mahmood's Birth Sponsors (a Reformer term meaning approximately his parents) were also present. The room was large and airy, with landscape screens instead of windows; it could have been anywhere. They did not look at each other. They knew that the small, grey-haired, withered being behind the big desk, cloaked in the purple uniform of justice, was looking at *them*, but they kept their eyes low. They weren't sure if he was really there. He could be in Xi'an, and just appearing here. He could be anywhere.

'Your behaviour has been exemplary,' said the small man, in a small, dry voice. 'You must not regard the consequence of your actions in defence of the Republic in any way as punishment or censure: but evidence must be taken. Social Knowledge Officer Grade Five Mahmood Al-Farzi MacBride will bear witness, with Honesty and Bibi's informed consent, for all three—'

Mahmood didn't move a muscle, but the blood drained from his face. His Birth Sponsors had known this was coming, but they didn't like the fact that Mahmood was being singled out, and they protested, with deference—

'Social Practice Officer Grade Five Gwibiwr and Domestic Servant Grade Seven Honesty are exempted, as they are assigned to the staff of General Yu's Diplomatic Mission, which will shortly be leaving for Speranza. A deposition interview, so close to the transit, would present a danger to their mental health.' The grey man smiled, paternally: an eerie effect. 'I trust, Bibi and Honesty, that you are willing to affirm Mahmood's statement?'

'Yes, sir.'

'Yes, sir.'

Mahmood had been taken home from the Church of Self. He had obeyed the police orders: say nothing to anyone. He had managed to behave normally, to get himself to bed; he'd even slept. He'd woken in the night, drenched in sweat, his heart pounding, fully realizing what had happened, and what lay ahead. And here it was. He was going to be interrogated. You can't lie to them. On the morning of his deposition he woke strangely calm. He wore his dress uniform again, he thought of Bibi. By that time rumours were beginning to circulate: a shocking discovery, a terrorist network penetrating the highest circles, arrests imminent. But nobody knew about Mahmood Al-Farzi, and what he must do for friendship. For love.

'You have nothing to fear, if you're innocent,' said the orderly in the evidence room, a robocop several powers above the bulky black-visored dolls on the street. Which was not reassuring, because who is there who *never* had a thought the Starry Arrow might find guilty? His bowels were water, he prayed they wouldn't betray him; he prayed he wouldn't wet himself. Although he knew, he'd been told, that in this chair there was no shame in letting go.

He felt an intimate touch, the breath of a moth's wing, like the time he'd accepted that download from Nightingale—

'See,' said the cop. 'Nothing to it. You're a brave little gang, you and those young women. But leave the police work to us in future, eh?'

The courier known as 'Jing' had been a highly qualified cypher clerk at the Elevator Base Station. He'd arrived in Baykonur on a legitimate errand, with a head full of very sensitive, stolen, virtual materiel. He had escaped from the secure accommodation where visiting Elevator staff were routinely confined, assumed a well-prepared false identity and left the Hall of Government in General Yu's Limo (the bluff, unsuspecting General, in all innocence, having been targeted for this purpose by the conspirators). It was believed that 'Jing' had died the same night: due to complications during the download process. Clandestine couriering was a hazardous occupation.

The Republic had never been in serious danger. The plot had been discovered at an early stage. Messages smuggled to 'Prisoner Haku' had been intercepted, and events had been allowed to take their course, in the hope of rounding up the whole cabal. The virtual materiel had been missing vital components, and the couches hidden in the crypt of the

Church of Self had been useless shells. But who were the ringleaders of this appalling conspiracy to bring Buonarotti Transit Devices to Earth—? The police reported only a successful intervention, and the death of 'Jing'. If arrests had been made, at the Church of Self or elsewhere, no information on that topic was released.

Accusations proliferated, questions were asked in the World State's news pages, and in the Diaspora parliament. Why were supporters of the so-called 'Young Emperor' still occupying high places in Baykonur? Why had Councillors and financiers – known sympathisers with the lost cause, who liked to dress up, meet in noisome cellars and toast their 'sick friend far away' – not been under surveillance? Big names were named, and tossed into the rumour mill. Councillor Javed Scolari made dignified statements. Ehsan Lukoil, the financier, directed an orchestrated media attack on the 'innocence' of the Xi'an government. The Starry Arrow continued to 'sift evidence' and 'weigh blame against blame', assuring the public that further arrests and interrogations were imminent. Some thought the scandal would grow until it engulfed Baykonur's whole upper caste—

For Mahmood time passed in a daze, until there was a note on his desk asking him to meet Bibi, usual time, usual place. He decided that he wouldn't go, then realised that he *must*. He must behave normally. He waited for her and she came towards him, with a radiant, tender smile, on the terrace where the dragons leapt from the chasm. 'Come with me,' she said.

They walked hand in hand, in silence. It was one of those days when winter suddenly, deceptively, gives way to spring. She had a keycard for the Palaces Ward's most charming Love Hotel, Street Level but expensive. They left their shoes in the narrow hall, Bibi chose an option and they stepped into a tiled courtyard where a willow tree with catkins grew in a pot. Above them floated a convincing blue sky, white clouds. The tiny private room was furnished 'Japanese style', which in Baykonur was considered elegantly erotic. Bibi took off her coat and cap.

'I want to give you my body. I owe you this.'

She removed her grey tunic, took off her trousers, her socks, and set them neatly aside: unpinned her long black braid, took off her chemise and pants and lay down flat. She was like a snowfield with two rosy peaks, a dimple of a dewy pool at her navel; and one black, rich hollow. Her eyes stared up at him, wells of despair, eyes of a suicide.

'Please, Mahmood.'

'I can't. We're not married. It would ruin you.'

There was a burning, pulsating sensation in his chest, his head was swimming. 'Auuhau,' he howled, like a baby in pain, throwing himself on her clothes, beating them and rolling around. 'Auagh! Auagh!' Bibi lay still.

Mahmood stopped howling when his throat was sore. She sat up, and groped for his hand. 'It's a great honour,' croaked Mahmood. 'Going to Speranza. I'm p-proud of you.'

'I'm p-proud of *you*. You gave evidence for us.'

'Nothing to it. It was my stupid fault, Bibi. If I hadn't said, "Tag the half-caste." If I hadn't said, "After him!"—'

'It was not your fault,' said Bibi. And that was all.

XIV

In the Great Concourse that Bibi had invaded, fearless and bewildered, on her first night in Baykonur, the Diplomatic Mission Lists had been posted. The hubbub around the Boards was tremendous: wild excitement, a great relief that could never be spoken of, an outburst of Family pride. A Mission to Speranza, and beyond! Didn't we say so? Didn't we always say this would happen? Ogul Merdov read Honesty's name among the domestics with indifference, but with foreboding. She looked for Bibi's name and found it; bile rose burning in her throat.

Mahmood had come to see Bibi. He'd announced himself to the AI concierge and been permitted to enter. He found her standing on the edge of the crowd, with Honesty. Honesty, who had not seen him since that terrifying interview, grabbed his hand, pumped it without a word: and slipped off.

'I'm sorry,' he said. 'I'm sorry for howling like a stuck pig and carrying on the way I did, the other day.'

'I'm sorry for what I did,' said Bibi. 'I went a bit crazy.'

'I'm going away, too. My folks are sending me on a trip, for my health. Until it's all over, until the arrests have been made and everything. I have leave of absence. So I think this is goodbye, Bibi. Until we meet again.'

She nodded. Five years. It would be five years, not for ever.

'I'll be here.' Mahmood attempted to be cheerful. 'Working away. You'll send a note to my desk. We'll meet on the Dragon Terrace.'

'Yes,' said Bibi, fervently. '*Yes.*'

She turned and left him. As he headed for the street doors another young woman came up, boldly. She was rounded and neat, with sleek hair and very pretty make-up: she had reddened the cleft above her upper lip, 'Aleutian' style. 'Off she goes to glory,' she said, with a mocking smile. 'Our high-born girl. Leaving us all behind.'

'Do I know you?'

'No, but I know you! You're Mahmood. I'm one of the Savage's oldest friends. I've known her since she was a destitute refugee.'

As Bibi hung up her dress uniform for the last time, it turned, in her hands, into the bloodstained rags that had been taken from her in Cymru, when she was a child. The illusion was gone in a moment, but it woke memories. The bare crags, the swifts, on crescent wings ... She shut the closet, sealed it, made the *recycle* gesture and sat on the floor, her arms around her knees.

> *Cariwch medd Dafydd fy nhelyn i mi*
> *Ceisiaf cyn marw roi tôn arni hi—*

Now I am going away again, she thought, when she'd sung all the words she could remember. *Far, far away.* Her cabin-bag was packed. It nudged against her, its hide shivering; picking up on her mood. It was an alien thing, grown from Aleutian cells, and now she was going there, where the aliens came from. Elation suddenly filled her heart. *I'm young. I'll see other worlds, and then he will be waiting for me, on the Dragon Terrace—*

Catch the knife by the blade, with joy.

INTERMISSION
GLIMPSES OF A TRANSIT

O

Bibi sat in the neuro-suite at Small Torus Station, wearing nothing but a paper exam gown, vulnerable and docile in her nakedness. She hadn't seen anything tropical at the Elevator Base, not a glimpse of a mangrove swamp or a palm tree: now there was nothing to tell her that she was already in outer space. She knew she weighed maybe half what she'd weighed on Earth (gravity was expensive), but she couldn't feel the difference. The games arena at Gagarin Circle had been more convincing.

Honesty had elected to make the transit to Speranza in dreamtime. Bibi wanted to be awake. That was why she was here, having passed the physical that everyone had to take. She was terrified of the Buonarotti process, but the idea that she would be having a fake experience, which was like being in prison, while her real mind and body were taken apart, scared her even more.

'It's a case of whether or not you want a blindfold when you face the firing squad,' Honesty had said, grimly. 'I do, you don't.'

'Does everyone have to do this, every time?'

The doctor was a dark-skinned woman in reassuring lab whites. 'The physical? Yes, but we streamline it except for newbies. You'll get a thorough medical scan every transit: it'll take seconds and you won't feel a thing.'

'What about the brain scan for staying awake?'

'Same thing. This assessment happens once, but you'll always have a health check. The couches themselves are cognitive scanners, you know.'

'Thank you, er, Doctor—?'

'I have no name, I'm a bot. I'm a facet of the Small Torus System.'

Bibi felt a shock. A doctor couldn't be a bot! It was only whores and robocops ... She looked around wildly: when had she entered the virtual, why didn't she remember?

The bot laughed. 'No, Bibi, this is the still the material world.

The Torus Station is 4-Spaced, therefore I can be visible to you. Speranza is the same.' She passed her hand through a piece of shiny desk furniture. 'And it's legal. See, I'm not an embodied!'

'Now I feel like a country bumpkin.'

'That's because you are one.' The facet of Small Torus smiled, with the cool, amused kindness that belonged to her kind: as Bibi would come to know. 'Don't worry, it'll pass. You're going to Speranza now.'

They went through a bland questionnaire, patently designed to calm the victim, then she lay down on the scanner bed. 'You know too much, don't you?' said the doctor. Bibi froze, bug-eyed in panic. 'About the Buonarotti process, child. That's why you want to make the crossing awake?'

'Y-yes.'

'Well, let's talk through it. What do you know?'

'The couch will use the forbidden powers of the void to break down my body, and, and my mind, into information space code, the 0s and 1s that are the building blocks of being. The code "me" will be t-torn in two, and the two halves will be thrown into a collider, a kind of particle accelerator called the Torus. When they collide I cease to exist. All that I am will be written into the code of a different place. Another couch will make a body for me there, out of the ambient chemistry of the universe.'

'That's nice and clear,' said the bot. 'And over five years old, I see. You have a retentive memory, Bibi. One correction: you are not "torn in two". A facet of your informational self is generated. There could be any number of them, without diminution of the source; but I believe humans don't like to think about that. When the facet collides with the original – a manner of speaking, as both are original, of course – at very high energies, you achieve fusion, and make the crossing. In the old days you had to know the 4-Space coordinates of your destination, and became embodied there by an act of will: which gave the traveller a very shaky, demanding psychological platform. Nowadays everything is programmed, and there's a trained crew on board to do all the work. One more correction. You do not "cease to exist" at any point. You exist, throughout, as much as you ever did.'

'How do people have "nightmares", if the transit takes no time?'

'Time is not what the embodied think it is,' said the bot. 'Fusion with the simultaneity, although at several removes in the Buonarotti process, is an intense experience. Your consciousness may process the intensity as duration, just as brain activity in certain kinds of sleep is perceived as dream, with false duration. But context is everything. Crossing to Speranza you probably won't feel a thing, as there is now a consensus that it is "a short hop" out to the Kuiper Belt. Some people, for reasons we don't yet understand, make transit after transit "awake" and *never* experience duration—'

Bibi had been waiting for the cognitive scan to begin, but she'd been lulled by the bot's calm voice. She only realised that an ephemeral shell had formed, a half-dome over her head and body, like the reader for a virtual avatar, in the moment that it dissolved. The bot stood by the couch, looking up and sideways: smiling, warmth in her eyes, as if listening to a voice she loved. Bibi thought of Nightingale's coding face.

'Yes ...' she said. Her attention returned to Bibi. 'I see you've never had an eye soc', that's good.'

'I don't like them.'

'Nor do we. Well, Bibi, you may join the Active Complement. In fact, whenever you transit, you *should* join the Active Complement.'

'Thank you.'

She didn't like the 'should', but she didn't dare to ask what it meant.

'You'd be a welcome addition to any crew.'

The Transit Lounge was a leveller: it did not separate grades and ranks. Bibi walked into it blind to her surroundings, blind to the knowledge that Lady Nef and the General, Honesty and Francois, everyone else on the Mission List, plus the soldiers who would act as their Household Guard, were all with her, lying down with her, on this departure. She was telling herself (a simple trick that had been recommended to first-timers) that this was a simulation, a practice run, no need to be anxious. She was thinking, another time when people's brains give them false-duration dreamlike experiences is at the point of death. She was wishing she did not know that ... and was not aware of having shut her eyes when the lid of the couch was opened. A young man with vertical pupils to his golden eyes, and sleek-furred ears that stood up like a cat's, stood there, in a fine-looking uniform of a pattern she'd never seen before.

'Welcome to Speranza,' he said.

Bibi covered herself with confusion by trying to put her hand through his arm. He was not a bot; he was a sentient biped from the Blue Planet who happened to have some cosmetic body-mods. He was just like

Bibi, a member of the community of numinally intelligent species, five of them so far, who were able to use instantaneous transit: who had the freedom of the stars.

This was their capital city, their native home.

She'd had no dreams but she felt, as if waking from a vivid dream, that everything behind her had just vanished. She was in the real world now.

O

At induction they were given something called an 'aura tag', which was their proof of identity, and denoted their status in the Speranza System. They couldn't see anything in a mirror, but they were told that to anyone who had clearance it looked like rays of coloured light. The colours were code for General Yu and Lady Nef's Commission, the Mission to Sigurt's World.

Their berths were two very small rooms, furnished in pared-down luxury, lined with yielding grey-green ceramic fibre, in one of the newer Standard Accommodation sectors. It was night, on Left Speranza. They were told to rest, and let the adjuvants in the air adjust their body clocks.

The air on Speranza smelled of nothing.

There was no connecting door. In fact the rooms were not adjacent, but Bibi kept thinking there *was* a door, becoming so convinced that she had to get up and search for it, in a designer-bathroom smaller than a shower stall. The confusion was a 'shaky psychological platform' effect. She would learn that this was not a solved problem. People got used to it, blanked it out; or gave up making transits.

She could not sleep, so she read the briefing on Speranza's history. Long ago, before the Aleutians arrived on Earth, there had been plans for a city in space, out here. The core habitat had served the asteroid miners of the Conventional Space Age, during Aleutian Colonial times, and had become the jumping-off point for exploration in the perilous early stages of Buonarotti Transit development. At one time it had briefly become a transit camp for condemned criminals – 'Prospectors' without any choice in the matter. When three more inhabited planets had been discovered, the Hegemony, the Group of Five, had been founded, with the Diaspora Parliament as its executive. The Kuiper Belt base had become its capital city. In less than sixty years (the Blue Planet's year had been adopted as the Hegemony's standard measure) a minimal space habitat had expanded; had inflated, suddenly, like a new universe, to become the Speranza of today.

The Large Torus, the Starship Crews—

Long, technical entries that she skipped.

The design of the original construct had been retained, for heritage reasons. Speranza was an asymmetric dumb-bell, spinning in a void strewn with spinning rocks, in the outermost reaches of the Blue Planet's system. Left Speranza, the big end of the dumb-bell, was now a captured, hollowed asteroid, like Aleutia. Left's gravity was about three-quarters Blue, except in non-standard sections. These were the facilities for detention, and refuges for failed colonists and others (restricted access). 'Right' was all restricted access: it housed Speranza's military capability. The whole dumb-bell was 4-Space mapped, and everybody was written into the code. Speranza System knew where you were, who you were with, what you were saying and doing, at any moment: but there were privacy protocols so nobody else did, unless they had clearance.

It was a turned-inside-out planet, with a protective shell of rock instead of gases, seamlessly woven with the virtual AI systems that supported it. A material world where sentient software entities could walk and talk, and human beings were made of code. It was a tiny room, hardly bigger than a coffin, speeding through eternal night.

O

On their first Speranza 'day', Honesty arrived at Bibi's door 'mid-afternoon', almost bent double, her arms cradling an awful pregnant tumour under her tunic. She crab-walked in, and emptied herself onto Bibi's bunk. A flood of glowing, vivid, gravid globules rolled and bounced—

'*Oranges!* Are they real?'

'Real as real, and piled up lying there for free on the breakfast bar in our lounge, which is in the Mission Suite, in Parliament Building. We can go there any time we like. You can eat oranges, and honey, and buffalo yoghurt, and cakes, and *bread*, until you're sick, and no one minds.'

'I won't test that,' said Bibi. 'Is there alien food, too?'

'Maybe. When I run out of things I love, and I've never had nearly enough of—' Honesty dug her nails into a fire-gold ball, spraying the whole cabin with the zing and sting of sweet citrus '—then I'll start on weird things. Come and be greedy with me, mistress. You *need* to come and be greedy. If you sit in here brooding, you'll never get over your embodiment nausea.'

'I'm not nauseous. You want to eat, I want to think.'

'You'll make yourself ill. It's in the briefing. It says *do not* try to think about what's happened to you, don't brood, or you'll probably go insane. Did you know, nobody knows where the Aleutians' real home planet is? Except the Aleutians, I mean. The place we call "Aleutia" is just an asteroid that the ones who deal with the rest of us use as a habitat.'

'Yes, I did know that.'

'I think it's antisocial ... Everyone knows where *we* live, of course. And the Balas/Shet, and the Ki/An, and Sigurt's World, where we're going. Oh, mistress, we have struck it lucky. This is the life. This is where we belong. I keep thinking *we did this*. Speranza is in *our system*, the Buonarotti Transit was invented by *one of us*. And my brain just soars.'

She tossed the peel in the recovery slot, reached for a paper plate from Bibi's dispenser, deftly split the orange into a petalled star and presented the delicacy with a beaming smile. 'Enjoy, mistress ... Did you know *all* the numinal biped species are supposed to have come from Earth? All descended from the same hominid, that had a huge civilisation, *millions* of years ago? So long ago there isn't a single trace of it? It's called the Diaspora.'

'It's a theory. There's different versions. Strong Theory says we're all descended from an ancient Blue hominid spacefaring species that vanished without a trace, and I don't think it makes sense. Weak says all numinal bipeds are alike due to convergent evolution. I don't think *that* makes a lot of sense either ... We learned about it at college.'

'All these things you knew, and you never told me!'

'You wouldn't have been interested,' said Bibi, after a voluptuous pause, sweet juice running down her chin. 'It was nothing to do with us.'

O

They had no duties, other than morning drill – which they performed assiduously, because if they didn't, they'd never be able to stand Earth gravity again. They were not required to attend the meetings, briefings, receptions that occupied their superiors; and they had no companions of their own age among the Mission's staff. They missed Nightingale. But if she'd been here she'd have been locked up in the Sensitive Visitors Facility with the Household Guard. The only military allowed to roam loose on Speranza were the Diaspora Parliament's own Green Belts.

The 'Hegemony' was the official name for the league of five sovereign, planetary nations (Balas/Shet counted as one nation). It was all people talked about on Earth. On Speranza it meant pretty much nothing. The Diaspora Parliament was the thing.

Having been trained from birth to subsist mainly on low-grade protein, they gorged on carbohydrates: made themselves ill, and recovered. They found the parks, the orchards, the museums, the games arenas, the theatres, the concert halls, the fashionable concourses; the shopping (but one thing they didn't have was money). They discovered (Honesty discovered) that the aura tag gave them free, first-class entry to an abundance of shows and games. The *best* show, ironically, was transmitted live from Chicago, in North America. To the girls' astonishment, it seemed there were places on Earth where the forbidden powers of the void were in everyday use ... It was *The Sleeping Beauty*. The ballet was at the end of its run, so they had VIP direct-cortical seats, which was like nothing they'd ever known. They were children, engulfed by the make-believe. They were great dancers, in the power and sweat of their perfect bodies; their superb artistry. Thoroughly intoxicated, grinning like maniacs, high as kites, they staggered around the concourse of the fabulous Nebula Immersion Theatre for hours afterwards—

Honesty kept grabbing onto Bibi and gasping, saucer-eyed ... *Oh, Carabosse, oh, that wicked, wicked fairy. She's going to get her vengeance! Wasn't she great! I LOVE her!*

Bibi thought it was strange that the new, babbling, buoyant Honesty didn't seem like a stranger: then she realised that Honesty hadn't changed. She was still saying exactly what she thought, with unhesitating candour. She'd just never had any reason to be buoyant before.

Transit had made Bibi look differently at the bots, who were everywhere. She was like them now, part of a huge system, borrowing a local appearance from the ambient code. Were bots less conscious, less *real*, because they didn't have material form, because they didn't have the illusion of autonomy?

It made her look differently at her own possessions too. Her cabin-bag, her few non-uniform clothes, her iface. Little souvenirs of lasting meaning that she'd carried with her since she first left the Great House. The pincushion Honesty had made for her, the New Year they were twelve; which she'd never used because she didn't sew. A tiny red jade pony from Nightingale. A Vlab 3D image of a sprig of pine, from Kushan resort. These homely things had travelled to Speranza intact, as part of Bibi's information-self. If they were still real objects, it made you wonder what 'real' meant.

The iface was useless, its software wrecked by the crossing. She could have got a new card for it, but there was no point: it would only get wrecked again on the voyage out.

Sigurt's World was getting a new Buonarotti facility, to replace the Old Port, which was out of date. DP engineers would be building the Torus and the new station, out in space. General Yu, Lady Nef and their staff would be on the ground – representing the Diaspora Parliament in the ancient capital of a rich and fascinating culture. Bibi and Honesty could have found out more, but they didn't bother. The briefing docs, which came with the aura tag, had to be accessed by talking to Speranza System in your head: it was too spooky. 'Time enough to find out about

"Sigurt's World" if we make it,' said Honesty. When you were on Speranza, you quickly grasped that *no* transit 'outward' was guaranteed a safe landfall. And it didn't worry you. Much.

Bibi knew she had to put what had happened, what she knew and what she guessed, out of her mind, *for ever*. But without telling Honesty, she had a look at the lists of names. (Bibi was down as *Assistant to Lady Nef's Secretary*, a big promotion, but she wasn't proud of it: she knew the real reason why she was here). The Mission staff roster told her nothing. The Household Guard troops were in the same file, and one of the private soldiers was a *D. Doyle*. So then she found *Phu, C. B.* and *Aswad, R. Sgt.* There was no mention of dishonourable discharge, or dreamtime.

Orange Company ... She thought of the ragged miscreants by that drinking fountain, talking awful sedition, and chills went down her spine. Lady Nef must have had to do some serious, *serious* fixing! Her powers were awesome indeed.

O

At the single reception they'd attended, Bibi and Honesty had seen their mistress treated like *somebody* by the DP high-ups: like an important person who belonged here. This had reassured them. But it was Francois who'd really come into his own. He was nobody's secretary here. He was an adventurer, freshly returned from a long voyage among the barbarians. He'd shed his cutaway coat, and those close-grained, pale pantaloons. He wore a second-skin pressure suit, called a 'squeeze-suit', under dun-coloured Aleutian overalls, casually as if he'd always been a spacer; and he didn't mix with Blues (except maybe, in private, with Lady Nef).

But Left Speranza was a small world. On the morning when they'd been summoned to the Mission Suite and told that their 'starship' was 'cleared for departure', they saw him having breakfast at La Tartine, a coffee kiosk on the great concourse outside the Parliament Building. They wouldn't have dared to approach but he called them over, and asked them how they'd liked Speranza.

'Very much,' said Honesty. 'How did all the meetings go?'

'I have no idea. I saw no need to bore myself to tears. Let me introduce my friend, Goraksa—'

An Aleutian built like a bear, at least two metres tall, with a dusky yellow complexion, gave the two human girls a shrug and a tucked-in chin, the gesture for *yes*, or *hi*—

Bibi knew that the Sanskrit name meant that this person had lived on Earth during the Expedition, as the Aleutians had called their empire. Maybe he'd even been with the party who made First Contact. Overwhelmed by so much history, she bowed deeply.

'I ... I'm honoured to meet you, er, noble sir.'

The yellow bear raised his capacious nasal, and gave his opinion in the Common Tongue. <You can't be *honoured*, kid. Have some self-

respect. I'm one of the pirates who raped and pillaged your planet. And I had a great time, by the way. A very tasty world.>

Bibi recoiled; the bear was astonished. Francois laughed, and gently punched Goraksa's shoulder. 'Careful,' he said aloud. 'I brought her up.'

Honesty covered the awkward moment by looking politely to the other alien, raising her eyebrows. She loved being a Blue, and having the right to patronise the lesser members of the Diaspora. 'And this gentleman?' She was blanked out by a black stare that didn't recognise her right to exist.

'That person doesn't have a name, not as you would understand it.' Francois stood up. 'Names are for undignified tourists. And he doesn't talk. Come with us, Bibi, Honesty. I want to show you something.'

The Aleutians had a better class of clearance. In their company Bibi and Honesty were allowed onto the Horizontal RT: which they rode a long way out. When they disembarked they were in a different Speranza: a grey space, a low 'sky', desultory plantings of low-gravity-tolerant shrubs. Off in the distance, aimless figures were hanging around the plinth of an ugly corporate sculpture. *This looks like the place where the clients live*, thought Bibi, intrigued, and wondered if she would find the old city around here: the shifty canteens, the seedy markets, the fried grasshopper stalls.

'We're taking you across the Umbilical,' announced Goraksa, speaking aloud this time. 'You'll have to suit-up on the other side. You know how to do that, I hope? You won't panic, in a hard vacuum?'

They assured him that they would not.

Left Speranza was a great city, warm by day, cool by night; where it just happened that you never caught a glimpse of the boundary, through the appearance of mellow sunshine or soft dark. The Umbilical was a shocking challenge to that illusion. Suddenly they were bouncing off the concertina walls of an interminable, freezing-cold passageway, in nakedly artificial white light; and perilously close to the void. There was a massive lock to pass through at the other end, then a chamber where programmable suits were tethered in rows, like rank on rank of drifting, swollen, faceless corpses—

'Are they in case we have to abandon ship?' asked Honesty.

'Nah,' said the yellow bear. 'They're for techies, security, particle cannon gunners, fighter pilots, if they ever come this way. Usually they don't, they come around the outside. In an emergency, civilians would leave by the transit. Or more likely not at all.'

'We don't need overcoats,' said Francois, giving Goraksa a quelling look, 'we're not going outdoors. But you should get dressed, children, or we'll never finesse you past the nanny routines.'

Bibi had enough simulation experience to pretend she was confident. She felt the embrace of the suit (strangely, unexpectedly), like a return to solid existence, to the world the transit had taken away. Cold, blackness, vacuum, danger of death. *Ah*, she thought, this *is where they keep the old city*—

She knew that Francois was smiling.

At first the suit store refused to open its onward lock, because the Aleutians had merely picked up facemasks and airpacks. It read them a terrifying list of Right Speranza Hazards for the Embodied. Radiation Peaks, Space Debris Impacts, Hull Fractures, Pressure Loss, Unpredictable Torus Effects and other no-exit situations. But they argued with it, and in the end it let them pass. They were members of the elder race, after all, and feared permanent death no more than a bot did—

Goraksa in the lead, the person who had no name bringing up the rear, they floated across a vast, girder-braced cavern, tethered together. It was very dark, the sense of cold and void *intense*. The murmur of the Torus, which haunted Left Speranza like a half-heard whisper, had become a subliminal thunder that throbbed in their bones. Bibi and Honesty tumbled, grabbing at anything solid with their gecko-palms and bootsoles. The Aleutians tugged them like ballast towards a pattern of winking green and red lights – that became, as they approached, the telltales on a row of ports, each about three metres in diameter, on the complex inner face of this huge dome. *Are they taking us outside after all?* wondered Bibi, wheeling over ominous sleek shadows, ranked 'below', then suddenly 'above'. *Are we going to die?*

Goraksa entered code, manually. There was a short delay, then he led them through onto a caged platform, with barely enough space for the five of them to set their boots, and sealed the lock behind them. Francois pulled off his mask, and rapped on Bibi's faceplate.

'Open up, we have air and pressure. What do you think?'

Far 'below' the platform, a single sleek and gleaming pod floated loose in a mist of light. Bibi had lost perspective; it could have been big as a city tower, small as a toy.

'It's a beautiful ship. Is it alive?'

'He's called *The Spirit of Eighty-Nine.*' Francois sighed in proud affection, not bothering to answer the absurd question. 'He's coming to Sigurt's World with us. He's transit capable, but he'll travel in the hold.'

'Safer that way,' remarked Goraksa, 'since you can't navigate.'

Honesty finally got her faceplate to open, and gasped like a fish. 'Is she *yours*, Francois? You must be incredibly rich!'

Every departure from Speranza was called a ship, and the ships had names and crews, they had payload capacity that varied. It was a tradition of the young history of 'starflight' that helped Buonarotti travellers to stay sane. In reality only the Aleutians, with their information-cell technology, had developed instantaneous transit *ships.* They were top secret, inordinately difficult to grow and unstable in performance (Bibi had seen this somewhere); dangerous playthings except in the hands of skilled military pilots. Maybe it was different if you were an Aleutian.

The yellow bear and the nameless one found Honesty's naïve deduction hilarious, and expressed this crudely (hampered by their suits) in the Common Tongue.

'Services rendered to the mighty,' explained Francois. 'Ignore them, Honesty, they are boors.'

There was a long silence. The Aleutians seemed prepared to gaze at the shining pod until the air ran out. 'You should call him *The Failed Renaissance*,' remarked Goraksa at last, aloud. 'Or *Darkness at Dawn.* Call a spade a spade.' He turned to the girls. 'Are you two looking forward to your trip?'

'I wish people wouldn't keep telling me how cultured and cultivated the, er, Sigurtians are,' said Honesty, darkly. 'It makes me suspicious.'

'Ha ha ha.' The yellow bear probably hadn't used his human laughter for a life or two, it was rusty. 'You're not alone, little one, methinks. Did you notice how your drill is mostly weapons training?'

'Weapons training is good for the soul,' said Francois.

'*Sure* it is ... What d'you think of Nikty, kids?'

Practically every 'alien' Honesty and Bibi had encountered – aside from the Balas/Shet Green Belt officers on duty at the Mission Suite – had turned out to be a Blue Planet biped, with body-mods. It was embarrassing. They'd had no idea that *Baykonur*, the great city, gateway to the stars, was such a dull, repressive dump ... They'd glimpsed the Sigurtian attached to their Mission once. He'd looked just like the ones in the induction simulation: slender, less than human height, wearing a metallic jumper with gleaming soft folds between arm and flank. A dark

velvet on his head, running down the back of his neck, prick ears ...
But they'd only seen him from the back.

'We weren't introduced,' said Bibi, ruefully. 'We're very junior.'

'We've hardly met *anyone* but Blues and bots.' It was Honesty's big disappointment. 'Other numinals here are likely to be high-grades, crews or government, aren't they? We see them passing, on their way to places we can't go. Oh well, two new Aleutians today. That's better than nothing.'

<You're welcome!> said the nameless one, with a graceful, ironic gesture.

'Time's up,' announced Francois. 'Let us return to the fakery.'

The pod hung in darkness in Bibi's dreams. She was 'on board' the *Rajath*, the imaginary vessel that was carrying them through the formless ocean of information space. Something more fundamental than air and pressure had failed, she was being torn apart, the void was in her. She woke, shaking, and stumbled around trying to find the connecting door that she'd left behind in the Town House in Baykonur: until the sensible part of her brain got scared that she *would* find it, and she returned to her bunk.

Nothing is real, time isn't what we think it is. Twenty-six thousand light years will separate me from my home, how can I bear that?

OO

'Sigr't.'

'*Sigr't.*'

'Sig-*r't* ... No, I can't. Why can you do it, when I can't?'

'Namibian ethnic origin,' said T'zi, the Navigator: who had befriended Bibi as they waited to be couched, all together, crew and Mission, the Active Complement and the dreamers. 'But I can't echolocate.'

'Can they?'

'Apparently so ... Don't you want to check that bag?'

'It always travels with me,' said Bibi, locking her fingers tighter round the cabin-bag's pull-bar. 'It's alive, you know. It'd be frightened.'

The navigator knew who would be frightened. '*D'accor*, well, there's a locker at the foot of your couch, just like coming from Earth, you put it in there, keep it in mind, it should be with us when we arrive.'

If you get your calculations right, she thought. She wanted to ask about the Aleutian podship in the 'hold'. Wouldn't it be an impossible burden for him, even if he did have special, extra, virtual neuronal architecture—

Whatever that meant.

'Will I see you on the voyage?'

'People cross differently. You may be able to spot me.'

False duration is what happens at the point of death. *If you die outside time*, she thought, *you could go on dying for ever*—

The lodge stood among fir trees, its outline blurred by a white smoke of driven snow. It was as cold inside as outside, and everything was covered in dust and grime. The stove was out. 'That's the first thing we must tackle,' said Nef. She took an apron from a hook on the wall of roughly shaped, overlapping planks: handed it to Bibi and took another for herself. They wrapped themselves in their aprons, and immediately felt strong and confident.

'This is our house,' said Bibi.

'We *know* how to keep house,' said Nef. 'You and I.'

They set to work, with Francois and the General: lighting the fire, heating water, bringing in logs. The hunters came and went, stamping their boots as they entered, bending their heads and shouldering the wind as they left. The lodge was called Haru'om; he was just one room, with a sleeping gallery up above. The elbowed timbers of the roof, which reached right down to the floor, must have come from some *mighty* trees. Nef and Bibi cleaned and scrubbed him, aided by their willing cohorts, and kept his every surface glowing. The four of them talked about all kinds of things, sharing the housework, wrapped in their aprons, looking after Haru'om, while he looked after everyone. 'This is real life, Bibi,' said Lady Nef.

'Baykonur was a bad dream,' agreed Yu, the Swimmer. 'It's over.'

The salt-horn in its silver cradle stood beside the brass pepper mill, with its pattern of acanthus leaves, in the middle of Haru'om's long table, where everyone came to eat and talk, safe from the storm outside.

'Everything is as it should be,' said Nef. 'Everything is new.'

But Bibi kept the sprig of pine from Kushan safe in her pocket, so that Mahmood would still be with her when she arrived.

The mess of the *Rajath* was clad in silvery-green, traditional starship décor: with extruded furniture of the same colour and material, in the old Left Speranza style. The salt-horn and the pepper mill were an incongruous touch on the mess table, but the crew were pleased to have them there. The fragility of every crossing made Buonarotti adepts as superstitious as old-time sailors on the water-oceans of the Blue. Every lucky charm was welcome. In the hold, 'down below', the engineers and their couriers, the soldiers and the Mission staff lay in their couches: Honesty among them. The Aleutian schooner, *The Spirit of Eighty-Nine*, was dreaming too, in its own compartment.

The crew came and went; they had their duties in other sections. The Navigator was rarely seen. The wakeful passengers spent their time talking to the off-duty officers; providing vital incident and novelty. Starship crews, the wetware of the Buonarotti process, were a rare breed. Everyone knew everyone else; it was hard to find a ship where you wouldn't be forced into the most intimate contact with at least one person who drove you crazy. But they did not fight, because they had learned forbearance; and because they knew there was hell to pay.

The Chief Engineer lost another game of gin rummy to Francois, who showed his fangs in triumph, a gesture he'd never have allowed himself on Earth ... Navigator T'zi, Reformer by birth and conviction, explained the validity of the undecided gender to Lady Nef – who had always thought there must be a better term.

'You want to call us a third sex,' said T'zi. 'But Undecided means what it says: fluctuation, drift, a mosaic sexuality that never "settles". It is the will of God: in time all Blues will pass beyond the either/or. A process which the Fundamentalists of your party are trying to reverse by force—'

His dark hands flashed, in emphatic gesture. His timbers bent to the storm, elbows and knuckles standing out. Knots in timber are hard but weak, they can be dislodged, leaving open wounds—

'The erosion of sexual difference was self-evidently caused by pre-Aleutian and wartime pollution,' said Lady Nef. 'It was a phase we went through, a problem that can now be solved.'

'I take that as a compliment! It's good to be a problem, a cause of thought, a nexus of development.'

General Yu got into an argument with the Payload Officer, about Strong Diaspora Theory versus Weak Diaspora Theory: something he'd been warned and warned that he *must not do*. He was charming, old 'Simian' Yu, and Lili Hellier, the honeypot (there's always a honeypot) was enjoying the combat, but Strong Diaspora is something crews won't have questioned—

'Not a single fossilised silicon chip—?'

Bibi thought that Francois looked like a werewolf in a squeeze-suit. He was giving her the shivers. And the Sigurtian in the hold, the matt-black mask, the loose cut of that silvery jumper, were his eyes open in the dark? She was frightened, but nobody else seemed to notice the rising tensions.

'The "Shelter and Storm" scenario is common,' said Viv Khan, Medical Officer, who wore the captain's armband on this trip. 'Also "Climbing Impossible Heights", and "Breaking into the Invincible Fortress". Believe me, this is a *good* crossing. When we go into fugue, we have a consensus. I've known flights where that doesn't happen, and it's *bedlam*.'

There was a hairline crack in the willow-coloured wall. Frozen air squeezed through, like puffs and rods of crispy white smoke.

Bibi wanted to say, *There's a chink in the wall, we need to go out and stuff the logs with moss*, but she knew that not even the hunters could go outside now. She laid her head on her arms, and concentrated on matching the pattern, almost in a trance. A one for a nought, a nought for a one, a one for a nought, a one for a nought. How could simplicity be so complex? Interminable, and very tiring.

General Yu sat facing her, holding her hands. She never came back, he said, without speaking. She's gone cold on me for a while, I thought. She'll get over it. But she never came back. Oh, Bibi, it was the end of me— When he saw that he had her attention he gave her hands a little shake.

'You're a good girl,' he said. 'A very good girl. I'll take over now.'

The hunters came in, stamping snow from their boots. Lady Nef was blood to her elbows. The Aleutian in running gait crouched beside her, a naked baboon with a gape like a shark's. They'd brought down the Medical Officer in mistake for a deer, they were skinning her and she was howling—

The Spirit of Eighty-Nine screamed in his sleep.

'The closing phase is always hell,' said Roscoe, Chief Engineer, who was building a card house with the gin rummy cards. The pack belonged to General Yu; it was very old. The face cards were characters Bibi had heard about at her grandfather's knee, but none of them looked the way she'd imagined. 'The Navigator makes a slip, and in the country of no duration it seems like a knot in the wood of a table, a wounding remark, an awkward confession, but when you come to the closing phase there's a transcription error, and it's too late—

'We don't *know* this, you understand. Usually nobody lives to tell the tale. There are no lifeboats on starships. We only know that ships are lost, and that voyages are fraught with strange little dramas.

'This is actually a very calm crossing.'

Everyone watched the cards. An errant Jack fell towards the floor. The Active Complement watched it drift, frozen in horror. The Aleutian leaned forward, very slowly, and took the slip of antique pasteboard from the air. The back was all interlinked circles; he turned it so only he could see the face.

'Whose card is it, Francois?' whispered Nef.

∞

It was the Navigator who opened Bibi's couch. She sat up, unable to speak for the tumult of things, the rich, sweet adventure she was trying to remember. T'zi's seamed face, familiar and beloved (but why? I only just met him …) split into a grin. 'Don't try. It's gone. Welcome to Sigurt's World Old Port.'

'You were our house,' she said. 'Your name was Haru'om.'

'Was I?' said the Navigator, the grin fading, so she knew she'd stepped on a void-sailor's superstition. 'I don't remember.'

'Where are the others? I must say goodbye. Where's Lili, where's Roscoe, where's Viv?'

T'zi shook his head. 'Still on board. The Port is nothing to look at. We don't bother to go planetside much, it's the bureaucracy—'

Then Bibi saw that she was surrounded by people climbing from their tombs, people standing around dazed like the newly resurrected dead; and Honesty was there, crying, 'Bibi! We made it!' She scrambled out of the couch. They hugged each other, frantically relieved, and when they broke out of the hug, T'zi was gone. A party of Sigurtians in fancy uniforms had arrived to greet the Mission, looking like the induction simulation but prouder, full of ceremony. General Yu glanced over his shoulder, across the drab Arrivals Hall: spotted Bibi, and winked. A flash of memory burst on her from the void, from the country of no duration.

PART TWO

XV

Nikty, the Sigurt's World attaché, gave Bibi and Honesty vocabulary
lessons in a dark hall, half-underground, where light and air came
plunging in broad lances from above. She spoke English, the language
of Hegemony diplomacy, very well. They could never *truly* learn either
to speak or to hear a Sigurtian language. They lacked the necessary
cranial and brain-structure organs. But there were phrases they could
attempt, for politeness's sake:

Please

Thank you

Good night

Good morning

Dinner is served (literally, an arm is offered)

The light bulbs need replenishing

Please switch on the windowscreens, there are flying things

She was not male, as they had assumed, but unlike the whores around
the Church of Self, she was not insulted by the 'he' mistake. 'We are
male and female, approximately like you,' she said: 'but with us it has
no effect on status.' The language she was teaching them was called
Myot, but she was a Neuendan, a native of the First Contact state,
which had until now been the only 'Sigurtian' culture to deal with the
Hegemony.

'That has to change,' she said. 'Other voices must have a say.'

Bibi had a transit hangover. She'd made the crossing in a world built
of intensity; now everything was overcharged with meaning. A room
could be an emotion, a piece of furniture a metaphor. The phrases she
was being taught to mimic terrified her, because she could tell that the
Sigurtian 'words' had no congruence with the English 'meanings'. She
could not map from one to the other, it was impossible, and the void
was in her head.

She clung to vital fragments of protection—

A card house

An apron, what a strange device for empowerment and control

—and tried to behave normally, while the Mission's first days, scents, sounds, landscapes, swam in and out of focus. Nikty was pretty and grave, and gently condescending: with a gleam of soldierly courage in her black-masked, diamond-rimmed eyes. (But why did Bibi think of soldiers?) A day (including the dark hours) was a *g't'z*. The other common unit, a half-moon, ten days, was *n'g'tcz* ... The play between the two moons was holy, and made the Sigurtian calendar beautifully complex, but the terms 'day' and 'half-month' were adequate for aliens; for politeness's sake—

Bibi's perceptions calmed, and she realised why the crews tried *not* to remember. She decided not to ask if her feelings were normal. If she complained of shaky psychological platform effects, they might say she had to travel home in the dreamtime, and Bibi was already addicted to the country of no duration, although she couldn't remember why. She was left with a lingering conviction that there was something spooky, something *haunted* about the beautiful house where the Mission was accommodated, close under the towering wall of the 'Chipshop' Crater, in the temperate zone of the south-west continent of the planet called Sigurt's World.

In this unease, as the *g't'z* and *n'g'tcz* went by, she was not alone. Neuendan, seat of Planetary Government, birthplace of the famous Sigurt himself – where they'd have met and mixed with people who'd dealt with Speranza agents before – was far away, and telecoms were not secure. The Mission was considerably more isolated than had been expected.

XVI

'What's sex like?'

'You mean, with another person?'

Bibi shrugged. Honesty continued to smooth out her mistress's fall of black hair, with long strokes of the brush. It was hard to be sure, because the Savage was the kind likely to hold out for *very* private moments, but she had a suspicion that Bibi did not masturbate. She was a real, real true virgin. How had this happened? Honesty would probably never know; probably the reason was long buried. Looking back, maybe all of the foundling children raised in the Great House had had past experiences, horrors of babyhood, hunger and shame, that they would never, ever disclose—

'I've heard you don't miss it if you leave off, after a while. The lust for it fades. Me, I take it when I can.' She paused in the brushing, and made an impish face at Bibi in the mirror. 'If you like, I could show you. Why don't we? Just as friends? It might be very nice.'

'Thanks but no.'

'Ah well.' Honesty fantasised that she would travel home in the Active Complement (if that were possible, if she could be brain-scanned at the Port); and in the 'fugue experience' there would be a dream sequence where she and her mistress shared an erotic encounter—

She braided Bibi's hair and fastened it for the night.

'I wish you had long hair,' said Bibi, 'so I could return the favour, it's so soothing.'

'You may get your wish. I badly need a haircut right now, and I don't trust Rashit, I don't think she likes me.'

Rashit was Lady Nef's personal maid, and the only hairdresser in the company. The Mission was designed to be self-sufficient and to present a stylish shopfront, elegance being prized by their hosts, but they were starting to notice, as time went by, awkward gaps of this kind.

Who cuts the junior officers' hair ... ? The dislike, as far as Bibi knew, was purely imaginary: petty slights and rivalries thrive on boredom.

They moved to their window embrasure and hopped up onto the cushioned stone benches, on opposite sides of a small stone table. All the furniture, the doorsills, the windows, the steps of Underwall Manor required a little *hop*. The Sigurtians were not tall; nor were they really, in any scientific sense, related to bats, but they had a way of entering a room, taking a seat, mounting a staircase, that involved a distinct upward lift and fall, like a flying creature alighting. The sanitary arrangements, and just moving around the place, had taken some getting used to: with the amused assistance of the local domestics. Bibi turned down the lamp by passing her hand over the mouth of the clear flask. The bioluminescent bulb at the bottom of it responded crudely to the warmth of a palm; or precisely (if you were fluent) to the right click.

The manor was, in Sigurtian terms, a romantic, mediaeval, fortified house. It did not have mains lighting. Or bathrooms en suite – except for the apartment occupied by Lady Nef and the General. There was no connecting door to rouse puzzling memories in the middle of the night: only the challenge of dark, irregular corridors, with more often than not a spectacular stumble along the way.

The assistant secretary and her maid shared a guest chamber intended for the juniors of a noble household. (They had to keep reminding themselves this huge promotion wasn't real.) It looked towards the crater wall, which towered immediately beyond the Manor grounds: fissured with black crevasses and yellow-green forest clefts, through which plunged jets of purplish water, with aquamarine spume – very picturesque, but a little too close. It was floodlit at night. Off to their left, where the wall dipped at the site of a crevasse that had once been very significant, they could see the feudal castle of their sponsor, Lord Hongfu: spidery and forbidding against the violet sky. The royal family still lived there – although they spent half the year in the city, Myotis, which sprawled over the centre of the crater floor.

Above the lights, and a layer of haze, stars began to shine. The small, smooth moon was up, half-full, the big lumpy one just emerging. This was their best time. During the day they were kept fully occupied, and the strangeness was lost in routine. The naked, starry sky, the riot of compelling night-scents that drifted through their windowscreens, made them feel they really were on an alien planet. They'd been given a Sigurtian entertainment centre, which would play the leisure records that had been couriered from Speranza on the *Rajath*; some of which were their own requests. But they didn't bother with it much. They'd rather gaze; and talk.

Honesty counted on her fingers. Twenty Sigurtian days, two half-months, should make one month. But then you had to do the big moon/little moon calculation … Was it add 7.5 and divide by 3? Or divide by 7.25 and add 3.5? And how many 'odd' moons had there been, with the extra days? There were Moon Tables, but they only made things worse. And then the Myotian 'year', unlike the Neuendan Standard 'year', had a great gap in the middle of it, because they hadn't modernised their liturgical calendar—

'Oh, I give up. I'll never get it. How long have we been here, Bibi?'

The Savage, most untypically, hadn't managed to memorise any of the polite phrases. She was relying entirely on a Neuendan-made translation aid: and sticking to Blue time. She intended to keep this up for the whole Mission, which Honesty thought was rude.

'Six months.'

'*Hm* …' Six months is a worrying chunk out of a five-year project, when the project has yet to begin to get off the ground.

'The Human Renaissance made Buonarotti transits from the surface of Earth,' said Bibi, 'from a gaming arena in Europe, before the Departure.'

'It wasn't hideously dangerous, back then?'

'It was as dangerous as it is now, I suppose. The Human Renaissance people didn't care, they were striking a blow against the colonial power. And nothing terrible happened – I mean, we're still here.' Bibi drew up her knees, wriggled her bare toes on the cool stone, and pondered. 'But there've been horrific transit disasters, I mean besides "ships" simply disappearing. *Spookily* horrific. Neurophysics isn't called the forbidden science for nothing; transiting interferes with the whole fabric of reality, nobody can deny that.'

Honesty pulled a face. 'So on Earth, where we invented the ideas, we don't use them. We rely on Aleutian biotech, which lines pockets in Xi'an and keeps us all dependent. I think when we built the Torus out in space, far away as we could, *that's* when we got left behind. *That's* when everything moved to Speranza.'

If you had transited awake, thought Bibi, *you wouldn't be so cynical about the spookiness, or the fear.* But she kept that to herself.

'Mm.'

Flying things danced against their window, some of them big enough to be annoying. Bibi made the *go away* gesture (in some respects, Sigurt's World was familiar: there were effective gestures, much easier than the clicking language). The night fizzed and returned, swept free of pests.

'But the *Torus*!' exclaimed Honesty, suddenly realising. 'How did they have a *Torus* inside a *gaming arena*? That's *impossible*, that doesn't make sense—'

'The Torus doesn't have to be in the same room as the couches.'

'I know, I know, but how could there be a Buonarotti Torus in the middle of a city ... Oh, I suppose it *was* in a city?'

'I think it was underground. Colliders used to be laid down flat, and buried underground. They had a particle collider that was 26.67 kilometres in circumference buried somewhere in Europe, before the Aleutians came.'

Honesty imagined, thrilled by her Blueness, a vast fairground wheel, tall as Baykonur's towers, laid out flat ... 'And we knew nothing, you and I. *Nothing* about our former glory. At the Great House we were brought up to be Aleutian-lovers.'

Bibi felt this to be a criticism of Lady Nef. 'We were taught non-living science, a bit, I'm sure we were ... But what good would it have done for us to have our heads filled with confusing ideas that would lead nowhere? We were educated according to our station, which sounds bad, but *it was our best bet*. Nobody thought we'd end up on a Diplomatic Mission to another planet. '

Honesty rubbed her brow, displacing the fringe that badly needed cutting. 'I'm going to take my nail clippers to this ... We're looking at our world from the outside, aren't we, Bibi? That's something we never did before.' Civic pride asserted itself. '*D'accor*, Baykonur wasn't paradise, and maybe we were in a cage we couldn't see, but I bet other Blue cities were as bad, and didn't have our fantastic architecture, or the cosmodrome. Or hot apple wine. Legal body-mods aren't everything.'

'I'm sure *Speranza* has its horrible problems,' said Bibi.

But she noted the past tense. It disturbed her that Honesy, the unerring realist, had begun to see Baykonur as an outgrown shell, to which they could never return. *That can't be*, she thought. *My life is there, waiting to begin.*

'I wish there were more seasons,' she said, 'so we could count them off.'

'Huh. You'll get enough of a season when the winter comes. I hope they move us into the city centre well before then.'

The 'Chipshop' Crater's present climate would have been called semi-tropical on Earth, but there was a plunge into much lower temperatures and stormy weather coming. All the lurid, rampant foliage, the vivid pollen-mounded flowers in the Manor gardens, would vanish. The wind would whistle (the young women imagined) icy-cold, along those dark, trap-filled corridors – and all the Sigurtian flyers, large and small, which they saw crossing their daytime sky, would be grounded.

There were no surface roads in the 'parklands', the outer reaches of the vast crater. The Myot aristocrats who lived here, in their historic manors and castles, didn't think that way. When the flying season ended they packed up and moved into the city – and moved back out again as soon as the skies opened in the spring.

In the early days at Underwall, a local servant had come to them at bedtime with the customary 'nightcap', a strengthening drink to help the young ladies through the dark. When they'd discovered that this salty infusion was based on dried blood they had decided (before they knew where the blood came from) that they'd do without. But some kind of supper would have been welcome. The meals the company took together were difficult to eat – if you followed Sigurtian manners, as they were obliged to do – and meagre, even by Baykonur standards. They wished they'd thought of packing rations. 'A year's supply of Speranza-crafted Swiss chocolate,' said Bibi.

'*Oranges*,' said Honesty, with passion.

They discussed the idea of informational oranges. If you bring them as personal possessions, do they still have calories? The window-embrasure talks were perfect for topics of this kind: questions that were too silly to ask, comments on a situation they weren't supposed to have noticed—

'So,' said Honesty, after a drift into silence that meant they were both ready for sleep, 'the first planetary nation to have a Buonarotti facility on the surface could be cutting the crap. Especially now that we can transit material goods. They'd be ahead of the game.'

'Or opening a back door to invasion.'

Bibi had spoken without thinking. The couches in the crypt, the topic they could *never* discuss: the reason why they were here, enjoying this life of exotic privilege, came looming up from the depths. Briefly, they thought of the Starry Arrow, criminal interrogation; and couldn't meet each other's eyes.

'I'm going to bed,' announced Bibi.

'Me too.'

Honesty lay ensconced in alien bedding, planning her future. *I'll work for my Grade Six exam.* And if she passed, why not college? *Business studies, I'll be an interplanetary entrepreneur.* Meanwhile (sleep drifting in), she had short-term plans for that nice, curly-headed Grade Five attaché. *He has to be past forty: but everyone's old except us, so that's not worth worrying about. He smiles at me, I know he's interested.*

Or longer term plans, why not? *Still got four-and-a-half years to kill.*

XVII

Francois and Nikty went riding with Prince S'na'ulat'tz' and his Blood-men. The Royal Myot Achievements Office had decided the Aleutian must be nobly born. They'd translated his lowly-sounding post into something exalted and archaic, perhaps 'Grand Vizier': so now the king's son could meet him without ceremony, opening a precious conduit for informal communication.

The riding animals were curious creatures, serpentine and segmented, varying in hue from glossy blood-colour to matt charcoal, and standing about as high as Francois's shoulder. They had a great many legs and no necks. One made a leap and settled, with what dignity one could muster, on a species of howdah, with perfectly useless bucket stirrups. One attempted to steer by means of a barbed girth, passed around the underbelly between the second and third pairs of forelegs. There was also a quoit, with a tassel that could be switched across the creature's bulging eyes, but *Brt'tz* (the thing had a name) reacted to that treatment with such mute, patient distress that he couldn't bring himself to slap her often—

The ride had become a morning ritual, since Francois's patent of nobility had been established. The prince would come to the Manor gates – a great condescension – to collect his Aleutian friend, and the Neuendan interpreter: one of the 'Bloodmen' leading Francois's mount. They'd roam the Manor grounds, sedately. Today they were making a longer expedition, to the summit of one of the volcanic plugs that littered the tangled savannah of the crater floor. 'It's over here!' called S'na'ulat'tz' with boyish informality. He was riding ahead, alone. The Bloodmen on either side of Francois turned their helmeted heads and silently glowered at Nikty: who obediently translated the fluting consonants and the vowel clicks into English.

'His Highness has discovered the path, sir.'

The prince's bodyguard refused, in defiance of the evidence of their eyes and ears, to believe that Francois already spoke and understood both Myot and Neuendan. It was patently impossible. He did not have the right kind of palate, the right kind of ears, worst of all he had no nose—

The Bloodmen were feudal lords of a city-state where all power had long since been swallowed by the Crown: glorified servants, doomed to squabble over who changed the prince's toilet pad for him. They deferred to Francois; they didn't know what to do with Nikty. They settled for being mildly rude. Clearly they believed, deep down, that any Neuendan was their social superior. Equally clearly they resented the attaché. She was not an aristo and should not be allowed so close to their prince.

Francois watched the lords carefully, more carefully than he watched S'na'ulat'tz': but unlike the Blues, who were legendary for their incontinent babbling in the Common Tongue, Sigurtians controlled their non-verbal communication. Which told him much, but it was unwelcome news.

'It's a little overgrown, but passable.'

'I hope the noble alien lord won't take a fall—' muttered a Bloodman.

'I'm sure I'll manage,' cried Francois. He twisted the girth-bridle so that his serpent picked up speed, and raised itself abruptly on its third legs before plunging onto the upward path.

Aleutians, traditionally, regarded 'animals' – uncanny free-living commensals, not budded from the information-cells of the sentient – with deep distrust. But Francois had lived on the Blue, in the days of cavalry charges: he was becoming proud of his Sigurtian riding skills.

They emerged at last from trees and vines, heads and shoulders splattered with pollen from late-summer flowers, onto a naked red-brown dome. The plain stretched in immensity: the city of Myotis a blur in the middle distance, spangled with the red eructations of telecom towers. Closer at hand, ragged moving blots glinted: hordes of *Brt'tz*'s distant relations, wandering about. The 'Chipshop' was a huge impact crater, (the volcanic activity a secondary effect) and – according to local science, which Francois saw no reason to doubt – alarmingly modern.

The prince waited, complacently, for his new friend's reaction.

'Magnificent,' chirped Francois. 'Truly magnificent.'

'The Aleutian lord praises the great plain of Myot,' repeated Nikty.

'The game's superb, too. See the herds of *vv'r'x*? Very fine animals. Of course, the numbers have to be controlled; you must come out with me for the autumn cull. *Nobody* lives on the surface of our planet, except the traditional Lar'z, who are more or less a remnant, scratch-farmers. Why should we?'

Sigurt's World was ocean-poor and water-poor. Much of the land above sea level was currently desert. Impact craters, moist and sheltered, scattered over the three continents, were enclaves of life and civilisation: a situation familiar to the Aleutian. Outside of its cities, and the life-corridors that joined them, the planet he called Home was a harsh, empty place—

Home, however, lived in a nice clean orbit, and did not have large, fresh pockmarks all over its face. *Why don't their moons shield them?* Francois wondered. Surely that could be fixed. Now *there's* an opportunity. Aleutian technology had helped the Blue Planet with a problem on a similar scale, a few hundred years ago. Maybe they'd used a little too much *force*, but still: uncontrollable warming was certainly no longer an issue.

The concrete expanse of the major flyerport could be seen on the edge of the urban area: flanked by vicious arrays of solar power stations. The sun of Sigurt's World was small (or far away: Francois was indifferent to the figures) – but very bright. Its spectrum seemed to be shifted towards the region the Blues called ultraviolet. Amplified, it was intolerable.

The prince moved close, so their beasts were almost touching, and peered at him with concern. 'You don't like bright daylight, my lord?'

'I do not.'

S'na'ulat'tz' bared his pointed white teeth. 'You'll enjoy our winter. The sun is hardly ever seen.'

'I look forward to it. Except that I understand we'll have to leave our beautiful Manor – where it's been such a privilege to stay, and we can't thank your Family enough – and move "indoors". But every cloud has a silver lining. Perhaps we'll take the opportunity to visit Neuendan.'

'Ah,' said the prince, and looked away. 'Hm.'

Nikty suddenly had difficulty with her beast: it didn't like the drop, perhaps. She was forced to move off, leaving Francois and the prince in privacy. The Bloodmen kept their distance—

Planetary Nationhood was a Speranza fiction, inspired by the official current situations on the Blue, and on Balas/Shet. Aleutia itself only met this 'condition' of Hegemony membership because the Big Pebble dealt with Speranza. Home definitely did not! Sigurt's World was a federation, apparently dominated by Neuendan. Some Crater-States were industrialised; some were not. There was a thriving conventional space age going on: and then again, there were places like ancient, cultivated, cultured Myotis . . .

Politics is the art of stupidity. Nikty's government seemed to have awarded the Buonarotti contract to the most poverty-stricken, reactionary and arrogant of their federal partners: no doubt in the hope that this boost would improve the lot of Myots in general. The Myot ruling caste, however, had seen an opportunity to throw their weight around – and had grasped it with enthusiasm. Hence the difficulties into which the Mission was plunged.

'It's amazing how well you speak our language,' said the prince at last, quite gently. 'In spite of your disability.'

The Sigurtian nasal protuberance was small but ornate: like a baroque little fleshy ear, set in the midst of their otherwise unremarkable features. The Neuendan nose was less convoluted than the Myot version: and this was a mark of exalted caste – which no doubt added to the friction between Nikty and the Myot Bloodmen. But to have no nose at all was a deformity, social disgrace. Francois took the insult with disdain, merely inclining his head.

'You are too good, my lord prince.'

'But you do not, forgive me, you do not *understand*. The Mission cannot visit Neuendan in the middle of our negotiations. It is impossible, a slight to our sovereignty. It is completely out of the question.'

Balancing perfectly in his saddle, hands free, S'na'ulat'tz' brushed sticky orange pollen from his shoulders and licked his fingers, delicately, reflectively. 'It's going to be a long winter. The parkland folk say you can always tell, from the consistency of the late-season pollens.'

And that's the end of the Neuendan topic!

'Your winters vary markedly in length?'

'They do.' Nikty had returned, quietly, to Francois's side.

She was no courtier. She was an academic linguist turned diplomat, but she knew when to be oblivious to words spoken aloud in her hearing.

'Winter is a misnomer, since our change of season is not tied to the lessening of exposure to sunlight, but to a change in atmospheric conditions, which envelopes the whole planet. It's cold here in the south, and the days are short, it's the opposite in the north: but the severe weather keeps us all indoors, sometimes more than half the year.'

A Sigurt's World year was somewhat less than twice the length of a standard Speranza year. Just how long would the skies be closed this time? *And here's something else Speranza didn't tell us, or that we didn't fully understand. One meets the alien through a haze, a fog composed of the vital questions that nobody thought to ask—*

'Your cities must become very isolated.'

'Not at all,' said the prince, complacently. 'There are the Tunnels. All the Crater-States are connected. The network is ancient, and partly natural.'

'Ah, the *Tunnels*.' Francois shook his head, apologetic. 'You have discovered another abyss of ignorance, sir. I didn't know that this world's magnificent natural caverns housed an all-weather transport network. There are trains? Motorways, vacuum-tubes?'

'Not quite.'

'If Your Highness will permit me?' The prince made the brusque gesture of assent one gives to a servant, and Nikty continued: 'As my Lord Francois implies, "tunnel network" is another misnomer. These are *caverns*, riven by unbridged chasms, subject to quakes, falls and shifts. Small flyers get through: but there's no commercial service, and no "network" that can be relied on, year by year. The tunnel-pilots of Myot are an elite, specialist corps, selected, trained and maintained by the Royal Household.'

'Admirable.'

'Isn't it,' said the Neuendan, avoiding any ironic inflexion. 'Winter is a time of consolidation with us, my lord. A time of rest, of dreams, and waiting for the spring.'

The prince leaned over and took a clawed hold on Francois's arm, to recapture his attention. 'You have served as Vizier to Lady Nef and the General since the Departure, my Lord Francois? Forgive me, but isn't that a *very* long life, for an Aleutian?'

Myot aristocrats kept their claws long, and razor-sharp, allegedly as a sign of privileged idleness. The ruling caste at Home did the same: and idleness was not the real message there, either—

Francois shrugged. 'I'm an obligate adventurer, which tends to curtail one's count of years. This time around, what can I say? There was a story I wanted to follow, which has not yet come to the end.'

S'na'ulat'tz' let fly a volley of piercing clicks: he was laughing.

'No, no, my dear sir. I know better! You've been taking the Blue longevity treatments!'

'Well, you have found me out.' Francois compressed his nasal, annoyed.

'I am the age I look,' remarked the prince, much amused. 'Many of the people you will meet in my company are not. We don't need "longevity treatment"; time passes differently for us.' He still had his claws in Francois's sleeve. 'But it's interesting that the treatments worked for you.'

He dropped his hold, signalled to the Bloodmen, and the party began a slow descent. The prince stayed beside Francois, inconvenient as this was on the narrow path: wickedly steep and littered with loose stones.

'Do you believe in the Diaspora?'

'The Weak Theory,' allowed the Aleutian, not wishing to give offence, 'is halfway plausible, I suppose. But I'm not a scientist.'

'Nonsense!' The bat-prince tugged Francois's hand from the rein and matched it against his own. S'na'ulat'tz'''s mighty beast, the dull charcoal of an extinguished ember, jostled close, shoving ruddy-chocolate *Brt'tz* off the trail. The prince's diamond-rimmed eyes glowed with a mysterious excitement. 'Convergent evolution? Pah! *Strong* Theory, the single descent, is the only rational explanation for the way we are made.'

The ride back to Underwall Manor was thereafter enlivened by an evidently well-rehearsed monologue on Strong Diaspora Theory ... Numinal biped Heritance Molecules, the Blue's 'DNA' and its analogues, show *clear* indication of a Blue forbear, a common ancestor. Why are there no remains of this starfaring ancient on the Blue; or anywhere else? What could be more obvious? They have been destroyed by cataclysms!

'Take our example. Our planet, like the prison moon, is riddled with great caverns: hollow right through. These two bodies have been shattered, literally *shattered* and reformed, time and again. The Blue must be the same, although Blues have lost this knowledge, and it has been disguised by vulcanism. Cataclysmic disturbance, our scientists agree, being one of the precursor attributes of life—'

'The prison moon?' Francois broke in. 'That's the big one, with an atmosphere? The one Speranza has named *Fenmu*?'

They had reached the trickiest part of the descent. 'The Grave,' agreed the prince cheerfully, over his shoulder, as his beast flowed, almost vertical, down a cascade of boulders. 'Of course, yes, very suitable. It's more secure than any tomb. We're selling space there to other Planetary Nations. We may have some members of the Hegemony in residence now: I'm not sure.'

Francois concentrated on staying on board, until he and *Brt'tz* reached the foot of the rockfall. 'How is that?'

'Pirates. Our near-space traffic is plagued by bandits, and some, I believe, were originally Buonarotti transiters. Riff-raff as well as heroes, naturally. Adventurers, and the like.'

The sun was very bright now, and yet there was an edge, a chill under the white blaze that warned of change.

'Nobody lives on the surface,' repeated S'na'ulat'tz'. '*Nobody!*'

XVIII

The Speranza Code was a mess, and that should have been a warning. The planet had been named Sigurt's World by starship crews, commemorating the famous Neuendan archaeologist, with 'Sigurtians' as the natural corollary. This nomenclature had been thrown out, along with an accretion of naughty bat-people references, for the first Diplomatic Mission – replaced by 'code' that would be used until the former 'Sigurtians' themselves had decided how they wanted to be known. But then, at the last minute, several terms approved by DP committee had been rejected by the bots as having negative psychology for the Mission's staff, who were exclusively Blues—

Hanging Manor, The Fallen World, The Underworld, Diyu—

A king called Red-Wing the Blood-Drinker—

So it was a mess, and they clutched at inferences. Was the king, whom they were to address as *Lord Hongfu*, hostile? Was Prince S'na'ulat'tz' friendly because he allowed them to try and pronounce his name? Or was it the other way round? S'na'ulat'tz''s father, the king's consort, was dead, which at least saved them another layer of complication. (Although maybe he *wasn't* dead, just in a coma somewhere. Between newly met numinal bipeds, the wildest misunderstandings may occur—)

General Yu and Francois walked around the stable-yards of Underwall. Ostensibly they were planning to purchase riding beasts, *serpents*, for the Mission; with the Royal Family's permission. This area, however, had been passed as (probably) bug-free by Mohabbet Soltani, Counter-Surveillance Officer. Francois was presenting his latest unofficial report.

'Nikty had the sense to get out of the way,' he said, having delivered the latest bad news. 'She didn't officially hear or "translate" the prince's veto, capped with an insult that left him no way to retract. So we *could* appeal to Neuendan: but I feel that would be unwise. We are trapped.'

The General scowled. 'Nikki's a good girl, but I wish the Neuendans had sent us an aristo. They must have a few of them, idling around, everyone does. They should have known she'd be hamstrung.'

'Perhaps that was the point. Whether or not our friend knows it—'

'Huh ... Well, she *seems* like a good girl.'

Maybe the charming, witty, sophisticated Neuendans were the ones who wanted the Transit facility on the surface, and they'd cunningly enlisted a difficult Developing Nation to do their dirty work—

They peered into the stone burrows, lined with smooth clay, where the serpents would be housed. It was dark in there: the stale air carried a dry, vaguely unpleasant smell, a hint of rustling, crawling things.

'Are we supposed to call them *serpents*? Shouldn't they be *wu-gong*?'

Blame my aversion to every being of that kind, Swimmer. I confess I didn't give the appellation much thought. Snakes, however, are beasts of auspicious omen in China. Centipedes, I believe, are not.'

'By all means, let's have a good omen.'

They moved on. 'You still think he's a wrong 'un? Your friend the prince? Or was he just the messenger?'

The Aleutian hitched his shoulders: a dry smile. 'S'na'ulat'tz' may be a "right 'un" according to his lights, but I'm convinced he's no friend of ours. Yet he's *fascinated* by me, Swimmer: and I don't know why.'

'Nonsense, it's simple. You've no nose and you can talk.' The General, who had never learned to handle the 'Common Tongue', was enjoying Francois's helplessness: although the loss of that secret weapon was mighty inconvenient. 'I should think he looks on you as a privileged freak. Court jester, holy fool, that kind of thing.'

Francois ignored the jibe – pacing with his clawed hands behind his back, nasal compressed, chasing the elusive meaning of the prince's manner. 'He's perfectly indifferent to the location of the Buonarotti Transit facility, but he wants *something*, and I wish I knew what. Well, *revenons á nos moutons*: the cavern network. It's a piece of luck that we have a small, eminently manoeuvrable flyer at our disposal.'

'We can use the *Spirit* as a light plane? No screwy business?'

'*Pas de problem*. He was built for the Speranza market, like all his kind: conventional flight is in his repertoire. There are other difficulties, which may be insurmountable: but the question in my mind is what to tell Liam and Alis. At this point.'

Liam and Alis were the Mission's Speranza agents.

'What the apparatchiks don't know won't hurt 'em,' said the General, after a brief pause. They walked on. 'Don't fuss, Francois, don't fuss. I'm not asking *you* to fly your pretty boy-racer through the rocks.'

The light in the stone-clad yard was blistering at this hour, shortly before the abrupt, colourless dusk. They'd been told they could look forward to splendid, mellow sunsets soon: before winter, when everything changed.

'I'll be glad to quit the bat-people's anti-UV medication,' Yu grunted. 'It makes me feel sick.' He tipped back his head and aimed his voice at the beetling, red-brown cliffs. '*Chipshop, Chipshop, Chipshop*— Do you hear the echo? I damn well can't. Why couldn't Speranza issue us with a gadget for improved hearing, eh?'

'Because the software wouldn't have made it through the transit?'

'I've heard that excuse too often. Well, the flyer idea. It'll do no harm to investigate, my Grand Vizier. See what you can work out.'

The Aleutian betook himself to the barracks, a shed connected to the Manor by a basement passage. The teardrop door opened to touch: he hooked his claws into the holds, hopped onto the sill and down into a long, blessedly dim room lined with rows of sleeping mats. A pile of folding Myot cots, rejected, were stacked against the far wall. The common soldiers, dregs of society, many having brains and limbs *littered* with horrible non-living devices, scrambled frantically to attention. He was not on the warpath but he prowled anyway, staring down the known miscreants; taking an interest in the unlucky cyborgs who'd suffered in the transit (happily there'd been only one fatality); picking on small infractions in uniform and kit.

They trembled and they loved him. Recall to General Yu's service had been glorious salvation for these men and women: from disgrace and penury to a Diplomatic Mission on an alien planet! *Self help us,* thought the Aleutian, *if it should dawn on some of this murderous rabble that General Yu brought them here so they couldn't talk. And he perhaps has everything to lose by taking them home again—*

'Ah. Col Ben Phu.' He studied the tattooed lady darkly. She was no more untidy than her neighbours, but her mat was *not* aligned dead square. 'Outside, if you please.'

Col stood backbone-cracking straight, in the middle of the barracks yard parade ground, staring over the Aleutian's drooping shoulder.

'You have your pilot's wings, Col. You lost nothing in the transit?'

'Got no code to lose, sir, 'cept the shadows in my grey an' mushy, an' no hardware 'cept if you count the patches. Nothing gone, sir. Sar'nt says I'm a hopeless skills addict, there's no *me* without *them*. Unlike poor Uko, got here with 'is brain dripping out his ears—'

'Thank you, that's enough. Navigation skills?'

'Sir. Yes, sir, full whack. I was Flying Bomb Squad.'

'A suicide warrior! Commendable indeed. And yet you are still with us, Col. How is that?'

'Never got farther than the sims, sir. I've only served with the General, an' we were never in an airstrike situation. But I've died thirty-six times, sir.'

'Very good.' Francois unbent a little. 'You beat my count, Col. In the history of the moving image, that is, which is all I allow. It's impossible truly to *know* who one was, before that era, don't you agree?'

'I would if I knew what you was talking about, sir.'

'Stand at ease and follow me, I want to introduce you to someone.'

Underwall Manor's flyerport was almost as empty as the stables. *The Spirit of Eighty-Nine* stood in lonely state, beneath a sectioned dome of translucent, chitinous synthetic 'glass', in a hangar large enough for a brace of passenger jets from the Blue's Age of Consumption. Col Ben Phu had heard about this machine, but this was the first time she'd actually set eyes on Francois's boy-racer. She stared, with candid hunger—

'Do you think you could fly him?'

Col hesitated. 'Are we, er, permission to ask are we allowed, sir?'

The glimmering Aleutian pod was grounded: literally tied down by ropes of black and red tape. The Mission had been informed that the noble Aleutian lord would have to apply for a licence before he could take the *Spirit* anywhere. No diplomatic exceptions, and the application, if all went well, would probably take, oooh, a good five or ten Sigurtian years.

The Sigurtians didn't know what *Spirit* was. Col Ben Phu, Francois discerned, definitely had an inkling. The Sensitive Visitors Facility on Speranza must have porous walls ... All to the good: if she knew, she didn't need to be told. 'As long as we don't leave the Manor's airspace, we'll get away with it. I repeat, do you think you can fly my pod?'

'I– I dunno, sir,' quavered the soldier, rattled by the Aleutian's steady, penetrating appraisal. 'If you say so. All I *know* is Flying Bombs—'

'Let's see how you feel at closer acquaintance.'

They went around detaching the tape and mounted – with a hop and a scramble, like old Sigurtian hands – into the shell. Francois reached inside his collar and ran his fingers, laden with red wandering cells from his throat-glands, over the instrument panel. Col looked around. The *Spirit* had the same appearance inside as outside: a stylish spaceplane, two-man cockpit and four-berth habitat, with a luminous silver décor. Powerful and robust enough to breach the Blue's lower atmosphere, for suborbital hops: but not at all dissimilar, essentially, from the private flyers that the Myots used all the time.

'Take a seat.'

Col, with betraying haste, attempted to take the co-pilot's couch, but Francois corrected her. 'I shall be your co'. Easy, Col. Let's hook up, helmets on, and masks, tho' we won't need oxygen on this trip.'

Col slipped into the body-hugging couch, hooked up with practised speed and donned the pilot's helmet. Francois took the co-pilot's place.

Connections found their homes in the patches set in Col's skull: and the luxurious interior of the boy-race shifted, swift as a dreaming thought. They were in the stark cockpit of a terrestrial fighter pod. Col Ben Phu pulled off her breathing mask and turned to stare, open-mouthed, at the Aleutian: but she did not panic, she didn't break sweat. She was with Francois the Noseless. She was impressed, but nothing surprised her. Ah, the beauty of being regarded as a person of unlimited powers.

'And people wonder,' murmured Francois, 'why degenerates such as myself keep returning to the Blue—'

'Sir?'

'Could you fly him now?'

Col's small, dark eyes flickered, checking her skillcard. 'Yeah.'

'Then let's go.'

There was a phlegmatic pause. Col ran over her instruments, checking the panel against her head-up display. The *Spirit* and the hangar system engaged with each other: the pod thrummed and rose, eerily quiet, sections of brownish, lucent chitin parting like insect wings. Col's emotional reaction (intimately shared by the Aleutian) at taking the chameleon aloft was wild panic: but her performance was unaffected. The *Spirit* reached a height some few hundred metres above the treetops of the Manor grounds, far below the regulated flight-path band: they commenced a circuit. The wall of the crater was a ruddy line beyond Myotis, like an ocean horizon.

He handles very nicely, sir.

Indeed.

Bet he can go a bit. Slippery as a fish, too.

Not now, Col. I fear if we tried his paces, in plain sight, we might alarm our friends the Myots. Let's make this an interface training session.

Uh, sorry, sir—

Enough, said Francois at last. Time to get back in the box.

The sudden dark had fallen, but the hangar was waiting for them, landing lights a cup of gold. The *Spirit* descended, spot onto his mark: Col Ben Phu pulled off her helmet and the interior became what it had been before. She gazed upward, stoically silent, at the closing dome.

'Very good,' said Francois. 'I'll want you to take him out again, before the skies are closed. A semi-AI needs to be exercised.'

They restored the cat's cradle of red and black tape. Col stood to attention, expression blank, eyes aimed correctly over his shoulder, her whole presence struggling with the need to speak—

'You have something to say?'

'Sir, I– I don't have red cooties, er, I don't have wandering cells.'

'Oh, that. I was giving him a treat, Col: he doesn't need to be primed. He will adapt to your skills unreservedly, as long as your wishes don't conflict with mine. He is, of course, intimately my creature. You are dismissed, soldier. Return to quarters.'

Too intelligent, decided the Aleutian, as she marched into the gloom, and he turned to the glow of the Manor's lamps. *Implicitly loyal, but tends to think for herself: which is why she's still cannon fodder ...*

Well, so we have a pilot. If we can find a way to use her.

XIX

Night temperatures dropped. The garden walks were clogged with sticky masses of giant, fallen flowerheads. Bibi and Honesty took their morning weapons training in a pall of white mist – under the exacting eye of Borgush Dunblane, Household Trainer (whose title at home, in the archaic style of Baykonur Traditionalism, was 'Master-at-Arms'); and there was no break in the impasse. Just a *g't'z* before the *Rajath* was due to return, on his first visit to Sigurt's Port since the Mission had made the crossing, the Speranza agents called an extraordinary meeting of the Mission Executive.

It was almost noon, but the dining hall they used for private meetings was below ground level and always gloomy – reminding the Senior Blues, nostalgically, of the bunker-architecture of their youth. The red-gold varnished table was lit by a row of standing bulbs; daylight fell through tall lancets, dissecting the outer darkness. The agents took the head of the table, flanked by the General, Lady Nef and her secretary. The rest closed ranks: mounting with a hop and a scramble into the cup-shaped seats that extended, like buds from a stem, from beneath the table.

The Exec was selected by a Mission's leaders: a system meant to ensure effective decision-making, with no voices that would not be heard. General Yu and Lady Nef had included their Master-at-Arms and their Housekeeper; but not the Cultural, Social, Trade or PR officers. An idiosyncratic choice, but prescient. Survival was the issue now, not a showcase for Blue imports—

'As you're all aware,' began Agent Alis, 'we've run into more trouble. Today the General received another strongly worded memo—'

The Myots claimed that they'd made their intentions known from the start. They had a site for the facility mapped out, in the badlands above their crater. They had a mass of surveys and reports, in which tame regulatory bodies gave approval to the scheme. They insisted that their use of a term meaning *outside*, or *far from all life*, had been perfectly clear, and they further claimed that they had the support of their Planetary Government. The Mission had spent the last six months (standard time: nearly seven now) trying to get Neuendan to refute this: Neuendan had been putting them off.

Probably.

Since every communication from the planetary capital was intercepted 'for translation' by the Myots, it was hard to be sure. By this stage, it was hard to be sure if they'd ever had *any* genuine contact with Neuendan ... But unfortunately, finally, something definite had broken through the fog. The DP engineers, out in orbit, had been communicating freely with their Sigurtian counterparts. Someone had let slip that the material couriered from Speranza *could*, quite possibly, be adapted for a surface build—

'His Majesty's a damned insulting fellow,' growled Yu, restless as a monkey in the uncomfortable seat, 'if you ask me.'

Mohabbet, on Counter-Surveillance watch, winced—

'Problem with my colourful language, Soltani?'

Mohabbet, not known for her humour, shook her head. 'Not in here, right now, so far as I can tell, sir. But the software isn't as reliable as I'd like.'

Intractable 'transit bugs' plagued all their couriered data; reinstalled in freighted hardware. Mohabbet, who couldn't safely convert to locally written code, had the worst problems—

'Well, let's try not to embarrass ourselves,' suggested Liam. 'But my proposal is not sensitive. Is there any other business, before I present it?'

There was a glum silence. Everyone knew that the success the General had needed was slipping away from him. Obviously the agents were going to send back a progress report with the *Rajath*, and it wouldn't be a shining one. Ariane Rasoul, Lady Nef's Housekeeper, raised a hand.

'I'd like to know if we can keep the Sigurtian domestics out of our personal quarters. I'm sorry if that sounds rude, but it could be put to them politely, and, well—' She appealed to her mistress, with the familiarity of long service. 'We'd never allow a situation like this on campaign, ma'am. It's regulations to minimise contact with all locals, when we're in talks. But *they're* in and out, and any little thing could cause friction—'

The agents and the Mission leaders exchanged sharp glances. 'Ariane, could you be more specific?' said Nef. 'Do you bring this up because there have been incidents?'

'Not anything to put on report, but they move our things about, and we know they've been poking in our personal details: Hari will tell you—'

'Personal details,' Francois repeated – recalling a conversation with the prince. 'Really? Exactly *what* have the, er, inquisitive locals been looking at?'

Hari Colmar, Admin Chief, grimaced and shrugged. 'What have they not? It's their software, their hardware and a node of their net we're using, for everything non-classified. I can tell when they've been in our files, but I can't keep them out. I've found the bat-brigade's clawmarks, so to speak, all over the place.' He shuddered. 'Like mouse droppings in the larder.'

'I think you'd like to rephrase that, Hari,' suggested Lady Nef. 'If we can't control our negative psychology, we can choose what is spoken aloud.'

Hari took the reproof without much sign of contrition. 'Excuse me, Lady Nikty, didn't mean to offend *you*. Excuse me, ma'am. Forgot myself.'

Personal details, thought Francois. The Strong Diaspora, a princely interest in an alien's use of Blue longevity treatments—

'Shall we move on?' suggested the General. 'The domestic problems can be dealt with, politely, as Ariane says. Well, Liam—?'

The Execs braced themselves, resentfully, for a criticism session. They disliked the Speranza agents on principle. This was supposed to be General Yu's command! But at least Alis *looked* respectable. (She even claimed to be a Traditionalist, but they didn't believe her.) Liam, the senior of the pair, was something else. His hair, which he wore long and loose, was silvery-blue, each strand flattened and slick, Aleutian style. His eyes were yellow and cat-pupilled, his skin had a sheen of metallic gold, his ears were pricked and pointed as Nikty's. He'd have been arrested walking down the street in Baykonur, and quite right too.

The offensively modified cissy looked at his tablet, looked up, and drew an audible breath. 'May I say first that there is absolutely no negative reflection on the Mission leaders or their staff. We've found a situation for which none of us was prepared. It's a normal hazard of our work, and your conduct has been, er, exemplary. In short order, then, what we propose is that Alis should return to Speranza on the *Rajath*, with the engineers and a Myot delegation, for a much-needed rebriefing. Hopefully this will solve our problems, and the project will resume.'

He paused. 'But we'd like you people to stay. For the Mission, or even part of the Mission, to leave at this juncture would be a gesture we hope to avoid. Alis will be couriering a full report of our situation. If Speranza deems the position here unsafe you'll be pulled out at once. Within days; or hours. There's no doubt of that.'

The Execs tried to conceal their relief: a few heads nodded.

'But the skies will soon be closed,' added Alis, spelling it out. 'If Speranza System deems the current situation safe, you'll be here on the ground, with no way to retreat to the Port, until the spring.'

'That doesn't sound unreasonable,' declared the General, after a moment. 'We knew what we were in for, it's a frontier posting. We're not going to scurry home at the first setback.'

'What does *Nikty* think of this plan?' enquired Lady Nef.

Everyone looked to the Neuendan. As far as they knew she was in the same position as themselves: cut off from direct contact with her superiors, struggling to keep the negotiation with these touchy poor relations going.

But they could not be sure. Blues unconsciously, universally, read expression and identity in the band of tiny muscles around each other's eyes. The velvet mask that covered the upper part of Bat-woman's face, framing her curled-up nose, disturbed them more than they were aware—

'I need to consult with my government,' said Nikty, carefully. 'But I am sure a rebriefing is highly necessary. When the surface facility was "impossible", that was straightforward. "Ill-advised" is difficult and puzzling. As Hongfu says, how can aliens know what is "ill-advised"? Interstellar transit is new to all of us, and Pendong science is far from inferior. '

Pendong, 'Bowlcave', was the new, official Speranza codename for Sigurt's World. Everybody forgot to use it, most of the time.

'Of course, meanwhile, I shall stay with the Mission.'

She set her hands (fingers unnaturally skinny and long; claws trimmed

147

to the quick) palms down on the tabletop, with finality – and some of them wondered, what did that gesture mean?

'I'll be staying too,' added Liam. 'Of course.'

'I see no difficulty whatsoever,' announced Lady Nef, smiling. 'Speranza must examine, in good faith, the question of a surface build.'

The Exec gave their assent, unanimously.

The agents were impressed and relieved by this firmness of purpose. Liam and Alis knew about the Baykonur Conspiracy, but they had no idea how close the General had been to arrest, or how much his household feared the prospect of a sudden recall to Earth. The meeting broke up in a surprisingly positive, cheerful mood: Liam and Alis winning more smiles and warm looks than they'd ever seen before.

XX

The last 'double moon night' of summer was an important date. It was no longer the day that the skies closed – the great shut-down was now decreed by super-computers, not the religious authorities; but the festival survived.

The whole staff of the Mission, at the invitation of the prince, joined the traditional royal visit to the Upper World.

It was the first time Bibi and Honesty had left the Manor grounds. Not that they'd felt confined, but they were thrilled to be going properly outdoors. They rode up the Crater Wall in a gondola with Ariane, Hari – and Nikty, who was still their good friend, though she'd given up trying to teach them Neuendan. The weather was really changing now: the chitin-glass car was wrapped in a thick mist that made frost-flowers when it touched, visibility out there almost zero—

'We'll be above it soon,' Nikty promised them. 'You'll see.'

'Is this goop why you don't fly in winter?' asked Honesty. The whiteness looked edible, rich as cream. She stared though the transparent shell, pleasurably disoriented, thinking the mist itself was a fine spectacle.

'Not at all! We don't fly by sight, Honesty. We're not insects!'

'Then why didn't we fly to the surface?'

'Tradition. And it's early, but there might be a little passing storm, you wouldn't have liked the turbulence. Are you getting chilled?' Nikty brought out an underarm flask from the folds of her overcoat, unscrewed the cap from the nipple and offered it to Ariane. 'Try this, it'll warm you.'

'Is that the blood tea?' asked the Housekeeper, doubtfully.

'No, it's, let me see, it's, er, *schapps*.'

'Schnapps?' suggested Hari, with interest. 'Strong liquor?'

The Blues had not met Sigurtian spirits before: only the ubiquitous pollen beer, which tasted foul; and a tart wine made from vine fruit that was highly prized, but definitely an acquired taste. The distilled spirit had a faint, sweet scent and was almost tasteless, but it burned down into their stomachs in a very satisfactory manner. They'd finished the flask, between them, when their gondola popped out of the mist as if bobbing to the surface of a well, and they saw the Upper World: a flat desert, a wilderness of red boulders and grey scrub, and fissures that stretched and branched like cracks in old paint. The cold was fierce, contesting with their cheerful inner warmth.

'We are now, of course, let me see, about three thousand metres above the crater floor,' announced Nikty. 'From here we ride. There's a little—' (she consulted her transaid) '—er, *café*, where an arm will be offered, it's a lovely, homely, rural place and it's not far.'

Hari was not keen. The 'serpents' gave him the creeps: he'd never touched one yet. 'Is there a car, or one of those hovers, for non-riders?'

Nikty laughed, a melodious tumble of clicks. 'No, no, not today!' She seemed scandalised. 'Today you must ride the animals, like everyone else. It's Communion with Nature Day. Don't worry, they'll be very tame.'

The desert wind was icy, the sky thick and low: the gondola station stood alone on the bare red ground. There was a herd of 'serpents' waiting for them: jostling and nosing around in a pen. They were smaller than the riding beasts from the royal stables, and had thick, curly blond hair between their segments. Strange bat-people, wide as they were tall in bundles of dark, felty garments, hooked the animals out of the mill, one by one, with pronged poles: saddled them up, handed each member of the party onto a saddle, and slapped the bridle into gloved hands. The hired beasts were roped, two by two, in short strings, with a guide at the head of each.

Prince S'na'ulat'tz', his Bloodmen and the leaders of the Mission were mounted on superior animals. They watched from a distance, until the last of the soldiers had been boosted into the saddle. Bibi and Honesty were knee to knee as their string set off, into a squall of stinging hail. They could see nothing but Ariane and Hari's backs. If they turned their heads, hail dived into their bristle-trimmed hoods, and punched them in the face.

'How can anyone *live* out here?' howled Honesty.

'I expect they don't!' shouted Bibi. 'After today, they'll be in their burrows with the serpents until spring.'

Conversation was impossible. The undulating movement of Bibi's mount was hypnotic, and unlike virtual horse-riding, which she'd tried and liked, there was nothing for her thighs to grip, no purchase for her heels. Whenever she relaxed she began to slip. It was all balance: and for two or three seconds together she'd get the idea, but then she'd lose it again. The serpent ignored her; it just rippled on, nose to the armoured rump of the animal in front, mindless as an animated scrubbing brush.

If there was anything to see on this ritual journey, they didn't see it. The squall never let up until another blot of buildings came looming through the veil. The serpent-herders led the strings into another pen, and hauled the inept riders to the ground. The lovely homely café was as big as a bus station, with a floor below ground level, like the lower halls at Underwall. A bounce up, a hop down, into warmth and gloom. Heat rose through the floor, as if there was a furnace under it. Café servants took everybody's outer wraps. The Blues filed onto benches along rows of tables, where there was a meal already laid out: jugs of pollen beer, loaves of pollen cake, bowls of dried fruit, seeds, flowerbud pickles; dishes of a gluey kind of hot brown paste that (from the odd smell) must be somehow produced by the 'serpents'.

'Centipede snot,' suggested Honesty. 'Centipede turd butter.'

'Ooze of boiled carapace, I think—'

The high-grades must have been doing something else, probably something ritual about the last day of summer. They came in later, wrapped in their splendid Sigurtian weather-wear, trooped through dining room and disappeared through a teardrop door in the far wall: which was glossy and translucent, made of slabs of real chitin ...

'Must be the first-class dining room through there,' muttered Honesty. 'I wonder what *they* get to eat?'

Bibi suddenly remembered the cabin in the otherworldly blizzard of the crossing, the hunters stamping their feet. *I will have that again*, she thought. *I will be friends with Lady Nef again, on the way home.* The promise filled her with happiness, though she was daunted by the endless days between, weapons drill and make-work. Lucky Honesty, she had her Grade Six studies.

If we make the crossing 'outside time', why can't we get back the same day that we left? Why can't our whole tour of duty be a dream? If twenty-six thousand light years can just disappear, why can't five tiny standard years?

She decided she would start asking questions, and learn something.

The 'nobodies' who lived on the surface passed to and fro, sweating and beaming, renewing platters and jugs. Would they be relocated if the Myots got their way? Or would they stay, and suffer some kind of terrible blight? *It's no different from what someone like Prince S'na'ulat'tz' would say on Earth*, she thought. *Nobody* lives outside the Enclosures, *nobody* ... And yet people do. The Magnet had used her mysterious powers to make sure they were sitting next to Zidane, the well-connected but dim Second Assistant to General Yu. Bibi didn't like him. He was too old and he reminded her of Lady Nef's son: but beggars, Honesty said, can't be choosers. He and Honesty were giggling, feeling each other up under the table, eagerly downing the pollen beer. *You're going to regret that*, thought Bibi, *when we have to get back onto those scrubbing brushes*—

She realised there was someone at her elbow, a spidery hand on the sleeve of her dress-uniform tunic: blue with red piping, because she was now an office assistant, not a social worker. It was Nikty with another Sigurtian, a young, half-masked one (which meant a woman, more or less), dressed like the café's staff in dark felt – but her arms were bare to the shoulder, loose skin visible between arm and flank; bunched against her sides.

'Bibi!' Nikty's eyes were bright; she looked rather drunk. 'Bibi, look, an arm is offered. You are invited to drink.'

'Oh—'

Sigurtians didn't have real flesh-animals: not on this continent anyway. Wild 'serpents' and their relations were hunted but they were poor eating, like meagre giant shellfish. The chitin, although nourishing, was time-consuming to prepare. Myot peasants ate the laborious porridge. Myot aristocrats still, although the custom was dying out, supplemented their diet with the blood of the lower orders. It was tradition. It wasn't cruel; it did the peasants no lasting harm. It was the same, essentially, as taking the energy of someone's labour, and eating well on the profits—

Scenes from the induction simulations flashed into Bibi's mind, along with the carefully worded script, which she had both accepted and rejected, *Yes, all right, fine, but it's never going to affect me.*

'Oh,' she said again, consternated. 'Oh, but—'

'The prince especially wants you to have this honour. And let me see, of course, Honesty too!'

The strange Sigurtian grinned and nodded. Her face was rounder and fatter than Nikty's, her nose an elaborate little swirl. She held out her arm, a flap of skin hanging under it, the inner flesh all puckered, drops of blood welling from two neat new punctures in the crook of her elbow.

'*Holy shit*,' mouthed Honesty, eyes like saucers.

'Go on,' urged Zidane. 'Honour of the Mission, eh? You've got to do it, girls.'

'*Please*,' said the young Sigurtian, or maybe it was, '*Thank you.*' She was beginning to look worried. Quite likely she'd be punished, or something, if her blood was refused. Blushing to the roots of her hair, Bibi bent her face and licked the two drops. A tumult of clicking broke out. The café servants were pressing around, clicking and fluting.

'They're saying you have to *suck*,' cried Nikty.

'Move over, Savage. I'll show you how!'

Honesty sucked with energy. She raised her bloodstained mouth, and the clicking redoubled. The peasant girl spat on her arm, and said something to Nikty. The Neuendan laughed. 'She says you drink like a princess.' Honesty jumped up and hugged the blood-offerer. Zidane jumped up, and thumped Honesty on the back.

'Good girl! You're a trooper, Magnet, a real trooper—'

After the meal there was dancing. The Upper World peasants shed more of their clothing and kicked off their boots. They laid their arms across each other's shoulders and swayed in circles: flaps of skin, vestigial or wide as wings, swaying with their motion, like sheeny leather veils. The Blues got up and danced in turn, the circles mingled. A half-masked Sigurtian, who seemed to be the café proprietress, led the mouth-music. Ariane joined her, to the peasants' delight: clicks and flutes and human ululation falling into phase, while stamping feet and snapping fingers kept the beat. Zidane took Honesty off to find the toilets, as she wasn't feeling very well—

When they left the café everything had changed. The hail had vanished, the ground was dry, the air was strangely warm. The 'double full moon', lost in haze but drowning out the stars, drenched everything in a juicy, ochre light, like the flesh of a plum. The serpent-drivers were all drunk and the beast-strings had dissolved. It didn't matter. Bibi and Honesty swayed along as before: the serpents weren't going anywhere but home to their own familiar pen.

'I feel awfully sick,' mumbled Honesty. 'I drank someone's blood. That's terrible. I think I'm poisoned—'

'You drank a real lot of that disgusting beer, Magnet.'

'I wish I was like you. I wish I had an ab-, ab-, abstemious nature. Why have we got soldiers on either side of us, Bibi?'

Bibi had wondered about that herself. 'Because you're drunk, and they think you're going to fall off, and roll into a crevasse.'

The Magnet, stung by this insinuation, attempted to sit up straight in her saddle. Bibi grabbed her and they rode on, Honesty's head on Bibi's shoulder, through the thrilling, plum-flesh twilight of an alien night.

Nef and Liam were riding with the prince. General Yu, Francois and Nikty had escaped from this honour, on the grounds that the Mission personnel needed a sober eye on them: which was undoubtedly true.

'I want those two young women kept indoors,' muttered Yu.

'Yes,' said the Neuendan. 'It would be wise if they are never alone.'

The hostages had been exchanged, to put it bluntly. A Myot delegation had left for Speranza in the *Rajath*: with Alis, and the engineers. There had not been a swift return, so the Mission wasn't going to be pulled out. The Myot royals seemed in benign high spirits, as if the victory was won; and the skies were closed. There was nothing to be done now except hold out, keep calm, and wait for the spring.

XXI

Imperial Restoration had probably been inevitable since the end of the Civil War. 'Prisoner Haku' had failed, but his supporters had prepared the ground: there was no doubt that the people wanted the Empire back. Lady Nef had called in her favours just in time – the Republic had been in its death throes when she spoke to her old friend Xue. The actual coup – precipitated by the scandal of the Baykonur Conspiracy, and the working out of certain deep-laid plans – was almost bloodless. A staggeringly high proportion of Earth's population watched, or attended in bi-location, as the shy recluse, who'd stepped down so long ago, was reinstated on the Dragon Throne, and became once more the Han Gaozu Emperor – resuming the name he'd chosen, to honour Liu Bang, the 'peasant boy' Emperor of ancient times. To the people, his four billion or so subjects, he was 'Old Tai Bai', the 'Big White One', an affectionate nickname awarded on account of his large, pale moonface.

During the ceremony he renounced immortality, among other concessions: declaring he was comfortable with a Senior's lifespan. This signal, promising that the Xi'an mandarins were not planning to hide behind 'Old Tai Bai' indefinitely, removed the liberal opposition's last objections.

The fallout on Blue-dominated Speranza was much more dramatic. The recall of the Republic's MDPs, swiftly followed by the revelation that Buonarotti materiel had *almost* fallen into criminal hands (a potential disaster that had been kept very quiet), led to blows in the Parliament Chamber. Members from the Liberal cities, furious at the Earth's 'return to tyranny', refused to quit, and grappled physically with Empire-lovers. Other numinal bipeds, panicked by the Buonarotti issue, took sides. Unauthorised weapons, forbidden since Speranza's founding, mysteriously appeared. Shots were exchanged under the Great Banner of the Diaspora. Left Speranza was in an uproar for days.

Fortunately Domremy Li, a Blue from the moderately Liberal city of Rio, and a Permanent Secretary, took charge with a strong hand: but before the unrest was quelled six citizens, including one Green Belt and one MDP, plus twenty-three hapless 'Prospectors', had lost their lives. Murder and violence were not unknown in the capital city of the Diaspora, which had its criminal underbelly. These casualties were different, each of them a terrible fall from grace. The names of the fallen would be enshrined for ever.

An appearance of normalcy was swiftly restored. Everyone wanted to forget the horrible sight of armed Green Belts deployed on the beloved concourses of the only really civilised world. The outgoing Blue MDPs, deeply chastened, made no further protests. Domremy's takeover was ratified, to everyone's relief, by Speranza System. 'Prisoner Haku', who had known nothing of the upset until it was over, was recalled to Earth. At first he sued for asylum: but he took advice from his Legals, and departed quietly.

The *Rajath* had been on the return leg of a round trip when he picked up Alis and her party. The crew had spent their Port time at Balas/Shet station 'on board'. They hadn't caught up with the big Speranza story; so they'd told Alis nothing. She was surprised when she didn't get her aura tag back in the Arrivals Hall, and when the Sigurtians were taken straight off to the Sensitive Visitors Facility. But it wasn't unknown for delegations to be housed there, particularly if the VIPs declined to be separated from their armed guards.

She had crossed in the dreamtime, but she knew she'd be in better shape for a tricky debriefing if she took her disorientation allowance. She delivered the deposition she and Liam had prepared, and went off to her quarters. The 'enshrined names' kept appearing in her field of view. She paid no attention: she assumed it was an outbreak of fly-posting (to which Speranza was not immune). She had a shower, rested, and enjoyed a peaceful evening with friends – the *Rajath* had arrived mid-afternoon, Left Speranza. Of course her friends talked about the coup, but they were so anxious to forget what had happened that they made out that nothing much had happened. There'd been a regime change on the Blue, stormy exchanges in the Chamber: so what?

*

At her debriefing, held in a secure, in-person meeting room in the warren of Parliament Building, she met a formidable panel of MDPs, legal officers and a Permanent Secretary. She'd expected nothing less. She was steeling herself for awkward questions about that leak. She had been a scientist once herself: she'd encouraged the free exchange with the Sigurtians, she knew she could be held responsible. *It was inconceivable, you see, that any Planetary Nation would* want *a Buonarotti facility on the surface. The dangers are so enormous—*

We hadn't understood the implications of the 'winter' problem—

Nobody wanted to talk about the Buonarotti facility. A new protocol for Diaspora relations was being thrashed out, which would address the 'Pendong' issues. Meanwhile, far more urgently, there was the question of the Diplomatic Mission's leaders, and the Baykonur Conspiracy. Alis, bewildered that Blue home affairs were being raised at all, suddenly realised that she didn't recognise any of the MDPs. She didn't know the Legals either. The Permanent Secretary was familiar, a distant superior, but he looked strange. Wary? Frightened? She was hit by a jolt of the frightening disjoint that sometimes overtook her after a transit, though she always used the dreamtime. A feeling Blue transiters called, for reasons lost in the mists of time: *We're not in Kansas any more.*

'Is the Mission's present situation dangerous, Alis?' asked the Secretary, a warning in his eye. 'In your professional opinion?'

'Difficult,' said Alis. 'No danger to life, no, sir.'

—Thinking of Lady Nef, and the brilliant but unsettling Francois. Those two guileless young women, bubbling with energy and bewilderment—

'Then I conclude that an emergency intervention to pull them out would be inappropriate. Let them stay in place for the moment.'

XXII

There were protests in Baykonur when the Third Empire was restored. Angry young Reformers, and a few Traditionalists, took to the streets. Expensive advertising was hacked and hijacked by Artists for Civil Liberty, and the ringleaders enjoyed momentary fame. In the Palaces a fly-post message went round, inviting juniors to join an illegal Society for the Restoration of the Renaissance (*Renaissance* had become a codeword for *Republic*). Mahmood, having common sense, paid no attention – though he had a guilty feeling that Bibi might have wanted him to join the marchers.

Three weeks after the coup he got the shock of his life: a summons from the Starry Arrow, on his hardscreen, in his cubicle at work. In blind panic he deleted it: as if that would change anything, as if his superiors didn't know. Within seconds the summons was on his eye soc', and a lot more hostile. He had so often warned clients about this swift progression, and the awful consequences of ignoring any form of mail from the police, that he knew exactly what would happen next. Frantically he undid the damage, found out what was required of him, and won a breathing space.

It was spring again. Bibi had been away for a year. He knew the date of her passage out from Speranza: he knew that for many months now she had been gone from his world, so far from him that no flesh and blood could cross the unimaginable distance. But the loss did not fade, although his life went on at an even pace, without tears or fury. He looked forward, as the hope that guided him, to the distant era when he would allow himself to start counting the days until her return—

He took the horrible dilemma that faced him to Syr Darya Prospect, where he still did his morning drill, for old times' sake. He no longer saw Nightingale or Konoe; they'd vanished out of his life. But he'd made new friends, notably the pretty young woman who'd accosted him in Lady Nef's Town House, the morning when he'd last seen Bibi. Ogul was about the only person in the world he could trust with this, and the only person who might tell him what it meant. She worked in Lady Nef's son's office: Amal had taken over the Family's affairs for the duration of the Diplomatic Mission. She must know something. They found a table by themselves, which was easier these days. The Prospect had gone out of fashion; the human gallahs were never seen here now, although the winged flocks still chattered in the citified trees.

'What am I to *do*?' demanded Mahmood, elbows on the table, hands twisted together. 'What's behind this, Ogul? Do you know? There's been nothing in the datasphere, or if there has, it's buried on inside pages and I daren't search, I d-daren't seem concerned—'

Ogul had stopped insisting on the Merdov family name. She no longer needed to distinguish herself from a brood of nameless foundlings. She studied the helpless young man, thinking carefully. She was frightened too, but she mustn't let panic cloud her judgement. Her future was at stake.

'Either you affirm the deposition, or you get interrogated?'

'*Yes*,' gasped Mahmood. 'And the deposition says, well, basically it says I believe that it was Lady Nef who procured the clandestine courier delivery, last year, you know. It isn't true. I know she didn't.'

'You *know* that? For a fact?'

'Oh, she wouldn't.' Mahmood could only think of his own trouble. 'If I don't affirm, I get interrogated again. But I've been interrogated, last year. It would be the same questions, wouldn't it, so maybe that would be all right—'

Or maybe not. He could think of things that he might reveal, under involuntary interrogation, which would have been good for Bibi and her Lady *then*: not so good now. Bibi in the crypt, shouting *Long Live the Republic*, as she flew at those crazy conspirators, without a thought for herself—

'I can refuse to be interrogated, they have no *probable cause*, but then I'd go to prison for contempt.' He looked up, a strange light in his eyes. 'You know, Ogul, I've thought about it. Temporary suicide. To go to sleep and dream of I don't care what, and wake up when Bibi is on her way home. Say I get three years. That wouldn't be so bad.'

Shivers went down Ogul's spine. He was staring right through her, with an unearthly smile. The truth was that she knew very little.

Amal's takeover of the Yu household had not been to her advantage: he had his favourites, naturally. But the Master was showing no sign of anxiety for his parents, not so far as Ogul was aware.

When she'd walked up to Mahmood Al-Farzi that day, she'd made up her mind to steal him from Bibi – and thus claw back just a little, just a *scrap* of undeserved good luck from that high-born girl, that conqueror of the world. She was still determined to win him, and she knew she would succeed, in the end. But he wouldn't be much of a catch with a prison record. And nobody should *ever* volunteer for an interrogation—

'What is going on,' she said firmly, 'is that you are going to stay out of this. If you affirm the deposition, nothing happens to you?'

'Nothing, that's the end of it. But—'

'Then affirm. How can your word hurt someone like Lady Nef? There are wheels within wheels, up among the high-grades, and we don't know how they turn. We should just do as we're told.'

'I'm so scared. It was such a shock, after so long.'

'Think about it. The first interrogation was friendly. You know very well it had all been arranged, strings had been pulled. This time it'll be hostile, and *you don't know what you might tell them.* You'll have no control.'

Mahmood's wild smile faded. Ogul's arguments made him feel the way he'd felt the morning after that fateful night: as if he'd blundered into a waking nightmare, as if he was caught in a terrifying, invisible, clinging web.

'You know I'm right.' Boldly, in this public place, she took his hand and squeezed it. 'You have to trust me, Mahmood.'

XXIII

Their transfer to the urban centre was well overdue. The Myot society friends Lady Nef and the General had cultivated, during the months of receptions, visits, public engagements, had moved to their city homes. They were not returning calls. 'Seasonal signal difficulties' plagued all communications, according to the Royal Office. A half-month after the departure of the *Rajath* they were finally given notice to pack up. The next day a fleet of hovers arrived, in the thick morning mist: without the Royal livery, but with a troop of soldiers and Bloodmen in plain, armoured uniform. The soldiers helped the Manor's domestics to stow the Mission's baggage.

'Are we travelling like this all the way to the city?' enquired Francois. 'Is that practical? And our own troops? What about them?'

'Everything will be explained,' was the only reply.

Hovers resembled giant serpent carapaces, hollowed out and set on tech-concealing skirts of supple chitin-derivative. They were like closed cars, or the landships of a bygone age on Earth: sometimes luxurious, always disorienting, because from the passenger compartments you couldn't see out, and there was little sense of motion. After about an hour (standard time), there was a halt. The Mission staff disembarked, a hop up, a step down, into a large gloomy space, divided into bays by pillars of dark Sigurtian concrete, with distant walls that looked like natural, reddish rock. An ugly place: utilitarian, but they couldn't tell its purpose. There was a sound of groaning, clanking machinery, close by. A strange Bloodman (woman, because of the half-mask, but the term *Bloodman* was unisex), in court dress, approached. She bowed to the General and Lady Nef, arms half-spread in respectful welcome.

'Good morning,' said the General. 'And who addresses me?'

Batwoman clicked and fluted, adding in passable English, 'Call me N'tt'rr'z, Lord General Yu. I shall have the honour to be your factotum for the duration of your winter sojourn. Your train for the ascent will be ready soon.'

'For the ascent?' repeated Yu. 'What—? To a flyerport?'

'Forgive me, General, but of course the skies are closed. Your lordship and your lordship's people are to join the court in Black Wing Castle. His Majesty, in your lordship's honour, has decided to make a retreat this winter, in the old style. We shall not be going to town.'

The General realised that his new factotum was *not* speaking English. He, or she, was using a translation aid, and the brain that moved the mouth had little idea what the words meant. He felt an unpleasant shock, and looked around for Nikty. But the Neuendan attaché was nowhere to be seen.

'Well, that's interesting news. Where's my interpreter, eh? Where's Nikty?' The stranger looked blank. 'You know, er, *N'k't'yl'*?'

'Ah. The Neuendan ... has of course been recalled, unexpectedly.'

'Hm. And my troops? My soldiers? Why aren't they with us?'

She bowed again, gracefully: the half-spread arms like broken wings, the folds of her court-sleeves displaying rich gleams of colour. Evidently the little ceremony gave her time to think what she should say—

'Your armed followers remain at Underwall, my lord. The Manor is winter-ready and well supplied. The servants will care for them.'

'I see. And this strange place, where we are now?'

'The summer approaches to the castle are unsafe today, my Lord General. This is the inner vertical train access, used mainly for freight. We regret that we cannot accommodate you more richly, but there is a rough and ready waiting room, if you would allow us to escort you—'

'No, we'll stay here with the bags. Thank you for your attendance, Bloodman N'tt'rr'z. You may leave us, until our train is ready.'

The Bloodman hesitated, but accepted her dismissal: bowed again, and retreated. *Never let anyone stick you in a waiting room*, thought the General. *We may not be bugged out here, if they didn't mean us to stand around. And never let them march you out to the woods with a gun at your head and a spade in your hand ...* Which was effectively what he felt was happening. So this was the trap he'd been asked to walk into! Speranza agents: he knew their reputation. Hardened suicide warriors, the lot of them, and they don't mind sharing the privilege, for the good of the damned Diaspora.

N'tt'rr'z had vanished into the gloom, with the troop that had escorted them from Underwall. General Yu turned – exchanging a shrug and a rueful smile with his wife – to face his household. So it goes. Fortune never favours those who need her most. When only your luck could save you, *that's* just when it deserts you—

'Well, there we are,' he said. 'We're spending the winter at court.'

Every single one of them, barring the two girls, was past forty, and since they were all Grade Three and below – under the longevity threshold – *forty* was middle-aged. If it came to it, which Heaven forbid, only Dunblane, Rashit and his own valet, the Rus, Yevgeny Vasitch, had been under fire. The Speranza agent? Yu considered, narrow-eyed. *Yes*, he's *seen killing action, that blue-haired cissy; of some kind*—

'I know I don't have to tell you to behave yourselves. You've done well so far, keep it up. Use your transaids, but keep your eyes open and use your instincts too. The spoken word can be a trap, eh, Francois?'

'One should choose one's words with care,' said the Aleutian, 'and be discreet in one's silence. The art of a courtier is the same everywhere.'

'Quite so.' The General cleared his throat. 'It's a crapshoot,' he announced, in a timely burst of candour. 'The diplomacy game always is. We're in a pickle, but we could still come good, and then the whole trip will be set down as a triumph, including this episode. I've been in worse foxholes than partying with a king all winter, and come up smelling like roses. So bear that in mind, act confident, and don't be downhearted.'

If they'd been soldiers he would have said *dismiss*. As there was nowhere for them to go he walked away himself, with Nef beside him. They stood by their bags, smiling, talking quietly; like passengers waiting for a porter on some perfectly normal journey.

Bibi and Honesty clutched the friendly pull-bars of their cabin-bags. They had no other luggage. Buonarotti transiters travel light, and there'd been no opportunity to collect souvenirs. They were so much younger than everyone else, and why had Nikty deserted them?

'What d'you think's going on?' muttered Honesty.

'What the General said. We could still come good. The Sigurtians don't want to offend Speranza, do they? We just have to keep our nerve.'

Blatantly, they had been moved in secret and their entry to the castle was being hidden. This made Bibi and Honesty (and the adults, presumably, though nobody was saying) think of a rescue attempt. Had the Neuendans been about to appear, and snatch them away from Underwall? Was *that* where Nikty had gone? To fetch help? They didn't know whether to hope for the relief force to arrive, or not. It wasn't going to go down too well with Speranza if General Yu ended up starting a war—

Francois stretched his legs, in the direction of the mechanical noise. Liam followed him. They passed the doorless teardrop entrance of what must be the 'rough and ready' waiting room, which indeed looked rough, bare and ugly. The Bloodmen were in there; the soldiers could not be seen. Heads turned, eyes gleamed. Nobody accosted them.

'It's a funicular railway,' said Liam, looking up into the mechanism.

'A funicular-railway *analogue*, produced by convergent evolution.'

'My apologies. We won't pick a fight about the Strong Diaspora Theory of Industrialised Transport. I admire your General.'

'You surprise me, Liam.' Relations between the decorative Speranza agent and the leader of the Mission had not been noticeably cordial.

'An army commander is no better than the professional soldiers he leads, Francois: the dregs of any society. He's a mass murderer by trade, a necessary evil. A *great* commander, as lucky and successful as General Yu has been in his time, inevitably ends up with the manners of a spoiled brat. But I admire his powers of leadership, his blunt warmth. You must feel the same.'

'I do. Very much the same.'

Beyond the railhead, wan strip lighting died in the depths of a black slot like a giant keyhole. No telling how far the cave went back or how far it went down. Liam peered into darkness. 'Do you think it's true that the planet is hollow, fissured all the way through? That there's a cavern in the centre, filled by storms of magnetic energy?'

'I believe it's very *big*, for a rocky planet in this orbit,' said Francois. 'And Sigurtian science is held to be impressive. But really, I have no idea.'

Liam studied the Aleutian: his cat-eye pupils dilated by the gloom. '*When* did Nikty disappear? I didn't notice. Was she with us when we left Underwall?'

'I couldn't tell you,' said Francois. 'I was distracted.'

XXIV

'How much time has passed, if we went back to Speranza now?'

Bibi leaned her head back against the padded wall of the embrasure. There was no window open to the night in this new room: which was grander than the one in Underwall, with a thick, silky serpent's hair carpet, but on the same pattern. The winter shutters were closed, and sealed on the inside by an opaque, rubbery membrane, unpleasant to the touch. There was a storm going on. There was nearly always a storm going on. Sometimes the thunder was so constant, for hours at a time, that it was like silence. Other times there was a fizzing, crackling sound they were told was made by 'lightnings'.

It was disturbing that they had never yet *seen* the bad weather. In the Great House there used to be screens everywhere, showing the world outside, the changing landscape, fiery electric storms, veils of rain, white blankets of snow. The Myots didn't do that.

'Ten months, two weeks, four days.'

Honesty sighed impatiently. 'I *don't* get it. What about on Earth?'

'Since we crossed to Sigurt's World? Or since we crossed to Speranza?'

'Oh, shut up. I really, *really* don't get it. If it was no time at all, I could understand. *How* can it work like that? If a crossing takes no time, then we get back when we left, don't we? Or we have no idea, and it could be hundreds of years, forward or back. That's *got* to be how it works.'

'Don't think of it as "time", the way it passes in normal space. Think of it as us being inside a special kind of moment. In terms of the simultaneity we're still in the moment when we left Speranza, or, no, when we left the Elevator Station: but if we go back to Speranza, or the Elevator, or anywhere else, we take our own "elapsed time", everything that's happened in this moment, with us. D'you see?'

'Sometimes I really don't like you.'

'Why don't you ask Francois? I'm telling you what *he* says, as far as I can remember. I'm not claiming I understand it.'

Honesty rolled her eyes. 'I'm just making idle conversation.'

In Black Wing Castle the time was late at night. They'd endured the fascinating ordeal of a dinner in the Great Hall, at which the king had been present (she wasn't always), so everything had been twice as long, twice as ceremonious. The party had broken up right after the meal, because the current storm was the kind called '*irritating*' by the transaid. It affected people's tempers, and social congress was ill-advised.

They'd been glad to escape to their room, but neither of them could sleep. They were half-watching a show from their Speranza collection, with the density turned down, the images hovering above the concave screen of their entertainment centre (known as the tzamer-kin, the nearest they could come to pronouncing the Neuendan term). The transit bugs were so familiar by now they were like old friends. They waited for the odd bits of twisted dialogue, the back-to-front music, like children who know all the stories by heart and like them better that way—

'I keep wondering what life's like in a *proper* Sigurtian palace,' grumbled Honesty. 'It can't be as primitive as this.'

'The court doesn't usually winter here, that's the problem.'

The windows were sealed, but there was always a draught. The lamps, which hung in inverted bowls from the high ceiling of their chamber, made flickering shadows as the chains swayed. The leathery bedcurtains shifted and whispered as if ghosts had taken roost inside. The room was persistently cold too, even when the brazier-chimney, in the central hollow in the floor, glowed red, so hot that the seats set around it were unbearable.

It was some consolation that the Myot royals, and their hordes of entourage (the lesser royalty, the Bloodmen, the lower nobility, the upper-poor-relations: degrees of status were very complex), were having to endure the same discomforts. And though things had looked bad at the start, nothing worse had happened. No news from the Port or from Speranza, because there couldn't be. No communication from Neuendan, either. But they were being treated as honoured guests; and they'd known winter would be a time when nothing got done. Maybe the Mission would come good, as General Yu had said.

The worst thing Bibi and Honesty had to suffer was General Yu's decision to treat them like 'young ladies'. It was relentless, like living in a costume drama. At night, if they wanted to reach their bathroom across the vestibule, they'd fall over Borgush, or Rashit, or even Francois, perched out there on a comfortless Sigurtian 'easychair': guarding their virtue. Thankfully, they were still allowed to do weapons drill in the winter gardens, one of the high spots of their day: but the vigilance was cramping Honesty's style.

'That so-called lightning makes very weird noises,' muttered Honesty. 'It sounds like something with claws, climbing the walls.'

Bibi watched the coloured shadows of the dancers, and wondered if she was hearing present thunder through the music, or the echo in her brain of thunder she'd heard last night. If you listened too hard you could hear voices you thought you knew, in the white noise—

It could sound like someone calling your name.

'Bibi! Honesty! Let me in!'

They stared at each other, and jumped down from the embrasure.

'That's *not* lightning, Magnet.'

'Is it outside?' breathed Honesty. 'Or is it *in here*? Is it a ghost? We should call whoever's on guard, mistress.'

'No!' Bibi listened again. 'Don't you recognise her? That sounds like, like—' Suddenly she realised where the eerie whisper in her ear was coming from. 'Oh, I get it! Take out your earbead! Clip, thing, I mean—' Sigurt's World didn't do earbeads. The tzamer-kin had come with wifi clips, coated in a black, velvety finish like Sigurtian head hair; they had to hook over ears that were the wrong shape and size. They pulled these off, the ballet music died and the voice that had been coming through the music was abruptly cut off too. 'Someone's short-range hacking our tzamer-kin.'

'You think it's Nikty?' demanded Honesty, eyes wide. 'It could be another bat-woman. How would you *know*?'

'You said the name, not me. I'm guessing someone's outside that window, anyway.' They held the clips to their ears and listened again.

'Bibi, Honesty, it's me, Nikty. Open the window! Let me in!'

'Can we open the window, mistress?'

'I think so.'

'What if it's not her? What if it's a trick?'

They knew they were supposed to be in danger of rape. Nothing had been said, better not to spell out an idea like that about their hosts, but it was obvious. So this could be trouble, an immemorial kind of trouble, a cunning ploy to get inside their bedroom, and insult the

Mission irreparably. But if they called for help and Myots came, and it *was* Nikty out there—

'Then we'll deal with it,' said Bibi. 'We're not helpless.'

'Right.' Honesty fetched their weapons and checked – as she had been taught to check, always – that they were ready. Bibi stuffed hers into the waistband of her trousers and clapped her hands, the gesture that dissolved the seal: getting the right percussive snap on about the third try.

She used the manual override on the shutters, hoping this wouldn't set off an alarm throughout the castle, and wrestled with the heavy bolts.

The right-hand side flew open. Something that had been clinging to the outer sill dived into the embrasure, like a rush of clear liquid, like gleaming water over a weir. Borrowing shape and colour, it rolled and tumbled to the floor. Bibi flung the upper half of her body out into the black, electric gape of the wind and hauled the shutter back into place. She slammed the bolts.

The liquid creature had become visible. The Neuendan attaché crouched on her heels, looking into the muzzle of a pulse firearm, steadily trained on her. She was wearing a dull grey jumper suit that covered her hands, and grey half-boots. It struck Bibi as strange that her half-masked face, and her velvet head, were dry.

'Please don't shoot me, Honesty.'

Honesty lowered her weapon. Nikty looked carefully at them both, as if checking they were still the friends she'd known: let out her breath in a *huff* of relief, and dropped her face on her knees, forearms crossed and pressed to her brow. They got down by her on the carpet.

'You'd better get out of that wall-climbing gear,' advised Honesty, hoarsely. 'It looks like spy stuff, and spies are probably shot.'

'You must fetch Francois, bring him here. Quickly!'

Rashit, Lady Nef's confidential maid, was on duty in the vestibule: a raw-boned Khasakh, her grey-streaked dark hair pulled sternly back, dozing over a soft-lit reading tablet. 'Rashit? Could you go and get Francois? We're dying of boredom, and he said he'd come and tell us a story.'

'Are you serious, child? It's late.'

'Please, *please*. He said he'd come if we needed him.'

Rashit looked consternated. Francois must be with Lady Nef: she hated to interrupt them. Bibi touched the pulse-gun in her waistband.

'Don't worry, I'll stay here.' The maid, devout Traditionalist, struggled with the idea: imperilled virgin on guard outside her own bedroom. But she went.

Rashit returned, with the Aleutian. She resumed her post; Honesty opened the bedchamber door. Nothing had stirred, no rush of bat-people along the dark corridors. Nikty was by the brazier chimney, shivering and sipping from a steaming beaker. The smell of blood tea was in the room: Honesty had heated the flask from the bedtime tray that was always left for them. When she saw Francois, Nikty grinned with all her sharp teeth, and raised a clenched fist.

'Ah, my friend,' he cried, jumping into the well beside her. 'I'm in your debt. Well done, thank you!'

'Not so well done,' said the Neuendan. 'I couldn't get what you wanted. But I brought you this.' She set down her beaker, reached into the pocket under her arm and passed him something small enough to be hidden in her palm. 'That's a chart, route finder for our solar system, near space and the asteroids. You could hole up in the Port, there's still air, and supplies.'

Francois's nasal tightened sharply. '*Still—?*'

'The Buonarotti Port is standing empty,' said the Neuendan. 'You didn't know?'

'How would we? No ... We didn't know.'

'How can the Port be *standing empty?*' cried Honesty. 'What are you talking about, Nikty? Has my transaid gone screwy? How can the *Rajath* dock there without a ground crew?'

'Unexpectedly recalled,' murmured Francois, and his shoulders lifted in a wry smile, the smile of someone who accepts an inevitable twist of fate. He tucked the little case Nikty had given him away, inside his jacket. 'What makes you think I could have a use for maps of outer space, Nikty?'

The Neuendan gave him a look that said, as Honesty would have put it, *cut the crap.* 'The wafer's configured for Speranza hardware, and so far your pod is untouched. The Myots would rather not damage your property. Besides, they believe you have no fuel.'

'Hm.'

'Very well, admit nothing. But whatever you do, that flyer must not be left where it is.' Nikty made the gesture that meant, *This conversation is at an end.* She looked at the two young women, showing her teeth again, warmly. 'Honesty would have killed me,' she said. 'I saw it in her. And Bibi is the same metal. You have two soldiers there, Francois.'

'I know,' said the Aleutian, and recovered his sense of urgency. 'Nikty, we are eternally grateful, but now you'd better go. Can you get out of Black Wing the way you came in?'

'She was outside our window!' Honesty couldn't understand why Francois wasn't asking more questions, it must be Aleutian Silence disease— 'She broke into impregnable Black Wing, she climbed our tower and hacked our ballet music to call to us. Did you set this up, Francois? Do you know all about it? Is *this* why Nikty vanished?'

'There's no hurry.' The Neuendan picked up her tea and sipped it, visibly relaxing. 'Ah, that's good, I feel stronger. It's very draining, being invisible. I didn't break into the Castle, Honesty. Hongfu knows I am here. I have returned to my charges. Her Majesty accepts my decision, but she had housed me apart from you, and I did not agree with that.'

Bibi noticed that the king had been given a feminine pronoun: but Sigurtians believed masculine pronouns denoted higher status in English. Nikty, the linguist, was usually meticulous about those little touches—

The seal on the bedroom door hissed as it opened. A troop of Royal Myot guards came into the room, taking up a lot of space in their wide, armoured uniform. They were followed by Lady Nef, the General and Liam; several Bloodmen including N'tt'rr'z and, astonishingly, the king herself, in a heavy, gold-faced winter robe, with elaborately folded sleeves.

She glanced with approval at the two maiden warriors, the Aleutian's ward and her blood-offerer, and gave them a slight, tight smile.

Nikty set down her beaker, rose from the brazier well and made a court bow. She turned and raised her hand, palm outwards, to the young women. 'Excuse me.' When she spoke again it was in flutes and clicks, and their transaids had gone dead. Francois went to stand with the leaders of the Mission and the Speranza agent, acting as interpreter. (N'tt'rr'z looked miffed at this.) But the discussion that followed was between the Neuendan and the Myots. The Blues and their Aleutian friend were not involved.

It was as if they'd stumbled onto the stage, in one of those little b-loc theatres off Nelson Mandela concourse, on far-away Speranza – where a scene from a ritual drama was being played out: a performance they'd thought was their own, but they were wrong. This had nothing to do with them. They were props, furniture, used because they came to hand—

XXV

General Yu's soldiers had been told, on the morning the hovers came, that the Mission was going to Black Wing: they'd heard nothing since. Left alone, they'd quickly fallen prey to boredom and uncertainty. They saw nobody, they had no access to local data. The Myot servants had a system that meant they never had to have contact with the aliens. Meals were laid out, in the canteen adjoining the barracks hall: but the door wasn't unlocked until the staff had gone back to the house by the basement passage; and nobody cleared away until the soldiers had gone. Cleaning in the barracks hall and the toilet block was done by the soldiers themselves.

After fifty-plus days of this isolation (the Myot calendar marked no months or half-months in winter) the captain, a world-weary veteran called Ezeke Shammat, was spending his time still as death on his mat, locked in fantasy. The senior lieutenant wasn't far behind. Sometimes it looked as if everyone would be comatose, in prison without the life support, before the spring came: but the two sergeants, Aswad and Roy, didn't give up. Hernan Roy had the discipline. He was a mean bastard, but you hated him while you appreciated his efforts. Aswad had the belief. 'It'll go one way or the other at the castle,' said the Sarge. 'Nobody's going to send us reports. But whatever way it goes, the *Rajath* will be back to take us off. All is not lost.'

Col Ben Phu and Drez stayed active. They'd made a solemn pact, they'd keep each other off the junk. They did their chores, helped to keep the hopeless cases clean, worked like hell at their drill, and perfected their 'Evening Dance' (Dance was supposed to be optional, but the only remaining officer, a kid of a junior lieutenant who shouldn't be here at all, had changed that regulation). The only relief they allowed themselves was the stinking pollen beer. At least if you drank enough of it, you'd sleep for a few hours.

The stuff worked better on Drez. It gave Col nightmares. One night, there was Francois sitting at the end of her mat, with a face like thunder. In panic, she sat up babbling. 'I didn't get a chance to go to him, and then the skies were closed, an' we can't leave quarters, it's winter—'

Another funxing anxiety dream. She might as well give up and take the junk, if she was going to screw herself over like this every night.

'Keep your voice down,' said the noseless. She saw his nasal flare with distaste as he surveyed the deathly rows, in the gloom of the long shed's night lights: he knew what was going on. 'Come with me.'

'Is there a secret passage, sir? We can't go outside. It's winter.'

'Nonsense. How do you think I got here? I didn't *teleport*.'

She followed him, obedient and fascinated.

Outdoors the sky was the colour of a bad bruise: a hollow, purplish dome through which crazed patterns of pink lightning spat and rippled. The trees in the Manor grounds were bare; some looked charred. The air was thick and sultry as a thunderstorm, cold enough for snow, and full of strange noises: a yapping and shrieking, like mad dogs in a sack, a groaning like rocks being torn apart.

'Funx,' breathed Col. 'I know they call it winter, but it's like nothing on Earth. What causes it, sir?'

'Apparently it's analogous to a meteor shower,' said the Aleutian calmly. 'The residue of a huge electrical entity that once died in their system: which the planet has to pass through every year. It's perfectly harmless.'

Col was not afraid, with the noseless beside her, but she looked at the charred trees and thought *harmless* wouldn't be the word she'd use.

'But the Myots are terrified, sir. What are they scared of?'

'I have no idea.' Francois slipped his Underwall master key – literally, *safe-conduct* – in its thin gold frame, into the manual override at the hangar doors. 'Your own planet is very rainy, naturally enough, with all that ocean. Before the Enclosures, Blues had a bizarre horror of going out in it and getting wet. They believed it made them ill. And yet you people *wash* in water all the time. We never worked it out.'

Col had been terrified that he would make her open the dome and take the pod up into that tumult, for another spin around the Manor grounds. What happened instead was a second training session, in which she learned just what kind of fabulous toy the *Spirit* was – and how a mere Blue mortal could interface with him, in his transit-capable mode. She wasn't totally surprised, but she had serious fears, when the session was over. Not afraid of the *Spirit*, afraid of why she was being told all this.

'What's happening, sir? Permission to ask, I mean.'

'Nothing to worry about,' said the Aleutian. 'Not yet. Things are going fairly well, but the *Spirit* must be moved. You have the route finder I've just given him, you can take him to the Port. Don't stay there, because it's the first place any hostiles would look. Sigurtian space is a wild frontier, they say. Outlaws thrive, I suggest you join them.'

'Sir, I've only done Flying Bombs.'

'Don't worry, Col. The *Spirit* will look after you, and you'll learn. Don't go alone. Take a couple of friends you can trust. You'll need company.'

'How will I know when to come back in, sir?'

'Keep checking the Port frequency until you hear from me. It might be a while. You may have to wait around until spring.'

Col took off her helmet and unhooked. The cockpit looked strange, not just masked but *strange*, now that she knew the whole truth. And the fear had settled in her belly. 'Are you being kept locked up, sir?'

'Evidently not, Col, for here I am. No, no, nothing so drastic. We are honoured guests. I am confined to my room by the winter flu, brought on by my refusal to sup on the strengthening blood tea. My exit was unobserved; I shall return equally discreetly. I hope that assuages your concern.'

'Sorry, sir.'

'If you *haven't* heard from me by the spring,' added Francois, softly, 'you must make up your own mind what to do. But in that case, you'd be wise not to return to Speranza.'

'All right, sir. Understood.'

They climbed down. Francois's boy-racer stood as before, softly shining; still anchored by Flyerport Authority tape. The yapping and howling of the evil night was suddenly audible again. Col noticed that the noseless was wearing the baggy brown overalls that were his native kit; and that seemed like a weird touch. She still didn't know how he'd got here. It was fifteen, twenty kilometres from Underwall to the Castle, and some of that was straight up the cliffs. Did he have a vehicle hidden? Perhaps she was dreaming, after all.

'What'll I tell the officers, sir?'

'Very little, would be my advice,' said Francois, and she saw his formidable eyeteeth gleam. 'I'll see you back to your barracks.'

He saw Col Ben Phu safely indoors, dropped into running gait and cleared the outer wall of the Manor in a wolfish, scrabbling leap. Terrible energies fought in the upper air; the darkness was drenched, incessantly, in vivid washes of sheet lightning. Balls of fire the size of a numinal biped's head hissed and danced along the ground. Francois trotted, unperturbed, at a pace he could keep up for hours (although he'd pay for it). Electric storms didn't bother him at all. Sigurt's World in winter reminded him of Home, in fact. The wildernesses of Home, where the wild bluesuns roamed, the natural fusion reactors that could be trapped and tamed, or harnessed to power the pirate ship of a nation of obligate adventurers—

XXVI

The first of the traditional periods of full retreat approached, a landmark in the long winter. There were three of these retreats, varying in length according to the demands of the liturgical calendar. This year the first would be long: twenty-one days during which everyone at court would be confined to their rooms, except the most necessary staff. Fasting was usual: weaklings were catered for; sinking into a coma optional.

On the night before the 'clasping days' began, the king held a splendid banquet. Special dishes were on the menu; traditional dancing and other interesting ceremonies would follow the meal. The honour table, set above the hall on a canopied dais (rather too high for comfort), looked down on a colourful crowd. Bloodmen of the highest nobility, napkins of glossy grub-silk on their arms, vied to serve their Majesties. Personal blood-offerers – robust peasants with ruddy cheeks and veins bulging on their bare arms – perched on stools behind the great, looking placid and bored. The leaders of the Speranza Mission kept their places of honour, somewhat to their own surprise, despite the contretemps over Nikty's return. So had Nikty herself, which was perhaps even more surprising. The Neuendan said the situation was very difficult, but there was a traditional winter truce, which both governments had agreed to respect. In General Yu's experience any so-called 'tradition', supposed to bind determined combatants to a ceasefire, was invoked to be flouted. But this wasn't Earth, so who could tell—

'I think you may expect good news,' he remarked, expansively, to the king: and broke off to examine a platter of between-course appetizers some duke or other was proffering. 'Thank you ... mm, that all looks *delicious*. A couple of those black, liquorice spring roll things, eh? I like those. A blood-sausage sorbet, and a few of the fried pollen turnovers ... If they hadn't recalled the Port crew I'd have been worried. But this looks hopeful, sir. They've taken your views on board and their response

is a complete rethink. Come the spring you may well be on your way
to that surface facility—'

N'tt'rr'z murmured, clicking and fluting in an undertone. Transaids
were freely used on the honour table, but protocol forbade His Majesty
to do without an interpreter. The king listened with a contained smile,
eyes inscrutable in the shadow of her velvet mask.

'Once, the retreats were practised everywhere,' the Myot First Minister
explained to the Speranza agent, his blue-haired neighbour. 'In every
culture you'd find the same winter ritual: the retreat, the clasping days, the
fasting. Nowadays, of course, the modern people say it's inconvenient. In
Neuendan they live so much in an urban world, out of touch with
nature, they can hardly tell winter from summer. Even here in Myot,
it's changing.'

'That's a shame.'

'Yes, it's shameful, I'm surprised you agree. Some would say impious,
and I'm one of them. But you are a *space-person*, Liam.'

'I was brought up in a very traditional way.'

'You must tell me about your traditions. I would be very interested.
When one goes into full retreat, one should have a *full mind*.'

Lady Nef sat on the prince's left hand, Francois beside her. The General
was on the king's right. From her place between Nikty and Francois,
Bibi could hear General Yu spinning his line (he misjudged the volume
when he was using transaid). You had to admire his ability to keep up
a front ... although he must know that the Myots couldn't care less
about the Port right now. They'd make their own terms with Speranza,
once they'd dealt with Neuendan. But someone should tell him to stop
calling Hongfu 'sir'. The Myots weren't interested in Blue ideas of status
any more. They'd taken control, and the 'he' mistake made General Yu
sound like a dumb alien—

The appetisers were cleared, the leftovers passed to the blood-offerers,
who would make a good meal this way. Bibi's noble waiter set a large
plate of lumpy carapace porridge in front of her. The main courses at
these feasts tended to be dire: a sure sign that, until recently, live human
blood had been the business part of the meal.

Bibi wouldn't mind betting it was very recently indeed.

'I wish we weren't up here,' she muttered. Whenever she looked
down at the hall, the whole crowd seemed to be staring. (Or perhaps

the crowd was staring at Nikty, the enemy in their midst.) 'Why can't we be with the others? It doesn't make sense. If I was a *real* "young lady" I wouldn't be allowed out of my rooms.' Honesty, whom the Myots regarded as Bibi's 'blood-offerer', had a stool behind her: which put the Magnet and the Savage in an excellent position for muttering in English, hopefully under the Myot radar.

'Ah, but we're so beautiful, mistress. We're an ornament to the Mission. *Our* high-grades are more cunning, aren't they? They keep the cred and the power, and don't have to make a spectacle of themselves—'

'I don't know. Think of poor Caspian and the society pages.'

'Tuh, *poor Caspian*. It's not like having to let the low-grades *stare* at you, in person, right in your face, night and day.'

'I'm going to make you swop places.'

'Then I'd get first pick of the food. Can't wait for my share of *that* heap of turd. Eat up, noble young lady, yum yum. The fasting food for weaklings is probably much worse.'

Eat up, keep smiling. The Myots couldn't possibly want to fight with Speranza, so the Mission would not be harmed. All they had to do was hold on, and they were about to get a break. The 'full retreat', what a relief, was just a few hours away—

The hall was cleared, the diners moved to the sides in a long hubbub. The Mission staff could be seen up front, sticking together. The honour table was removed; the blood-offerers went to join the crowd. The leaders of the feast settled on so-called 'easychairs', like an after-dinner party on the society pages: except there was no need for them to adopt poses meant to defeat cunning, embarrassing camera angles.

The entertainment rolled out as announced: a costumed mouth-music ensemble, followed by a troupe of acrobats, or maybe clowns; followed by a solemn dance-drama, the narrative recited in metre by a world-famous Myot artist ... Bibi suppressed a yawn. It all had the slightly fake feel of tradition preserved, of the past recreated. *That's what Mahmood used to say about Traditionalists*, she thought. *I wonder if the Neuendans are, like, Sigurt's World 'Reformers'? Oh dear, and we thought they were the good guys.* But Honesty had gone down to join the staffers, so she kept her insight to herself.

Prince S'na'ulat'tz', untroubled by the drop that made the Blues nervous, strolled around with his favourite Bloodmen and alighted in a chair beside Francois. 'Shall I explain the drama to you? It's highly mystical, very religious, it's about our two moons—'

'Thank you, no,' said the Aleutian, pleasantly. 'We have religion at Home. Should I ever become interested, which I doubt, I believe I'll start with that brand.'

S'na'ulat'tz' let rip a burst of piercing clicks, visibly startling the ancient poet. He leaned close, his diamond-rimmed eyes gleaming with a lust Francois still didn't understand. Was this an amorous advance? Maybe he should be prepared for a discreet royal tap on the door of his room, under cover of the retreat.

'Your *innamorta* is a powerful woman among the Blues, isn't she? More powerful than her husband the General, by far.'

'Powerful? No, no ... S'na'ulat'tz', something has been lost in translation. For the last several decades my *innamorta*, as you say, has devoted herself chiefly to running a home for foundling children—'

The poet wailed with renewed vigour, words lost in a long, sad cry: a question that hoped for no answer, no consolation. The dancer, subtly enhanced or naturally endowed, set her neck-frill and the folds under her arms shivering in desolate ecstasy, and collapsed on the floor – to a long outburst of enthusiastic clicking and hand-flapping.

'Of course, this I know. As it were, a reservoir of blood-offerers, the best of them to be recruited as the most loyal Bloodmen. Superb!' The prince set his claw on Francois's sleeve. 'I am going to honour you now,' he said. 'Remember, it's a great honour, and sincerely meant.'

The king hopped down from her easychair throne. A Bloodman set an ornate sort of microphone before her (the hall had faultless sound technology: this must be a special, traditional microphone). Another noble held up an open tablet. *The speeches*, thought Bibi. There were always speeches.

'My lords, ladies and gentlemen. It is with great pleasure that I come to make this announcement, on the doorsill of one of our most sacred holy times. My son, the Crown Prince, has chosen, in the adopted daughter of the great Lady Nef, and ward of our noble, wise and subtle friend, Francois the Aleutian, an honourable bride. Although she comes to us from far away, we have learned to admire and respect her distinguished blood, her skill in combat, her noble bearing, her personal qualities—'

But that's me, thought Bibi. *The king is talking about me.*

The transaid English, bland and bizarre, floated away from her. She could no longer follow the words. She heard Nikty, who was sitting beside her, suppress a gasp of astonishment; or a wail of despair. And here was Lady Nef, on her feet, responding, what an honour, so unexpected—

Be confident, pretend nothing's wrong. The crowd was staring, clicking and fluting, seemingly thrilled by the news that their prince was getting engaged to an alien office assistant. Bibi realised that her speeches-face, a practised expression of attentive interest, had become a frozen mask. But that was probably all right. It was probably the way a young lady ought to look, listening to a conversation like this, not expected to say a word.

XXVII

Sen Mughal, General Yu's First Assistant, took charge of the non-Exec officers and the staff; Zidane went with him. The Exec gathered in Lady Nef and the General's reception room. They didn't know how long they'd be left alone. Lightning hissed and crackled, but there was no thunder tonight, except for the echoes rolling around in Bibi's head. She sat on a dimpled, serpent-lacquer sofa, Honesty on one side, Lady Nef on the other, while her superiors told her that they'd known about the proposal. That the approaches had begun immediately after their remove to Black Wing, or even before.

'Why didn't anyone tell me?'

'We thought we should spare you,' explained Lady Nef. 'We were sure it was a misunderstanding, we did everything we could to put them off.'

'Did you tell him I'm already engaged? I'm engaged to Mahmood.'

'Yes we did, Bibi.' Nef spoke gently, as to a child. 'I'm afraid the prince and his mother believe their proposal take precedence.'

Hari Colmar was slumped on the hot seats around the brazier chimney, head in his hands. 'This is an Admin disaster,' he groaned. 'I take the blame. I should have drawn your attention, ma'am, before we left Speranza. We should have deleted the information, but she's only a Grade Five! It never crossed my mind. They're aliens! We're aliens!'

'But can it be *true*?' cried Ariane, the Housekeeper, Hari's boss and partner. 'How *can* it be true? Who ever heard of such a thing?'

There had never yet been a confirmed case of natural live birth, or even natural conception, between numinal biped species. Given the mental and physical problems of the few reliably attested, lab-built hybrids, the DP was moving towards a Hegemony-wide ban on the whole concept. But there was no doubt that the king had been talking about fertile, sexual union—

'Intromission is anatomically possible,' snapped Bouasone, the Mission's brusque Men's Doctor, 'between humans and Myots, from what we know. Sexual attraction? Why not? There are no rules! Fertility, unlikely. Live birth? Insane. Try keeping a woman with full babies alive for nine months, or however long it takes, even with total life support, which I doubt the Myots can provide. They're brutes, they're insane.'

'But they know that Bibi is "a perfect XX",' countered his colleague, Persis Afar. 'That's what they read in her file, and the royal interpretation makes her a kind of universal donor, fertile with *any* . . . numinal biped. The prince is a fanatical Strong Theory believer. If we could talk freely to their xenobiologists—'

'Oh, spare me your cultural relativism, Persis—'

Lady Nef intervened. 'That's enough, doctors, thank you.'

<I have been wilfully blind,> said Francois, bleak and furious. <The prince called Bibi *my ward*, and I think the bastard knows what that means. This is my fault. I have been wilfully blind—>

No one heard him except Bibi, because he had retreated into Aleutian Silence disease ... The adults were talking over her head, arguing stupidly, or making obscure Common Tongue confessions. Bibi didn't mind, it gave her time to think. The serpent-silk carpet at her feet had a pattern of purple vines and golden flowers. She counted the repeat, and counted it over again. Honesty squeezed her hand.

'My God,' muttered the Master-at-Arms. 'I knew we were for it. But I wasn't expecting this, nothing like this—'

General Yu paced up and down, stooping to peer into the window embrasures, as if sizing them up as sniper roosts. 'It's just another ploy,' he growled. 'Are we alone in here, Mohabbet?'

'Yes, sir,' said the Counter-Surveillance Officer. 'So far as I can tell.'

'Well then, let's consider our options. Not forgetting that a few kilometres away from here, we still have fifty armed men—'

'We don't.'

'What's that, Francois?'

The Aleutian stirred out of his angry stillness. 'There seemed no point in telling you. Shammat's been letting them use the dreamtime.'

'He's *what*—?'

'As you may recall, General, we'd had to forbid that evil recreation because the software was full of transit bugs, and a danger to their mental health. The night I visited the Manor, to ensure that *The Spirit of Eighty-Nine* was moved out of harm's way, practically every man and woman was under. Self knows what state they're in by now; the soldiers or Shammat and his officers.'

The Exec officers looked at each other in renewed dismay. They'd been counting on those soldiers, although they knew it made no sense. General Yu controlled, with a visible effort, the fury that smouldered in his eyes. He would sacrifice them ruthlessly at need, but he loved his ruffians. 'All under,' he muttered. 'Someone's going to pay for that.'

'There's nothing we can do, General,' said Liam, speaking for the first time. 'And, forgive me, in a sense their fate is irrelevant. Armed response was never going to be a solution to our problems; it is no solution now.'

The Speranza agent knew what he was up against: Blue Traditionals, assaulted in the most sensitive, irrational issue for their culture, the rape of a sequestered 'young lady'. Useless to point out that Bibi was nothing of the kind – or that their outrage was pure atavism, absurd as the Myot proposal. He sighed. He knew how to calm them down.

'Let's review another option. Nikty?'

The Neuendan attaché set her palms on the arms of her chair. 'Yes.'

'Nikty, I appreciate the extreme delicacy of your position, but tell me what you can ... The fact that you don't seem to have suffered any coercion, or interrogation, since you returned to us, suggests that civilised rules of conduct are still being observed between Neuendan and Myot?'

'Just about,' said the Neuendan, with a very human little grimace.

Liam nodded. 'Which is something. But our hosts are accustomed to hostage-taking, as a tactic of realpolitik. Would I be right in assuming that the Myot "negotiators" on the delegation to Speranza are suicide warriors, ready to lay down their lives rather than let their nation be held to ransom?'

Nikty stared at him. 'You're right. But *I am here.*'

'We appreciate what that means,' said Liam, his romantic body-mods looking different now, cold-blooded as a merman in a fairy tale. He addressed the Mission. 'My point is that we have no hold whatsoever over our friends the Myots. We can *hope* that Speranza will send a ship in the spring, but we have no idea why the Port crew was recalled, in that unprecedented way; and they know it. They know we're helpless—'

'You don't pull your punches, do you, Liam?' snarled the General. 'Now it's too late, you tell us what a misplanned *cock-up* this Mission was.'

Liam gave General Yu a potent, cat-eyed stare. He seemed about to say that actually he *was* pulling his punches, that he knew something worse—

It's an ugly carpet, decided Bibi. *I don't like it.* She'd been trying to think, as every Traditional girl in this situation thinks, *what had she done?* When had she raised her eyes to the prince, when had she smiled at him? She couldn't remember ever glancing his way, but there's always a reason. In the café in the Upper World, when Nikty came to their table with the blood-offerer, and Honesty drank; but Bibi didn't refuse. It must have been then—

'There's a simple solution,' she said. 'I'll get engaged to him. Why not?'

Everyone stared. Ariane cried, '*No! Impossible.*' General Yu came over and patted her hand, looking at her kindly.

'You're a good girl, Bibi. But no, no. This isn't about you, child. I've seen this kind of thing before. If we say yes there'll be something else, and then something else. Appeasement never works, unless you're buying time for a surprise attack—'

'But we *are* buying time,' said Bibi. 'Time is what we need to buy.'

Nikty was looking at Bibi with respect, and dawning hope. 'She's right, General ... The Myots are testing my government, using their treatment of your Mission as provocation. That much is true. But the prince wants this marriage. He is convinced that the, the—' She had to use her transaid. 'That the Royal Household's "expert breeders" can make the union fertile. It's a genuine proposal, and the prince's obsessions are important, as important as policy here. We *would* have a hold on him, and through him on Myot.'

'You're sure of this?' demanded Liam.

'But there's one thing.' Nikty hopped to the floor and crossed the room to crouch at Bibi's feet. 'Bibi, I swear to you, I *didn't* see this coming. What you offer to do is rational, and may save all our lives, and many more. But you may not understand, with us the betrothal is a bedding. This is how lovers used to get together: in the winter, sharing a retreat. It's supposed to lead to marriage but there's nothing binding until, unless a child is conceived. So you see, if you "get engaged" you will have to, to "sleep with" him.'

Bibi looked at the ugly flowers, and remembered that moment in the crypt of the Church of Self, when she had touched the tomb that was a Buonarotti couch and said to herself, *I have no future.* It had been true then, and it was true now. She'd only managed to escape for a while from the disaster that had fallen on her, and on everyone here—

'Yes, all right. I see that. But when it's spring and the *Rajath* comes back, you'll take me home to Speranza, won't you? And I won't have to *marry* him, because I won't conceive, will I?'

Nobody spoke, but the guilty relief was palpable.

'Bibi,' said Lady Nef, at last, 'be careful: you are not under orders. Don't do violence to yourself for something that may achieve nothing. We'll try to put him off, but if you say yes, I think tonight is the night—'

'It's not so bad, mistress,' said Bibi, thinking aloud now. 'It's what would have happened at White Rock, where I was born. I'd have been married to a stranger, or to someone I didn't like, without any choice. And that would have been for life; this is for a few months.'

'Not even that,' said Nikty. 'They'll let you come back to us between the retreats. They have to, if they want the marriage to be legal.'

Liam drew a breath. 'Well. If we were to put this to the vote—'

'Which we will not!' snapped the General. 'This is *my* command!'

'*If* we were to put this to the vote,' repeated the Speranza agent, wearily, 'my vote would have to be for Bibi's solution.'

So it was settled. Bibi would become betrothed to the prince.

XXVIII

Bibi and Honesty waited, alone in their room, for the prince's sponsors to come and take his betrothed to him. Ghosts whispered in the bedcurtains, cold draughts snaked around them, winter outside the shuttered windows yelped and groaned.

'Bastards, bastards,' howled Honesty. 'How could they do this? They put a guard on our door, they treat you like a high-grade, making us look like tasty goods, and then they, they *hand you over*, like a side of meat—'

'It wasn't like that, you were there. I volunteered.'

'I'm coming with you, mistress. He may be a bat-eared alien doodah prince, but I never, ever met a feller that didn't fancy a threesome—'

Bibi wiped her eyes, and laughed. 'No, no, Magnet. You don't take my bullet. You don't have enough pull for that, I'm sorry.'

'You're crazy. *Why* did you volunteer?'

'Because I want to live, and I want you to live, and I want to see Mahmood again. I want us all to get home safe.'

'Fat chance of that,' said Honesty, true to her code. 'We're screwed to all hell. Don't do this, Bibi, don't do it, it's pointless.'

Then the chamber door opened, and a crowd of bat-people came in, dressed in their 'full retreat' robes, clicking and fluting and smiling happily with all their sharp teeth.

XXIX

She was given a drink of blood tea and put to bed, naked, by three women who were obviously blood-offerers. They looked like the peasant girl in the café, in the same brown felt tunics; robust bare arms and ruddy cheeks. They all had neck-frills, which was a lower-caste trait, not seen in polite society. One of them seemed as young as Bibi, one grown-up, and the third middle-aged, about as old as the king. They sat on the covers, crouched on their heels like Nikty, inside the glowing, leathery cave of the bedcurtains.

The one who seemed the senior touched her breast.

'*Vroucolocha*,' was what the transaid made of her name.

The second did the same. '*Goul*—'

The youngest said, 'I am *Broucoloka*. We will care for you.'

Vroucolocha took Bibi's hand and stroked it. 'There are things we must tell you, little one. First, if you have any barrier, or medicine, to take for contraception, don't use them. He will keep testing you, and he will know.'

'But if you have any kind of mental block, then use it,' said *Goul*.

'Don't get pregnant,' insisted the youngest, 'not now, not soon.'

'Put it off until you have your woman's strength,' said *Vroucolocha*. 'S'na'ulat'tz' earnestly wants your child. He believes you have the oldest, purest blood. But listen, the kings of Myot don't like to share the throne.'

'And we are not talking dance drama,' added *Broucoloka*. 'It was before *Vroucolocha* was born, and the public story is a cover-up, but everyone knows that Hongfu's own consort, a foreigner and a submissive type, didn't live very long once his son didn't need him any more.'

'I can't get pregnant,' protested Bibi, feeling nightmarish. She'd been brave and calm, but this was too much. The mouths making words that the brains didn't recognise, the bland received English. What were the women really saying? 'I'm *human*. Do you understand? A different species, from another planet. I don't know what he'll do to me, but he isn't even a man.'

They looked very grave, very sorry for her.

'Myot royals have world experts here,' said *Vroucolocha*, slowly. 'They have had months to study you, using devices that you never saw. They know how your people's bodies work. If they think it can be done, it can be done, Bibi. No matter what the Neuendan says.'

They were speaking to her simply and slowly, as if she were a child. It came over her, turning everything upside down, that these people were not backward, this society was not primitive, it was *decadent*. Then they took her transaid away, and she was lost.

An animal crouched on her bed, in the nightmare. A close black pelt ran down the back of its neck, covering its shoulders and upper forelimbs. Its belly was flat and muscular; the genitals looked human, but very small. It clicked, it fluted. It examined her body, handled her breasts, spread her thighs. It mounted, found her virgin, and used a razor claw to cut a way for itself. She didn't feel anything down there, except that the razor-cut hurt. S'na'ulat'tz' seemed content. When he'd done his business he wrapped himself in his robe, and slept. She lay still. The wild sounds of the winter night returned; almost homely now, almost comforting.

XXX

The General's assessment proved correct. As soon as the Myots had secured the 'young lady' they stepped up the provocation. The night that Bibi was taken, the Exec found that the other officers and staff had been moved, and could not be contacted. The lower floor of the Mission's accommodation was now out of bounds, and those Execs (Hari, Dunblane and Bouasone) who'd had rooms there would have to make do. N'tt'rr'z, the General's so-called factotum, claimed that these changes were temporary, for the convenience of the 'clasping days' servants.

Sometime during the next gloomy day (lighting bulbs were reduced to a minimum in a full retreat, so there was little difference between day and night) all their bedrooms were rifled. Bibi and Honesty's tzamerkin, on which the Mission had sometimes been able to pick up the sporadic *Winter News* broadcasts from Myotis City, disappeared. General Yu protested. N'tt'rr'z responded, in a newly frigid tone, that isolation from worldly affairs was a tradition of winter; and that the servants had a duty to remove contraband Neuendan items.

And so it went on.

By the time Bibi was allowed to return to her friends their rooms had been deftly ransacked on several occasions, although never in their presence. Their reduced accommodation comprised their lobby, reached by a short flight from one of the main stairways, and the five-star of corridors leading from it: one to the reception rooms and the Mission Leaders' apartments; three short dead-end corridors of officers' rooms, two dry bathrooms, the crooked hop-up-and-down passage to the 'winter garden' where they could exercise; and the vestibule outside Bibi and Honesty's chamber, with the little cloakroom across the way. They were not short of space, though Hari and Bouasone, the Master-at-Arms and Liam now had to double up: but both their means of access

188

to the rest of the castle were sealed and under constant guard.

The end of the 'clasping days' had brought no improvement. Just before Bibi returned N'tt'rr'z had arrived, and informed them that due to the growing tension between Myot and Neuendan, the Mission would be confined to these rooms for the rest of the winter. Their meals would be served here: they would receive no visitors, and they would no longer be invited to His Majesty's Winter Banquets. They need have no fear, however. They would be well treated, and their friends, now housed in another part of the castle, would come to no harm.

So they weren't honoured guests any more, and their fate seemed dependent on political events they couldn't even monitor. But they didn't *know* that any violence had been done to their colleagues, or to the soldiers left rotting their brains at Underwall – and Bibi was subdued but physically unharmed. Persis dosed her with onei, a gentle narcotic, to soothe her nightmares.

Morale was very good. There wasn't a shadow of reproach or recrimination between Liam and the General, now that the chips were down. It was a worrying situation: most of all because they didn't know what had happened to the others. But everyone was in good spirits, the servants weren't openly insolent (a hopeful sign); and spring would come—

Bibi and Honesty reverted to childhood. They shut themselves in their bedcurtains to keep warm, and told each other stories. They dressed up, in some Myot clothes they'd found in a closet, and devised rambling scurrilous sketches about their superiors: the unsuspected romance between Hari Colmar and a flirtatious Hairy Serpent, and what happened when Ariane found the couple in flagrante, in the royal stable-burrows—

'Why d'you think they never got married?'

'That's easy. Hari gets bossed around enough without Ariane having a right to review his accounts in bed as well. No, really, I know: it's because they aren't fertile, and Hari thinks only people with a chance of having children should get married. Except if they're high-grades, of course.'

'I never knew that.'

'Does he hurt you, Bibi?'

'Not really,' said Bibi, blushing in the shadows, hiding her hot cheeks in the whiskery shawl she had wrapped around her head, as the Flirtatious Hairy Serpent. 'It wasn't much, Honesty. It was just like a long bad dream: all vague. What he does doesn't hurt at all. It doesn't feel like anything. I don't think it can be real sex.' She hoped it wasn't. She hoped she was still a virgin, somehow: because otherwise she had betrayed Mahmood.

'What *does* he do?'

'Puts his thing in me, and, well, not much.'

'Is it big?'

'No, I think it's very small. But I have no experience.'

Persis, the Women's Doctor, said Bibi had taken no harm. On the other hand, Honesty had noticed that Bibi had stopped talking to Nikty, the one who'd encouraged her to get betrothed. So she wondered. But you would never get the Savage to spill the beans, if she'd made up her mind to keep her mouth shut—

They heard someone knocking at their door. Honesty went to answer it with her pulse-gun tucked inside her Ariane costume: whoever searched the girls' room hadn't yet taken their weapons. But it was Francois, not a Myot assassin, so they let him into their cave, and gave him a private performance of *The Flirtatious Serpent, the Admin Chief and the Housekeeper*—

<Bibi,> said Francois, <the second 'full retreat' starts tomorrow night.>

'I know,' said Bibi, who was trying to forget.

She felt hunted: she didn't want to talk to Francois in the Common Tongue. Things you say in that language are privileged, they can never be used against you, but she didn't want to share her secret feelings. She had never for a moment doubted that what she was doing was worthwhile. One life against twenty-five. Or a lot more, if it was true that she was keeping the peace between Myot and Neuendan: and Bibi wasn't even dead. But it was hard to look at the people who'd accepted her sacrifice, so greedily.

Harder still now it turned out she'd fixed nothing—

<Take this,> he said, slipping a pouch of soft, Aleutian skin into her hand. <It's my private supply of onei. It's all I have to give.> She could feel the small globules moving inside: throat-poppers, Aleutian style.

'I never knew you were a drug fiend.'

She knew she was being rude, speaking aloud when he wasn't, but Francois didn't care. He was beyond manners.

<Tell the prince,> he said. <Ask his permission. I think he's a drug fiend too, I see it in his eyes. He should allow it – they have 'winter warmers' to make these gloomy days pass more swiftly. I've heard them say so—>

XXXI

Bibi had believed that the second retreat would be easier. It was shorter, just seventeen days this time, and it would be like the first. Blood tea; and the meagre pollen wafers she was allowed because she was a weakling. The prince drinking from the veins of the three bat-women: who had never again been alone with her, and could not talk to her, but who seemed to look at Bibi kindly. The red gloom inside the bedcurtains, when the lamps were lit in the prince's bedchamber. The brief, painless act, the long hours of unbroken darkness when S'na'ulat'tz' lay comatose beside her.

But she was no longer protected by shock, suddenness and the pride of sacrifice. Everything was harder, and though she'd been determined not to do it (she thought she knew, better than an Aleutian, how a chattel wife should behave), she showed the prince the onei pouch, and asked him, in signs, if she could use this 'sleepy, dreamy' winter drug.

S'na'ulat'tz' was horrified. <How did you smuggle that in here?> he demanded, in the same manner, with startling fluency–

<I didn't *smuggle* it,> protested Bibi. <The pouch was just in my pocket.>

So then they had a common language, and the change was terrible. She began to know her betrothed, as a person; and to hate him.

<Make more passion,> he ordered her. <You're like a limp plant.>

<Make more passion! Show enjoyment!>

<I don't know how,> said Bibi.

(and her heart cried out for Mahmood, who would have taught her—)

<You think my thing is small? You think I am nothing much?>

<You don't feel anything? Well, I can fix that.>

He hit her, first in impetuous anger and then in calculated fury. She was back at White Rock, feeling the pity of the other women in the caves. Why, oh why had she enraged her husband? The other women felt sorry for her but what could they do? Marriage is a lottery, Bibi was just unlucky.

Then one time he came to the bed, and said: <Why don't you bleed?>

Because you're careful, thought Bibi, bitterly, feeling she'd known S'na'ulat'tz' for ever by now. *Because you've done this before. You always hit girls you 'sleep with', it makes you feel less inadequate. I bet you're what Sigurtians call a submissive type, like Nikty, like your father. Except Nikty is sweet and brave, not a craven bully. Maybe your father was like her, and that's why he's dead.*

<I don't know what you mean,> she said: in their shared language.

The bed was Bibi's territory, she never left it. The bat-women tended her inside the curtains, brought her the chamber pot, cleaned her teeth and skin: puzzled over her strange, abundant head-hair. She'd come to feel safe there. The prince was hitting her, for any reason or none, but at least he was still treating her like a bride. Now he flung back the curtains, an insult. He prowled around, glaring at her with his little diamond-rimmed eyes.

<Blue women bleed from the womb, periodically. I wanted to see that, it would be a spectacle. I wanted to taste it. Why don't you bleed?>

'Nobody bleeds like that any more,' explained Bibi, babbling, scared that he was going to drink her blood anyway. 'Nobody except real young ladies, of *really* old-fashioned families, and they have to have special hormone mix in their rooms. It doesn't mean I'm not fertile—'

<You're not a high-caste girl?>

He jumped onto the covers and crouched there, staring.

<You're not the Aleutian's ward?>

Then she realised that she had spoken aloud, and the prince, although he didn't deign to speak in return, had understood her. Something in his face warned her that there was no way to recover: this was the end. 'I'm his office assistant,' she told him, despairing. 'It's all in my file, the one your people have read. Everything about me is in there. But Francois has been very good to me, and I'm still an XX. I'm still what you wanted—'

'I have been deceived,' he said: and took his revenge.

XXXII

The leader of the Mission was called to account for the outrageous deception. General Yu insisted on knowing who was interrogating him, and by what right. He was in no mood to kowtow. He had just left his small army holed up in their last redoubt, where Persis was doing her best with limited resources (the room-riflers had confiscated most of the Mission's medical supplies) for an innocent young woman who'd been systematically, expertly beaten by her so-called 'betrothed'.

'I am the Myot State Examiner,' said the bat-person who faced him, an elderly-looking, authoritative male in a four-pointed cap fitted over his ears and tied under his chin, and a wide, stiffened black robe. But Yu looked at the two soldiers in armoured uniform, flanking this hanging judge, and doubted that the Mission's affairs had been turned over to the civil authorities.

'Your royals deceived themselves,' he said. 'Our files have been open to you, you had the facts. It was a mystery to us why S'na'ulat'tz' wanted to marry our Bibi, but princes have their whims.'

He demanded to know, since he had the chance, what had happened at Underwall. The Examiner told him he had no right to ask questions.

'Excuse me, I have every right. I'm the Ambassador of the Hegemony.'

The hanging judge rose. 'General, you attempted to secure the current charts of our tunnel network, through the offices of the Neuendan spy. This was incontestably an act of war. Your troops have been treated as enemy soldiers, invaders on Myot soil. They offered resistance, and perished. What did you expect, after such a blatant abuse of your immunity?'

'They offered no resistance. If what you say is true, it was a massacre.'

'On that topic, I have nothing further to say.'

'It'll wait until springtime,' said the General. 'We'll have a sorting out then. All right, so in the meantime, what now?'

'Her Majesty Hongfu and her son the prince have set the penalty, as is their right, for the deception that was practised on them. They have been lenient. All they require is the surrender of the Neuendan, and a tribute in fresh blood from Bibi's immediate relations. Which in this case shall be taken to mean, from each member of the Mission's Executive.'

The Swimmer usually detested transaid conversations, which lost all nuance and made him feel helpless as a puppet. But this one he'd quite enjoyed. He felt that he and the hanging judge understood each other splendidly.

'We'll think about it.'

He was escorted back to the redoubt, cast himself down in one of the stupid, comfortless lacquer sofas, and shook his head.

'What happened?' demanded Liam.

'It's over, my blue-haired friend. We are comprehensively screwed.'

'I could have told you that weeks ago,' yelled Honesty, furiously. '*Why* did you have to let this happen to Bibi! We knew it would do no good.'

'Because it's still a crapshoot, little lady,' said the General, in perfect good humour. 'And I never say die until I'm dead.'

He told them the conditions.

'Oh, no,' said the Aleutian, when he heard them. 'No blood from me.'

'No,' said the General. 'Thought you'd say that.'

'You should give me up,' said Nikty. 'It might buy some time.'

Her masked face was no longer inscrutable. She'd been 'breathing their air', as the Aleutians say, for months: the Baykonur Blues felt she was kin. The choices she'd made, the way she'd behaved, were exactly what they hoped they'd have done themselves. Loyalty, honour, obligation—

'You're a good girl, but no. It would change nothing, and Pendong, or Sigurt's World, or whatever you call it, is still part of the Hegemony. Come springtime, if we've survived, I don't want to end up telling the folks back home that I was fooled by the Myots, and then I wilfully screwed a chance to be a hero with the Neuendans ... Am I right, Nef, am I right, Liam?'

'You're absolutely right, Swimmer,' said his wife.

The Speranza agent agreed.

In fact, though there was no formal vote, the decision was unanimous.

XXXIII

Liam decided it was time to break out the concealed arms. They all went with him to the room he now shared with Dunblane. The heavy case he was about to open contained, apparently, printed books and other antique media. It had passed every scan, every scrutiny: though the servants at Underwall and the room-riflers at Black Wing had certainly been through the contents.

'My library,' said the Speranza agent, 'is my pension fund, and my treasured recreation. I never travel anywhere without it.'

He made the irreversible changes to the code of the lock. When he opened the case the antiques had vanished, replaced by disassembled weaponry, with the appropriate consumables, far more powerful than the Mission's regulation side arms: which could disable, but were unlikely to kill.

'*Magic*,' breathed Honesty: scandalising the older staff.

'Information space masking,' Liam corrected her. 'Dangerous, I know, and a capital crime where you come from: but effective. It's lucky that the Myots are not connoisseurs of alien fiction. They might have noticed that my Shakespeare and my Hollywood have survived multiple transits, uncannily free of the usual corruption—'

'Let us hope,' said Lady Nef, 'that the hardware is equally pristine. Get to work, Dunblane. Assess and issue weapons.'

The 'winter garden' was a long gallery, with an exterior roof, reached via a narrow passage that snaked alongside Lady Nef and the General's suite. Plants, flowers and full-grown small trees flourished, in synthetic summer daylight. Paths wound between false vistas around an open space of raked gravel; large enough for Dunblane's drill sessions.

General Yu and Liam went there the day after the General's pleasant interview with the hanging judge, to review the territory. Nothing further had occurred, as yet. Nobody had turned up to demand a final decision.

'Can't do anything about the skylights,' remarked the General, looking up into the coffered, amber roof-space. 'We'll have to seal this off.'

'We should harvest anything that might be edible, first.'

Ariane had had the foresight to bring all the stores she could muster, when they'd been moved from Underwall. With her supplies, plus the 'clasping days' rations remaining in the servants' closet, they could quite possibly hold out until the end of winter, though it would be tight. Water would not be a problem. They had an aggressive distillation plant in their survival kit, and the air of the castle was moist with the exhalations of hundreds of numinal bipeds—

'Good idea,' said the General.

Then they saw something pale in a thicket by their path, a glimpsed shape, broken by creepers and shadow, but instantly recognisable. Without a word they unshipped their weapons and approached with caution. It was the naked body of a tall, raw-boned woman. She'd been decapitated, and by the look of the exposed raw flesh, and her waxen skin, drained of blood while she was still living. The Myots, it seemed, had taken tribute.

'Rashit,' said the General, softly. 'My wife's maid, you know.'

'You knew her well?'

'Oh, for many years ... Well, that's torn it.'

A search revealed one more body, Yevgeny, the General's valet: he'd been treated the same way. Leaving the dead where they lay, they proceeded to the end of the gallery, where – because of the climate control in here – there was a solid door rather than a teardrop entrance sealed by membrane.

'My given name's Kristophe,' remarked the General. 'I don't use it. Not even my wife calls me Kris, hasn't called me that for a hundred years or more. What's your family name, Liam? I've forgotten the damn thing.'

'You never knew,' said the agent. 'It's Mallorn.'

'Oh.' The General took stock of this news. 'One of those.'

'Yes.'

Mallorn had been a 'virgin world' of the early prospecting days. The survivors of the Blue Utopian group that had named it and claimed it were now Speranza citizens. They were never going back to Earth, nor their children's children, if they had any offspring: not unless all the laws against Buonarotti Torus Failure Contamination were rewritten—

The General pulled his heat-shield over his face and shouldered his plasma cannon. The agent did the same. They sealed the door into Black Wing: it was no use to them as an escape route.

'I ought to share something,' Liam said, when they stood looking, with curious satisfaction, at the job well done, the river crossed: no way out. 'The *Rajath* may have foundered—'

'We're all aware of that, thank you.'

'Yes, but ... The recall of the Port, without warning, without any message to the Mission, is something else. Incomprehensible, unless Speranza has been forced, maybe because of whatever happened to the *Rajath*, to place Sigurt's World under quarantine. If that's the case, then we've been sacrificed. No one will ever come here again. Never.'

'You think that's what's happened?'

'Either that, or there's an entanglement effect. We're sharing the fate of the *Rajath*, and everything we've experienced, all our mounting disasters, has been our perception of an error in the Navigator's calculation: something akin to the fugue experience of transit. We are living in a bubble universe, a vacuum fluctuation, liable to wink out of existence at any moment—'

'What minds you apparatchiks have.'

The General poked at the fused mess of the door, which resembled a mass of seared, glistening human flesh, but was already cool, and hard as concrete. 'Liam, my blue-haired cissy friend, these *if, if, ifs* are worthless. We have adequate food and water, and the state of these doors will show them we mean business. They may decide to leave us alone. Who knows? The *Rajath* may turn up on schedule, and find us still holding out.'

'General, I salute you,' said Liam. 'Your ability to put a good face on things is a marvel; your bizarre optimism is the best resource we have.'

'It's a modus vivendi,' said the General, grinning. 'I like 'em.'

On their way back to the little army's command tent, that room with the ugly, florid carpet, they sealed the two servants' entrances, which – conveniently – also had solid doors.

A funeral party returned for the bodies. They were laid out in one of the dry-bathrooms, where they could be left to desiccate, Aleutian style. Perhaps everybody thought of later casualties, for whom there'd be no ceremony, but not even Honesty mentioned that their fate was now beyond doubt. The winter garden was stripped of everything Nikty declared edible, and the inner door of the gallery was sealed.

'What must you think of us?' The Neuendan, bitterly shocked, was the most emotional of them. 'The priests are right. We Sigurtians are ruled by the Fallen Moon. We think we are civilised, but our souls are crawling with monsters, and grace is like the sun, bright but very far away.'

They were left alone for four *g't'z*, an interlude of vivid intensity. Rationing was in force, which was a shame because they all had ravenous appetites: the drab carapace porridge and the slippery pollen wafers had never tasted so good. They toasted each other with recycled water and missed the comfort of alcohol: but on the whole they knew they were better off without. They played games, they talked; they danced together. Bibi and Honesty presented their scurrilous playlets, and the Hairy Flirtatious Serpent became a figure of legend. The whiskery shawl would vanish from wherever Ariane tried to hide it, and the Serpent would reappear when least expected – with a menacing bombast if it was General Yu who'd taken on the role, a piratical swaggering waddle if it was Francois ... Some people made short, or lengthy, personal deposions, recorded on the spare memory of one of the transaids: which was then concealed in Liam's deactivated 'library case'. Others, including Francois, decided not to bother.

'Doesn't that mean you won't remember being our Francois?' asked Mohabbet, concerned. She knew that an isolated Aleutian, unable to pass on his 'wandering cells' to another of his kind, had lost the normal way of maintaining continuity, from life to life.

'Recorded memories are so dull,' he said, shrugging. 'I have stacks and stacks, I never look at them.' So then his friends realised something they'd missed. The Aleutian was going to die like a human being this time, mortal like the rest of them. Some of them had been hoping that one day, Francois born again would tell their story. They gave up that hope and thought of what dying like this might mean to him. But he made light of it.

On the fifth day a party of Myots approached. Nikty, who had hardly left the five-starred lobby since the winter gallery had been sealed, heard them coming.

'Is this it?' asked Bibi, on watch with the Neuendan at the time. She had forgiven Nikty, wholeheartedly. If there was any blame due over what had happened with S'na'ulat'tz', Bibi was as guilty as anyone.

'I don't think so. N'tt'rr'z is with them, I can make out her step: she's not armoured, and there are unarmed servants. I think this is a parley.'

The Neuendan's acute hearing had given ample warning. N'tt'rr'z arrived, in court dress, at the foot of the short flight of stairs that led to the lobby: accompanied by four armoured Bloodmen, and servants bearing the official implements. She found herself facing Lady Nef, flanked by three of *her* 'Bloodmen', all of them armed with weapons that had not been in their possession a few *g't'ʒ* before—

'We have come to collect the tribute,' announced N'tt'rr'z. 'We also require access to your rooms, which we must search again for contraband.'

'I'm afraid you've had a wasted journey,' said Nef. 'We've taken advice from Speranza: there will be no blood tribute. Please convey our regrets to His Majesty, and our request for transport back to Underwall, since our stay at Black Wing has clearly become an embarrassment.'

'You have no contact with Speranza.'

'Yes we do,' said Nef. 'Of course we do, by means you cannot begin to imagine. You know nothing of our resources, N'tt'rr'z.'

The factotum seemed nonplussed. 'Then stay in your rooms. But you must surrender to me the prince's wife, and the Neuendan spy.'

'In a pig's eye!' shouted Honesty. 'Nikty's our friend.'

Then the Bloodmen made a rush at the stairs, possibly on their own initiative, firing at half-charge. Their standard weapon was a subsound rifle, which at full charge could shatter rock. A half-charge headshot would turn an unprotected brain to mush without cracking the skull, although it wasn't quite as effective on aliens. The Blues were wearing light body-jackets over their tunics, and ear mufflers: all the protection they had.

Honesty dropped to one knee and sent a thin lance of flesh-slicing heat between the foremost Bloodman's helmet and his neckpiece. The blood-taking servants set up a frantic clicking, threw down their bowls, arm cuffs and scalpels and took flight. *'Fire at will!'* shouted Dunblane, belatedly, but N'tt'rr'z had made up her mind she was outnumbered. The Myots fled back to the main stairway. Lady Nef's party let them go.

The rest of the small army hurried out of the corridors, where they'd been lying in wait behind barricades of furniture, decorative screens, slabs of carved stone from wall-niches, chairs, tables, chests. Together they dragged everything to the foot of the stairs that led to their lobby, heaped it up to block the teardrop doorway there, and turned a plasma cannon on the heap.

'I should put you on a charge,' Dunblane told the trigger-happy Magnet. 'You *obey my orders*, Honesty, or so help me I'll disarm you.'

'I just wish it had been that smarmy factotum,' said Honesty. 'But she was unarmed, the dirty cheat.' She was shaking. She couldn't remember deciding to fire, she couldn't remember taking aim. Another part of her had done it, without asking her permission, and now she'd *killed* someone—

'Well done,' said Nef, to her maiden warriors, when they had time to draw breath. 'But I confirm Dunblane's warning, Honesty.'

'Blood tribute to *us*, this time,' said the Master-at-Arms. 'But that'd better be the last time we use the cannon, ma'am, General. It's not healthy in closed quarters. Could turn the whole floor into a firebomb.'

'We'll have to bear that in mind,' said General Yu.

The Seniors and Francois were in good shape, and so was Liam. The others, without the protection of longevity treatment, were weakened by two lengthy fasts and months of poor nutrition. Nef found herself wondering, as they sat down to their next banquet, how she could sneakily arrange for them to get the lion's share of the calories in future. Pollen wafers, a little dried fruit, carapace porridge made with blood tea, twice a day for a Myot month, and then relief had better be near ... She almost laughed.

The Swimmer's attitude was infectious, and she blessed him for it.

'I propose a toast.' She raised her flask. 'To the many millions, all over Sigurt's World, and in Sigurtian Conventional Space, who are following the 'Myot Royals' situation on their newsfeeds, shaking their heads and feeling glad they are far away. On every world in the Hegemony, terrible, unforgivable things, much worse than our fate, are happening every day. Let's not forget that. And yet we have reached each other. We have made it this far. To us.'

Nikty raised her own flask, spoke in clicks, and took a reckless swig of the tasteless distillation. 'It's the blood-price of living,' she translated. 'That cannot be reduced. Do you say that?'

'Something like it.'

The third night after that, Hari and Ariane, on patrol, detected something going on on the other side of the fused door to the winter garden.

Nikty was fetched. She listened for a moment or two, and then made that gesture with the flattened palms. 'You can hear for yourselves, they've got some kind of heavy machinery in place. I'd guess it's a small rock-plough, used for clearing falls in the tunnel network. It'll take them a while to get through both doors, unless they want to wreck this wing of the castle: but they're coming in.'

They said their goodbyes, over a last dinner of porridge and blood tea. Bibi wept, because it was all her fault. Why had she let S'na'ulat'tz' know she could speak the Common Tongue? Why had she enraged him? If only she was still a virgin, so Mahmood could remember her with honour—

This display, so unlike Bibi's usual stoic calm, suddenly brought to Nef's mind the factotum's demand for the prince's *wife*. But her intuition defied all common sense, and it meant nothing now.

'Bullshit.' Honesty stroked her friend's face, where the bruises the prince had inflicted were still dark. 'Reformers think it's immoral to have an exclusive sex-partner. Now he'll be able to hold his head up.'

'It was *une marriage blanche*,' Francois assured her. 'In spirit, if not in body. You volunteered for a dangerous duty, such as many others have performed before you, in all the wars of history: an act of heroism under the orders of your superior officers. He'll be proud of you.'

'Why do you *talk* so much, Francois? I thought Aleutians weren't ever supposed to say things aloud, except when it was strictly necessary. But you never shut up. I've always wanted to ask you that.'

'My dear Honesty, *c'est tout simple*. I have no respect for the law.'

On the fourth *g't'z* after they'd sent N'tt'rr'z packing, the Myots broke through from the winter garden gallery. The first Royal Myot guards through the gap were sharp-shooters, using a weapon the Blues hadn't seen before, highly focused and deadly. They picked off Borgush Dunblane, Persis Afar and Hari Colmar in seconds. General Yu's depleted forces retreated. Ariane, sheltering behind Hari's body, stayed behind, firing rather wildly (she had never really learned to use a lethal weapon), and covered their retreat.

The rest of them reached the room with the ugly carpet. Liam, Nikty, Francois and the General flanked the two doors, watching for an assault from the lobby, and taking turns to make the narrow passage from the gallery too hot for the Myots. Mohabbet Soltani had been hit. She'd insisted she was fine, but had collapsed as soon as they reached –

relative – safety. Bouasone gave her diamorphine, as emergency first aid, scanned her torso and belly, shook his head and gave her another dose.

Lady Nef knelt holding Mohabbet's cooling hand, and called to her husband: 'Swimmer, have we any breathing space?'

'Possibly, Beauty. This pretty boy and I can hold the pass a while, the rest of you should refuel. I'm afraid we won't get any rest tonight.'

'We must eat, he's right,' said Nef. 'Bibi, get the—'

Then the thunder that they had stopped hearing suddenly rose to a roar that thrummed and shook in their bones, and set their eyeballs swelling. The air turned to jelly. Bibi saw Nikty turn, open-mouthed, in slow motion, as if through water, blood spurting from her eyes and her pointed ears—

'Bibi! Look out!' shrieked Honesty, shoving her aside, taking the bolt of sound that had been about to snap Bibi's spine.

Dunblane and the General had discussed sealing Bibi and Honesty's chamber, which had an exterior wall. But Dunblane had been very reluctant to use the plasma cannon again, and the General had been unable to bring himself to abandon that last, desperate escape route. The Myots had come up the wall, and sliced the bolts of the window shutters. Instead of advancing through the lobby, they'd driven straight through the internal walls. They were now pouring into the Mission's last redoubt. The room was full of hot dust, pulverised stone. Bibi coughed, her throat on fire, as she held Honesty in her arms. Francois came out of the fog, swooped down and hugged her. Red bugs from his throat glands, stirred up by his emotion, were creeping over his face, the dark-centred animal muzzle—

Let me remember this!

She heard the words in her mind: a moment later she saw him reach Nef's side and fall, his head bursting like a ripe fruit. Who was still alive? Where was General Yu? Where was Nikty, Liam? She could see Myots, in armour, no one else: and that was her last thought.

XXXIV

The relief force arrived on one of the first days of spring. General Yu, stubbled and haggard, was brought up from the detainment cells under Black Wing Castle. He'd been offered a chance to tidy himself up, but he'd declined. The interview room was clean and warm, with a view of one of the garden courtyards. Spring on Sigurt's World came like dawn on a battlefield. The small bright sun in a clear sky looked down on devastation: scoured ground, blackened skeletons of trees.

The General had been allowed access to the media, throughout his imprisonment. He'd had notice of the arrival of the *taikos*, a new Speranza taskforce in charge of policing the Buonarotti network. And later of the *Rajath*, with a high-ranking official on board. All these months, the Swimmer had had his own ideas about what might have triggered the recall of the Port crew: what might have been happening twenty-six thousand light years away. He could read the runes, but he still didn't *know*. He wouldn't know for sure until he saw the expression on the face of the man who was about to walk through that door. They say a week is a long time in politics. General Yu had been away from the front line for aeons, it felt like.

Although it wasn't really so long. A few months—

Everything depended on what kind of smile came through that door.

The Speranza Envoy entered with his aides, plus officials from neutral Crater-States, the Neuendan Ambassador to Myot, and the Myot civil authorities: who had been very busy rewriting the Black Wing Castle affair. Apparently the Myot 'Oligarchs', civil authority politicos, had known nothing about the murder of the two Mission servants. Hence their inaction when the Royals had 'defended themselves' from the Mission staff's unprovoked attack, using contraband deadly weapons—

The General had been holding his fire.

'Let us have a few minutes alone,' snapped the Speranza Envoy, turning on the pack indignantly. 'Can't you see this person has been through hell?'

He sat opposite the General; they looked at each other.

'So you made it, Swimmer.'

And the General knew that he was saved. The darkest, deepest of his fail-safe plans had come to fruition. A wise rabbit, as the old Chinese used to say, has at least three exits from his burrow, and the last of them he keeps a secret from his own heart. The two men talked – touching on the need to smooth over this tragic interlude for the good of the Hegemony. Enlarging briefly on future relations with Pendong, or whatever the Planetary Nation chose to call itself, on a new and more secure footing. They agreed that the General should make a deposition on the real course of events, to be vaulted in Speranza System's closed records, and that's where the truth had better stay. At last the Envoy raised the distressing subject of the Baykonur inquiry. Lady Nef's guilt, confirmed by innocent witnesses. Her trial in absentia: the penalty of the law mercifully commuted, in view of the great Lady's many honours, to life imprisonment.

'It was my painful duty to pass sentence.'

General Yu shuddered, and bowed his head.

'I'm sorry to have to make these demands,' said the Envoy. 'You should be in a hospital, and you soon will be. But there's one more thing, before a very short press conference. Could we go over the list of survivors?'

They went over the list of survivors. The General knew he was being given the opportunity to silence awkward voices, and he shuddered again. The soldiers at Underwall had indeed perished, which was no surprise. The officers and staff who'd been separated from the Exec had lived, but none of them knew anything dangerous. Greatly relieved, he broke into warm praises of his fallen comrades. Francois, Dunblane, Hari, Honesty, wonderful people, heroic to the end, faithful unto death. Bouasone, Persis; Ariane Rasoul, what a splendid woman—

'And then there's the prince's wife,' the Envoy continued. 'The Royal Myots insist she won't see us or speak to us, she's in some kind of purdah. Should we press it? They claim she's legally married. Is that true?'

General Yu blinked once, twice.

'Oh, yes. They got together just before things broke down in that unfortunate way. Legally married, of her own free will.'

INTERMISSION
POETIC TIME

O

Bibi lived. Her friends were dead, she would never see Mahmood again, she was alone in an alien world: but the life inside her had its own compelling logic. The spring came and her attendants let her know (against orders, in the Common Tongue) that the space-people had returned to their Port. But hearing words in her head, conjured from the body language of bat-people, was reading messages in raindrops on the window. Even if it was true, she had no way to reach the relief force. Almost certainly they'd been told she was dead. She was adrift in a timeless world, into which the hope of rescue floated; and dissipated vaguely.

The *Rajath* had foundered. Sigurt's World was quarantined. Nobody would ever know what had happened to the Mission. When the bat-women told her that she must take blood, or the baby would die, she offered no resistance. She was not asked to suck. The blood came in slithery poppers, affixed to her arm: she guessed, or learned, that it was from the child's father.

She got very sick. For a while there was nothing in her world but aching bones, open sores, nausea, fever and nightmares. She got better, and her attendants told her she could no longer be sedated, for fear of harming the baby. They were warning her she'd be restrained by other means if she didn't behave. She could have despaired, then: but her birth culture saved her. She'd been taught to admire the wilful choice of death in battle, *no surrender.* She had no respect for the suicide of a pregnant woman. What was so terrible? Unwilling brides had often, often been in this situation, and found consolation in their children, and made a life for themselves. At least S'n'l't"tz (her ability to hear Myot as it was really spoken was improving) seemed to be excluded from the pregnancy. *If I have to sleep with him to get pregnant,* thought Bibi, *and the rest of the time he leaves me alone, I'll be better off than a lot of women married to mean-spirited, violent men—*

She discovered, as the mists parted, that although her attendants were the prince's blood-offerers, she wasn't in his chamber. Her territory was still a curtained bed, and she supposed she was still in Black Wing Castle, but everything was different: less mediaeval, more alien. Medical people came and went, affixed gadgets to her arms and belly, read the runes and refused to allow her to get up. *Vroucolocha*, *Broucoloka* and *Goul* massaged her, groomed her and moved her limbs for her, endlessly patient, until she felt as if she were a precious grub, a queen bee helpless in the midst of the hive.

There was a visit from an important bat-man who seemed to be the leader of the medical team, though Bibi didn't remember seeing him before.

<Your baby is strong and healthy,> *Vroucolocha* told her, afterwards. <He's had all from your womb that he needs. They'll induce labour now.>

<But I can't give birth!> protested Bibi. <My body isn't ready, I'm nowhere near full term!> The medics never spoke to her, and she didn't trust the words she heard in her head, but she understood enough of her condition to know that. <I'm sorry, Bibi, but you must,> said *Vroucolocha*. <Her Majesty desires it. Her Majesty wants the birth to be natural, so that your baby will get the full benefit of his mother's admirable spirit. It's an old belief, but our king holds by it. Her Majesty is a Traditionalist.>

<The king is not like S'n'l't"tz,> said *Goul*. <She values you. We all know, though it can't be said, that she's been disappointed in her son: but she's promising herself you'll give her an excellent grandchild.>

Bibi's pride was touched. She fought valiantly to give birth like a princess, and never once gave way to panic, although the battle grew long, hard and bloody, and the medical team were all over her with their probes and gadgets. She woke feeling ravaged and torn but triumphant, with the blurred memory of having heard her baby cry like a good 'un. She pulled herself up in the bed, and immediately *Vroucolocha* was there, inside Bibi's curtains, hopping up onto the covers.

'Where's my baby?'

'He's a fine, healthy boy. The king is very pleased. He's with the medics, he'll need all their attention for a while.'

'But I want to see him. I have to feed him. Can I go to him?'

Vroucolocha took her hand, and stroked it. 'Poor child, poor child, I warned you not to get pregnant, not until you'd made a position for yourself, but I suppose you couldn't help it. You will never see him, Bibi.'

O

The medics took her blood, so much and so often that she became anaemic. She had an idea of why this was happening, and it scared her because she cared about that baby, the son she would never see. *They change his blood and change his blood, and still he can't survive unaided*... When *Vroucolocha* told her she must drink like a princess now, so that she could help the medics to keep the king's grandson alive, she sucked from *Broucoloka*, willingly.

'See, dear Bibi, an arm is offered—'

They let her take walks in her dressing gown, in a gallery like the Mission's winter garden, near to her room: she was never allowed any further. She saw no one but the blood-offerers now, and the timeless drift closed over her again. Sometimes when she was in her gallery she heard the unearthly thunder of a Sigurtian winter, but what winter was this? She didn't know. She remembered something Francois had said, explaining the laws of simultaneity. Poetic time, the time of mind, where years can vanish, and yesterday and today easily change places, is different and more true than the time of causality, where tick follows tock. She was living in poetic time.

<How long will my son need me?>

<A while longer,> they said, vaguely: <a while longer.>

See, Bibi, an arm is offered.

She realised she didn't want the baby. She wanted Honesty and Francois, she wanted Lady Nef. She wanted General Yu, and Dunblane, and Hari and Ariane. She'd been pumped full of alien drugs, alien blood, for so long, but at last she was developing a resistance. For the first time she was shaken by grief. She mourned her friends, she conjured up their faces, she remembered their last hours: she puzzled over what could have happened.

The *Rajath* might have turned up, but the Myots must have lied about the fate of the Mission. *They'll have said we all vanished*, she thought. *We went on an expedition and got vaporised by lightning; or some such story.* She thought she had to be the only survivor. When she recalled those last moments in the redoubt, the hot cloud of pulverised stone, full of armoured Myots, the bursting skulls and pulped limbs she had glimpsed, nothing else made sense. She remembered what the blood-offerers had told her about S'n'l't"tz's father, and got scared. She would probably be murdered when the baby didn't need her blood, and now that she was free of the drugs she wanted to live. But how could she possibly escape?

She had nightmares, reliving the 'full retreats'. The thunder of that far-off winter yelped and groaned. S'n'l't"tz lay beside her, comatose, wrapped in his robe, for endless hours. The horror was when she woke up and knew it wasn't true. This retreat would never be over. She would never be allowed to return to her friends.

O

Deliverance came when she least expected it. The demand for her blood had suddenly increased, to the same level (as far as she remembered) as just after the baby's birth. She guessed that the child, who must be about a year old by now, was having renewed health problems. If he died would she be killed? Or would S'n'l't"tz try and get her pregnant again?

Then her attendants brought her a set of clothes: serpent's silk underwear and ruched leggings, a wide-sleeved silvery tunic, cut for folds of skin she didn't possess. Soft boots for Sigurtian feet, too long and thin: but everything else fit quite well. Astonished by this development, disoriented from the amount of blood she'd given recently, she let them dress her.

'Goodbye, Bibi,' sighed *Vroucolocha*, kissing her hands. 'Your son is a fine, big, strong lad, everybody is extremely proud of him.'

'He can already ride any serpent in his father's stables,' said *Broucoloka*. 'He's wilful and headstrong, but gentle. Everybody loves him.'

Bibi imagined a toddler clinging to the barbed bridle, with hands that had barely learned to grip. She could speak and understand Myot well, considering her disabilities: but an unfamiliar idiom could still confuse her.

'What's happening? Please tell me. Why am I allowed to get dressed?'

They were out of their depths, they didn't know, or were afraid to say.

'The mother's retreat is over,' declared *Goul*, taking refuge in formality.

'Your son no longer needs you,' explained *Vroucolocha*, and gave the puzzle a hopeful spin. 'Of course you are returning to your friends.'

Bibi placed no faith in this announcement; blatantly the bat-women didn't know what was going on: but it was a luxury to have proper clothes. *If they are taking me away to murder me*, she thought, *I shall sell my life dear. I don't feel very strong, but I'm bigger than some of them, and I've always done my drill. I'll be the last of us to fall. I hope I can take one or two of the bastards with me.* A pair of Bloodmen came, and she left the room of the curtained bed with no regrets. They didn't speak to her; Bibi had nothing to say to them. They took her to the vertical train, and straight to the freight depot: she was to leave Black Wing the same way she'd entered it. No sign of the king, or the prince; or that hateful N'tt'rr'z. The back-door departure convinced her she was about to die.

When they let her out of the hover she was assaulted by a rush of sounds so unexpected and so evocative she barely saw what was really around her. She was crossing the concourse of the great Cosmodrome, a nervous cabin-bag pressed close at her heels, all her life's adventure ahead ...

It was Myotis City Flyerport. She knew the place, though she'd only glimpsed it briefly, long ago. She did not see the echoing bustle of the crowd that pained her so sweetly: she only heard it. The Bloodmen took her, by a discreet, VIP route, to a small flyer in a distant field. *They're moving me to the Royal Town House*, Bibi told herself. *The prince keeps his discarded girlfriends there, locked up so they can't tell the society pages what he's really like. Well, I shall* mobilise *them.* She still was sure she was going to be killed.

The flyer transferred her to Myotis Spaceport, a short hop. She was put onto a private shuttle, with a different pair of guards and not a word of explanation. Determined that she wouldn't speak until spoken to, determined not to be fooled, she asked no questions. The safety wings folded around her cowled seat, swaddling her in place; she felt the gravity of Sigurt's World release her.

So this was freedom. The Buonarotti facility seemed less familiar, ironically, than Myotis Flyerport. She didn't remember these drab corridors at all. Burdened by conflicting emotions, she barely felt the buoyancy of reduced gravity. She padded barefoot between her taciturn guards, wondering how she could endure to return to her old life. Her boots and liners had been taken away at the spaceport; they hadn't been returned and nobody had explained why. Soon, in a moment, she would see the faces of her own kind again. She wondered if she'd recognise a Blue when she saw one, it was so long since she'd even seen her own face in a mirror. She wanted to be back in her curtained bed, to sink into that endless gloom again. The corridor was naked, windowless. She realised she was very hungry and tired, and suddenly thought of the tricks captors played on hostages—

'Where are you taking me?'

A long silence. She guessed the guards had difficulty believing their pricked ears. Suddenly the alien was speaking Myot!

'You'll find out soon enough.'

She'd been steeling herself for a delegation, a welcome party that she didn't want to face. Instead there was a small room, featureless as the outer reaches of Speranza, in which a Sigurtian official perched behind a desk, knees up to his chin in one of those cup-shaped chairs. He wore a drab robe over a light pressure suit and a four-pointed cap with a scarlet badge, which tied under his chin. The extruded furniture was the same red-brown as the document pouches that lined the walls, like bulging pollen sacks.

Bibi stood, between the two guards.

'I understand you can speak Myot?'

'Yes.'

'Neuendan?'

Bibi gestured for *no*.

'Well, Myot is good enough. Prisoner Gwibiwr, guilty by association of involvement in the Plot to Assassinate the Third Emperor and Overthrow the Blue Planetary Government, otherwise known as the Baykonur Conspiracy, you have been sentenced to indefinite, humane incarceration. You'll be taken from this office to the cells, where you'll be issued with your uniform, with a copy of the regulations pertaining to political prisoners and—'

'*What—?*'

'Restrain her.'

Bibi calmed herself, clutching at her rational bewilderment, fighting the nightmare. 'Honoured sir, I don't understand this. I don't know what you're talking about. How can I be a condemned prisoner? I've been with my husband the prince of Myot. I haven't left Black Wing Castle since before our son was born, a year ago. How can I have plotted to assassinate anyone? And anyway, there is no *Third Emperor*—'

The official's bare face told her he was male, but little else. Small, diamond-rimmed eyes studied her curiously, impassively. 'The king of

Myot's grandson is ten years old. I don't think you can have been in the prince's company recently, Prisoner Gwibiwr: the prince has been dead for some time. A hunting accident, or that's the story. You were granted a commutation until the child was old enough to do without his mother; you'll now serve your sentence here on Fenmu. Everything is correct. We seem to be having language difficulties. If you wish, you may be issued with a transaid.'

Ten years.

'Let the prisoner sit.'

A stool rose from the floor; the guards set Bibi onto it. The official pushed a document case towards her, the frame attached to his desk by a short tether. For a long moment she could not read the English text. She stared at her own hand, smooth and slender and very pale: the inadequate claws trimmed long by her bat-women, who had wanted her to look like a princess. Sigurtians can go into long comas. Their medicine is expert, far better than ours. Ten years. Poetic time.

'If you have anything to say, it is your right to make a deposition, at this time and never afterwards. Said deposition shall be couriered to Speranza and delivered to the appropriate authorities without unreasonable delay; along with any personal messages you wish to append.'

Ten years.

Bibi set the horror of that news aside. She was not free, of course not, the guards had been telling her different all the way from Black Wing. But she was free from that bastard S'n'l't"tz, and though there was no one to greet her she *was* legally in the hands of her own people. With a fierce rush of energy, knowing that she saved herself *now or never*, she swept through blurring pages, and found that she was condemned 'by association' with her mistress, who faced a capital charge. *What* devil *did this?* she asked herself. A thousand things she could do, appeals she could make, damning evidence she could reveal, rose up in her mind. Even if it *was* ten years, she would not rest. She would clear her name and her Lady's. She'd demand to be sent home, to be interrogated by the Starry Arrow. That would settle it. At last she found the fatal indictment, and the lying deposition that had condemned Lady Nef and her 'accomplices'. Mahmood was an affirming witness.

'No,' she said, when she had seen that. 'No, I have nothing to say.'

O

The Governor of the Interplanetary Prison Moon, a fearful place in the young legends of the Hegemony, had his office and his residence on the surface. The cells were in the rock. A tract of the so-called 'habitable' inward face of the big satellite – which supported a bizarre ecology – was honeycombed with them. Limited-term prisoners were held in neat facilities just beneath the surface. The lifers were buried deep, in dungeons old as the Sigurtian Space Age: where they lay forgotten, minimally fed and tended, until they slipped from coma into death.

Fenmu's atmosphere was breathable but noxious; danger lurked in the jagged terrain and perennial fogs of the inward face. Prisoner Gwibiwr never saw the surface; or what passed for daylight. She was taken straight to the down train, and delivered to her final home. Here she was stripped, dry-showered, fed with blood tea and put alone into a holding cell. She was exhausted; the food stunned her: she fell asleep. The lifer guards gathered, on the far side of a heavy chitin grille, to stare at her – a savage, big-breasted woman with a bare face and no ears. They were fascinated by her head-hair, which the sanitary crew had decided they weren't obliged to touch. The women in the group, having looked the alien over, left the room. The male guards stayed, got themselves drunk, opened the grille and crowded around.

Bibi suffered the first rape with indifference. It was her husband, putting his little thing in, it didn't hurt, she didn't care. The second guard to mount her was more demanding, he wanted a reaction. Under his attentions she woke, realised that this was *not* her husband, and fought like a tiger. She was naked and unarmed, but well trained. The guards, slighter and smaller than most Blue males, were no match for the fury of Bibi's violated honour. By the time they'd dragged her off him, the demanding rapist was dead, and the rest had lost their appetite for bestiality. They managed to get her sedated, and dumped her in her designated cell.

She woke there some hours later, in utter darkness. She crawled around, seeking the dimensions of her prison, and found her lifer uniform in a heap, alongside a document case that presumably contained the regulations. She put the clothes on and licked her lips: tasting blood. '*Haha!*' growled the Savage, squatting on her bare heels, nodding her head in satisfaction. '*Now they know better. I think they'll leave me alone now.*'

Bibi didn't expect to see the light again, but she was wrong. There was day and night in the lifer cells: a red gloom alternating with the abyssal dark. When the day came she saw that the walls of her cell were natural rock, with intrusions of a thick, glassy, reddish concrete. There was a covered bowl for a chamber pot, and a mattress laid on a low plinth; but no blankets.

Each time the light came on, a tray was delivered through a hatch at the base of the door, one section holding a dollop of carapace porridge, the other full of tea. Sometimes there was also a chunk of pollen bread. Sometimes it was blood tea, sometimes a herbal infusion. The herb stuff was rare but better: the blood tea was often stale and foul. She never looked at the regulations. If she'd tried she'd have learned nothing: she had no idea how to read a Sigurtian text. Eventually she realised that if she dragged the full chamber pot to the hatch, it would be removed and returned, empty and more or less clean, with her next meal.

So there was a routine to her life.

A hundred times, a thousand times, she walked down the blank corridor. She faced the Sigurtian official at his desk, and felt the hope of rescue drain out of her. She saw Mahmood's affirmation, and she was lost. A hundred times, a thousand times, she hammered and clawed at the massive, glassy red door, screaming that she'd changed her mind, she wanted to make a deposition. A hundred times, a thousand times, she crawled around the cell, trying every crack in the rock with her nails and teeth. She searched for a mechanism for opening the door, and found none. She leapt and grabbed at the upper sill of the doorway, and fell back, howling. And nothing changed.

She was left alone. No face ever looked through the hatch, no guard ever came to check her status. If there was anything in the rules that said she was allowed exercise, or access to other prisoners, the rule was ignored. At first she'd lie in wait for the clawed hand that pushed her tray inside, took the pot or returned it: planning to grab and bite the crawling thing. But she was afraid of what they'd do to her if she attacked them again. Later she became very frightened of *the hand*, and hid in a corner when she heard it coming.

She listened, listened, listened, but the hand's footsteps were the only sounds she heard. Somewhere there was a prison, Fenmu. There was surveillance, there was cruelty; regulated and otherwise. Maybe there was decency. There were prisoners who could count off the days, the years until their release, prisoners who plotted to escape. For Bibi there was nothing. She had been buried alive. She must die here.

Gradually she sank into a subhuman state. The uniform infuriated her, for reasons she couldn't remember. She took it off, tried to tear it to shreds, and threw it in a corner. The cell was neither warm nor cold, she didn't need clothes. Thought became fragmented and fell away. *Something* ate the meals, used the chamber pot, pushed the pots to the hatch and retrieved them: but it wasn't Bibi. *Something else* gnawed in anguish at its own heart, and clung to life so that it could continue this hateful, cannibal feast.

'Poetic time,' croaked the Savage, rocking on her heels.

She slept, wrapped in the filthy nest of her hair.

Dimly aware that she was pregnant again, she had thoughts of clawing the child of rape out of her womb. She pulled serpent bristles out of the mattress and stuck them inside herself. But nothing happened, and then she was afraid that if she succeeded she'd bleed to death, so she stopped trying. She didn't want to die. One day, just before the onset of darkness, she gave birth, squatting on her hands and knees on the rock floor; without much pain at all. The rush of matter that slipped from her contained two moving things, one of them with limbs, the other smaller, shapeless and squirming. The afterbirth followed. She crawled away from the mess, and slept.

Feeble cries came from there for a while, but she covered her ears and ignored them. Then she woke from a heavy doze to find the shapeless thing in bed with her: it had dragged the other creature along with it. She examined, with revulsion and curiosity, a little white girl-dolly half the size of a human newborn, and was inspired to let it suck, to relieve the pain in her breasts. The other thing crawled all over her, rasping at her skin with its many-toothed underside. It devoured the blood and fluid from her thighs, and started on the detritus that clogged her naked skin, her hair.

O

The tiny doll fed from her, and *something* remembered a son she had
never seen. The phage oozed over her face and limbs, nibbling and
tending the body that had been Bibi: *something* thought of Francois's
creatures, in those quarantined rooms in the Town House in Baykonur.
But Bibi had lost all connection with the person whose memories flitted,
like a ghost's dreams, in and out of her darkened mind. She had
forgotten that she was in a prison, or that there was a body attached to
the menacing hand, the evil, vital invader from outside her world. She
wouldn't let the phage go near the hatch. She slapped it away from
there, and the baby too, when it began to crawl. She had no clear idea
why she did this.

Her commensals were essential to her, she protected them without
knowing that she did so; but mostly she ignored them. She spent her
time lying on the floor, in the corner where she'd found a crack that
breathed: picking at a fault in the rock with her nails. She thought she
could hear a tiny sound from beyond it: a tapping of stone on stone,
the dripping of water on rock. The sound conjured up a hollow space,
much larger than her cell, an idea that attracted her. There might be
living things in the big darkness, which she could kill and eat. When
she thought of water, real water, she slavered and licked her lips.

The baby made experiments in walking, clinging to the rough parts of
the walls: but it grew very slowly in size. The phage didn't grow at all,
though it could stretch out or reduce itself to a lump, like a slug. One
day, soon after it had mastered the art of stumbling across the cell
without support, the baby came and sat in front of Bibi. Head to toe,
the naked thing was no longer than her forearm; its limbs were bone-
white twigs. It disturbed her to look at it. She pushed it away, but it
came back.

'*Who are you?*'

It was the baby. It had spoken. It was looking at her, proud and trembling at its own audacity. It had little teeth, and a ragged thatch of hair. She'd never noticed before that it had teeth; although she dimly remembered shoving it from her breasts, when it hurt her there. That a baby should *speak*, when nobody had ever spoken to it, struck Bibi as so uncanny that she jumped up and backed away, for once afraid to hit out. She didn't know that she had often spent hours shouting, muttering, singing, holding conversations with her dead – or that the child had listened, learning what it could.

The uncanny doll came after her and repeated the question.

'I'm your mother, foul thing. You're a kind of shit. You came out of my insides. You're Dirt. I'm the Dirtbag.'

'I'm Dirt!' cried the foul little thing, showing its teeth.

It tried to climb into her lap. She repulsed it, as usual.

Soon after this – in Bibi's poetic time all incidents were soon, and the gaps between them measureless – something momentous happened. It was the middle of the gloomy red daytime. She was in her corner, picking at a secondary crack, while the phage worked far more efficiently on the original fault; which was now two fingers wide. She didn't want the phage in her corner; she resented its interference deeply: but it had persisted until she'd lost interest in shoving it out of the way. The phage oozed through the big crack. It oozed out of sight and came back, but it couldn't tell her what lay beyond. It had no voice, no eyes, no ears.

Dirt-baby was grubbing at her breasts, where the food didn't come as easily as it used to do. 'What you suck is my blood,' muttered the Dirtbag mother. 'What you suck is my blood, foul little thing.' She was starting to have bitter, greedy thoughts about the baby's toll on her rations. Sometimes, her stomach hollow, she'd look at it, scrawny as it was, and she'd distinctly hear a voice in her mind.

See, Bibi, an arm is offered—

She heard the hand's footsteps from a long way off, and noticed that they sounded different. She puzzled over the strangeness of the familiar phenomenon for a while, before it struck her that this was not hand time. It was the middle of the day. *It was not hand time.* She leapt up, grabbed the uniform that she never wore, pulled the tunic over her head and bundled her commensals into the darkest corner. The rest of the clothes she spread over them with frantic hands.

'*Lie still,*' she moaned, '*lie still!*'

The door of the cell scraped, a painful sound, and slid aside. It *opened.* A male guard peered in, holding a long serpent-prong or stun baton in front of him. He was more robustly built than the bat-people Bibi remembered, but shorter, and very grubby and slovenly. He wore drab leggings, a dirty singlet that let his generous skin-flaps hang free. A tool-belt was slung under his arm; an aged, red-badged uniform cap set at a casual angle between his pricked ears. *If he finds them I shall kill him,* thought Bibi, the fire of lucidity rising from smouldering ashes. *But he won't, because I will be calm, I will not look at the corner. With luck he will just rape me and go away.*

'My Grace,' the guard clicked and fluted, seeing the prisoner crouched on her bed, half-naked in her tattered tunic, her bare face overwhelmed by all that mad hair. 'My Grace, look at the state of you.'

Grace was a word Nikty had used, a religious word, sometimes an expletive. 'What are you doing here?' hissed Bibi, in Myot.

The guard made the gesture for *I don't believe this,* and poked his baton towards her, but without touching her flesh. 'I've come ... to change ... your mattress,' he explained, speaking slowly, as to a child. 'Every three years lifers gets a cell check. The facilities gets overhauled and a new mattress delivered. This is your big day. Didn't they tell you at slopping out?'

'Nobody speaks to me.'

He came into the cell, his barbed stun-baton *en garde*, a bulky roll of sacking in his other arm. 'You don't look dangerous. I bet you never killed anyone, did you? It's all talk. Now, see, your cell is nice, you've kept it well, *but* you've pulled your mattress apart, you've been sleeping practically on the bare rock, you'll get rheumatic. Why do lifers do that? Did you think you could weave a rope from the bristles an' shin down from Fenmu to the Crater-States? Strangle one of us and get away? You poor silly woman. Have you gone mad, like the other one down here? No one gets out, not from Fenmu, not once in history: and if you did, you'd be sorry.'

As he spoke, he tossed the remains of the old mattress into the passage, shook out the replacement and spread it. He found the regulations case, which Bibi had never touched except to kick it around the floor; discovered that it had ceased to function, and placed it in the proper niche anyway. She saw that he didn't believe she could understand him: but his language was enough like Myot for her to follow it. He'd left the door of the cell open. It took a frightful effort of will not to jump up and run.

'Why? Why would I be sorry?'

'Oh, for Grace. You're on the *Fallen Moon*,' said the guard, in kindly contempt. 'Don't you know what that means? You really are an alien political, aren't you? And friendless too, like the madwoman, or you wouldn't be down here. It's not for me to know, but I can tell: somewhere there's a file on you marked *forget this person existed*, poor girl—'

Holding the baton less cautiously, he reached under his arm and produced a snouted tube, which he set on the floor. It began to run over the rocky parts of the floor and walls, sucking up such minor debris as the phage had not consumed. The guard watched it, placidly.

'Have you got a secret an' all? The madwoman's got a moth in her head about a secret. Used to lie with her mouth to the hatch, shouting and raving that she knew something worth empires, worth more riches than the world can hold, and she'd tell it to anyone who'd get her out. But she's given up on that, long since. Decided we are not worthy, she says. She's quiet now, and likely to get quieter soon, poor thing. Lifers never last long: just wrap themselves in their skin, drift off and never wake up. When the food's left untouched, then we know. But apart from you two alien buggers, *this* 'orrible old section's been empty since I was taken on—'

'I have no secret.'

The snouted cleaning tool approached the corner where Dirt-baby and the phage were hidden. The prisoner leapt up with a howl, flung herself on it and threw it out of the cell, with such force that it shattered on the wall of the passage. Teeth bared, broken claws reaching, she sprang at the guard—

'*Grace!*' he yelped, waving his baton wildly. 'Holy *Grace–!*'

He fled. The door snapped shut with an evil, grating sound. The prisoner, wild with fury, searched for something to punish. She grabbed the regulations document case from the niche, and beat it savagely to bits.

'It's good to have a reputation,' croaked Dirtbag.

O

She was afraid the guard would come back with reinforcements. He didn't. The intrusion had no aftermath, but it marked an epoch. Bibi's innate resilience and toughness began to return – as if her recovery had only needed time, not hope: time, and that single flash of contact with another soul. She still woke, intermittently, in Dirtbag's mindless body, and knew that she'd been ranting, singing, talking wildly. Echoes drifted through the emptiness inside her head, the song of *Dafydd of the White Rock*, croaked by a dead voice, fading away down endless dark corridors ... But her lucid periods became longer, and she always recovered the thread of her days. She knew that she was in a prison called Fenmu, and it was a real place, not a nightmare. She knew that time was passing, that countless days had already passed: and she was violently determined that she was going to escape. Maybe she couldn't get off the prison moon, but she *would not die in this cell.*

'Humane incarceration!' snarled Dirtbag, working tirelessly, hour on hour, at the cracks in the corner. 'Bastards! Hahaha!'

She thought of the taste of water, and licked her lips.

She thought of Dirt-baby, the child who didn't grow, living and dying in this hole, and howled with frustration. '*You're going to get me into trouble,*' she yelled, smacking at Dirt, sharing reluctantly the food that disgusted her. '*You're going to make me do stupid things!*' Then she'd return to stabbing, hour upon hour, at the rock wall, with a sliver of the document case, or a chip of rock. '*I hate you, foul little thing.*'

Fenmu Prison held no prisoner as forsaken as herself: except maybe the madwoman who had howled that she had a secret, and then folded up and died. Perhaps the madwoman had died happy, dreaming of the people who loved her. Bibi had nobody. She could not tell herself that somewhere, far away, she was mourned, she was missed: that her old friends wondered what had happened. There was no one. There was *no one.*

The wall above and below the biggest cracks sounded hollow. She couldn't remember if this had always been so. She chipped and hammered and bit at the rock, in an agony. She could *smell* the sweet dripping water. She threw the phage aside, infuriated by its patient chewing, and slammed her calloused fists against the stone, with screams of fury. Something gave way, with a crack and a strange, whispering rush. Falling fragments rattled, rattled into stillness. Bibi knelt, holding her bleeding knuckles for the commensals to lick, and stared at a ragged black hole, a little bigger than her head.

The Dirt-baby tried to get near it. Bibi pushed her away. The phage crawled into the hole, and crawled out again. It oozed up Bibi's arm and settled on the back of her neck, under her hair, a pose she thought it adopted when it was scared. What had it found? A void, most likely. A bottomless abyss. The Fallen Moon was like Sigurt's World itself, she remembered: full of caverns, fissures passing all the way through, where it had broken apart and been reformed. Climb through that gap and fall, and fall, and fall, until your lungs burst in vacuum.

Dirt got by her again, and peered into the black place. 'What is it?'

'No!' snapped Bibi, grabbing her and dumping her roughly out of harm's way. 'It's dangerous.' She pushed her head and shoulder through, dropped another handful of rock chips, and listened.

'Not far,' she whispered. '*Not* far.'

'We need rope, and a light.'

She ripped up the sacking of her mattress and knotted the strips together, while Dirt slept on the bare rock with the phage wrapped around her. Did that thing sleep? Maybe it just rested. She had no stores of food: her daily allowance of porridge, tea and bread had barely been enough to keep her working. She didn't let this worry her. If they couldn't find a food source in the caverns, the three of them were dead anyway. But light she must have.

She had sacking and serpent bristle to burn, hard rock, and the resistant slivers of the regulations case. She had been well taught how to make fire, in survival drill: but she'd tried every means, patient or violent, and failed, over and over again, to strike a spark. It was hopeless.

The red gloom of her day returned. The glow came from a section in the thick reddish glassy stuff, just above the door. Every 'morning', every 'evening', she had heard the hiss and the click as the light came on, as the light vanished. She remembered Underwall, and knew that there were bioluminous bulbs up there inside the wall. She just couldn't get at them.

She jumped up and snatched the lintel of the doorway, but as she'd so often discovered, she *couldn't* climb her walls. It was impossible to get any grip on the glassy intrusions. She let go with one hand, beat her fist once against the glowing section: fell and lay winded, hugging her ribs and sobbing angrily. The phage climbed over her. It squirmed up the door, and oozed to and fro over the thick red glass. 'You can't eat your way through *that*,' snarled Bibi, jealous of its prowess. 'It's solid glass. You'll die first.'

She watched it. She pressed her raw knuckles to her temples, she covered her face, she rocked on her heels, muttering furiously, sickened by hope: she crawled away to lie on the bed with her back turned. When the hand's footsteps came, she didn't stir. Misery had buried her mind again. She knew that she *would* climb through that black hole, nothing would stop her, but without light she'd have no chance of surviving what lay beyond. Dirt pushed the chamber pot over to the hatch, and joined her mother on the bed. When the day came the little girl retrieved the empty pot; and their meal.

The phage worked for a long time, poetic time, aeons.

Bibi woke with the taste of blood on her lips, and an awareness of great change. Dirt was patting at her face. The child's tiny hands and feet were dabbled in blood. The floor in front of the cell door was scattered with ground glass, and glass splinters; a trail of bloody slime reached across the floor. But the great change was the light. Beside Bibi lay a row of five glowing bulbs: like the kind she'd known in Underwall Manor, but a strange species, knotted and wizened, each about the size of the baby's fist.

'Light,' whispered Bibi.

Dirt repeated the word, carefully. *'Light.'*

The phage was curled up beside the treasure, smaller than Bibi had ever seen it. Its skin had grown hard, like a shell. Maybe it was dead.

The bulbs were reactive. She couldn't make the *click hiss* that turned them on and off, but they responded to touch, glowing bright in her closed fist, dimming to charcoal if she blew on them; or if she left them alone. She wriggled her head and one arm into the hole and peered down, a bulb in her fist. There were hand- and footholds in the wall of rock: marked by the glisten of the phage's slime. The sight of them gave her a feeling of intense unease, but she couldn't think about that now—

She dressed herself in the ragged uniform. She'd reserved part of the sacking: she used some strips to tie the baby to her breast. The rest made a kind of pouch into which she stuffed the spare light bulbs, the dead or comatose phage, and her tray. She needed the tray, because she was planning to drink sweet water from the tea bowl. The chamber pot struck her as a useless luxury. One end of the sacking rope knotted round a cusp of rock at the edge of the black gap, the other secure around her waist, she struggled and squirmed into the dark, headfirst. She righted herself with difficulty and let herself down, foothold to foothold. The drop was not great: three body-lengths or less, maybe roughly five metres. She stood on a flat surface, Dirt's little arms clinging frantically around her neck, held up a wizened bulb and examined the wall that she'd just descended, the skin over her spine prickling. Someone, something, had chipped out those holds, and the marks did not look ancient.

'*Someone has been here,*' she whispered.

She untied the rope from round her waist: and turned, holding up the light. She was not in a natural cavern. She stood in a narrow passage, a smooth wall facing her; only darkness overhead. The floor was paved. In one direction this outer passage quickly ended in a blank wall. In the other it seemed to continue. She crouched down, holding Dirt and shuddering at the awful truth. She had not escaped. She was still inside Fenmu Prison. The air was harsher than the air in her cell, and had a bitter tang in her throat. She listened, listened. Not a sound. No dripping water, nothing but her heartbeat, Dirt's heartbeat; and their mingled breath.

'Looks like we go this way,' she muttered.

She left the rope dangling and began to walk, a bulb in one fist and a fragment of stone clutched in the other. Prisoners who'd escaped from their cells but could not escape from the prison might prowl these lightless corridors. Lifers turned feral, preying on each other. *That's me,* she thought. *I shall join that company, and I won't be the weakest.* The passage ahead was blocked too. It looked as if there'd been a rockslip: the wall

225

to her left had been tilted, boulders lay heaped against it. The baby strapped to her breast was very quiet. She sat down again.

There was no water. The tiny sound that had haunted her for years had been a mirage, a persistent delusion. There was no way out. She wouldn't die in her cell. But to crawl into that heap of spoil until she was trapped, and die there of thirst ... Was that the hard-won victory?

A voice began to whisper in her mind.

If we dreamt the same thing every night, it would affect us as much as the objects we see every day. And if an artisan were sure to dream every night, for twelve hours' duration, that he was a king, I believe he would be almost as happy as a king who should dream every night for twelve hours that he was an artisan ... If we were to dream every night that we were pursued by enemies and harassed by these painful phantoms, or that we passed every day in different occupations, as in making a voyage, we should suffer almost as much as if it were real, and should fear to sleep, as we fear to wake when we dread in fact to enter on such mishaps ...

The words were like poetry, full of strange expressions: but they spoke to her misery, with a dispassionate, rational consolation. She leaned against the rock and listened with her eyes closed, convinced that this voice was her own, that Dirtbag was muttering again: but much more pleasantly, more sensibly than usual. Dirt didn't make a sound.

But since dreams are all different, and each single one is diversified, what is seen in them affects us much less than what we see when we wake, because of its continuity ...

That is not my voice, thought Bibi. *My mouth is not moving. I feel I know that voice, but it is not mine.* Struck by revelation, she jumped up and began to tap with her rock fragment against the wall to her right. It was hollow. Of course it was hollow: it was the wall of a cell. She was still in Fenmu Prison, she'd just dropped a level below her own, and someone was speaking in there. Immense hope flooded through her. *Another prisoner.* Another banished criminal, someone of Bibi's own kind, someone who didn't click and flute, who *spoke*. Oh, but what crime had they committed to be sent here, abandoned, thousands of light years from home? To be buried alive on this terrible charnel moon? What kind of monster could have earned that—? The chanting had broken off when Bibi started tapping. She listened, listened, feeling scared: hiding the light bulb behind her back.

An innocent like me, she thought, setting her teeth. *The wicked are never punished ...* Suddenly, shockingly, she was tapping on a flimsy barrier that gave way, and fell apart as she grabbed at it, like the quarantine film in Francois's rooms in the Great House. She held up her bulb. She was looking, as if through a window, into a different cell, and though it surely should be prison 'night' by now, there was a soft flicker of light inside.

'Do come in,' said the prisoner, her fellow prisoner. 'You're very welcome, my friend: whoever you are.'

Bibi wriggled through the rent she'd made. It had sharp edges. She stood on the floor, the tiny girl's arms tight around her neck, and stared around, dumbstruck. She was in a cell like her own in size and shape, but otherwise so different it was like stepping into a fairy tale. The rock floor was covered in mats of woven gold, the walls hung with patterned fabric (one of these hangings lay tumbled at Bibi's feet). The light came from a bowl-shaped lamp that stood on the floor in the midst, giving off a faint scent of perfumed oil. Beside it lay a sheaf of paper, an inkstone, and brushes on a little stand. A withered old woman, shrunken and half-bald, sat on her heels by this workplace, her prison uniform hanging loose on her sunken shoulders, a stringy thread of white hair coiled on her nape. She beamed at the visitor serenely, showing the few teeth left in her head.

Whatever else had changed, the eyes were unmistakable.

It was Lady Nef.

PART THREE

XXXV

Bibi knelt, facing her mistress: bewildered as the little girl saved from a massacre, in Cymru, long ago. The baby wriggled around and faced Nef too. Mother and child stared, as if they'd forgotten how to speak.

'So you survived, Bibi,' said Lady Nef. 'I thought you might have done, from hints I picked up in my first detention, after the Myots had put me back together. For which I did not thank them, I'm afraid!'

She looked into Bibi's eyes, and touched the young woman's hands, her skin, her hair, with a fascination Bibi would not fully understand for a long time. 'The Myots are the experts,' she murmured, and offered her hand to the swaddled baby – who grasped the old woman's bony finger with the confidence of a newborn: although clearly she was far from newborn.

'And who is this? Is this the prince's child? It hardly seems possible, but time runs differently for Sigurtians ... Another thought I had, those last few days, before the end, was that *you* were pregnant, my dear.'

'No,' croaked Bibi, her own voice seeming to rise from the bottom of a chasm: miles deep, years deep, aeons deep. 'I had a child by S'n'l't"tz, a son, but the Myots kept him. When he was old enough they sent me here. I was raped the night I arrived, then I had her.'

'Ah, my poor girl ... What is the baby's name? Do you know your name, child? Will you tell me?'

'Dirt!' cried the infant, proudly. 'I am Dirt!'

Bibi had done a lot of crying, through the uncounted days and nights of her term in solitary, but her howls had been dry as bone, as far as she could remember. Suddenly, her eyes filled with stinging, painful tears – 'I c-called her that. I am the Dirtbag, she came out of me, she is *Dirt*.'

Lady Nef considered, and at last nodded in approval. 'It's a good name, Bibi. By chance, or whatever you care to call it, you have named your little girl "Earth", after our own planet, her ancestral home. If you don't mind, I shall call her *Di*, which is shorter, and has the same meaning in Chinese.'

The child was staring around her, hungrily. 'Perhaps you'd like to get down, little girl?' suggested Nef. 'Allow her to explore my domain, Bibi; and we can talk. You could tell me *how on Earth*, or on Fenmu, I should say, you got hold of the light bulb? The only light I have had for my nights, and my expeditions, is my miserable lamp: fuelled by the oil that can be extracted, with *infinite* pains, from our daily porridge—'

Bibi unknotted the straps, the naked child clambered out of her arms, and Bibi was shamed again. The phage had kept them both clean, but it had never crossed her mind to *dress* the Dirt-baby. 'She doesn't grow,' she muttered, hiding hot cheeks with her palms. 'She's, I don't know how old: she can walk and talk, she eats my food and she still nurses. But she doesn't grow. I think there's something wrong.'

'Hm. Yet she seems healthy, and well formed.' Lady Nef looked the tiny girl up and down, and offered no further judgement yet. 'Off you go, little Di. You may touch things, see what you can find to do. And the bulbs?' Nef peered covetously at Bibi's pouch, revealed now the baby had left her nest. 'Do I see you have *more* of them?'

'They're from behind the concrete glass, above my door.'

Nef's eyes gleamed. '*Really?* That's an extraordinary feat! How did you break the glass? What did you use, how long did it take?'

'I didn't do it. My ... I don't know what to call it.' She showed Lady Nef the phage, tightly curled up on itself, like a bug in a hardened shell. 'This. It was, it came out from me, when D-Di was born. It's alive, it cleans us. I don't know what it is. Maybe something the Myots put inside me, when I was pregnant before?'

'It's possible,' murmured Nef. 'But I don't think so. Well, it seems to be sleeping. We'll know more when it wakes up—'

'I think it's dead. It's been like that since it chewed through the glass.'

'It doesn't look dead to me. More likely healing itself; but we shall see.'

Di had picked up one of Lady Nef's brushes and was testing the tip with her moist tongue. Absorbed, she stroked the brush against her hand, and studied the mark she had made—

The cell looked like something in a fairy tale, but it was a prison cell, buried deep in the pitiless rock of the Fallen Moon, the place of horror Speranza had named The Grave. The shock of finding Lady Nef, finding her *alive*, worked in Bibi like a powerful drug, almost a corrosive joy. She and her mistress were innocent. Why had they suffered this fate? The truth, which Bibi had known since she read that indictment in the Prison Governor's office, burst from her like a bolt of annealing flame: restoring her to herself, restoring the person she had been – and horrifying her with its cruelty.

'*He* put you here! He betrayed you!'

Lady Nef nodded, at peace with something she'd known for a long time: ah, for how long? Only the first betrayal really hurts, the rest are expected. 'Of course he did, Bibi. I cannot make out the details: but if he had to denounce me, if that was the way out, of course he took it. He survives, my Swimmer. I benefited from that talent for a long time, you know, so I can hardly take the high moral ground now—'

'It was his fault. *He* killed Francois, and Honesty, and everyone who died, not the Myots. Our whole disaster was because of him!'

'*No*,' said Lady Nef, sharply and firmly, raising a hand. 'Bibi, stop that. You will injure yourself to no purpose. We will talk over what happened, and speak our bitterness, later: another time. Not yet.'

Bibi's cheeks were burning again. A rush of self-disgust had come after the anger. Appalling memories sprang up, how far she'd fallen: how she'd failed the test of Fenmu, failed by any standard to remain human. She saw Grade Five Social Practice Officer Bibi, snarling and yammering. Naked and filthy, grunting and giving birth, crawling away from the mess—

'I have been mad!' she wailed. 'Lady Nef, I have been *mad*! For years. I have been insane, disgusting, worse than a brute!'

'Me too,' said Lady Nef. She took Bibi's hands, in a grim, steady grip. 'I was mad too, Bibi, for *years*. I contemplated terrible things, despair shook me to my foundations. But it passed, and now we have found each other, so let's forget all that. How glad I am to see you. How happy we are going to be.'

233

XXXVI

They talked through the night, in the glow of Bibi's stolen light bulb, while the little girl slept: the young woman and the crone feasting on words, their eyes shining, their cheeks flushing, drunk on the sight of another human face, the mere sound of a human voice. Nef dismissed her own adventures, but she insisted on hearing every detail of Bibi's purdah in Black Wing, her lost years. How she'd been convinced she was going to be murdered, how she'd come to Fenmu. How she'd recovered from her madness, and made up her mind to escape. Bibi was startled to find how much came back to her. It was as if her mind had been dormant, never lost, only needing another person—

When the light above Lady Nef's door hissed and clicked, and the red glow propagated through the glass, Bibi went to fetch her daily meal. The hand mustn't know that anything had changed, and she couldn't be a burden on her mistress. Her old cell horrified her: it stank of despair, degradation, soul-eating loneliness. She snatched up her mattress and bundled it under her arm; grabbed her food, and the clean chamber pot; and fled.

'The right decision,' said Lady Nef when Bibi returned, uncertain of her welcome, with all her worldly goods. 'The lifer cells, if not much else, are generously proportioned. There's plenty of room for three. Now, if we are to keep house together, I must show you how things are done.'

The golden mats were woven from serpent bristle, recovered from old mattresses. The hangings were mattress-sacking, fixed to the walls with a carapace-porridge glue. To make paper Nef teased fibres out of the same sacking: beat them smooth, soaked them in tea, layered them together in sheets; dried and beat the sheets again. Her lamp was a broken cusp of food bowl, ground to translucence. Her ink was blood tea, partly dried, mixed to a paste with a friable black mineral, and shaped into sticks—

'As you'll observe, Bibi,' she said, 'the grinder and the black mineral are not native to my cell. Like you I have been exploring, and occasionally I have brought back treasure. I have a nub of metallic ore, from which I can strike a light; and there's another stone, a kind of quartz – I believe it's colonised by a microbe tolerant of complete darkness – that gives a scented powder when ground, which I add to my lamp oil.'

To make the oil she reserved the shards of tooth-cracking chitin that appeared in their porridge. When she had enough she pressed them between two flat stones, one of which she had pierced: she bound the press tightly, and increased the extraction by means of a screw, chipped and smoothed from the spine of the case that had held her lifer regulations. Ink, paper and light were vital to the project of her leisure hours: a history of Fenmu Prison, which might throw startling new light on the history of Sigurt's World itself.

'I draft in memory as I work on my chores,' she explained, 'and allow myself an hour or so of calligraphy, after Evening Dance, whenever I have lamp oil. Your bulbs will make a wonderful change . . . The brushes are my own hair, trimmed with my teeth, and bound to slivers of document-case. I use serpent bristle for the coarser stroke I've used to decorate the hangings.'

Each process had its place. The oil press, dripping infinitely slowly into another cusp of broken bowl, was relegated to a corner. The mat-weaving, in abeyance at present, had a corral against the wall, marked with ink, from whence no untidy fragment of bristle was allowed to escape. The paper factory stood by a natural depression in the floor, stained red by the soaking process. The ink mineral, scent stone and other stone tools were laid out in a hollow under the plinth that formed Lady Nef's bed . . .

Bibi felt that she was back in Kirgiz, astonishingly honoured, being shown the wonders of the Inner House by Lady Nef herself: but a frightening unease struggled with this welcome ghost. They returned to Lady Nef's study, the spot in the middle of the room where she wrote her history: and then Bibi knew why she was scared. She was aboard the *Rajath* again. Nothing was real. Everything was made of symbols, and *there was a rift in the wall*. The fallen hanging, that Lady Nef had replaced, shivered wickedly. From behind the magic characters chaos came creeping in—

'I wonder how long they'll last.' Nef was examining one of the light bulbs. 'I suspect the air in the lighting system channels is unfiltered. If these bulbs are native to Fenmu, which may well be the case, they won't like our scrubbed atmosphere. We'll keep them in the outer passage when not in use: that should help.'

'We must block the hole!'

'I wonder, could you *spare* one of them? I would love to dissect one, and make an accurate drawing ... What's that, Bibi? What should we block?'

'The hole in your wall!'

Little Di had been copying the character *Di*, which Nef had drawn for her. She'd spoiled half the paper, but she'd managed it at last. Bursting with pride and joy, she pushed her triumph under Bibi's nose.

Bibi shrugged the baby off, without a glance—

Lady Nef noted Bibi's coldness towards the child, but she wasn't too concerned. *Someone* had fed Di, and cared for her; and the infant's cheerful confidence was evidence of a hidden bond. Bibi could not bear to express her affection directly: but this little girl, child of rape, knew she was loved.

'There's something out there, Lady Nef. I think there are prisoners who broke out of the cells, and went feral when they found they were still in prison. Something with feet and hands had climbed the wall I climbed down. There were footholds and handholds, they'd been chipped out, they weren't natural, and they were quite new!'

'Ah.' Nef set down the bulb, and sighed. 'I'm afraid the feral prisoner was me, Bibi. I "broke out" long ago. Before your time here. I had no light, but I'd taught myself to echolocate, a little, while I was in detention – a skill you and the child must learn, by the way – so I wasn't afraid of falling into an abyss. I found what you found: the outer passage, sealed at one end, blocked at the other. Near the sealed end I felt the phantom of a breath of moving air, from overhead. I chipped those holds: it was my occupation for quite a while, and then I climbed: I was much stronger then. I found a crack, and knew the wall was thin, but by testing the echoes I discovered that the space beyond was another cell. So I gave up without breaking through.'

'So there's no way out,' said Bibi, softly.

'There are no feral prisoners.' Lady Nef paused to admire the shaky *Di*. 'That's *very* good, child. Now, see how you get on with these two: 公主. They make your mother's name, in Chinese ... There is no need to block the hole. On the contrary, we'll have to keep it open, because it will seal itself. You'll have to go back to your cell daily: I don't think we should let the prison staff know of our new arrangement. And since we're numinal bipeds—' Nef smiled, and the gently mocking courtesy of a society lady shone through the crone's mask. 'I've no doubt we'll get tired of each other sometimes.'

She sat back on her heels and looked up at her 'ceiling', which was one mass of glossy, murky red. 'The concrete glass, as you call it, is programmed to mend breaks in the walls. It flings out strands of molecules, like spider thread, and builds them into a lattice. The barrier becomes glassy and thickens over time: but it's not an effective way of preventing break-outs. I think it's a very ancient building material, dating from before Fenmu was a prison – telling us, by the way, that the Fenmu atmosphere has been noxious, but not acutely poisonous, to the local numinal bipeds for a long time.

'Perhaps one could say that the glass has "gone feral", having been abandoned for aeons. It's almost enough to make one entertain a belief in the Strong Diaspora, isn't it? But it's easy to make absurd mistakes about the age of alien artefacts. There were equally sophisticated materials in use on Earth, five hundred years ago: which hardly takes us back to the dawn of time.'

She has been talking to herself for years, thought Bibi. *While I was screaming through my madness, Lady Nef was here, just a few tens of metres away: composing her history, pondering on archaeology—*

'But I was saying ... There's no one out there. Very few lifers have been housed in this block since the Old Wing, as it's called, was abandoned after a rockfall. The others are accounted for, you and I are the last: and there is no common wall between the Old Wing and the modern installation. I have questioned P'p"st, indeed, you could say I have plumbed the depths of his mind. I believe I know all that he knows about this place: and he's been in service for over a hundred and fifty of our standard years – including his breaks for recreational coma, a very important item for the Fenmu staff.'

'Who is *P'p"st*?'

'Our guard. He's almost a friend of mine by now, and has been generous in many ways. You must have met.'

'Once. I think I frightened him.'

'I'm sure you did! I have heard rumours of your career, Bibi. I didn't dare to hope that my ferocious alien neighbour was you – but I wondered.

No way out, thought Bibi. The lost years formed up behind her; a different darkness took shape ahead, shot through with gleams of comfort. She would be serving Lady Nef. What else had she ever planned?

'How long have we been in here?' she asked, feeling the words drop like stones. 'I have never kept a count of days.'

'I have,' sighed Nef. 'Several times. I found one of my attempts, recently, on the wall over there.' She pointed to the corner where the oil press lurked. 'The longest stretch I managed, as far as I know, was just under three years. But it was so dreary, making the marks. There always came a day when I didn't want to do it: when I could see no reason. I *think* I have been on Fenmu, in this cell, for around fourteen or fifteen years, Bibi, and I *think* I was brought here just a few months after our last parting. But I cannot be sure, of course I cannot be sure.'

Like stones onto a grave.

For life is a dream, but a little less inconstant.

The little girl worked carefully with her brush, oblivious.

'What were you reciting, Lady Nef?' asked Bibi. 'When I came through the wall, last night? It was like poetry. I thought the voice was in my mind: but I sat down and listened—'

'That was a passage from Pascal's *Pensées*,' said Nef, after a moment's thought. 'Rendered into English, I'm afraid. In spite of Francois, I have no Ancient French on my skillcard! It's my recreational reading at the moment. Would you like to hear more?'

'Yes, I would.'

'Good. I enjoy reading aloud. Like calligraphy, it gives one a deeper engagement with the text. But I intend to give you a copy of my library: so you needn't listen to my croaking old voice just for politeness. We'll start with the ancients, and the histories—'

'I can't take a copy of your library, mistress,' Bibi pointed out, embarrassed to have noticed this slip. 'I've nothing to download it onto. I have no eye soc' and I'm not augmented.'

'Nor am I, Bibi: except that all Seniors have significantly increased neural plasticity. Otherwise we'd spend the latter phase of our long lives as mumbling idiots.' Lady Nef looked into Bibi's face: once more assessing something remarkable she found there. 'We shall see.'

XXXVII

Every morning, Bibi went to do her duty by the hand, breaking through the film of glass-fibre that had formed overnight, over the gap in this wall, and in the wall above. She learned to wrap her own hands in her ragged sleeves, to protect them from tiny, vicious splinters. Then they ate together, but not until Lady Nef had searched both bowls of porridge for chitin. Some of the blood tea was preserved for household industries. Pollen bread was put aside for a lunch or supper treat. Then it was Morning Drill, including the echolocation game; then it was school time. Di learned her characters. Bibi had to practise mental exercises, and memorise code strings: apparently in preparation for the feat of copying Lady Nef's library into her memory (a project Bibi still believed a fantasy). At lunchtime, whether or not there was any lunch, they had a nap.

Afternoons were devoted to the household industries. Once she'd trained her apprentices, Bibi and Di worked while Lady Nef read to them from the *Pensées*; or else she'd add a few sentences to her history. In the hour before lights out, the household gathered for Evening Dance.

Nef didn't seem afraid of the hand, but she paid it no more attention than if it had been a mechanical process, like the light and darkness. At random intervals, when it had done its business it would rap on the door. A voice would click, faintly, '*All right in there?*' (This had never happened to Bibi.) Nef would click in reply, '*All right, thank you,*' – and the intrusion would be over.

My poor mistress is not mad, thought Bibi. *But she's not sane either. She's created a starved, pitiful version of our life in the Great House to fill this emptiness, and protect her from reality. And I'll join her in her delusions, why not? What is the use of mental agony, what does it achieve? Why not use the trapped power of your mind to convince yourself that all is well? What if the people who hurt you, who betrayed you, who buried you alive, could see into this cell? Would you want them to see you reduced to a naked, filthy lunatic, would you want them to see you howling in despair? So be happy, live in a dreamworld, if that's the only defiance possible.*

Later, she revised her opinion. Nef was not deluding herself, she was keeping hope alive. A hope that would never be fulfilled, but which had become an end in itself.

Later still, she changed her mind again.

Sometimes for days, for measureless time, they hardly spoke aloud, except for Lady Nef's readings. The Common Tongue was all they needed, as they passed and repassed each other in their treasured, unvarying round. The Aleutian respect for Silence drew a veil over the jagged words that Bibi occasionally heard, in her mind, in a voice she hardly recognised as Nef's. She knew that Nef must sometimes hear her screaming, too. They never mentioned this phenomenon. The little girl took to Silence as if it were her mother tongue, and one day Bibi had the shock of hearing a tiny voice, whispering in her head. *Mymi ... Mummy ...*

Bibi, who was beating paper, whipped her head around as if she'd been stung. The child beamed at her, and returned to her characters: brush poised, one tiny hand pushing back her black hair, in a curiously grown-up gesture, the inert phage safely tucked between her feet. Her strange twin was still her favourite toy. Where had Dirt-baby found that word? She had not. It was Bibi who had given her child's loving glance the shape of *mother*.

Di, although she'd never been exposed to Sigurtian language, soon beat both the grown-ups hollow at echolocation. Securely blindfold, she ran around clicking softly, often at a pitch that neither Bibi nor Lady Nef could hear: fearless, unerring, avoiding obstacles, darting straight for 'hidden' treasures (a writing brush, a knot of sacking). Nef wanted to try her skill in the outer passage, but Bibi was fiercely against this idea. One night, after Di was asleep, she woke Lady Nef and begged her to stop the lessons.

'She can't come to any harm inside the cell, Bibi.'

'I don't want her to be like *them*,' she whispered. 'If I could, I'd rip her rapist bat-freak father out of her with my bare hands—'

She reached for the light bulb, which they kept between their beds, and coaxed it to a glow. Dirt-baby lay beside her, hugging the phage; occupying as little of her mother's mattress as possible. She was no longer naked. Nef had made a crude dress for her, sacrificing a piece of one of the wall hangings, with a hole cut for her head, and a sacking belt. She looked even more like an eerie, skeletal toy, clumsily dressed by a child. Bibi's feelings choked her: love and revulsion, barbed hooks in her heart.

You are not *my life, Dirt-baby. This is not a life. I don't want to have emotions. I am dead.*

'You'd be wasting your time,' mumbled Lady Nef, from her mattress up on the rock plinth. 'One has only to look at her to see that she's no hybrid. I think she has no Sigurtian element in her Heritance Molecules at all.'

Bibi set her teeth. 'Then what *is* she? Was I not raped?'

'I believe she may be what is known as a haploid dwarf. She has only half the genetic material she should have, and it is yours. That would explain why she's so small, but without any disproportion.' The old lady turned over impatiently. 'What does it matter? She's just as quick at reading and writing. And if you wish to hate her parentage, you have as much grievance against the Blue as you do against a miserable sot of a prison guard. Now, please, let us sleep. I sleep too little; and I enjoy sleeping very much.'

The *Pensées* gave way to von Clausewitz *On War*, and then Jane Austen. The first of the light bulbs died, collapsing suddenly into a fine, grey powder. Oil production had increased – they seemed to be getting more chitin. Lady Nef decided they should conserve the rest, out in the passageway.

Sometimes Nef talked, after lights out; if they'd managed to save a little tea to moisten their mouths. General Yu's treachery was never mentioned, but the Mission was discussed, in the forbearance of hindsight. 'We were absurdly mistaken about the Myots, who are by no means poor relations, or a "Developing Nation"! Did Neuendan intend to deceive us? On the whole, I think not, although one might accuse them of deceiving themselves ... But the older I get, the more I realise how difficult it is to hear what *anyone* tells us, through the barrage of interference from our blind assumptions, our self-obsession ... I look back on my personal relationships, and years later I grasp the meaning of a word unspoken, a turn of phrase, an inexplicable little grimace. Yet the truth was always there. *Ars longa, vita brevis.* How long it takes to learn to be a numinal biped! But politics, even Hegemony politics, move at a sharper pace.

'We knew before we arrived that the Myots were obsessed with Strong Diaspora. The belief we heard of from Nikty, *the Fall*, is prevalent throughout the Crater-States, stronger than the legend of "The Flood" in Eurasia at home: the Sigurtians regard themselves as a fallen race. It's a metaphor known to other numinal bipeds, perhaps a "symptom" of consciousness itself: one day you will read the great Sigurt's work on the subject. The Myots tend to Fundamentalism, as we might call it. They weren't the ones who objected, when Speranza suggested we call the planet *Diyu*. On some level they like the idea that they live in hell—'

'They drink blood,' whispered Bibi.

Nef laughed. 'They're not alone! Cannibalism is a family trait, Bibi. We Blues slaughtered the whales and ate them, broiled. We extirpated the elephant, and the great apes, when *we knew* that they could think and feel. We're unusual in that we haven't literally fed off our own poor, not in modern history, not on an industrial scale. But we *consume* them: we are doing it still. No, no. The numinal bipeds of Sigurt's World are no more vicious than the rest of us. What happened to the Mission was an accident: but if we had listened, if we had understood that the Myot Royals *wanted our blood* to add to their own, as their route to a higher rank, the Mission would have been handled very differently.'

Lady Nef sighed in the darkness.

I would not have been here, Bibi realised. *Or I'd have been sterilised before we left, it probably isn't illegal on Speranza: and I wouldn't have minded. Mahmood and I were never going to have children.*

'Still, all was not lost. As I told my Swimmer when things started to get difficult, we must keep our heads and remember: Speranza Code means something. The system has intuitions, and there is no such thing as eternal torment in the Chinese hell. Everybody gets out alive, from *Diyu*.'

But we are not getting out, thought Bibi. *Only he lives.*

'Personally, I'm more and more convinced,' continued Lady Nef, placidly, 'that the Sigurtian "Fall" was historical. I believe they "fell" from Fenmu, so long ago that when they returned here in their Conventional Space Age, they found few traces of previous occupation; and ignored them. Which presents us with the conclusion that this large satellite must once have been much more congenial to life – raising the possibility that the Sigurtians engineered their own "fall", through overuse of resources. However, before we leap to that conclusion we must remember the "winter" phenomenon, and that natural cataclysm is also a vital concept in Sigurtian thought ...

'It's a shame we have no vermin. When I was alone I dearly wished I had fleas or lice. I could have befriended them, and taken an interest in their doings. But it's a curious fact that numinal bipeds have few parasites, except on the Blue, which teems with them. (The Aleutian "wandering cells" are something completely different!) That's very telling.'

She spoke often of the Buonarotti Device, that fatally flawed means of opening up the 'empire to be' of numinal intelligence ... The feats of the first Prospectors, often condemned criminals: a naked soul, the informational self, swinging out into the abyss on a string of bare coordinates. Most of them never heard of again. The perilous 'journey' through the Sum of All Possible States. The fearsome statistics of loss. No communication except by courier. Commerce prohibitively expensive, mass transport inconceivable—

'The Blue Planet gave interstellar contact to the world, Bibi, but *even now* nobody really knows what to do with it. On Earth itself the Buonarotti transit is regarded as magic: an evil invention, breaking the sacred barrier between matter and mind, bound to destroy us all. And I'm not talking about the people, I'm talking about Heads of State, Powers That Be—'

Bibi thought of the fortune-tellers of Gagarin, with their branded faces. 'It breaks the barrier, but it's *not* evil. It's dangerous, and, and spooky when you try to think about what's happening, but how can it be evil?'

Lady Nef chuckled. 'Aha, a convert! They say every Blue who makes the crossing to Speranza is instantly a convert to the Buonarotti future, which would seem to be a self-fulfilling prophecy, but one takes the point. Don't be complacent, Bibi. The Buonarotti Device is not mere technology. When time and space are once annihilated, who knows what else goes with them? Do you know, there is a version of Strong Theory, called Paradoxical Strong, that says *we, ourselves,* are the "Ancient Blue Hominids"? We transit into our own far future. The numinal bipeds we have found are our distant descendants, differently adapted to our different landfalls.'

Bibi struggled. 'Surely that's impossible?'

'Is impossibility an obstacle? Francois, you know, who viewed the "Theory" with distaste, had a weakness for "Paradoxical Strong". Naturally, in his eyes the Aleutians represent the final, perfected model of the numinal biped: ungendered, immortal, their superlative technology subsumed into the cells of their bodies—'

They laughed, remembering Francois's vanity, but Bibi was puzzled by Nef's tone. 'But you're not serious? It's a joke, isn't it?'

'Not at all, Bibi: just the normal antics of high science. Some of the greatest minds in the Hegemony go further, and say the simultaneity *changed* when the Device was first used. In that instant everything was recreated, a new universe sprang into being, and everything we think we know of what went before is an artefact of the shift.'

Bibi struggled, determined to refute this sophistry, which made her head spin. 'What about the Aleutians? They existed before the transit, they crossed the galaxy without it. *They* discovered *us*.'

Nef turned on her mattress, a comfortable rustling over Bibi's head.

'Apparently so. However, Bibi, it was a close thing ... All sources agree that a strange, solitary genius called Peenemunde Buonarotti had built and tested her device before the Aleutians made themselves known. The original records are lost, we have no dates. Who knows exactly *when* she first lay down in the embrace of her magic couch, and wished for company?'

The prison cell whirled away. Points of light glittered in a fathomless void, where time ran backwards and forwards at will, and thought itself became one with the stars, stretching into immensity, spinning into logic-defying webs and skeins. Bibi lay gazing into her own mind, mysteriously expanded by the knowledge Nef was giving her: with such a sense of space and freedom she felt she could leap from her sacking bed, and the walls would be gone, *everything* would be gone—

'I must teach you how to install 4-Space coordinates in memory,' remarked the cracked old voice, with its beloved, slightly archaic diction: the thread that would always lead Bibi home. 'We'll start on that as soon as we've finished copying the library.'

Bibi was so much in thrall to the power of Nef's imagination that she lay awake, on nights when they didn't talk, waiting for something to happen in her brain: for the strings of symbols she'd memorised to blossom into the works of Shakespeare, or Li Xifeng's Commentaries.

They never did. '4-Space coordinates' was better. Nothing *happened*, but it was fascinating, as she got the code by heart, to contemplate the patterns it made. Like a section of a kaleidoscope, contained yet limitless, ever-changing in her mind's eye.

One night, after Evening Dance, Bibi and Di were invited to join the director on her plinth. 'Come, sit with me,' she commanded. 'You did that very well.' Two skeletons climbed up to join the third, glowing with pride. 'As your reward, I shall tell you my political history.'

She spoke frankly of the poverty of the Republic of Earth, except for the élite. The captivity of the masses, their mayfly lives: the hidden cost in lost children. The unremitting surveillance, the savage punishments. How far the Republic had fallen from the Human Renaissance, the light that failed—

'We had been colonised for three hundred years, our own culture insolently sold back to us, wrapped in Aleutian technology. Our fratricidal struggle – I mean the Gender Wars – was behind us. It was inconceivable to us, young activists, that the mummified Empire could be exhumed: though of course that's exactly what happened. *We* took our inspiration from a time of dreams, the year of seventeen eighty-nine, Christian Era. The Spirit of Eighty-Nine, when the *Illuminées* of the Great Nation, men and women "enlightened" by reason and science, truly believed they could build a better world—'

'I didn't know you hated the Aleutians, Lady Nef.'

'Did I hate them? I had an Aleutian lover. I have lived, in many ways, an Aleutian life ... Bibi, child, you will never get on with modern cosmology if you can't accept that paradox is essential to our being. But I was speaking of the Renaissance, my flowering time.

'*Liberté, Egalité, Amitié ...*' Bony hands flickered in the lamplight; Nef counted off the ancient words. '*Liberté*, the liberty of the individual. *Egalité*, the concept of equality, which checks and balances the first term. We can only be as free as our neighbours, and our "freedom" must never be at the cost of theirs. The last of the triad vexed us. *Fraternité* was impossible for the Reformers, so we exchanged Brotherhood for Friendship, in the Old French. But *Amitié* resists translation, it is not an English concept; and where there are friends there are enemies, whereas we wanted universality. I was one of those who favoured *Agape*: thrown out as too intellectual. *Affection* I always thought a weak compromise—

'How it all comes back. Reformers and Traditionalists, fresh from centuries of mutual hatred and scrapping over a comma: it was so annoying, we always had to give way because *they* were the good guys—'

'Did you believe that?' Bibi wondered: more cautious this time.

'I did, and I do,' said the great Traditionalist Lady. 'I believe that the Reformers are right, and that they must always be defeated, because in power they are monsters. It's a difficult position, but one learns to put up with it.'

Loyalty, honour, obligation ... Little Di whimpered in her sleep, and pressed closer to the old lady: who stroked her hair, smiling down at the last of her foundlings. *I was wrong*, thought Bibi. *You haven't taught yourself to be content in this cell as an act of defiance. You are truly at peace, and it's your greatest victory. The Traditionalist Lady, the General's Wife, was the shadow. I've been privileged to know you, mischievous, gentle scholar, as you might have been. The real Nef, buried alive for so long—*

'Ah, my people,' sighed Nef, tugging at her skinny braid, and grinning with her few teeth. 'Those Traditionalists! They must win, they always win. And after each crushing triumph, their territory is a little smaller.'

XXXVIII

Towards the end of *Persuasion*, Lady Nef announced that Di would have a birthday, a ceremonial occasion, a whole holiday from normal routine. 'We shall say you are seven: it's known as the age of reason, and though you are very young, you will be given your Grade Seven rank.'

'But *Anne*—!' protested Di, wide-eyed in panic.

'On her birthday a good girl gives the orders. You won't miss Anne Elliot's adventures. We'll have *Persuasion* in the afternoon, in the usual way. In the evening, to celebrate your junior majority, I shall begin to read Proust. You are young, but a sensitive, intelligent seven-year-old is old enough to profit from the *Combray* chapters.'

Overwhelmed, Di grabbed the phage and ran around, hugging it in a strangling grip. A new dress was in secret preparation. The presents were almost ready. 'How are we going to arrange special food?' murmured Bibi.

'Simple. The next time we have pollen bread, that will be her day.'

They laughed. Di settled by the inkstone, looking over her morning's lesson. She might be seven, possibly: she was no bigger than a toddler.

'Could she be treated? Could she be made normal? If, if we weren't in here?'

'Maybe she could be treated,' said Nef. 'You'd have to get her to Speranza: before she reaches puberty would be best. But what is *normal*? The choice should be hers, not yours.'

The phage, which had woken gradually during *On War*, came crawling back to them, and oozed onto Bibi's knees. As soon as she saw the thing in its active state, Lady Nef had known what it was: and Bibi's eyes had been opened too. Bibi must have ingested one of Francois's "wandering cells" – usually a harmless accident – in the close quarters of the siege. It must have been stimulated into migrating to her womb, by whatever the Myots did to her, and it had grown there with the haploid pregnancy.

It seemed much attached to its human twin, and to Bibi. It shrank from Lady Nef in a way that made Bibi feel as if she'd stolen something. This keepsake should not be hers. But Nef was philosophical, and mocking. 'It's the fate of old, discarded lovers,' she said. 'They make each other uncomfortable. Perhaps in time it will forget, and we can be friends.'

On the birthday, Lady Nef didn't get up. She complained she'd had a bad night, creeping to the chamber pot time and again, without any results. She was still lying down, curled up like a shrivelled old leaf, when Bibi came back from the cell above, with a second piece of pollen bread for the feast. Her hands and feet were cold. Bibi pulled down a hanging to wrap around Nef's shrunken shoulders, and tucked her own mattress over her mistress, like a straw-filled quilt. Nef directed the celebrations from her bed, and everything went well. The Grade Seven was awarded. The new dress, inked in a pattern of stars, was declared a perfect fit. The ingenious necklace of paper flowers, made by Lady Nef, the new brushes made from Bibi's hair, the new stick of ink, were received with awe. At bedtime they lit the lamp, and sat together on Nef's bed. The child, blissfully exhausted, fell asleep between one word and another, as Lady Nef read aloud from the first pages of *In Search of Lost Time*.

'Bibi, I have to give you some serious advice.'

'Don't say I should take my mattress back. You need to keep warm, you have a chill. There are mats on the floor, I'll be fine.'

Lady Nef took Bibi's hand in her withered claws, fixing her with eyes like crumpled holes in a paper skull. 'No, this is *serious*. Listen to me. I know your mind, child, as you know mine. I know you are still brooding on the idea of revenging yourself, on those ... those who survived our disaster. You must let that passion go, Bibi, or it will ruin your life.'

'I'm not going to get the chance.' Bibi tried to laugh.

'Take my advice. You don't need to even the score on my account, I have done that myself. I've committed, and condoned, plenty of evil in my time. *You* have never yet been guilty of a wicked deed. Don't start.'

'You will always be my guide.'

Nef patted her hand. 'There, I'm a shameless old crone, employing emotional blackmail and I don't care. I've spoken, and I shall sleep easier. Please put out the light.'

Bibi piled the slippery mats together, and lay on her side. All her senses seemed more acute. The rock floor was very hard, the darkness very black, her mouth was sticky and parched. The phage mopped up the effluvia of their skin and sweat, but the smell of the chamber pot, which she often forgot for days, was intrusive tonight. *This fragile wonderland is dying*, she thought. The phage crept under her hair, and settled on her neck. She'd known for ever that Lady Nef had an escape plan. Sometimes she'd wondered, *If it's real, if there is a way out, what are we waiting for? For Di to get bigger and stronger? For me to be sane? For a rare event, that Nef knows about, that will give us our opportunity?* She'd never asked; Lady Nef had never spoken.

She'll get better. She's been poorly before.
She was doing Drill and dancing with us, not long ago (how long?).
It's nothing, just a chill.

XXXIX

Lady Nef stayed in bed. She had to be helped to use the chamber pot, showed no interest in food and hardly sipped her tea. Bibi formed desperate plans to grab the hand when it came through the hatch. To scream, if it rapped, that someone needed medical treatment. But it didn't rap, and she knew that Nef didn't want her to interfere, so she did nothing. One afternoon Nef woke from a doze, and looked around her slowly, wonderingly. The walls of the cell were almost bare. The floor was naked, except for the heap of mats, cracked, unravelling and no longer golden, where Bibi and the child now slept.

'Ah, it's nearly time. Even in Fenmu there are seasons, and one can detect, at the end of winter, the buds pushing on the bare twigs. Three years, and we've had our differences, but we never did get tired of each other.'

'We never had any differences,' protested Bibi. 'Never!'

'Nonsense. There were several periods when you were frosty with me. You'd better help me up, we have plans to make.'

Nef was expecting the lifer maintenance guard. Energised by this prospect, she seemed to make genuine recovery. She ordered her papers, hoarded food and tested Bibi's knowledge of the codes, so cheerful and active that Bibi was fooled into thinking she was really stronger. She was out of bed, making final revisions in her 'study', the day her intuition was proved correct. The child knew first, then Bibi and Nef. They heard the distant, uncanny sound of approaching footsteps: when it was not hand time.

'Go to your cell, Bibi,' said Nef. 'Quickly. He'll come to you first. He'll find you present for inspection, but too crazy to be approached. Di, you and your pet must go with your mother, and stay hidden in the outer passage.'

They obeyed.

Bibi's cell was ready. The glass dust had been swept into a corner, the bulbs had been replaced in the hollow section above the door. She wriggled through the membrane, pushing her mattress in front of her; and shoved a heap of rock fragments, prepared in advance, in front of the gap. If P'p"st made a thorough inspection, if he even took a good look around, they were lost. The guards might not care how Bibi had destroyed the glass, or why the forgotten lifers, having 'broken out', were still in their cells. But the prisoners would surely be moved, they'd be parted, a terrible thought.

She stood in front of the door, breathing hard, clutching her mattress. The footsteps approached, halted. She heard a grunt and a muttered sigh.

'Ah, this one. Poor thing, hope she's feeling better.'

The door ground open. The prongs of that long baton appeared. A fresh mattress was thrown in, and landed at her feet.

'You can keep the other one!'

The door slid shut, the steps moved on. Bibi dropped to the floor, squirmed through the hole, twisted around and shot down the wall. Di and the phage were waiting in the outer passage, crouched where the light from Lady Nef's cell welled through the last of the sacking hangings. Bibi grabbed Di and hustled her into deeper darkness, to the rockfall that marked the end of their first exploration. They squatted on their haunches, and listened. Lady Nef was talking to herself, too low for them to make out words: rehearsing sentences of her history, conversing with her dead. She sounded happy.

A grating shriek of concrete glass against glass—

'My dear P'p"st, how nice!' exclaimed Lady Nef, in Myot. 'Do fold down, I hope you have taken blood. And your family news is all good?'

'Not so bad, ma'am.' There was a heavy thump. 'There you are. All the dirty old mattresses you could wish for. Hangings for my Lady's chamber, paper for my Lady's memoirs.'

'You're very good.'

'They'd only get incinerated, so why not?' The Sigurtian heaved a gossipy sigh. 'Well, I'm afraid you'll soon lose your neighbour.'

'The fierce alien?'

'The same. Not so fierce this time. Not a peep out of her. I didn't go in, best not to disturb them when they're going into coma. Funny, I was sure you'd leave your food untouched before that one.'

'Perhaps I will, even yet. And when she "leaves her food untouched", she won't be disturbed?'

'Nah. We don't need the cell. She'll dry out in there for a few winters, it's more dignified than putting them straight in the incinerator.' There was a murmuring too low to follow, and then: 'So you think it won't be long?'

'Not long at all. Our last decline is mercifully brief; and it has begun.'

Bibi clutched her head in her hands, and shook with pain. When she could hear again, Lady Nef was saying, 'Is everything prepared?'

'All set. A send-off like a princess.'

'Could we go over it? I'd like to have the details in my mind. You know how old people love to think about their funerals.'

Bibi and the child listened, listened, lips parted, eyes wide, straining at darkness. At last the guard had satisfied Nef's curiosity. He clicked wordlessly: a trill of concern. 'Ma'am? I've tired you out, you're looking very peaky. Could I offer an arm? It'd be no trouble.'

'That's so kind, but no thank you.'

P'p"st stayed a while longer: as if, for politeness' sake, it was his duty to ignore an old friend's fatigue. News from Sigurt's World, Fenmu gossip, the miserly increase in coma allowance this winter. Finally they heard a faint scrabbling as he hopped to his feet and pattered to the door.

'May I say, ma'am, it's been a privilege. You've kept this cell lovely, and even when you were mad, you never offered violence. I'll see you soon, but you won't see me, so pardon the intrusion; and Grace be with you.'

Bibi tumbled back into the cell, blinded by tears—

'I could give you my blood! I never thought! I'm young, my blood will make you strong again. *See, Lady Nef, an arm is offered.*'

'That is not appropriate.'

'I won't leave you! I can't leave you!'

Lady Nef sat back on her heels beside the inkstone, a radiant smile transforming her withered face: casting a glamour, a fugitive veil of youth.

'What a true friend P'p"st has been! We have met only three times – or was it four? – but it was such a friendship. Do you know why it is so difficult to do good, Bibi? It's because the world, the universe, *being* itself, is almost as good as it can possibly be: we are struggling to add touches of perfection. So much that we take for evil – including nearly all our suffering – is simply natural process: not wicked at all. Happiness is made of moments, it belongs to the country of no duration. And one finds kindness everywhere.'

Bibi wiped her tears with the backs of her hands. The little girl watched them both, with grave anxiety. The phage, which had been clinging to Di's throat, slithered to the floor and approached Nef, for the first time, of its own accord. It touched her knee with its blind prow.

'Ha,' she said, 'so *now* you want to kiss and make up!' She ran a finger along its body: still radiant, her dark eyes shining.

'I don't want to escape. I'll stay here, and keep house, everything as it should be, the way it has been, beautiful, in memory of you.'

'Oh, hush. Let me tell you what will happen. Very soon, in days or possibly hours, I shall be dead. It's nothing to cry about, Bibi. I am, at my best guess, nearly a hundred and sixty years old. If we had returned to Earth, or Speranza, as planned, my rank would have entitled me to decades of hale old age, but even a Senior's lifespan has its mortal close. Whatever the Myots did to me, they didn't enhance my longevity. The symptoms of the last decline are clearly established. I can no longer piss, shit or digest my food. Parts of my body are shutting down, so are parts of my brain. It's rather pleasant, in fact, very pleasant. I am not afraid. Could you help me back to bed?'

She lay on the prison mattress, curled on her side. Bibi knelt beside her.

'As I know, and you have guessed, there is a way out to the surface through the Old Wing. I found it. I broke through the rockfall at the end of our outer passage, and found another corridor beyond. I followed the fault-line, where what seems to be native rock is really the glassy repair, until I reached the open. You can do the same. It won't be difficult; it was harder for me, but the "concrete glass" thickens very slowly. Di will help you find the places. Remember to wrap your hands well, and cover your eyes. Once you're on the surface you'll be in a rocky, fissured terrain where it should be easy to hide. The atmosphere is harsh but not poisonous, and you'll appreciate the oxygen content, which is a little high for Sigurtian taste. Breathe through sacking masks.

'Now comes the important part. I reached the surface and realised that my case was hopeless. I was as trapped as ever. *You* can leave Fenmu ... The Myots haven't got their Buonarotti facility on the planet yet, but there is a transit lounge on the surface of Fenmu, essential for the Diaspora's High-Security Prison. It's run from Sigurt's World Port, and rarely open. There've been only a handful of interplanetary transfers so far, all of them notorious: we're in dreadful company, but never mind. What matters is that my body is to be returned to Speranza, in recognition of my rank, and my lifetime achievements. Your cell will become your tomb: but when *my* food remains untouched the governor will be notified. He'll send a message to the Port, a courier will take the news to Speranza. A different courier will return, and transit to Fenmu to escort my remains. During the time between my death notice and the arrival of the courier, the transit lounge will be active. *You* will be on the surface, keeping watch.'

She paused, and Bibi moistened her parched lips with tea.

'The installation is close at hand, it will be unmistakable. It is physically isolated from the prison. Prison staff await the arrival of couriers and prisoners in a storm shelter close by; or on the surface in summer. You must choose your moment, and enter. You will find two couches, one intended for a prisoner, and one for the escort. In the hideous "normal" procedure, the escort has a lien on the consciousness of the prisoner. *My* mortal remains will transit as couriered freight. This actual flesh will be annihilated, so pointless, but perhaps well meant, we won't look for sinister motives ... Everything is "automated", as P'p"st puts it. You will see a touch panel at the head of each couch; you will select the destination Balas/Shet. I would send you to Aleutia, but the Big Pebble repels all uninvited boarders, *viciously*, for historical reasons—'

'And no one will stop me?'

'No one will stop you.' Nef raised herself, slowly, on one elbow, moving her limbs as if they were dead weight. 'Bibi, do you know that I have a treasure? A treasure of unbelievable worth, unsurpassable riches?'

'Yes, yes.' Bibi tried to get her to lie down again. 'You have an incredible treasure, you are immortal, you are in a beautiful place, you have succeeded in everything you ever desired—'

'No, no. This is real. I have a treasure: it was given to me in trust when I was made immortal-designate. When I was mad I tried to trade it for my freedom, but that was stupid and wrong. I have entrusted it to you, instead. Do you remember the 4-Space coordinates? The exercise we practised?'

'Of course, of course. I remember it perfectly.'

'Now you're babbling, but your mind is open to me, and I know you have it secured. That wasn't an exercise. Those figures and symbols specify a unique destination, in the sum of all states. The Sigurt's World Torus will insert you into the manifest of a ship bound for Balas/Shet. You'll reach the arrivals hall, where I advise you to declare yourself a destitute Prospector. You will be given subsistence. You should take some rest, then go to the planet. Find a library, a good public library, and say you have some new files you wish to install ... Rest, eat, sleep. When you are quite recovered, take a shuttle out to the Buonarotti Port again, and say you wish to make a "private transit". You'll be shown how to use your coordinates. You will reach the destination I have given to you, and there you will find the treasure.'

Nef sighed, closed her eyes and gestured, faintly, that she wanted to lie down. Bibi helped her, and moistened her lips again with a little tea.

'Disgusting stuff. I kept the secret, to prove that I was worthy to be immortal. I would have kept it unto death; now I give it to you. You are to do with it *exactly as you choose*: with my unreserved blessing. Where is Di—?'

Di climbed up and bent her face, so that Nef could kiss her on the brow.

'I couldn't have wished for a better old age. I promised myself I'd retire to the Great House, and here I am. You were my best find, Bibi. I knew it the day we met.'

The silences punctuating Nef's instructions had been growing longer, and this one seemed to be the last. Then she spoke again, very clearly. 'It's been a constant delight to live with you, and help to bring up your little girl. She has such potential. An artist, I think, but who knows? Be *proud* of her, Bibi. A child needs, above all, someone to be proud ...'

Lady Nef drifted in and out of consciousness. '*Bunny rabbit,*' she murmured happily, in Putonghua, the language of her childhood. '*Little horse, little mouse, bunny bunny rabbit.*' The lighting system hissed and clicked, the cell was plunged in darkness. Bibi struck a spark and lit the lamp. Mother and daughter sat in silence. Later Bibi woke from a doze, huddled against the plinth, found the wick guttering in the last of their oil, and got up to see if Nef needed anything. The body on the bed was already cold.

'Was any of it true?' asked Dirt-baby.

'Some, maybe,' said Bibi. 'I don't know ... We'll die somewhere else, we won't rot in here. That's all I can promise. I'm going to take the phage, and get the light bulbs back from my cell. You stay with her.'

XL

Life is a dream, but a little less inconstant.

   Sometimes when life throws a deadly knife at us, we deserve it.

   *The great charm of the Guermantes Way was that we had beside us, almost all
the time, the course of the Vivonne ...*

   Fortuna opes auferre, non animum, potest.

The first adventure of the Old Wing had been intense. Bibi had
beaten at the weak place in the rockfall, passionately: with her wrapped
fists, with a rock, then with her fists again, a strip of sacking round her
eyes, terrified that she would not break through, that the whole idea of
escape was a delusion. The glass had shattered; she'd muffled the jagged
edge and climbed over into a new world, with the child and the phage
in her arms. The second time she'd felt she was getting into her stride;
after that it had become brute repetition.

   She'd had no reason to deviate from Nef's minimal instructions.
When there was no way forward, Dirt-baby found a weak place and
Bibi worked. (The child was Dirt-baby again, she was not *Di.* The time
of Di and Lady Nef was over.) She had nothing to do but walk through
the dark, husbanding the light bulb in her fist; and break glass; and
wonder why these particular bubbles rose in her mind, this delicate,
random spray of memories. Why such sleek, airy, fragrant coolness
attached to the word *Vivonne?* The taste of the fried grasshoppers she
had never found. Lady Nef, in immaculate uniform, on a big screen
that dominated a hall full of uniformed children. Tadpoles sounding up
like tiny carp from the depths of a great pot, filled with dark, clear
water ... When they'd broken through the fifth blockage they walked
level for what seemed a long way. The bulb, which Bibi was using as
little as possible, because darkness was her greatest fear, showed the
same features over and over: she was afraid they were going round in
circles.

'I can hear something strange,' said Dirt-baby. 'It's coloured, it flashes.'

Bibi was carrying her; it was easier on both of them. She realised that she could hear something too. She kept walking, clambering when fallen blocks or intrusive boulders made it necessary: bad news swimming into her mind, sinking the bubbles. They reached another place where rockfall filled the passage, and here faint sheens of pink, grey, yellow propagated through the darkness. Dirt-baby found the thin glass; Bibi set the phage and the child out of the way, and attacked.

She didn't need a rock: outer forces had slowed the repair here. One blow from her wrapped fist, and light and thunder crashed in, through the rent Lady Nef had reopened (how long ago?) in an ancient rockfall. Bibi's eyes began to stream. She pulled up her sacking bandanna, over her mouth and nose, and looked around to make sure Dirt-baby had done the same.

'Oh, hell. It's *winter.*'

It was winter outdoors. The sky of the prison moon, if that was what Bibi was seeing, was a black theatre laced by violent, lurid traceries. Pink, acid green, yellow, violet. Rocks looked up, so close-packed she couldn't see the floor they stood on, if there was one. Fresh lightning burst overhead, shattering the black dome, revealing spires of stone and rafts of mist, letting loose a fresh yelping, hammering scream of thunder. *If it's winter*, thought Bibi, *there'll be no daylight.* Maybe there was never any daylight on Fenmu. She told the child with a gesture that the lights and the noises were harmless (Francois had said so): and carried her out onto the surface.

The terrain was horrible. Bibi quickly decided that she wasn't going to try to reach the ground. She clambered, stepped or jumped, from the crown of a boulder to a ledge on the side of another, from the ledge to a massive arrow where she had to cling with arms and legs ... Fortunately her feet were very tough, and once she'd seen that she would not fall, that the clutter-heap was navigable, the bubbles of memory rose again ... *clifftop vista of clouds and sky, a bowl of noodle soup, a rosy face, the little stones she had buried in Cymru, a flock of gallahs rising from the citified trees* ... She recalled the dimensions of Fenmu, and imagined a whole, two-thirds-of-Earth-sized, planetish moon, covered with this monstrous scurf. Why not? Except that Lady Nef had believed the place was once inhabited. From choice, that is.

She found a flat rock and they rested: ate some lumps of pressed carapace porridge and sucked the tea they'd brought with them, in the form of soaked rags, wrapped in oil-waxed paper. They dozed a little, and went on. Thunder boomed and snarled, lightnings lashed the sky. Whenever she saw the chance, Bibi headed for higher ground. The hateful boulders broke up into clumps, separated by scoured rock and patches of earth. Bugs crawled, and things like lichens, mosses and matted creepers grew. Suddenly feeling exposed, she ducked in the shelter of a boulder clump and looked back.

Fenmu Prison lay below her. The visible installation, packed close to the rock, was a complex of long, pale-coloured blocks, pocked with rows of darker storm shutters. To one side stood a more expansive building, with a barrel-domed extension that made her think of the winter gardens at Black Wing. In the distance she could see (unmistakable, painfully nostalgic) what must be the spaceport. No roads, not even a covered way, above ground. The prison buildings and the towers of the port rose up, naked and isolated, like the fruiting bodies of fungus. Bibi could not imagine that she'd ever lived under them. The world she'd shared with Lady Nef – the two cells, their industrious days, the sound of the hand's footsteps – no longer existed.

The transit lounge was as unmistakable as the spaceport: a half-dome, starship silver-green, planted close to a dry channel – like a river bed but too regular to be natural – that swept around the slope Bibi had climbed, and disappeared from sight on either side of the buildings. There were no watchtowers or warning signs, but, '*I bet that ditch is armed*,' she muttered.

So they were still in prison.

Bibi looked up into the angry sky. No surveillance in winter? *Will no one stop me?* In sudden determination she got up, clutching Dirt-baby, the phage pressed between them, and headed downhill. The half-dome looked oddly familiar: as if a section of the imaginary *Rajath* had been dropped here, casually, in passing ... Near it there was a big sealed hatch, flush with the rock, and signs of temporary structures that had been removed. The dome was surrounded by a pattern of small beacons, tough-coated bulkhead sensors. When they detected Bibi, a cage of light sprang up and a bot voice clicked and fluted. 'Do not approach. Sigurt's World nationals may not enter. Prison staff must await the courier in the storm shelter.'

'I'm not Sigurtian,' said Bibi: but of course it was a recorded message. She stepped between the beacons: nothing stopped her. The flat face of the truncated dome had a panel, marked in brighter strips, that could have been a doorway on Speranza. But there were no visible fittings, no lockpad, no screens. She touched it, in case the featureless surface was a mask: her touch found nothing hidden; wakened nothing.

'It's not active. We don't know when it will be active. We don't know how long her food has to "remain untouched" before they go in and find her dead. It could be a long time. She forgot to tell us.'

'We forgot to ask,' said Dirt-baby. 'But everything's been true so far.'

Bibi had been talking to herself, but she nodded. 'True.' She felt elated, not disappointed. The boulder clump they'd just left seemed a possible shelter, a place where they could keep watch, but for how long? She licked her lips. She was very thirsty. She was *always* thirsty, she'd been thirsty for ever; but the accustomed, harmless feeling was a threat now.

'We'll need water. We must find water. Can you help me?'

'No. But maybe Slug can. Shall we put it down?'

'Let's get to somewhere more hopeful.'

They put the phage down among the creepers. Bibi thought it had grown bigger since its 'full retreat', but otherwise it was unchanged: a reddish, slimy, rubbery blob that could stretch and contract.

'Dear Slug,' said Dirt-baby, squatting on her haunches, 'please find some water for us—'

'Do you think it understands English?'

'It understands a lot.' Dirt-baby patted Bibi's arm. 'Slug will look after me, and I will look after you. Even if you go mad again, we'll be all right.'

This was a long speech for Dirt-baby. Bibi nodded, brusquely. The phage crawled; they followed through the lightning-shattered gloom. Bibi pulled at creeper stems, hoping for moisture: but they were too tough to break, and the taste they left on her palms was foul. They were being led back to the channel, further along its curve.

<Watch out,> she said, Silently. <I think the ditch is dangerous.>

<Slug says not.>

The gully they were following cut straight through the bed of the channel, which was reassuring. Maybe it had *once* been live, but Fenmu had ruined it, long ago. Bibi insisted on throwing stones ahead of them, but nothing fizzed and burned; except the lightning balls that roved around on the ground. They crossed over, and the gully plunged, becoming a cleft full of much more varied vegetation. Bibi looked back, and wondered, *If it's not to do with the prison,* how long *has that construct been here?*

The ground became damp and finally they found a spring, buried in mosses and succulents, that welled from a bed of glittering sand to fill a tiny, rocky cup. The phage extended its prow and touched the quivering surface. It seemed to approve, or at least it didn't recoil. Bibi tested the liquid with a leaf, and then a rag, before she touched it herself, or let Dirt-baby near. She dipped her hand, pulled up her bandanna and sipped, and swallowed. It was bitter, rusty and strangely warm: but heavenly.

'This is water,' she whispered. 'This is life.'

The gully continued, cutting deeper but heading upwards, towards a black split in the roots of one of the spires. Bibi took out food, and pondered while they ate. She distrusted caves and mountains: they were traps. <We shouldn't go any further,> she said. <But we could stay here for a while.>

<I don't know if I like it or not,> said Dirt-baby, licking water from her tiny palm. <It's a bit runny and thin-tasting ... >

I don't want her to be normal, thought Bibi, passionately. *I want her to be the way she is now, so I can pick her up and carry her, and never let anything hurt her ...* Something rustled: she looked sharply around. She was looking into the face, the snout, of a four-legged creature the size of a large dog. It had a scaled hide, big glossy eyes and a toothy grin. It peered at her out of the foliage. Bibi reached, slowly, for Dirt-baby. The child came to her arms, bringing Slug. The phage crawled round the back of Bibi's neck.

The Fenmu animal was not afraid. For a moment Bibi wasn't sure of its intentions, then a ridge of flesh on the top of its snout flared up, like a warning signal, and she knew. She leapt to her feet, charged straight at it, got by and kept running. Thunder had broken out again, like a yelling pack of beasts in the sky. She risked a glance over her shoulder: it wasn't thunder. The animal had been joined by several others: they were yelling as they hunted Bibi. She flung herself at the wall of the gully, the harsh air tearing at her throat, stinging her eyes, buoyant in her greedy lungs. Dirt-baby's arms tight around her neck, little heels in her ribs, she shot from foothold to handhold, grabbing at roots, rocks, clawing her fingers into the earth, and came bursting over the brink. Something reared, huge and clattering, right in her face. Bibi choked a scream, flung herself down and rolled, jutting her elbows to protect the baby, kicking out wildly—

She got to her knees, half-stunned, holding Dirt-baby tight with one arm. A few metres away a dark shape moved uncertainly in the gloom. She saw the gleam of segmented chitin. It was a riding serpent, and it seemed to have a saddle on its back.

That's what I ran into, thought Bibi. A wash of vivid lilac flung itself across the sky. In the shock of light a heap of rocks, right beside her, turned out to be the rider. He was in uniform, with an armoured breastplate and helmet, marks of rank on his wide sleeves. The air-filter over his mouth and nose, black chitin chased with silver, looked like the proboscis of a giant insect: but it was a male bat-person. Thunder came pelting after the light, like a shrieking cascade of broken glass. Was this the governor? The bastard who had dispensed her fate, how many years ago? No, it was a much younger man. He seemed to be dead; maybe he'd broken his neck.

She could still hear the hunting beasts; in a moment they would find her scent and come clawing up the wall.

'Sir, sir? The blood-seekers picked up a trace, in Metal Spring Gully—'

'They're heading back your way. Are you there, sir—?'

The voices, eerily distinct, came from the dead officer's wrist. 'Blood-seekers,' whispered Bibi, aloud. 'That's what they are.'

The serpent was just standing there, quivering. Bibi thought it was afraid of the dead rider, and afraid to be outdoors in winter. It wasn't a big riding beast: no bigger than those placid, animated scrubbing brushes Bibi and Honesty had once 'ridden', with a leading rein and a guide, in the cold desert above Myot. It let her approach, it let her get hold of the barbed girth. She scrambled into the saddle, Dirt-baby clinging to her, and found the stirrups. Instantly, the serpent took off like a rocket.

Bibi was horrified, sure it would deliver her to her enemies. She couldn't get her feet free, she couldn't fling herself off. She clutched the girth, trying to change its path, but she had no control at all. Lights, a cluster of lights and the shapes of riders, flashed by, away on her left. She realised, when they were gone (thunder after lightning), that she was on the other side of 'Metal Spring Gully'. She was being carried away from her pursuers, but away from the transit lounge too.

The serpent sped on. It poured over the side of another gully, parallel to the first, lowered its blunt head and drove through tall plants that whipped at Bibi's arms and legs: onwards, upwards, slowing to a sinuous trot as it climbed. Bibi saw the lightnings paint their banners on a narrowing strip of black sky, and then the sky vanished. The serpent, having found its way underground, slowed to walking pace and began sniffing around. Bibi took a light bulb from her sacking pouch, and held it up. Rock. Strange glints of colour, marbled shields, pipes and towers built from the dripping of time.

Dirt-baby's eyes gleamed as she stared around. 'What is this?'

'It's a cave. A slit in the side of a mountain. It's not a good place to be, but I couldn't help it. I had to get us away, and then the thing wouldn't stop.'

The serpent had detected a bay in the wall of the fissure. It scrambled into this refuge, and settled on its belly on the sandy floor, nose to tail. Bibi got down, Dirt-baby in her arms. *How can they be hunting me?* she wondered. *They're supposed to think I'm dead.* She put the bulb on a rock, loosed the child's grip: set her down and gave her the phage to hold.

'What is that thing that carried us?'

'It's called a riding serpent, Francois called them that. It's an animal.'

'What were the other things? The ones that chased us?'

'Hunting dogs. Blood-seekers.'

'Like the bad Myots?'

<Stop talking aloud. Bad Myots might be near.>

Dirt-baby approached the coiled serpent, hugging Slug. <I want to touch it – will it let me?>

<*Don't,*> snapped Bibi, arms folded, brooding. <Leave it alone.>

They must have gone into Nef's cell. They must have found the hole in the wall, barely sealed over. That set them off, and then they found I was gone. Or else P'p"st betrayed us. Or else there is surveillance, but I don't think so, Lady Nef would have warned me. It doesn't matter. They'll still send Nef's body back, and we can get back to the transit lounge.

She was dismayed, but utterly determined. Her faith in Lady Nef was absolute now: she would follow her mistress's instructions, or die in the attempt. She examined the serpent and found a bulky handgun attached to the saddle; a water flask, which was empty, and another flask, which had traces of schnapps. Dirt-baby squatted as near as she dared, watching.

<How far did it carry us?>

<I don't know. I'm tired. Let's have some more food, and a suck of tea, and sleep for a while. The serpent seems to think it's safe here.>

But the serpent was not native to Fenmu.

Bibi slept and woke to the underground darkness, the harsh bite of Fenmu's atmosphere; the sound of thunder. Was it morning? She longed for night and day the way she had longed for water. She decided it would be safe to leave the child, and took the handgun and the water flask; intending to fill the flask if she could find a spring, and see if she could fire the gun. When she reached open air she climbed to get a view of the surface. She couldn't see the prison, or any feature she recognised. There was a glow around the horizon, could that be sunrise? Then her heart jumped. There were moving lights on the plain. She heard the faint whistling of amplified Sigurtian voices. The hunters were coming this way. She raced back to the cave.

'Come on, wake up, we've got to go.'

<Are the blood-seekers coming?>

<SHUT UP! Stop asking questions, foul thing. Bring the phage, give me that light bulb ... > The serpent seemed docile when Bibi led it down to the passage floor, but it was very reluctant to go further up into the dark. The gun stuffed in her sacking belt, girth twisted around her free hand, Bibi slapped at its eyes with the authority of desperation.

<Can't we just let it go?> pleaded Dirt-baby.

<NO!> snapped Bibi, Silently. <The hunters will have found the dead person. They'll have figured out that I took the serpent, they mustn't find it wandering in this fissure ... > She bullied the beast into submission and they began to climb. <This had better be one of those mountains that's fissured right through,> said Bibi. <We'll have to find a way out the other side, we'll ride the serpent back towards the prison, leave it near where we found it, and hide ourselves where we can watch ...>

Dirt-baby led the way, a tiny barefoot ghost in a sacking dress, clicking softly and incessantly: testing the darkness ahead, and each side passage, for hazards. They were lost in a black jumbled maze, but the baby always found a safe way forward, always climbing. The serpent, resigned to its fate, rippled at Bibi's shoulder. An upward passage levelled, and opened into a wider chamber where the glow of Bibi's light bulb reached no walls. Suddenly the air was fouler. Did that mean they were near an exit? The child dropped back and squeezed her mother's hand. She tried to stroke the serpent, but Bibi shoved her away. <Don't. It might snap at you.>

<Does it feel? Is the hard stuff its skin?>

It's the stuff you've been eating all your life, thought Bibi, and felt the child's touching, doubtful reaction: catching the unspoken words, making no sense of them. *You are my life*, she thought. <Pull up your bandanna,> she said: and then the serpent began to fight her again, silently, with all its strength. Bibi couldn't hold it this time. She was flung to the ground, the girth torn out of her hand, the bulb went flying.

The serpent shot away. Bibi groped on the floor for the light bulb–
<Mummy! Look!>

They were surrounded by shadows of light.

They were in a complex chamber, with natural windows onto the winter sky: some distant, some near and at floor level. Bibi decided to abandon the serpent (they didn't have a chance of catching it). A few metres more and they were climbing out, through a three-cornered gap in a tumbled pyramid, onto a ledge among the spires. The glow of that false sunrise was still in the sky. There was no sign of the hunt, and the descent didn't look impossible. In the pale band above the horizon Bibi saw the crescent shapes of winged things, coming closer. Did Fenmu have birds, or were those giant moths of some kind?

'The swifts,' she murmured.

Dirt-baby tugged her hand. 'There's our serpent!'

The riding beast had found its own way out. It was crawling over the rocks, a dark, moving gleam twenty or thirty metres beneath their feet, heading swiftly downwards. Bibi watched it, wondering if she and Dirt-baby could use the same route. She felt a shadow over her, glanced up, and saw that the winged things were a lot bigger and a lot closer. Suddenly one swooped. It became enormous. Leather wings flapping, horribly clumsy, horribly efficient, it plunged on the serpent, and grabbed it from the rock.

Bibi saw for the first time the kind of debris that lay on the ledge. She grabbed Dirt-baby and shoved her back into the chamber they'd just left. <Get on my back. I'll need both my hands.> She grasped the grip of the handgun, a light bulb closed in her other fist—

These winged things, adults often attaining a monstrous size and wingspan, were called S"nt"lz, Summer-Wings, on the grounds that they only flew in summer: but in mild winters, such as this one had been, they often made forays. They could glide and soar, but were mainly ground hunters, using their wings to extend their leaping attacks on the marmot- and lizard-like things that lived among the boulders. They haunted the prison site, often penetrating the tunnels, where they set up roosts: but they were protected animals. In summer, the breeding season, they couldn't be touched. In winter the officers were permitted to cull the brutes, tracking them on the ground with blood-seekers – pack animals that could surprise a feasting Summer-Wing, or leap up to take one from the air. The hunters Bibi had encountered had not been looking for her. They'd been on their way to a hide in the foothills. They'd found the young officer dead, but seen nothing suspicious in the absence of his riding-beast. They were only surprised that they'd found an untouched body.

As Bibi lifted her light bulb, looking for the exit passage, the half-grown juveniles, sleeping among the rocks of the nursery chamber, stirred: winter-sluggish but disturbed by the light. They scented their parents and screamed for food, rousing completely, so the chamber seemed filled with flapping wings, flailing claws, gaping gullets, rows of jagged teeth. Bibi kept her head. She stuffed her bulb away and retreated, levelling the unfamiliar weapon, trying to get her back against rock. Behind her, the dim light from the ledge was suddenly blocked. An adult was thrusting herself through the gap. Bibi felt one cry, '*Mummy*,' as Dirt-baby was snatched from her back, one tug as the little twig arms relinquished their hold.

The adult Summer-Wing tossed a morsel of flesh to the brood, and Bibi was overwhelmed by the rush of the juveniles. Wings beat at her, fangs and claws stabbed. She fired and fired, the children shrieking in fear and pain, the bolts of sound recoiling, proliferating: she could not get to the adult that had taken Dirt-baby. More adults came thrusting in, through every rift in the chamber, she kept firing, hurting them, battered by their panic, she fell, and went on falling.

She woke at the bottom of what she found, in perfect blackness, to be a narrow, rugged chimney. She did not know if seconds had passed, or hours. The gun was in her hand, completely discharged. The phage was still clinging to the back of her neck. She started climbing at once, feeling no pain, only an insane urgency: as if there was still something she could do, as if she could rescue Dirt-baby. When she emerged through the floor again, all was deadly quiet. She held up a bulb: the nest chamber was empty. The adults, very frightened at finding a predator in the roost, had fled with the surviving juveniles, after devouring the dead and injured victims of Bibi's fire. Many of them –

more than the permitted number, on the strength of that dead officer –
had already been slaughtered by Fenmu Prison's hunters.

Bibi searched everywhere, behind rocks, in dark corners: as if there
was a chance that Dirt-baby was hiding there, as if she might be hurt
not dead, hurt not dead. She found fragments of the half-eaten juveniles,
fresh shards of serpent chitin, and at last a grey bolus, the ejected
remnant of a Summer-Wing's recent meal in which scraps of pure white
gleamed. She broke it apart, and picked out a handful of tiny teeth, like
seed pearls. The delicate brain pan of a baby skull. Nothing more. She
crouched, hugging her child, rocking her close and crooning to her, as
she had never done in life, her soul in the grip of agony, grief and
remorse, loss deeper than she had ever known. 'Oh, I shall mark your
grave,' she keened aloud. 'Oh, I shall mark your grave.' The phage clung
to her neck, soothing her as best it could.

XLI

The first real storm of that winter kept Bibi under shelter. When she emerged, and made her way back to Fenmu Prison, the creepers and lichens – which would regenerate in spring – were black remnants and charcoal tracery. She approached the dome, wondering what she would find: whether Lady Nef's funeral cortege was long gone, or was the governor still waiting for the right liturgical moment? On the plane face, which had been completely blank, the Diaspora Banner had appeared. The worlds of the planetary nations, including an artist's impression of the 'Aleutian Home', turned solemnly, beautifully coloured, lined up and rationalised to approximately similar size. Bibi went to the door, on which a virtual scanner had become visible, and pushed the bright plate. The Sigurt's World Port system read her, recognised the tokens of her authority: and let her in.

There was a roaring in her ears. She hadn't heard the thunder since she'd fought with the Summer-Wings, but now she'd brought the snarling and groaning of Fenmu with her: into this cool, innocent, silver-green space. Skeletal, charred, battered, dressed in rags, she chose one of the two couches. The touch panel was as Lady Nef had described it, the couch active.

Balas/Shet?

No.

'Die somewhere else,' muttered Bibi. She left the destination field blank, as it would have been if Lady Nef's corpse had been laid here. Only numinal consciousness can have a destination, in Buonarotti transit. *Take me to those who love me*, she thought. *Take me to my friends.* She lay down. The phage spread itself, like a veil, across her face and throat, and she prepared for annihilation.

XLII

Bibi had lost all sense of the place where she had gone to sleep. She could not even be sure at first who she was. She had only the most rudimentary sense of existence, such as may flicker in the depths of an animal's consciousness. The memory of places where she *might* be, places where she had slept in the past, came like a rope let down from heaven to draw her up from the abyss of non-being. Was this her mat in Juniper dorm, the regular breathing hummocks of Nightingale and Honesty on either side? A tent on a field trip from Hanoi, green, dripping night through the screen, and her mind drifting up from dreams of Mahmood? Was she in the mediaeval bedchamber at Underwall? She understood at last, with an unexpected, bodiless sense of continued existence, that what she had taken for her own thoughts were the words of a story, read aloud in a familiar voice.

Was it her own?

'Is Honesty here too?' she whispered.

'I'm sorry, Miss Bibi. Honesty's been dead a long time.'

Bibi opened her eyes and saw Col Ben Phu looking down at her, Col disfigured but perfectly recognisable. Still bodiless, she knew she was alive, and remembered, *appalled*, that she, who had such obligations to fulfil, had tried to kill herself—

'Oh funx. It's all ri', it's all ri', Miss Bibi, don't panic, it's over, you're safe. Dunno how you got out, how you got here, but you're on b"rd the *Spirit*. You're s"fe, amon' fren'—'

She had arrived, by means she couldn't imagine, in the cramped cabin of a little pirate ship, one of those scrape-a-living freebooters that plagued conventional Sigurtian Space: an annoyance to the mining companies, a hazard to tourism. The pirates, last remnant of the Baykonur Mission Household Guard, gave her sweet water to drink, and fed her. They cleaned her up, applied first aid, and put her to sleep again, under medication.

When Bibi had slept, off and on, for thirty standard hours, she seemed coherent, and her vital signs were strong. They let her up, stood down from the weighted gecko-boots they used to keep their bones in trim, and told her what had happened. They had returned to the vicinity of Sigurt's World Port, the old rendezvous. It was a trip they made regularly, out of respect, they said: because Francois's last order had saved their lives. They'd 'felt something', one of those minor disturbances, hard to describe, that happen when you're schematically 'near' a Torus – especially if you're riding in a transit-capable Aleutian pod. One of the couches in the four-berth habitat had 'come to life': Col had opened it, and found Bibi lying there.

The interior of the ship that had been Francois's boy-racer retained something of its former, sleek and classy identity. Everything integral was in perfect shape, all surfaces pristine. The piratical additions were a miscellany: military drab, colourful commercial packaging, old and new, expensive and basic. There was a rack of well-worn weapons, an air of combat readiness, hardened living. Weightless, the three old soldiers were easy as monkeys in a tree. Bibi wore a harness like a toddler. She didn't have her sea legs, and the Sarge – Rohan Aswad, formerly of Orange Company – didn't want any accidents. He tried to keep the *Spirit* in military order.

'We've been coming back here for more than twenty standard,' said Drez Doyle. 'We thought *you* were long gone. We knew Lady Nef was in Fenmu, owing to that bastard. D'you know anything, like how she is?'

'Lady Nef is dead,' said Bibi. 'She died of old age. I escaped because the transit lounge was opened, to take her couriered body back to Speranza. She had planned it all, for years: but I ... I lay down without a destination. I don't know how I got here.'

They nodded, grave and tactful. They understood what she had done, and were ashamed for her, and passed over it in silence. Col jerked her chin at the phage, which was drifting in the sweet air, curled in a ball.

'Is that one of *his*, you know, body-critters?'

'Nef and I thought it must be.'

'Then that's how, because the *Spirit* is another, in a sen'. The Port Torus read them as one, and put them together. Obvious.'

Drez gently took an emptied half-litre of pure, fresh, activated water from Bibi's hand, hung upside down to select an option from the *distributeur* bolted to the fuselage (evidently a fairly recent acquisition), and wrapped Bibi's fingers around another pack. 'Blue Tomato soup. Suck on the nipple, Miss Bibi, and it'll warm up nicely.'

Bibi wondered why the honorific. Surely they had never called her *Miss* before. When she'd last seen them (how long ago, how long?), they had not been young, but they hadn't been very old. Now they were grizzled veterans, in faded singlets, and voluminous ragged shorts that drifted around them. Drez had lost an eye, an injury that looked old and permanent. She wondered what she looked like herself (she had yet to see a mirror). How old was she? She examined her hands, skeletal, ageless, daubed with skin-repair gel. Her body, withered by starvation, draped in the same undress as the pirates: no way of telling, was she maybe forty?

'How has it been with you?'

'Bad and getting worse,' growled Drez. 'We were scrap merchants, scav'in' our fuel. Now every cubic metre of plas is funxing *owned* by some funxer, all the free docks are getting closed down, and it's getting harder all the time to keep out of the way of the law.'

'Put it this way,' said Col. 'If y're not S'g'rt'n, an' you don't b'long to a consortium, ther' no r'm for y' no m're.'

'Everything's changed,' Sergeant Aswad translated, pained at these admissions, and at Col's dreadful clicking. 'It's another world from what you knew, Miss Bibi. There's no moral standards.'

From the look of the packaging, the fresh water had been liberated from a luxury cruiser. A different fancy logo adorned the exotic soup. Bibi noted these speaking details. The old soldiers gazed at her in wonder and delight, as if it was *she* who had rescued *them*. And perhaps she had. She had released them from their long vigil, she had given meaning to their exile—

'What are your plans, Miss Bibi?' asked Rohan, at last. 'Where d'you want us to take you?'

'When she's *rest'd*—' protested Col. 'Giv' Miss a *ch'n*—'

Bibi guessed that Col did most of the talking, in Sigurtian Space. The clicking set her teeth on edge, but she could bear it. She thought of Lady Nef's warning. I should not ruin my life? Ah, but Nef didn't know half of what the General had done. She had never seen the indictment, *or the date on it*, and Bibi had never told her. Ah, but my baby, my baby—

'I'm rested now. I have plans that will involve Speranza, and the

Blue. It'll be dangerous, but could you take me back there, in the *Spirit*?'

Drez's single eye kindled. 'You're going after *him*?'

'If I can find a way.' Bibi touched her breast, fleshless bone under the soft, clean fabric. 'Did I have some papers with me? Strapped to my chest?' She had been conscious when they took her out of the couch, but she'd already lost the experience of waking. The papers were fetched. They'd been stowed in the same tethered pouch as Bibi's filthy rags, with everything else she'd brought through the transit. She loosened the sacking strips that bound the History of Fenmu together. On the top sheet of reddish rag-paper a few big characters, vividly drawn, blurred before her eyes. She heard Lady Nef's voice, old-fashioned and precise to the last. *When you are quite recovered* ...

'I forgot. I need to get to Balas/Shet. I have to find a library.'

'Can do,' said Col, instantly. 'Easy.'

'But first, there's somewhere else.'

The 4-Space coordinates were in her mind, secure and accurate, the code felt solid, but how long would that last? She freed herself from the harness, and assumed the command she knew was hers: the dominion over them that she needed, and that they were asking her to take.

'We should go now, because what I know I learned in a world that doesn't exist. It might vanish, like a transit fugue narrative. Col, I'll pilot this trip, you will be my co'. Show me how to hook up.'

'B't, exc'se, you g't no skillcard patches, Miss Bibi.'

'The phage is my connection.'

The Spirit of Eighty-Nine left normal space and made a transit in which Bibi, at least, experienced no duration. Francois's boy-racer kissed the ground; the couches shaped themselves upright. The outside cams reported sunny daylight, green savannah, trees, or something like trees, gathering into forest. All under a sky of eggshell blue, a yellow-tinged sun.

'Are we on the Blue?' asked Drez.

'No,' said Col, staring at head-up, reverting to vowelled English in her consternation. 'We're still in the *galaxy*, an' more I can't tell you. Conditions are Earth-perf' out there, but that makes no sense. There's no such place as this. This is not a landfall. This is not on the Registry.'

'We should get out an' have a mosey round.'

'Will we funx. This is not right.'

'Is this where you wanted, Miss Bibi?' broke in the Sarge. 'What are we here for?'

Here I am, thought Bibi. *What do I do? Where is the treasure? Is it marked? Do we dig on the spot where the* Spirit *came through? You didn't tell me, I forgot to ask* ... The simple answer dawned on her, dawned and dawned, filling her head with light. 'Col? Could you take the *Spirit* up into the atmosphere, in normal space, and get some global samples? Can we do an orbit? Do we have the fuel for that?'

'Easy. Fuel is all around. Don't look like there's anyone here to tell us we can't scav' the particles.'

'Let's change over.'

The *Spirit of Eighty-Nine* put an unhurried girdle around the planet, in some twenty standard hours, and returned to his starting place. They had located a single, large, high-albedo moon *sans* atmosphere, and two other planetary bodies, gas giants, well outside the comfort zone. They'd seen two large, sprawling continents that clasped the globe, a pattern of islands spilling to the north and south, and one awesome tall plateau, rising from sea-ice, near the south pole, to an unearthly height. Forest upon forest, and not a sign of numinal biped population. The *Spirit* detected none of the chemical or e/m signatures of civilisation. Nor any of the more esoteric information-space markers for either numinal intelligence or borderline sentience. There was every sign that this was El Dorado, a virgin world.

Bibi stepped from the *Spirit* onto yielding turf. Col, Drez and the Sarge followed, after a slight interval of respect. The soldiers stayed by the pod. Bibi walked into the majestic silence. A cool breeze fingered her thin shipboard clothes; the air was honey-scented. A short distance from their landfall, trees fringed the shore of a silvery lake. Beyond the waters, in the new-named west, the sun, descending between two hills, had begun to colour the sky, green, rose and gold. Something between a large, shaggy blue heron and a two-legged deer came stepping out of the forest, glanced at Bibi incuriously, and dipped its crested head to drink. She heard the wings of the wild geese, beating over the snowy wilderness of Kushan. She understood what this secret meant; and why it had been kept for so long. Were there other virgin landfalls, or was this the only treasure the immortals had kept in trust?

My unreserved blessing, said Nef's voice.

Her small army was waiting. It crossed her mind to disappoint them. It crossed her mind that it was three against one, she was unarmed, and they were ex-soldiers, hardened outlaws, unlikely to hesitate at murder. But this latter thought was unworthy; and not the reason why she returned to them, smiling, having made her choice for better or for worse.

'My friends,' she said. 'We are very, *very* rich.'

A virgin world is an awesome gift: difficult to know how to begin enjoying such a feast. They were agreed they wouldn't kill or eat anything: for an hour or more they hardly dared to touch the grass. But before dark they had collected dry fronds of the starry-flowered, thorny, fruiting vine that tangled the forest eaves, and built a fire on the small shingle of the lake shore. If the stuff wasn't wood it burned like wood. Sparks flew upwards, blue smoke wreathed between the landing party and a rich strew of nameless stars.

'This is where the hordes of giant, vicious, air-breathing, deadly poisonous piranha fishoids jump out of the water,' suggested Col, 'an' eat us to our bones.'

'There may be problems,' agreed Bibi. 'We'll let someone solve them for us.' She took the flask of (tested and proven) lake water Drez passed to her, and sipped it with a connoisseur's lingering delight.

'Have you thought how you're going to tackle the actual job, Miss?' asked Rohan Aswad. 'You know the one I mean.'

'I shall commit no act of vengeance,' said Bibi, smiling at the flames. 'Vengeance is wicked, and I refuse to join them in their infamy. If any one of those I consider guilty is proved innocent, or if they've *become* innocent over the years, they have nothing to fear. I shall lay traps for criminals. I shall be nothing but the instrument of justice; the judgement of Heaven.'

The small army nodded, grimly satisfied. They liked eloquence.

'We've got ourselves a good officer,' said Drez. 'Told you so. I always knew it. She's a princess, our Bibi.'

XLIII

The twin worlds of Balas/Shet – always represented as a single planet, in shifting, equal superposition, on the Diaspora Banner – had known of each other's existence for millennia. Just before they were 'discovered', dubious evidence had emerged for the existence of the inhabited planet now known as Ki/An, the fifth Hegemony world, which was (relatively!) close – but fundamentally they had believed they were alone in the universe. Their peaceful coexistence, their enlightened standards of civil rights, equality and justice, had seemed like a miracle … Closer acquaintance, inevitably, had revealed that the dominant powers of Balas and the dominant powers of Shet had made repeated attempts to exterminate each other, since they'd reached spaceflight-level indus-trialisation. The first Blues had simply arrived in a phase of benign exhaustion and remorse. But the birth of the Hegemony, and the existence of Speranza, cast a powerful spell. The peace continued, bringing riches and spreading prosperity with a lavish hand.

Bibi walked up the steps of the great public library in Kalia'aan, the City of Lilies, capital of Va. It was winter, which meant temperatures of a spring-like coolness; if a visitor remembered Baykonur. She wore a long grey coat, full-skirted, with a sheen like velvet, over her elegant grey suit; and carried the phage at her throat, like an oversized jewel. On either side of her, great banks of black and white variegated roses bloomed. They were virtual: but they reminded Bibi of the gardens of the Great House – just as the mighty, sculpted portal of the building, several hundred years old, made her think of the Palaces, and the Luna Boulevard.

She was struck by the number of what seemed like interplanetary visitors, in the crowd in the famous foyer. So many! Were they here in the flesh, or bi-locating like that ballet from Chicago, long ago? What had happened to the worlds, in twenty years? Maybe these weren't aliens, maybe they were locals with body-mods. But she was wrapped in the past, and didn't really care where the tourists came from. She was not afraid she'd be recognised. She approached the information desk.

'I'd like to install some new files.'

'Certainly,' said the bot. 'Are you a resident of the city?'

'No, just passing through.'

'I'll give you a visitor's pass.'

In an instant, in the twinkling of an eye, a virtual screen appeared in Bibi's field of vision. The codes she had memorised in a prison cell flickered by, faster than she could follow. She felt Lady Nef's library begin to unfold: lines and paragraphs and single words catching her attention, gleaming in the rush of riches. The process was over in under two seconds, standard.

'Is there anything else?'

'Yes. I should like to view whatever information you are holding on the Baykonur Conspiracy.'

The library bot, presenting as a small, fragile-looking Aleutian with a scholarly little stoop, hesitated. Bibi held her breath. She didn't believe she was about to be arrested, but she prepared to be told that the information was classified; that it had been removed. Or else (a variation on the above) that the library had no knowledge of something called the Baykonur Conspiracy.

'Is that difficult to arrange?'

'Not at all. It's just ... There's a lot of material.'

'Never mind. As the Aleutians say, *time's cheap*. Is there a charge?'

The librarian saw a tall young Blue woman, dressed in severe, expensive high fashion, with a perfect, luminously pale complexion, regular features, a firm mouth; and great sombre eyes that gave her youth a look of sober, darkling permanence. If she was really, as she appeared, around twenty years old, she was a very wealthy, very well-connected young mortal indeed, because she was evidently a Senior. But with those eyes, she might easily be two hundred—

'There is no charge for any public information service. You might care to make a donation to our couriered archive fund.'

'Let it be done.'

Bibi was shown to a private viewing room, a fine little data-secure cabin, furnished luxuriously with the soft, colourful hangings, the big cushions and little glass tables that the City of Lilies currently admired as furniture. She asked for a hookah – an item that had been 'couriered' to Balas/Shet a generation ago by an enterprising Blue Prospector, in the form of craft skill; and had met with approval. Settled in one of the generous cushions, the scented mouthpiece at her lips, the phage in the crook of her arm, she prepared to review all the data on record about the course of events, on Speranza and on the Blue, so long ago – that had doomed her friends, destroyed her beloved mistress, and left her trapped in a living hell.

XLIV

Two Sigurtian tourists waited for attention, at the Independent Transiters Assistance Desk. One of them was unusually tall and robustly built for his kind, with curiously round, wide-open brown eyes. The fluffy down of childhood lingered on his cheeks and brow – giving him, since he was clearly a young adult, a rather feminine appearance. The other was more typical: slight and wiry, long in the arm and short in the leg for the notional ideal of numinal biped proportions, with small, dark, diamond-rimmed eyes. The folds of a neck frill were visible at his throat – a so-called 'regressive' trait some Sigurtians considered a deformity.

The office was virtual. They'd been offered business-suited avatars at the gateway, but they'd opted to be captured as they stood. This had possibly been a mistake. They faced a senior Diaspora Affairs Officer wearing the sloppy embroidered shirts and baggy short breeches they'd picked up at the Twin Planets Port, in a naïve attempt to look like seasoned spacers. The avatar of their officer – a massive, furrowed, grey-skinned Shetian in an ominous black uniform – seemed to be very busy doing *something* on their behalf. But the Sigurtians had a nose for obstructive bureaucracy: they feared the worst.

At least their boots were respectable.

'Maybe we should stand on our heads,' suggested D''fydd, the tall youth, looking at his. 'We'd make a better impression.'

'Sssh.'

Datalines and notices flashed around the virtual walls, in several languages. Ch'r''o'p''x, companion and mentor to the orphaned prince of Myot, had been trying to read the English bits (there was no Sigurtian script on offer), but everything moved too fast. He feared he was ill-equipped for this interview: but needs must. They'd been running around trying to get Special Registration for days. The Help Desk was their last resort.

In the spacious breakfast bar of The Caprice, from whence they were making their call, fashionable society took 'coffee and cake', Speranza style, amid preparations for extreme weather: the modesty of the breakfasters preserved by a façade of prismatic supple-glass. Newcomers came glowing through this screen, from the Lateral Canal Promenade, as if they were being born, fully formed, through falls of rainbow. The young men kept forgetting to attend to their avatars, distracted by the spectacle.

The coming festival, and the superior coffee at The Caprice, drew Twin Planets celebrities, Detta'aan aristocrats and artists, plus the more cautious interstellar tourists who hadn't really left Kalia'aan: uniformly old, rich and closely attended by Official Guides. But what about the lone Aleutian, in his characteristic brown overalls? What was *he* doing here? He never seemed to speak. Was he one of the Silent? What about the party of Ki, looking around them nervously and talking in whispers? The Blue woman who appeared every morning and was greeted with such reverence had arrived, beautifully dressed as always. Ushered to her usual place, she sat flicking the pages of a Detta'aan journal. A fragrant bowl of mélange was swiftly delivered. She was addressed as *Princess*, which intrigued the Sigurtians, but they hadn't dared to look her up. Princess of what? Princess of where? The pet, ornament or weapon that she carried intrigued them too. It lay coiled in her lap: a bud-limbed serpent with sleepy, watchful little eyes.

'It must be a toy. Live animals can't survive a Buonarotti transit.'

'It's not a toy, it's a weapon. No, it's a person. The "Princess" is a chauffeuse, an escort. The little chap in her arms is a fabulously wealthy interstellar gangster, an extreme case of the Blue passion for body-mods.'

'You're completely wrong. That's a Blue domestic animal called a pangolin. Intelligent, affectionate and also edible. It just can't be a real one.'

'*Pangolin?* There's no such word. You made that up—'

YOU MAY APPROACH. Silver capitals leapt into their field of view, recalling them to business. Their avatars approached the desk. The Shetian official looked them over carefully, and opened her large mouth, displaying teeth like tombstones in a motherly smile.

'Well,' she said, in English. 'Messir Chiiiroopopx, Messir Dahahaafop—'

'It's pronounced *Chiro*,' offered Ch'ro, which was near enough. The Shet were incapable of pronouncing a clicked language. 'Most honoured Ma'am Officer, I am, as you'll have noted, Neuendan nobility. My charge, the Myot prince, is Messir D"fydd, pronounced *Dafydd*. I should explain, we came to Detta, what a wonderful city it is, at this time, *particularly*, to … to experience the illustrious Air-Fish Festival of the Inundation in its full glory.'

The official smiled more warmly, displaying her blueish gullet. 'Your passports are in order, your credit is adequate, your port of entry processing indicates that your transit was perfectly normal. This is all good news. I see you spent several months on Shet — I hope you enjoyed your visit.'

'Tremendously!' exclaimed Ch'ro, plunged into despair.

'Now, I'm very sorry, children, as to your request. I wish I could help you, but I've tried every approach. It's just far too late.'

'We need an invitation, don't we? If we had an invitation to one of the great balls, it would make a difference, wouldn't it? But you see, in spite of my employer's rank, we're strangers in Detta. We don't know how to get one, it's rather embarrassing, we'd be *so very grateful* if—'

'It's impossible, child. I've given this case a *term* of my time, I can do no more. If there was a way I would have found it. I'm sorry. '

The virtual office winked out of existence.

The Princess had left; the breakfast bar had lost its charm. They walked out into the burning, golden sunlight, just to be somewhere else.

'Did you notice that she was watching us?'

'Who?'

'The Princess.'

Ch'ro shook his head. 'Your vivid imagination again. *Pangolin*. Why would anyone be watching two dirty little tourists?'

The light didn't bother them; they were used to a more piercing sun. The noise levels did. They fled the crowded Promenade, took to the back streets and wandered at random, until they met the bright limb of a minor canal, and folded themselves down on a stone-built dock. On the farther side the buildings were lower, flat-roofed. They could see the city vanishing into haze, into an empty land of reed forests, marshes and lagoons.

The Inundation was a few days away, according to the ubiquitous satellite forecasts. The lower floors of the housing 'reefs' by the canal had already been sealed: they looked as though they'd been dipped in ice. The dock was empty. Small boats hung on davits beside high windows, out of harm's way. Most of the housing would be empty too. At flood time the rich threw parties, and Twin Planet tourists poured into Detta'aan: ordinary citizens moved out. Some kind of crawling, flying machine, banded orange and red, the City Council's colours, droned above the canal's surface.

They hadn't read the small print. They'd escaped from Shet, where they'd spent the first tranche of their Grand Tour in the rather annoying company of Sigurtian expatriates; reached Balas, impulsively decided they *must* see the Air-Fish of Detta: arrived in the holy city and discovered that (for their own safety) foreign visitors were banned from physical presence at the event. Unless they had Special Registration, and nobody would tell Ch'ro and D"fydd how to join this secret society. They could not swim with the fishes, and they had never wanted anything so much.

'What if we apply to the Embassy?' suggested Ch'ro, desolately.

'I'd rather drown myself.'

'You could try.'

The lipid surface of the canal mocked them. There was plenty of liquid water on Balas, riches compared to the meagre supply at home, but it all came bonded to a fatty surface layer, like the scum on porridge: rich with peculiar life and in some places, at some seasons, mountainously thick. The vessels, large and small, that plied the canals of Detta'aan were called *knives*. They sliced through the lipid with wicked-looking prows of honed metal. You could walk on the canals, if you knew what you were doing, and you weren't afraid of the neurotoxin escapes. If you wanted to drown, you'd have to shove yourself face down into the goop until you suffocated, entombed in grease.

'Why did you say I was your "employer", Ch'ro? That's ridiculous!'

'If I'd said I was your Bloodman it wouldn't have sounded good. We have a bad reputation, you know, and the Shet are vegetarians. I tried to bribe our friendly Diaspora Affairs Officer, did you notice?'

D"fydd showed his white teeth, the long, gleaming incisors of his royal race. 'Good for you. Maybe you were too subtle.'

'Oh, she understood. A wheedling note in my voice, a twitch of rejection and contempt in her jowls. It was utterly the wrong move.'

'You don't know that. The Aleutians make out that if you don't

280

'I need to find out how to repay a favour,' muttered Ch'ro, scanning the notables for any dress-uniformed Shet.

Their benefactor had not contacted them. There'd been no discreetly vague transaction on their local credit account, no developments at all.

D"fydd made the gesture for *don't*. 'Let me dispense the worldly advice for once. Do nothing. Whoever wants to be paid will get in touch.'

'Maybe you're right.'

'Excuse me. Are you the lads I found by the canal?'

The Blue from the stone dock, in her green, silver-braided uniform, was at Ch'ro's elbow, proffering a small glass tray. On it lay a slip of card, white with a margin of thorns and flowers. The legend across the centre read, in English, *The Princess of Bois Dormant*.

'That's us.' D"fydd stared at the card, tingling to his bones—

'I hardly recognised you in the formals. It's an improvement! Could you walk this way, Excellencies? The Princess would like to meet you.'

The uniformed woman grinned, crinkling up the strange marks around her eyes and mouth. They followed her, in astonishment. D"fydd noticed that the silver braid on her cuffs and shoulders, and around her neat cap, was like the margin of the business card: white-petalled flowers and thorns.

'We don't know any Princesses.'

'Yes you do, Excellency.'

'If you say so! But what shall we call *you*?'

'Col, if you get to know me. Secretary, if you don't.'

She walked with a spacer's bounce and a fighter's alert readiness. The uniform was a perfect fit. They observed the excellence of her musculature: and noted that she was as physically present as they were themselves.

'*Some "secretary",*' whispered Ch'ro, in his own language.

'*Some Princess!*' chirped D"fydd, in the same. '*Even her servants are on the Special Register.*'

Their guide turned her head and winked.

Mechanical dolls, the older form of Remote Presence on the Twin Planets, stared as the Sigurtians passed. Graceful Balas, imposing Shet, virtual dignitaries whirled around them: laughing, greeting, embracing. Dancing, sniffing, drinking, snacking. They were delivered to a group of supple-glass chairs and sofas, set to face that mounting bar of light: which had just become visible, from this high vantage point, to the naked eye. One of the sofas was occupied by the same strikingly ugly person whose avatar had greeted them down below, or someone exactly like him; another by the Aleutian from The Caprice. Beside him, the 'pangolin' draped across her shoulders like a living scarf, was the Blue woman from The Caprice. The Zeldi sprang up and babbled, courtesy of transaid, in halting Neuendan.

'Oh, here they are! Delighted to meet you, dear Messir D"fydd. And Messer Ch'ro. A ... scholar and a prince, from so far away! You're about to ... experience the most sacred wonder of the Twin Planets! Of the Diaspora! We must talk, anything you need arranged ... tickets for my library ... anything. Later, later. I must fly, I have a hundred relatives to embrace ...'

He kissed their hands – a swooping, ritual gesture, no actual contact – and flew. The Princess sedately invited them to sit, on the sofa the Zeldi had forsaken. Col the 'secretary' stood behind the Princess's sofa: her cap with its braid of thorns and flowers tucked under one arm.

D"fydd and Ch'ro were speechless with dawning understanding—

'You've made a conquest,' remarked the Princess of Bois Dormant, in English. 'Don't hesitate to call on him. LaLa means what he says.'

'But it's to *your* generosity we owe our presence here, Princess,' D"fydd exclaimed. 'We are overwhelmed! If we can ever serve you—'

She nodded, a gleam of amusement in her sombre eyes. 'Be sure I will let you know, my lord prince. But it was nothing at all. It's my custom to take coffee in the lobby of The Caprice, where one finds the best mélange in the Diaspora – aside from a certain kiosk in Parliament Square, on Speranza. I happened to notice that you were in need of an introduction; I took the liberty of mentioning this to our host. Really, I am in *your* debt. LaLa adores a novelty: I was able to bring him a Myot prince, and a Neuendan scholar into the bargain. I stand high in favour tonight.'

She turned to Ch'ro, bowing slightly from the waist, and switched to Neuendan. 'But isn't it a little unexpected for a compatriot of the great Sigurt to serve the Royal Myots?'

'Not my idea – I was chosen by the prince's off-world guardian,' said Ch'ro, caught off guard: and then stumbled into inadequate explanation: 'As Your Excellency says, we are known for our scholarship, and I was ... I was. There were special circumstances.'

The Princess laughed. 'Well! It's a long time since I visited Sigurt's World, but I know when to stop asking questions. I shall have to change the subject! Tell me, noble Neuendan, could the Myot Oligarchs actually lose control of your Planetary Government over the "History of Fenmu"? That seems extraordinary!'

D"fydd and Ch'ro had heard of this cause célèbre on Shet. A study of the pre-history of the 'Fallen Moon', Fenmu – famous for its high-security prison – published anonymously, by some reclusive scholar, had become an instant sensation throughout the Crater-States. For reasons they'd have thought only a Sigurtian could understand, the 'History', with its *factual* treatment of the mythical 'Fall', was a rallying point for the opposition to the Myot Oligarchs, the party that dominated the planetary nation—

They were astonished: and more so when they realised that the Princess was not using transaid. She spoke impeccable Neuendan.

'I've heard it's very well written,' offered Ch'ro, cautiously.

'Wouldn't that be strange,' chirped and clicked the Princess, 'if a little scholarly treatise could topple the Oligarchs. Sigurt's nation might become again the gentle, mocking voice of Sigurt's World. And you might be restored to the throne, Messir D"fydd—'

'No thank you,' responded D"fydd, cheerfully. 'I like my freedom!'

The Princess smiled. Conversation reverted to English, and became general. The Aleutian, who turned out not to be Silent, told a story of the first 'Zeldi' generation. Balas 'Heritance Molecules' injected into Shet embryos, and vice versa: a bizarre and some might say unscrupulous peace initiative ... But how astounded the peacemakers had been when the 'infection' of graceful Balas and majestic Shet with each other's traits produced such stellar ugliness! 'They made the best of it. From henceforward, they declared, all peoples shall recognise and revere the innate awkwardness and *difficulty* of peace, as opposed to the beauty and simplicity of war. Which explains a lot about the constitution of Speranza, don't you think? Speranza having copied so much from Twin Planets post-war idealism—'

Everyone laughed. 'Yet the Zeldi became very rich on those HM patents,' remarked an exquisitely lovely Balas lady. 'And not *all* of us are delightful golden-hearted grotesques like LaLa, my dear Conrad—'

They were still talking when the tocsin rang: a thrilling, vibrant note that grew until it shook the gondola. The last bi-locating guests winked out of existence, banished to their sealed hotel rooms, or to faraway home locations. Remote Presence dolls froze, woke again and marched, empty-eyed, to stack themselves in the cloakroom coffers.

The Inundation had reached the city limits.

XLVI

Out in mid-ocean (Balas was one-third ocean; this part was called The Cauldron), the Inundation weather system, regular as the seasons, marginally chaotic, had done its work. The lipid layer, rucked and crumpled into vast folds, had been forced on shore along the isthmus, dragging a mass of water with it. Several times, in the ages of its existence, the Isthmus Ridge had been buried. Several times in the life of the current numinal biped civilisation – the enduring success story that had suffered colonial oppression, attained its own space travel and three times waged interplanetary war – the city in the path of the flood had been utterly demolished. But the Dettans always came back, and rebuilt their capital in the exact same perilous spot.

As the lipid piled up along the shore, folds became cracks, cracks became open wounds. Great loops and coils of force formed within the mass, breaking bonds, igniting change. Gushes of pure, sterile water burst through the paradoxical water-repellent layer at the base of the scum and shot to the surface like geysers, carrying an ephemeral chemistry that formed itself into a slippery crust and poured onward, racing faster and faster, diffusing upward, gathering speed and height.

Ch'ro and D"fydd abandoned the group of 'air-fish' veterans around the Princess and joined the frantic throng. Everyone was fighting, laughing, gasping, good-humoured and ruthless, to be among the first who were engulfed. 'This is insane!' shouted Ch'ro. 'I've never heard of anything like it! If we were at home, would we rush out to get fried by a winter storm—?'

'Completely mad!' yelled D"fydd, and they linked arms—

The glass walls of the gondola were a yielding lattice, preventing falls, but offering no obstacle to the racing foamy tide. People were shrieking. Here it came, the diffusion layer, at its most concentrated (the effect was far weaker on the Promenades down below). It poured over the

Zeldi's guests, it drowned them in pearly light, and in the light there were moving shadows, whip-tailed giant bacilli, finned serpents, huge diatom spheres, squirming tori: shapes beyond any comparison, nameless colours. Eyeless, limbless, the creatures of the flood danced in the vapour, their natural and only habitat.

Air-fish passed between and around the human revellers: playful, fearless, exhibitionist, seeming to show off their tricks, seeming to peer into faces, in joyful curiosity. They were aggregates, temporary colonies of the microorganisms that lived in the lipid layer, individual cells hardly alive, hardly more solid than the vapour itself, but it was hard to believe that en masse they weren't conscious – capricious children, distracted from their sole purpose in life by the fascinating two-legged things. The first wave was no more toxic than a night's merry drinking (as the veterans put it). The second would be thicker. Left stranded, Ch'ro stared around, recovered his wits and grabbed the breathing mask from D"fydd's breast, where it had been dangling in readiness all night.

'*Mask—!*'

'Extraordinary! Extraordinary! This is the *best* thing we've done—'

'You're right, but you're babbling. We're mad drunk, you know.'

'If we stand on our heads, the air will be clearer.'

'Put on your *mask*—'

Between the third and the fourth surge there was a backwash of quiet. The floor had disappeared; the city beneath their feet was sunk as in the depths of a mirror, pale in the dawn. The air-fish swimmers stared at each other, goggle-eyed. Some stripped their masks off, because from this point there should be no real danger. As the fourth wave broke like bubbling silver wine, couples parted, linked groups unravelled. Each person wanted to be alone with the incalculable beings of the flood. They were drifting, filled with a dreamy hunger for more, for another wave, for just one more dance ...

After the sixth the tocsin rang again, and it was over. The diffusion layer rushed on, sinking as it flew: carrying the 'air-fish' to their breeding grounds. Floating screens reappeared, data and images showing the progress of the heavy lipid. Not much serious damage this time, apparently. The guests began to depart (LaLa had already slipped away). Doll-servants moved about, bearing trays of breakfast confectionery and a sour, warming drink: the traditional wake-of-the-flood hangover cure.

In hours the canals would retreat into their channels, the vapour would have dissipated, the Dettans would start cleaning up.

The ballrooms would be rendered back into fluid glass and sucked up into dirigible reservoirs again; the fantastical lamps, the fabulous costumes would be stored away. All over for another year. Ch'ro and D''fydd sat on a safety-barrage by the gondola stairs, looking down at the dishevelled streets and eating '*koulis* curls' (their favourite Dettan cake).

'If there's an eighth wave the city drowns,' remarked Ch'ro. 'Isn't that strange? They have the same fatal number as we do.'

'That's because we're one species. We are the Diaspora: numinal bipeds, all from a single origin. Can you doubt it, after what we've just experienced? Those creatures were *aliens*, Ch'ro. They have mind, a ... a form of mind we can't understand. That's why Balas are mystics, different. They *know* ... I wonder when the Princess left? I wonder who she is and why she helped us? I mean, really. Shall we try to find out?'

'I think not,' said Ch'ro. 'She frightened me, a little.'

'Me too.' D''fydd sighed. 'She's so perfect, so utterly perfect.'

Ch'ro glanced at his friend, sidelong. The Princess's *perfection* wasn't what had scared him. He decided not to pursue the matter.

'There's a trip we can take, D''fydd. We can hire a guide and go into the marshes, following the fishes: maybe see their courtship behaviour. It's hard for tourists to get permission, it can be dangerous country. But now—'

'We can enlist our dear friend LaLa! Yes, let's do it.'

D''fydd had spotted the Princess of Bois Dormant, strolling along the temporary elevated walkway by the Median Canal, with Conrad the Aleutian. Her green-liveried secretary (or bodyguard!) followed behind. Everything was shrouded in mist, but he thought he detected intimate conversation. Had the Princess and that world-weary noseless immortal known each other before? Were they old friends? Did they travel together? He was stung by unreasonable jealousy.

'Ch'ro, I've just realised. I must *do* something with my life!'

XLVII

<So that's the ex-prince of Myot,> remarked Conrad. <A charming boy. And may I say, an improvement on the Balas/Shet attempt at 'hybridising' two numinal biped variants! You know what I think about *noses.*> He touched the rim of his own dark, bristled nasal space fondly. <Awful excrescences: but the Sigurtian version, my Self! Like a nightmarish little Blue ear, stuck in the middle of one's face. The Neuendan suffers less than most of his planetary nation, but even so! The prince is lucky to have escaped. Well, almost escaped.>

<You are shameless,> replied the Princess, amiably. <Aleutians believe they have the best manners in the universe, because their disgusting habitual rudeness is subvocal: refined gesture, pheromone exchange, which few of your victims can read. Actually, you have the worst. Arrogant, conceited brutes.>

The Aleutian laughed, soundless and delighted, and made the gesture of *accepting a just chastisement.* <Princess, you and I are going to be great friends.> 'You know the story, I presume?' he continued, in spoken English. 'Of the young man's birth and parentage, I mean?'

'I do.'

'Tragic.'

'Tragic,' agreed the Princess of Bois Dormant.

They continued along the Median, stepping around the places where overspill had invaded the walkway in heaps of gleaming slime. The Aleutian had rarely met anyone, even of his own 'arrogant, conceited' race, as hard to read as this Blue. He wondered what she was thinking now. Nothing escaped; there was only the perfect control that itself betokens secrets. But her expertise in the Common Tongue only confirmed the air of mystery and power that surrounded the Princess, and all her works.

'I'm puzzled by that creature you carry around with you, Princess.

Where does it come from? It resembles an Aleutian commensal—?'

'It *is* an Aleutian commensal. At least, I believe so.'

The thing seemed to dislike Conrad's scrutiny. It shrank closer around its mistress's throat, and she raised a hand to soothe its slick hide.

'No, that's impossible. We grow our commensals from the cells of our own bodies, as I'm sure you are aware. They are *not* transferable.'

The Princess shrugged. 'Then my familiar must be an ingenious fake. Never mind, it still pleases me.'

'Hm.' Conrad's curiosity increased, but one did not interrogate the Princess. They reached the Lateral junction. A large red and orange machine sat in front of The Caprice, cleaning sealant from the façade with huge slurps and grunts. 'Time to move on,' remarked the Aleutian. 'I'm going into the marshes, to "follow the fishes", in a day or two: and perhaps to do a little business. Would you care to join my party? I'd appreciate your company.'

She smiled. 'Thank you. That would suit me very well.'

XLVIII

After the flood the whole isthmus was sunk in fog, the persistent cloud-
bath of the humid season. The sky over the marsh forests, when it
could be seen between the swaying tips of the reeds, was lightless at
night, diffuse gold at the clearest part of the day ... Ch'ro and D"fydd
lay on their backs, on the pillowy bare ground, and stared upward. The
'reeds' were towering masts, wrapped in the tattered silvery banners of
their immensely long leaves.

They'd been following a troupe of the little mossy creatures called
'weepers' or 'reed monkeys': but there was nothing moving up there
now except a flock of small Blue birds, cute alien invaders. The *sparrows*
were a pest, they could be shot. Ifraa"k, their obligatory bodyguard,
aimed his gun at the flutter of wings, but he wasn't going to waste his
ammunition—

'I wonder why the Guide was so negative,' remarked D"fydd, idly.

The Independent Traveller's Guide had described this trip as an
obscure experience worth missing. Monotonous, sinister scenery, miserable weather, dreadful food; chances of seeing the air-fish: about zero.

'The English word "reed" is the name of a marsh plant they have on
the Blue,' said Ch'ro. 'But the original reeds are about knee-high; these
are twenty metres tall. Blues must feel crushed and tiny here, how
upsetting for them. "Monotonous" is fair, I think.'

'*Sinister* is unjust ... It's quiet here, not menacing.'

Ifraa"k snorted in disgust. 'Speranza-isation. Two thousand years the
Va tried to take over the Isthmus, and never succeeded. Two hundred
years the Shet carried us off as slave-labour, tried to destroy our culture,
and they couldn't. Along comes First Contact, and soon no one will
know the name or measure for anything, except in English.'

'You've got to admit, Ifraa"k, it's useful to have a contact language.'

'I like talking to strangers, it's true. But enough is enough.'

'I tell you what. I'll dump my transaid, and you can teach me Dettan—'

'You couldn't learn, Messir Cro. It's hard.'

'You'd be surprised,' said the Neuendan.

They were five days out from Detta'aan. They'd visited traditional settlements, been escorted round a mud mine, observed wildlife, and were learning to walk on the lipid streams, wearing marshland *plates* – a kind of flat-bottomed overshoe, customised for their Sigurtian feet. But the Guide was probably right about the air-fish; once you were out here it was obvious. Tourists travelled in style: it was the only way you could get a permit. At every halt a whole village of supple-glass huts went up to accommodate their expedition, including the Approved Tour Leader, the Isthmus Natural Reserve Officer, the gendarmes, the porters. You'd have to be on a much more rugged itinerary to have a chance of tracking down those elusive creatures.

What do the so-called 'brigands' prey on when they can't get rich tourists? wondered D"fydd. *There can't be many of us ... It always puzzles me when people say a lonely wilderness is 'haunted by robbers'. Wouldn't they be better off in a busy city? And if this country is so lawless, wouldn't* we *be safer with less show? Without offering the temptation of the baggage floats, a glass-extruder and all the rest of it?*

'One day you'll go to Speranza, Ifraa"k,' said Ch'ro. 'Then you'll never look back. You'll be a space person, a citizen of the Diaspora, and forget the Isthmus: apparently it happens to everyone.'

Ifraa"k set his long gun on the ground and pillowed his head on his feathery golden arms. 'What is it like, Messirs? The Buonarotti transit?'

'Like nothing much. No tomb-couches, not any more. An Aleutian starship is one big Buonarotti couch, I think; er, technically. You sit in a row of seats, you fold the safety cowl over you. You pull on your headset, you play a game in what's called "false duration"; you disembark.'

'You travelled in the dreamtime?' The Dettan sounded disappointed.

'You bet,' said D"fydd. 'I don't want to risk being driven insane.'

'Everyone travels in the dreamtime, on commercial flights,' explained Ch'ro. 'It's a safety regulation. In *theory* you can apply to join the Active Complement, but it doesn't happen—'

'No time has passed,' D"fydd broke in. 'But that doesn't mean anything. Say it's fifteen o'clock standard when your flight "leaves" Sigurt's World, and it's the same fifteen o'clock – so to speak, in the simultaneity – when you "reach" the Twin Planets Port. You still have to travel to Shet or to Balas through conventional space, and it takes weeks on the Superfast, er, I mean thousands of *term*. Or is it hundreds ...? Unbelievable distances disappear, but they were unbelievable anyway, so who cares? The believable distances are still there. The weirdness vanishes, d'you see what I mean?'

Ifraa"k groaned. 'I can never fly to Speranza.'

'Why not?'

'I would *love* the transit,' declared the Dettan. 'I would transit awake, and know the weirdness. How could you miss that? I can't believe you had a chance and missed it. I just can't stand the idea of a thousand and a half *term* on a spaceship, locked in a box with irritating people, so dull, so deadly dull.'

'The Isthmus isn't dull?'

'Never. There are always more funny tourists.'

The Sigurtians heard the *knife* first. 'Company,' said D"fydd, sitting up. They watched the boat approach, pleased at any incident. There were four people standing in it, a fifth hunched over the steering bar in the stern.

'Can't be tourists,' murmured Ch'ro. 'As we know, the vibration of an engine can cause the aggregates to fall apart. That's why all gullible foreigners have to pay a troop of porters, if we want to follow the fishes.'

'Can't be marshfolk,' added D"fydd. 'They use reed-bole dugouts that they push along with those brush-things. Or is that only for show?'

The steersman cut the engine; the *knife* slid to a halt. It occurred to Ch'ro that the strangers were now between them and their camp – just visible through the reed boles, on the far side of the lipid stream they'd crossed on their 'plates', half an hour ago. But Ifraa"k didn't seem worried. He hadn't touched his weapon.

'Mud-eaters!' exclaimed Ifraa"k.

'*Mud-eaters?*' repeated Ch'ro, carefully.

Mud-eaters were marsh quadrupeds, three or four metres long. They ate huge quantities of the jellied mud that passed for solid ground, for the sake of its freight of microorganisms: but they also had large teeth for chewing up reed leaves, and could be aggressive.

Ifraa"k made the gesture for *I didn't say it right*. 'Mud ... mud-diggers. Treasure-seekers. They come after the flood, look for special silicates: the mud that makes you rich, and makes you poor. This is good, good luck.

Maybe ... If they know anything, I shall call Keelian.'

The mud-diggers climbed out of their boat and advanced. Two of them had the Dettan pattern of sparsely feathered limbs and sleek gold heads; the longer feathers trained into curls behind their small ears. Three, including the older man, the steersman, looked as if they came from further afield, either Va or the Southern Continent. Their clothes were battered cast-offs with touches of second-hand finery, the uniform of rural poverty everywhere. A supple-glass torc, a smart-looking iface tucked in a grimy waistcloth, glitter-studded headbands. Ch'ro could see no weapons, but he could *feel* them. *A gun here, a knife there*, he thought. *Kept out of sight, and why not?*

Ifraa"k talked to the older man, and became excited. He used his radio to call Keelian, the Natural Reserve Officer. Shortly, she appeared through the reeds: dropped from the bank and crossed the lipid without breaking stride. There was more discussion. The tourists waited to know their fate.

'D'you think we should join in?' wondered D"fydd.

'Keelian's in charge. Let's not mess it up.'

The other mud-diggers were neither ignorant nor hostile. A young woman in a grubby 'traditional' kilt and an embroidered shirt that had once been a fashion item made the gesture for *permit me?* and touched the transaid barrette on the side of Ch'ro's skull. She obviously knew what it was.

'Would you guys like to come fishing? Party? Exchang' culture?' She raised an imaginary snifter to her vestigial nose.

'Sounds good to me,' said D"fydd, grinning.

Keelian came over. 'Messirs, we have an opportunity. Messir Piric here knows where the fish are active this year. He can take us to a complex of lagoons where he says we have a good chance of a sighting. If you agree to my conditions we can go there.'

Chro frowned. 'In their *knife*? What about engine noise?'

Keelian screwed up her mobile Balas features. 'Yes, it's a problem. If I had my way I'd ban *knives* from the Reserve, but the Prospectors, so-called mud-diggers, are something we have to live with. We keep relations friendly, and they *do* know the marsh. The *knife* will take us partway, then we'll go in on foot. Spend the night, come back to camp the next day. I think this is your best chance of seeing something, Cro, a better chance than most tourists get. You understand, it's forbidden to make any recording?'

'We were scanned,' said D"fydd. 'Why is it so important?'

'No secret cameras,' promised Ch'ro. 'I swear by the Mighty Void.'

'Forget that Shet nonsense. I'm Balas ... The fish are ours, that's all. Not yours. Ifraa"k's coming too, and we'll maintain radio contact. You'll let me haggle for you? And while we're on this trip you do as I tell you, at once, without question. Is that agreed?'

They gestured eager assent. 'Agreed.'

'I'll talk to Piric again.'

Supply packs were brought from the camp. The fee was agreed, the certified transaction stored on Keelian's iface, pending datasphere access. Everyone got into the *knife*, tourists up in the curve of the prow. There were no fittings inside the shell. Bundles of possessions, pipes of the refined scum used for engine fuel, oddments of mud-panning equipment littered the bottom boards. Ch'ro and D"fydd crouched on their haunches, facing front.

'What d'you think? Are we being cheated?'

'I'm sure we could have done better ourselves, but it's only money.'

'Keelian says transaid spooks the natives, but I don't think so. She just likes her tourists to be helpless ... What about the fishes?'

'I don't know, I think we have to trust Keelian.' Ch'ro shivered, struck by a chill of excitement. 'Incredible, if it's true ... What you said, at the ball.'

'Alien intelligences, making love. When you put it like that, Ch'ro, it sounds weird, but in a bad way. Should we even be—?'

'Nobody "puts it like that", on the record. The air-fish are a species of slime mould ... But I know what you mean. This is something holy. I wouldn't *want* to make a record; if we were allowed.'

'Nor me.'

It was hard to judge distances. Time slowed to the rhythm of the engine, the lipid stream twisted and turned, and every direction looked the same. In a clearing like the one where they'd met the mud-diggers everyone had to get out. The *knife* was dragged along a slick track, through a neck of forest to a different kind of channel, straight and broad.

'This is very ancient,' said Ifraa"k. 'Old canals. Somewhere here, Buonarotti made the first transit landfall. But it's lost.'

'We read that,' agreed D"fydd. 'It's in the Guide.'

'You don't believe it, because we have nothing to show.'

'She must have landed somewhere.'

They reached the lagoons as the heat of the day began to build, and here they left the *knife*: just sitting by the bank, unattended. The diggers seemed confident it would still be there when they got back. Now they had to traverse a string of mud islands, Piric leading the way. The diggers crossed the channels barefoot, splay-toed. Keelian and Iffraa"k were at ease in their light marsh-boots. The tourists had to keep putting on their *plates*, and taking them off again. The mist – which should have been thinning, as much as it ever did – grew thicker. Keelian made them check their breathing masks, and they noted that the diggers were doing the same. Glimpses of a pale expanse, dotted with islands, appeared when the fog shifted. The grey, silver-speckled ground quivered underfoot, hardly more stable than the lipid.

They'd been told not to talk. Voices couldn't disturb the fish, but there were mud-eaters around, it was dangerous. They didn't mind. Silence was welcome. There was a nervy tension in the party: and transaid is disturbing in such situations. Sounds you don't recognise become intelligible speech in your mind. Your mouth makes uncouth shapes and noises, but the foreigner seems satisfied ... Sometimes the bridge breaks. Sometimes you know you're misunderstanding everything, and that every word you utter is offensive—

Nobody sank, nobody drowned. They reached a large lump of mud, bare of vegetation, where Keelian said they would make camp. 'In the early hours, very early, Piric will take us from here to the sink where we might see something. I'm going with him now, to check it out. You stay here, with Ifraa"k. Have a rest and a meal.'

The mud-diggers had collected sheaves of fallen reed-leaves on the hike. They spread and layered the leaves to make a dry floor: apparently this was 'making camp', digger-style. Everyone sat down in this sketch of a house, with roof and walls of warm, mineral-smelling fog. Everyone took out food and drink. One of the diggers had a carrying cloth full of ruddy oval fruit. He split and examined them, before offering one to D"ffyd.

'You like *koulis*? You eat our food? These are very fresh.'

'Absolutely. We love *koulis*.'

The fruit had wriggling maggots in it. D"fydd picked them out with a claw, trying to do this unobtrusively, and ate it anyway. The duties of a tourist are sometimes onerous. The mud-digger looked more puzzled than offended, and tried another. '*Koulis*. Alive, much better flavour.'

The *koulis* were the worms.

'You like to party now?' asked the girl in the embroidered shirt.

Ch'ro and D"fydd consulted. 'What do you think *party* means?'

'Let's ask Ifraa"k,' suggested Ch'ro.

'It's up to you,' he said. 'You may be sorry later. You're the ones getting up in the middle of the night.'

'Aren't you coming to see the air-fish?'

'I'll sleep. It's for tourists. You paid, I didn't.'

The tension that they'd felt, or imagined, had dissipated; the mud-diggers seemed perfectly relaxed, but this response made them uneasy. The English words sounded strange. What was Ifraa"k really saying?

'Ifraa"k—' Ch'ro made the gesture for *please take me seriously*. 'Are we doing something wrong, coming here? Are we stepping on holy ground?'

'I don't think there's any harm in it,' said Ifraa"k, looking away from them, into a wall of fog. 'It's just not for me.'

They decided to decline the party.

Nobody seemed offended. Two of the diggers took folding shovels from their packs and went out onto the lipid. They disappeared into the fog and returned, balancing a big lump of scum between them. They dumped this on the shore, and all the diggers gathered around it. The young woman gave the lump a hefty slap with a shovel. She fell back, gasping and giggling, her arms waving and her legs kicking the air. Someone else took the shovel, and repeated this process.

'I think I get it,' remarked D"fydd, grinning.

'Me too. Neurotoxins.'

'Shall we try a sniff? It'd be a new experience.'

'No!'

'Shall we tell them to stop?'

'Why? I don't see why they should listen. On what grounds?'

By the time Keelian and Piric returned it was nearly dark, and the junior treasure-seekers were laid out, comatose: giggles rising from them occasionally, like bubbles of gas. Keelian got extremely annoyed. Piric tried to calm her down. Ifraa"k suffered the brunt of the Reserve Officer's displeasure (the diggers were feeling no pain) and became sullen. The tourists, who had wrapped themselves in their sleeping bags, pretended to be asleep. The sound of a powerful engine interrupted the exchange of views. D"fydd and Ch'ro sat up. Keelian swore, fluent and furious—

Everything was pearl and charcoal. Keelian, Piric and Ifraa"k were gesticulating shadow-puppets, haloed in the dim light of Keelian's chemical lantern, which she'd set down on the raft of leaves.

'Nothing to do with me!' cried Piric. 'I don't know what's going on!'

'*Ifraa"k!* Where is your weapon?'

'I don't know! I put it down somewhere!'

Keelian took out her dart-gun and marched angrily toward the sound. Ch'ro and D"fydd freed themselves from their sleeping bags and hurried after. A big *knife*, its prow looming huge and predatory through the fog, stood by the sloping shore and had let down a gangplank.

'What are you doing here?' demanded Keelian. 'You can't use an engine that size in the marsh at breeding season!'

The first figures to step from the gangplank were carrying bright lights, which made everything more confusing. Two of them grabbed Keelian, a third relieved her of the dart-gun and used it to shoot her in the chest, point blank, with a dose of animal tranquilliser meant to subdue a mud-eater. Keelian slumped; the other shadows dropped her.

'I will protect you,' babbled Ifraa"k, holding back D"fydd, who had started forward, shouting. 'Be calm, they're just brigands. I will call for help. Only I don't know where I put my gun—'

Piric crouched beside his comatose crew, watching and waiting. His eyes glittered. The tourists shouted and protested. The brigands hauled Ifraa"k away from them: took his radio and shot him with the dart-gun, point blank, like Keelian. Someone dealt Ch'ro a stinging blow across the side of his skull. The world went black. He was still standing, but he could not see or move, and his hearing had gone crazy. His head was filled with howling feedback, he didn't know what had happened to D"fydd.

XLIX

They woke in pitch darkness, and listened to each other's breathing. 'Did somebody put a bag over my head?' mumbled Ch'ro.

'No. I think we got a sniff of something, like a punch in the brain.'

'Wearing off now. Is this is the same night?'

'I *think* so—'

Their wrists and ankles were bound, and their boots had been taken. Echolocation told them they were alone in a bare, four-walled shack — nothing like the dwellings of the traditional marshfolk, who built giant nests and hung them in the reeds. The ground under them was mud. So, no longer on that island, but probably still in the marshes.

'What d'you think? Interstellar sex-pet slave trade?'

'If we're lucky,' said Ch'ro.

'These playful, charming Sigurtians must be homed together.'

Ch'ro laughed. 'Thank Grace we had no implants, no desirable gadgets stuck in the back of our eyes. That might have been nasty.'

'What *did* happen to Ifraa"k's gun, I wonder?'

'Maybe they were all in on it, my Prince. Whatever it is.'

'Why not? Tourists are lawful prey, anywhere in the Diaspora. I hope what we saw wasn't a double-cross. I liked Ifraa"k. And Keelian, mostly. Shall we start planning our escape?'

'Soon. When we know what's happening. But don't fall asleep.'

Sigurtian metabolism was liable to shut down, dramatically, in the face of serious illness, trauma or simply hardship: it was a winter survival trait. But the prince and his companion were less likely than most to succumb: they had learned to resist coma. D"fydd thought of nights in his childhood when he had lain awake, never beaten or tied up, but often very frightened, and very glad of Ch'ro's breathing presence across the room.

Images of the old manor house where they had lived, alone except for servants they couldn't trust, drifted through his mind: nostalgic, haunted.

Some time later they were hauled out into a dim humid-season dawn. A roof of fog, walls of fog obscured their surroundings, but they made out the angles of squared, Shet-type buildings, alien to the Isthmus. The faint smell of heavy-metal processing, which they'd already noticed, was stronger outdoors. The brigands who did the hauling were a pair of big, armed Shet, in military-style uniform; and that was a bad sign. They were taken to the balcony of a reed-bole longhouse where they met Piric, the steersman: with an escort of armed guards, Dettans this time. He wore uniform too; he was looking very pleased with himself. They'd wondered if they were being punished for sacrilege, but there was no mystical glamour to any of this.

'My name is Piric the Marsh Lord,' announced the mud-digger, in English with a Shet accent. 'I'm also known as *Tsunami*, or the leader of *Tsunami* ... You will have heard of me. I've never taken a Sigurtian before. Bat-people, the Blues call you. What does *bat* mean? Is it true you can walk in darkness?'

'Untie us,' suggested Ch'ro. 'Blindfold us, dump us out in the marsh. We'll show you.'

'Very humorous, children. I could put out your eyes, of course. But I won't do that. No harm shall come to you, if things go smoothly.'

'How much do you want?' demanded D"fydd. 'We have funds, we can make freeing us worthwhile, no delay, no police, no questions asked.'

Piric made the purring in his throat that was Balas laughter. He flipped out a virtual screen from the iface bracelet on his wrist and made a show of studying it. *The Help Desk*, thought Ch'ro. *Never go near the Help Desk—*

'That's not what I'm reading here, Messir Prince. What I see here is pocket money: enough to pay your bills at The Caprice and so on. Your funds are controlled by your guardian, on Speranza. This is what I intend to do. I shall send to the Sigurtian Embassy in Kalia'aan, with proof that I am holding Prince D"fydd of the Myots. They'll send a discreet courier to Speranza, your guardian will obey my instructions, and all will be well.'

'There's no need to send to Kalia'aan,' said Ch'ro. 'We have friends in Detta'aan who would stand surety. And be very discreet.'

'Frankly I doubt that. Allow me to know my own business. I am not a cruel man. You will stay here, in secure custody, unharmed, until my terms are met. If there is unreasonable delay, or if your *friends* do anything stupid, I'll have to start harming the prince. But you needn't worry. They will know my reputation, they will know I mean business, you are safe.'

Ch'ro's attention had been caught by something that stood beside their guards: a cube of silvery basketwork, finely woven from split reed-leaf, big as a packing case. What was it for? Was it contraband in a box, was it art?

The brigand's disastrous terms fell on him like something ordained, like fate.

'We're not worried,' he said. 'Why should we worry? We'll dine out on this, it's an adventure, worth the fee.'

'Very humorous. I will speak to you again, later.'

Tsunami and his guards went inside the longhouse. The Shet picked Ch'ro and D"fydd up like toys and put them in the basket. One of them leaned down and cut the slick bindings at their wrists and ankles; the other dropped a reed-leaf package in with them. The lid was secured. The whole cage was then carried, jolted about, and finally hauled, swaying, up into the air. They watched the process, as well as they could, through the weave. Their prison was suspended on a line between two tall, shorn reed boles that stood like banner poles in the midst of the brigands' camp.

L

They sat facing each other, backs against the walls, rubbing at their stinging wrists and ankles. There wasn't enough room to lie flat, or to stand. Evidently they weren't the first residents in this hotel. A small hole in one corner, dark with urine, greased with traces of faeces, gave off a seasoned, powerful stink.

'I wish they wouldn't keep calling us child, children,' complained D"fydd. 'They all do it, here and on Shet. I hate that.'

'It's not meant as an insult; it just means all foreigners are minors.'

Ch'ro reached for the package. His hands were still clumsy: he was smaller, the nerve gas had done him more harm. It held a bundle of mud-eater jerky strips and a traditional marshfolk flask, full of liquid. He unstoppered the flask and sniffed. Not water, alas, no chance. Plant sap. Hopefully not one of the varieties that would make them sick.

'We've been untied, and they mean to feed us: two good signs. We'll have to explain to our friend Tsunami that we can't eat flesh.'

The Sigurtians couldn't digest Twin Planets animal protein. Hence their pleasant carb diet of cake and alcohol. Plus grain porridge, fruit, the plant sap 'dairy' products that agreed with them; and vitamin pills. It wasn't a problem, except they were prone to energy crashes.

But they had no tourist supplies with them now.

'So it's over,' said D"fydd, quietly. 'So soon ... I didn't think it would be so soon. I'm sorry, Ch'ro.'

'Don't talk like that. Never say die till you're dead.'

'Oh, agreed, my Bloodman. I wouldn't consider saying die. We must plan our escape, of course. I insist on that.'

'This is to demoralise us. They won't keep us in a cage for long. They'll transfer us to one of the buildings, they'll be nice as long as we're docile. You need to eat something, D"fydd, you're having an energy crash.' Ch'ro pushed up his shirtsleeve. 'And since this is an emergency, my feudal lord, you'd better take your dues. See, Prince, an arm is offered—'

D"fydd made the gesture for *don't be a fool*. 'I drink your blood, you drink mine, noble Neuendan ... Very romantic, but not very logical. In the stories they forget to mention those useful other ranks in the besieged fortress, whose blood is drunk and not replenished—'

The prince broke off, fired by a sudden realisation.

'Ch'ro, you're right. They *won't* leave us like this. They'll put us on the ground. Tsunami will want to take us out, and play with us. This could be our only chance. We're helpless against giant Shet gangsters with machine guns, but we have our teeth and claws. And certain other advantages ... Surely we can fight our way out of a *basket*. Where d'you think we are?'

'In a derelict mining camp—'

'Yes, but *where*? How far from Detta'aan? From anywhere?'

'I have no idea. But a mine must be on a canal route. We can find our way to some kind of civilisation, it shouldn't be too hard.'

They could get no purchase on the fastenings of the lid. The hinges and the catch were like the ligatures that had been used to tie them up: immensely tough, designer material. The basket-weave itself was almost as resistant. The weak spot was that fetid hole. They looked at it, grimly.

'Advantage number one,' said D"fydd, 'Tsunami not only thinks we'll wait and hope, like his usual prey. He thinks we are soft.'

They worked on the shit-hole for hours, indifferent to the filth as two trapped animals: rinsing their mouths from time to time with the plant sap; taking care that nothing fell through; saving the fragments to disguise their work, should they be interrupted. No one came. The brigand camp went peacefully about its business. Occasionally they heard tramping feet, or the distant hum of a *knife*; or caught snatches of Balas conversation, which they could no longer understand. In the end they ate the jerky, because they *had* to eat, and blood-drinking really didn't make sense.

When the hole was big enough for Ch'ro's head and one shoulder, D"fydd was ready to stop. 'I can't fly, noble Neuendan. Off you go. I'll tell them I sucked you dry and you disintegrated, I'll tell them I ate your husk: and you'll come back with the rescue party.'

'Don't be so childish. We can both go, and still leave them with a mystery.'

They worked on. The camp became noisy at nightfall, but it calmed down again. They took a break, roused themselves from a state near to coma, and finished the plant sap. A little light escaped from Tsunami's longhouse: otherwise the camp was dark, except for the hissing, blue-white lanterns carried by the guard on patrol. They measured the interval between his crossings, and wondered if it was time enough. Maybe, maybe not. Ch'ro slipped off his shirt and shook out the folds of skin between his flanks and his upper arms. Silently, they hugged each other; Ch'ro dropped headfirst through the hole. He clawed onto the underside of the basket, hung there for a moment, clicking at a pitch that was unlikely to alert anyone below, and launched himself, arms spread.

The reed bole came to meet him as it had promised, like a trusted friend. He embraced it, shinned ten metres or so to the ground: and located the pulley mechanism. He was very tired. It took all his strength to lower D"fydd slowly, and to hold the cage above the ground, leaning against the weight, while the prince scrambled out.

Dead silent. They started to haul the empty cage up again. The pulley squeaked, a squeal of glass-fibre rope on metal. They stopped, groped at the mechanism, tried to ease it: tried again. Another squeal. The guard was far off, his pacing unperturbed, but Ch'ro touched D"fydd's arm: *leave it*. Then there was a new sound, someone coming out of the longhouse, not carrying a light. Unaware of D"fydd and Ch'ro, probably tipsy, this person passed them and blundered right into the empty cage.

He yelled; he fired a fusillade of shots, spraying the darkness. Lights sprang up. Figures exploded from the building. The Sigurtians sped for cover, but D"fydd stumbled, he fell: and that was that. Ch'ro had reached a maze of unlikely shapes, huge cones, bellied pots for giants. He turned and saw D"fydd upright, one leg dragging. He was fighting his captors, but purely to distract them from Ch'ro, he hadn't a chance—

'Go on!' he shrieked, in Neuendan, into the dark. 'They won't hurt me! I'm the *money*! Get out of here! Fetch help!'

LI

Tsunami's Bloodmen hunted Ch'ro for hours out in the marsh, wasting a lot of ammunition. They didn't find him, because he hadn't left the derelict refinery. He was hidden aloft, in an upper storey of pipelines. It was dawn of the next day before he could bring himself to abandon D"fydd.

He had no iface, no printed Guide, no food or water. Everything they'd been carrying had been taken when they were first knocked out. No boots, not even a shirt. He must find help, but not around here. A 'traditional settlement' or Prospectors' camp in this vicinity would be a death trap. He ran, straight into the reeds, hearing no pursuit but instinctively expecting a brigands' flyer, invisible in the fog, to hover and pounce. It didn't. The Isthmus in the humid season was like Sigurt's World in winter: atmospheric conditions had closed the skies.

He thought he would hide in the reeds and follow the channels to Detta'aan. The passage of a *knife* or a dugout left lasting traces: more 'cuts' in the lipid meant denser traffic, which must lead him towards civilisation. But how far could he run? When he swarmed up a mast, at dusk, he could see no glowing shadow of a city on the unbroken overcast. Not a star, not a glimpse of Balas's pretty ring of moons. His hands wouldn't grip, his vision blurred. He glided down again, blundering from bole to bole, and collapsed. When he woke it was daylight: he felt stronger, he went on.

He was afraid he was going round in circles, trapped in Tsunami's domain by a cordon of wide old canals. He tried to make *plates* the primitive way: from strips of reed-leaf knotted into cord, and the round leaves of the 'dry-foot plant'. His clumsy attempts came apart as soon as he stepped onto the lipid: and he discovered that the channel he'd chosen was corrosive, it burned bare skin. He could not tell dangerous surfaces from the safe ones. He searched for sections of fallen mast, small enough to be handled, and managed to lash three pieces together. When he shoved his raft over a bank it wallowed and vanished. He stood and stared at the sullen eddies, his limbs shaking, his heart thumping, helpless. This was the end of his attempts at handicraft—

In the refinery he'd lapped condensation from glass and metal surfaces, some of it tainted, some sweet and pure. On the second day he had the great good fortune to find, and to recognise, a wild food plant that Ifraa"k had showed them. The tubers were easy to dig. They were infested with maggots, like the *koulis* fruit (and the scholar in him started to wonder, *Are these 'maggots' symbionts? Or actual parts of the plant, mobile tissue?*). He gobbled the thick sap and ate the worms live: thinking of crisp *koulis* curls, delicately served in the breakfast bar of The Caprice—

—Thinking of the shock in Ifraa"k's beautiful large eyes, as the dart-gun was pressed against his breastbone. The way the Dettan's chin had dropped, abruptly as if someone had snapped his cervical spine.

Within an hour he was suffering vicious cramps. Time after time he had to scrabble a hole and defecate, though nothing came out of him but a foul, dark gruel, then nothing but slime, but his bowels kept on retching. He was terrified because no matter how he tried, he was leaving a stinking trail. But Tsunami's men must have given up. Nothing moved except the weeper monkeys, the little alien birds; and once a family of mud-eaters, feeding in a stand of saplings. They went plunging away from him, thick bodies swaying, their crashing progress audible for a long time.

The cramps subsided to a dull ache, and thirst grew imperative. *Water is all around me*, he thought. The small, hollow-stemmed reed Ifraa"k had called 'drinking sticks' grew everywhere. He pulled a stem, broke off the ends and poked it through the scum. The tourists had been told that they must not attempt this trick, but he was desperate. His mouth filled with explosive, bitter goo. He spat and choked and rolled on the mud, clutching his chest. His eyes were bursting from their sockets; he thought he was going to die.

He did not die. The worst of it passed: he got up and went on.

*

Footprints vanished in the elastic surface; the patterns of *cuts* on the lipid were meaningless. He could be crossing his own trail over and over. He remembered Tsunami's iface, and the ease with which the gangster lord had penetrated D"fydd's local credit account. This is *not* a primitive land. Any of the flying things that buzzed around him might be artificial, or augmented: sending back realtime video of Ch'ro's misadventures. Tsunami's men were watching him and laughing. No, they didn't care. They'd let him run because they knew he could do nothing.

The fog-laden reed forest, threaded by oozing streams of fat, was unspeakably alien. Even the colours were subtly impossible. The green was not green, the silver was not silver. The air he breathed, tainted like the dead refinery, was not air. The unbelievable distances crawled out from wherever they'd been hiding, from crushed and minutely folded extra dimensions. His past mapped so perfectly onto this new existence that he wondered if he had ever left home. Life had always been like this. Trying to protect the boy he loved, groping in fog, failing to guess where the real threat lay, which servant would betray them, what course of action he should follow. Always a new threat, always realising your last decision had been a hideous mistake—

On the fourth day (if he hadn't lost count) there was light through the reeds. He worked towards it. A silvery expanse opened in front of him, curtained in mist, strung with mud islands. He could see the channel, with its cusp of beach, where they'd left the mud-diggers' *knife*.

'I have seen all this before,' he whispered.

He sank into a crouch on the shore, bare arms and skinfolds wrapped around his knees. He was the original numinal biped, lost in space. His mind drifted free of his body, into a void that grew, and grew, until the whole universe was inside him, looking out of his eyes. He knew all time, all space. He had a huge conviction that *this was the way it had been*. Long ago, aeons ago. And out there on the glimmering surface of the lagoon, where the pearly fog was thickest, the aliens were waiting for him—

I'll be back, he promised: forcing himself upright. *After I've rescued him. I shall find you again. Wait for me.* Now he was untouchable. Black dots danced in his eyes, he staggered as he walked, but by some miracle he was where he had aimed to be. The clearing where Ifraa"k had asked them about Speranza was within hours of here, but he must not go back there.

Listen, listen, listen. There will be another camp.

LII

'So it was here.'

'Or hereabouts. Allowing for the temporal-spatial shift of the Twin Planets system, relative to her position on the Blue, several hundred years ago, in terms of normal space, if that makes any sense—'

'A moot point,' said the Princess, amused. 'I tend to feel the Dettans are right, no location can be marked. Have you met the idea that the whole Diaspora is still caught in that journey without duration? That our universe and everything in it only exists in the moment of first transit?'

'Mere wordplay if you ask me.' Conrad put his Speranza-made 4-Space sextant back in his overall pocket. 'An untestable theory is not a theory.'

Aleutians were supposed to despise both 'scientific method' and Blue gadgets, but this adventurer made his own rules. The lagoon shone in the dark, with an eerie silver glow. The reed forest whispered at their backs. Somewhere out there the mating of the air-fish, alleged object of their expedition, was in full flow; according to the marshfolk. After a few minutes, silently agreeing that they'd paid their respects, they moved away.

'You're not interested in spying on the aggregates?'

'Not really ... Will Aleutia ever make those coordinates public?'

'I doubt it,' said Conrad. 'It might be embarrassing to explain how we acquired Buonarotti's lost working record. You're lucky,' he added. 'The last time I was here, the notional site of first landfall was a toxic sink. The marsh changes every flood.'

'And remains the same ... I like this place.'

'Because it's dangerous and lonely? I like it too. I wonder how our Sigurtian friends are getting on. Probably still puttering around the outskirts of Detta'aan. Those "Official Guides" are all crooks, and the lagoons *are* quite risky. By the way, did you know that a compatriot of mine was a member of the doomed Mission? He died in the massacre – alleged massacre, I should say. The prince's mother survived until the child was born, and then succumbed to her injuries; or so the Myots tell it ... A murky business, that affair, a blatant political cover-up: but you probably know more than I do.'

'I am indifferent to politics,' responded the Princess, placidly. 'It's a game for greedy fools, and the criminals who prey on them.'

'Ah, shame, then you won't have an opinion on the momentous event that doomed the unfortunate diplomats and their staff? I mean the Speranza Revolution?' He corrected himself. 'Excuse me, perhaps I'm mistaken, I'm no judge of Blue Senior ages, but you must have been alive at the time?'

The Princess laughed. 'Conrad, what is this interrogation? Are you auditioning me for a business partnership, or afraid I have connections with the police?'

'Neither. I'm just curious.'

'Isn't it strange the way it never rains here, in the wet season.'

'I don't find it strange at all,' said the Aleutian.

Their camp was a spruce and secure affair, a discreet distance from the lagoons: moated in lipid (the moat partly natural, partly dug by Conrad's Dettans). There was one guarded, temporary bridge, which was drawn up at night. When they got back, Rohan Aswad, the Princess's grave housekeeper, had prepared an excellent meal: which they shared with the Princess's muscular secretary; the Princess's equally formidable valet in attendance. Conrad's Dettans were not domestics. They excelled at security measures, and at taking long walks into the marsh, from which they returned with mysteriously laden baggage floats.

After dinner Conrad spent an hour or two in his camp-laboratory. He emerged to find the Princess alone by the fire pit: where a substance called 'Dettan charcoal' glowed, warding off the damp chill of the night. The reeds, untreated, could not be persuaded to burn; at a high enough heat, they melted. The friends-of-passage settled in companionable silence, with a flask of Aleutian whiskey, another of spring water, and a pair of Conrad's handsome freefall beakers. Reed monkeys chanted a doleful chorus; harmless flying things pestered the chemical lanterns. The Aleutian sipped his spirits, the Princess savoured her water.

Conrad watched the creature that she had called a commensal. It was capable of independence – he had seen it creep about the camp, active and inquisitive: but it was happiest on her body. It had crept up her sleeve, a favourite roost. Its eyes, peering from shelter, seemed to return the Aleutian's attention with a touch of warning, or challenge. Perhaps it perceived Conrad as a threat. Perhaps it expressed the Princess's own feelings.

<D'you think those two boys are lovers?>

<Still fascinated by your Sigurtians.> The Princess proffered her snifter case. <I'm afraid a romance is unlikely, given the obvious mismatch.>

<Difference in rank? Oh, no, I've made some mistake about *gender*, haven't I? I have no patience with that idiocy, can't understand why it's so popular with you mortals. You'll grow out of it.> Conrad selected a slender vial. 'Thank you.' He gazed into the embers, pleasantly melancholy. <Have *you* ever been in love, Princess?>

She tapped a vial of Twin Planets mix into her own holder, and inhaled. <Once. We were very happy for a while, but it didn't last.>

<You may find him again.>

<I won't be looking. I've grown out of that fantasy.>

<I don't believe in the eternal flame myself. But you have a past, evidently. Maybe, like an Aleutian romantic, you need to find your *trueself*, the same person born in an older or a younger generation, and nobody else will do. When one has lived many lives, no matter how fortunate, there is a core of darkness in one's heart, things that cannot be shared – unless with someone who already knows. Who was there at your worst moments, when you were completely alone, in the most terrible hours of your soul—>

<Immortal love sounds like a gloomy business,> remarked the Princess. <Are you nursing a broken heart, Conrad?>

<Drowning my sorrows in the risk and profit of Dettan silicates?> The Aleutian shrugged, his eyes brimming with laughter. <Not at all! When it comes to love, I travel light. *My* bond is with the others of my obligation, the loners, rogues: *alien-lovers*, as our compatriots very rudely name us.>

He set down his beaker. 'It's getting late. Shall we dance, Princess?'

'By all means. Let us have *The Bones of the City*.'

She was familiar with Aleutian customs. This, along with her expertise in the Common Tongue, told him plenty about her background on the Blue, and (though she would not be drawn) her likely views on the present Speranza Regime. The Princess's officers, who never missed Evening Dance, came to join them. Conrad's mouth-music kept the beat, and his Dettans gathered to watch: fascinated by the alien figures bowing and rising, swaying together in the lantern light, pacing the shivering mud in graceful measure—

The Princess listened to snores from the tiny vestibule of her hut (where Drez insisted on sleeping, fully armed); the warm, familiar weight of the phage coiled at her throat. *You are my one true love*, she thought, *strange little thing. No human soul will ever share what lies at the core of my heart, that hell where Bibi and her little girl-child lived and died.* The Aleutian's insight had made her uneasy. Perhaps the Princess and her familiar would have to part, and it would be a cruel loss. But not now, not just yet—

LIII

In the middle of the night Conrad was woken by his guards. An intruder had tried to cross the moat, and had been dragged out of the lipid, insensible.

'What *is* it, Messir Conrad—?' demanded the Dettan captain, holding up his lantern over the body. 'I never saw anything like that. It has flaps of skin, falling down under its arms, as if it is half-flayed. And look, something nasty has grown on its face.'

'My Self ...' Conrad had dropped into the running-gait crouch, his hind limbs reversed, beside the emaciated, prick-eared, half-naked thing. 'It's one of the Sigurtians.'

The Princess had arrived, roused by the uproar, her greatcoat wrapped over a snowy night-shift. 'How extraordinary. Is he injured?'

'Not so far as I can tell, aside from the lipid burns, and they're not serious. Mainly starved, dehydrated, feverish ... But what do I know?'

He rose to his feet, his nasal pinched, and expressed his uncharitable feelings in Silence. <This is *most* unwelcome. He must have got lost, there'll be search parties, questions. *Self*, most unwelcome. I suppose we must try to contact his Tour Guide by radio—>

<I think it will wait,> countered the Princess, in the same mode. <Let's see what Ch'ro himself has to say.>

<I bow to your prescience,> said the Aleutian. <And I take your meaning: the Isthmus is a lawless place. Will you talk to him? You know his language.>

'Of course.'

The Princess's officers stood around her in the blaze of lantern light, peering at the body. Something passed between them, a profound disturbance that Conrad couldn't read. They didn't have their mistress's control, but they were remarkably continent Blues. But the Princess was calm.

314

'What shall we do with him, Messir?' asked the captain.

'Carry him to the supply hut,' ordered Conrad. 'Move some stores, make up a bed. Treat his burns, that can't do any harm, and wrap him in a life-support blanket. Then take your orders from the Princess ...'

Ch'ro dreamed that he was at the Zeldi's ball, lying on his back, mad drunk, wrapped in a blissful cool cloud. The Princess of Bois Dormant looked down on him, all-knowing, surrounded by mystery and darkness; and he was afraid. *'Who are you?'* he gasped, trying to rise, very embarrassed—

'Lie still, Sigurtian. You know who I am, we met in Detta'aan. Conrad and I have been following the fishes: you stumbled into our camp. You tried to cross a corrosive channel. That's why you can't move, we're treating your burns. What happened to you out there?'

She had bared her left arm, and was tightening a cuff around it. 'What are you doing? I can't, you are an alien, I am an alien ...'

'I won't poison you. Your errand seems to be urgent, and you aren't fit to talk. This is the quickest way for you to gain strength. Drink.'

Next moment, it seemed, the Princess was gone and Conrad, the Aleutian from The Caprice, was holding a freefall beaker for him to suck. Foggy daylight welled through the rough-cast glass walls of a small hut. 'A nourishing soup,' explained the Aleutian, in English. 'No animal protein, plenty of variant-neutral numinal biped restoratives. You have remarkable powers of recovery, young mortal. I thought you'd be obliged to die on us. Sip and breathe, sip and breathe, don't choke yourself.'

'D"fydd ... We were kidnapped. Tsunami holds the prince.'

Conrad stood up quickly. 'Good! You're ready to talk. You'd rather speak in your own language, I'm sure. Excuse me, I'll leave you two.'

Ch'ro was alone with the Princess. He had dreamed of drinking her blood, how bizarre. But he was awake now, and his mind was clear. She knelt, slipped her arm around his shoulders and administered the rest of the beaker of soup. She wouldn't let him speak until it was all gone.

'Did I offend Messir Aleutian? What did I say?'

'Don't worry about it. Tell me what happened, take your time.'

She spoke in Neuendan. So he told the sorry tale, in the same language, while the Princess stalked the small area of the hut. Her pet

315

crawled down from her shoulders onto her breast, and she stroked it absently. The *pangolin*.

'I see,' she murmured, 'I see. What to do, what to do ...'

'Did you know we were missing? Have you heard from our team? I think it's been five days. Have there been search parties?'

'I don't know. We've been maintaining radio silence: Conrad's business interests require discretion.'

Her whole manner, impatient and distant, told him not to presume on their slight acquaintance. There would be no miracles this time. She knelt again and looked him in the face, straight and stern.

'Have you told me everything?'

'Everything I can remember.'

'Well ... We can contact the Detta'aan authorities. They'll come out here in force, making a lot of noise. They'll achieve nothing, but they'll have to do that. This gang-lord "Tsunami" is notorious, and quite ruthless. Do you realise it might be safest, for D"fydd, if we kept the police out of this?'

'I know.'

'We may presume that the ransom note has been delivered to the Sigurtian Embassy by now. What will they do?'

It's over, and so soon ... thought Ch'ro.

'Nothing.'

She raised her dark brows, a Blue gesture meaning incredulity. 'What do you mean? To ignore the demand would amount to murder!'

'I'm sure it won't be obvious. They'll cover themselves. But they won't pay a ransom, and there'll be no message sent to Speranza. You don't believe me? You don't understand. Listen ... The former prince of the Myots got notice to quit, the moment he was legally of age. We could have taken shelter in another Crater-State, lording it over a court of obsolete monsters, hateful idea. Instead we agreed to stay with a certain household of émigrés, on Shet. It turned out they were rabid feudalists, isn't that strange? We tried not to say anything that could be twisted ... but ... but that's the way it is between the Oligarchs and the Feudalists, two kinds of utter bastards, in bed with each other. Traps are laid for us, we're watched. The Ambassador won't lift a claw to save D"fydd's life, far from it.'

The Princess paced again, her arms folded.

'Perhaps we could call on LaLa, he might help you.'

Ch'ro made the gesture for *I'm not a fool*. 'We have organised crime at home, Princess. The Zeldi is very kind and charming but he has his primary residence in Detta'aan, next door to the lawless Isthmus with its mineral wealth and its notorious brigands, and—'

'And we need say no more. You've been doing some thinking.'

'I have.'

'So why are you here? What do you want me to do?'

'He told me to run, and fetch help,' said Ch'ro. 'I ran. At first I thought I could reach Detta'aan, then I realised it would do no good and I couldn't make it, anyway. I had to find another tourist party. Not the team who brought us out: I think they were paid off, or some of them were. Other tourists. That's why I'm here, but all I ask is a weapon. And if you know it, the quickest way to get back to Tsunami's place.'

'Is that what D"fydd would want?'

'You don't know him. Princess, my mother died, my father followed her to the tomb, where he may be living still, for all I know. My uncle, who assumed the title, considered me a freak, a regressive, a stain on the family. He found me a place in service, far away. I was ten years old. D"fydd ... I don't know what you know about our medicine, but he'd been held back. He'd been very ill, all his life. He was my age, but he was *just a little boy*. He was going to be all right, by then. He got better, he sprouted up amazingly—'

'There is a point to this story?'

'He knew he was dead the moment we were captured. He organised me into escaping and ... the only reason I kept running was that I need to have a weapon. I'm his Bloodman. I'm going back to die with him.'

She stared, coldly curious, as if struggling to see him as a fellow creature. 'Who called the prince D"fydd?'

'Liam,' said Ch'ro, bewildered. 'His guardian: I suppose it was Liam. I don't know. It's a Blue name. His mother was Blue, you know. '

'Liam Mallorn,' said the Princess, softly. 'Now that is strange.'

'Do you *know* him? I think you know everything. Princess, whoever you are: please, *please*. Give me a weapon—'

She left the hut.

Ch'ro tried to get up, but his legs were bound, and he couldn't stand. Weakness and shame overcame him; he blacked out. When he woke there was a smooth green case beside him: it proved to contain a pair of Blue-designed automatic handguns.

LIV

It was daylight again. Ch'ro lay in his pallet bed, playing with the Blue firearms. The material was intelligent: the grip adapted itself in his hand. He rolled the ammunition pellets in his palm, small and dark and heavy. *Bullets.* He wondered how much damage such little things could do. You'd have to be a crack shot, hit some vital blood vessel or organ ... It was quiet out there now; there'd been a lot of activity, earlier. He guessed that the Princess and the Aleutian were packing up to leave this dangerous neighbourhood.

The Princess's response to his desperation was of a piece with her mystery, her cold omniscience. She had given him not what he needed, but exactly what he had asked for. So be it. He would find his way back there, or find out where D"fydd had been taken, and ...

All he'll know is that I deserted him.

One wall of the hut had a permeable panel that served as a door. This section gave birth to a large and solid body: a Blue man, in the Princess's livery. He was followed by Col, the strangely marked secretary, and an older Blue with a long, furrowed, solemn face.

'Put it down, Scrappy,' said the first of these figures. 'We're all friends here.' He squatted, and firmly removed the handgun from Ch'ro's grasp.

'It's not loaded.'

'Can you even use one 'er these? Sigurtians kill with sound, all scales, various ways and means of delivery, isn't that right?'

'I can handle a dart-gun. It's the same principle, isn't it?'

'Just point and pull,' said Col, settling her bulk at Ch'ro's feet. She laughed. 'You've never used a lethal weapon in your life. I can tell.'

'Don't tease him,' said the man.

He took Ch'ro's hand and waved it up and down, the Blue greeting. 'Drez Doyle, pleased to meet you, and this here is Sergeant Rohan Aswad, our Commissar. Col you've met. We're here to entertain you.'

He showed teeth. 'Et your way through the shit-hole, eh? Flapped your skinny armpits and flew down into the middle of Tsunami's camp? That's the style.'

'Ran four days through this toxic dump full of evil rapacious bastards,' added Col. 'Found your way to the lagoons, which you'd seen once, without a drop of water or a bite to eat, or a shirt on your back. You look like a snapped twig, but you're a tough little bugger, bat-boy.'

A terrible suspicion rushed over Ch'ro. 'Let me up. What's happening? Where has the Princess gone?'

Drez gently flattened him with one great paw. 'Calm down, Scrappy. Calm down. You're right, she's gone without you, but don't fret. We don't know how you did it, but you might, you just might, have saved your blessed Prince D''fydd's life.'

'For which we're in your debt.' Col bared her teeth, amiably.

'Not for your sake, or his,' intoned the Commissar, his hollow eyes burning with passion. 'We hate the Royal funxing Myots. For *hers*.'

LV

The former prince of the Myots had been moved from the broken cage to a cell he believed had once been a distilling vat. It had pitted walls without a join or an angle that tapered into a funnel high above his head. A heavily sealed porthole, or lock, in one bellied side, and that was all. His walking breeches and underwear had been taken, but they'd left him in his shirt. His wrists were bound in front of him, his ankles shackled in a figure-of-eight loop of the same tough ligature. He'd been warned that he'd be gagged if he spoke to the Dettans who brought his rations, so he didn't.

He felt there was nothing to be gained there.

They could have changed the chamber pot more often; otherwise he didn't have much to complain about. His bullet wound had been dressed, he was fed. You couldn't expect variant-neutral meals, in these circumstances. He knew he had no one to blame but himself. Like an idiot, knowing the truth about the situation, he'd failed to realise he *looked* like a tempting target: the brigands had just done what brigands do. He thought he was still in the old mining camp, since he believed there were no gaps in his memory – which was hopeful, but he curbed his optimism. He didn't try to keep track of time. He'd soon know when Tsunami began to get impatient.

He used some of his unmarked hours repeating a simple petition – addressed to the Mighty Void, to Grace, to Fate, to what the hell.

Let Ch'ro have escaped.

Let my friend have got away, or else been clean-killed.

Don't punish him. *I'm* the problem—

The rest of the time was spent resisting coma, and reviewing his favourite memories: the air-fish of Detta'aan near the head of the list, although they'd been his downfall. He was determined to enjoy himself.

If these were the last days of his life it would be a crying shame to waste them being miserable.

The door, or porthole, opened. One of the usual Dettans climbed in, followed by a stranger, someone tall, wide-shouldered but not heavily built. Neither a Shet nor a Balas. Lantern light blazed, blinding him.

'Why is the prince bound?' enquired a clear, calm voice, in English.

'He can see in the dark. He might jump us.'

'But why has he been left without a light?'

'I just explained that,' muttered the Dettan, sulkily.

The tall figure bent over him. A cold touch, and the ligatures at his wrists and ankles were released. D''fydd immediately scrambled to his feet: he was caught as he fell, and saw who was rescuing him. He'd known her voice, he just hadn't believed it ... The Princess propped him against the curved wall, supporting him with one hand while she stared around, her beautiful eyes taking in every sordid detail.

'Sorry about the mess,' croaked D''fydd. 'Can't get the help—'

'I've seen worse. But not much. Prince D''fydd, I am going to talk to your friend Tsunami. You will be present, but you are to keep quiet. If you are questioned, answer in Neuendan and address yourself to me.'

The Dettan peered at them, deeply suspicious of these clicks and trills.

The interview took place in the gangster lord's longhouse, which proved to be rather luxuriously appointed, indoors. Intricate supple-glass screened the reed-bole walls. There was expensive furniture; the air was sweetened by a fashionable ambience. A Speranza-style desk stood at one end, but the Princess had ignored it, and Tsunami had been flustered enough to accept her ground. The gangster perched, in his paramilitary uniform, on a sofa that might have graced the Zeldi's ballroom. His guards stood around, armed with big, rapid-fire versions of Ifraa''k's bird gun, which would deliver a furious shower of silicate pellets, designed to shatter in the opponent's flesh. The Princess was unsupported. Maybe her troops were waiting outdoors.

'Piric, Piric! You have put yourself in a difficult situation!'

She had set D''fydd in a surprisingly comfortable glass armchair, in all his bare-legged disarray. The dressing on his knee was conspicuously old and grubby. She paced the floor, between them.

'*How* many armed persons do you have gathered here?'

'I think it's sixty—'

'Sixty! Barely two *term* away from the lagoons. An alien prince. Are you mad? Do you have a death wish? Do you realise you're in danger of embarrassing the Isthmus's most generous protector?'

'I don't know what you mean. What danger?'

The Princess had turned towards D"fydd in her pacing. The look in her eye said she had the situation in hand: the hint of a smile that graced her beautiful mouth told him that there were no troops, her bluff might be called, and then they'd both be in extreme peril—

'He's been decently treated,' muttered Tsunami.

'*Have* you been decently treated, Excellency?'

'I can't honestly say I have,' said D"fydd, clicking ferociously. 'It's true I tried to escape, which was cheeky, but there was *nothing* to do in that cell. No exercise, no reading matter. I've been bored out of my mind.'

She turned again to the monster. 'You didn't do your homework, Piric. The authorities of Pendong, the planet formerly known as Sigurt's World, don't negotiate with hostage-takers, they won't allow the prince's guardian to do so, and they're *very* touchy. Whether you shoot this boy now, or later, it makes no difference. They'll make a hell of trouble, to satisfy their pride, and Detta'aan will suffer greatly. Am I right, Excellency?'

'Absolutely. My royal life is nothing, the honour of the Oligarchs is everything. Sanctions will be demanded.'

The gangster seemed less than convinced. He was rallying, visibly calculating, what to do with this reckless foreigner—

'Luckily, your ransom demand was intercepted. The Sigurtians know nothing, your idiocy has been covered, and this will go no further.'

Clearly Piric couldn't contradict this. He hadn't heard from the Embassy (how surprising). The Princess swept across the room, smiling, and offered her hand. The guards took fright, training their guns with a slam and a clatter. Perfectly unmoved, she grasped the gangster lord's reluctant fist. *Add this to the air-fish*, thought D"fydd. *Possibly the final addition to my favourites. If we aren't killed at once, I hope she has a weapon for me.*

The Dettan was gaping at a virtual screen, which had sprung from his iface at the Princess's touch. D"fydd could see it only from the side, a shining needle in the air: but the effect was miraculous—

'What shall I do?' cried Tsunami.

'Nothing,' said the Princess, withdrawing her hand. 'I have destroyed the evidence of your indiscretion, and the boy will remember nothing, I'll see to that. Don't thank me, my own interests are affected. Piric, Piric, there are rules! Overstep them, and you make yourself very unpopular. Count this as a lesson.'

'There should be compensation,' muttered the crestfallen Tsunami. 'I acted in good faith. I have staff to pay.'

'Are you joking? The compensation is that you are staying alive, and in business. Now, will you take a sniff with me, and with this promising young man? And then we'll leave, with no hard feelings.'

The scene in which D"fydd had to guess his part grew stranger. The gangster took a vial from the Princess's elegant case and drew on it deeply. The Princess returned the gesture, then offered the case to the prince. *We drink blood tea together*, he thought ... He had barely eaten or slept for six days, he was afraid the stimulant would knock him out, but he survived. The three of them abandoned the citified furniture. They sat at ease on cushiony mud-glass lumps, marsh-ethnic style. One of the guards brought fresh *koulis*, which the gangster himself broke and served. Piric/Tsunami and the Princess chatted, about the illicit silicate trade, unruly Prospectors, the bloodthirsty Shet gangs who kept trying to move in ... *She knows everything*, thought D"fydd. His heart was throbbing, he thought he might explode. Tsunami's face, the golden Balas oval, fine features distorted by bad-guy soul inside, thrust large into his view. *Oh, he'll remember nothing*, chirruped the gangster, in English that sounded like Neuendan. *Don't worry!* She *will change the data in his brain*. She *is one of* those *Blues*.

He was carried. He lay in the bottom of a dugout. There were two Dettans in the boat, and the Princess. Brush-paddles made an endless susurration. Later someone helped him into another open boat. A *knife* engine whined, disturbing the air-fishes; the *knife* flew to a place where Ch'ro suddenly appeared. Then he knew that his petition had been granted. Ch'ro had fetched help. The Princess had performed miracles. D"fydd would not die, he would live: and somehow, when he was sober again, all these bewildering fragments would knit together.

LVI

Detta'aan was very quiet, after the flood. The tourists and the Twin Planets celebrities, including LaLa and his relatives, had departed. The few visitors who lingered were seasoned travellers, air-fish veterans who'd learned to prefer the city in its normal state of drowsy, forgotten calm. Ch'ro and D''fydd, who felt they counted as veterans now, took breakfast with the Princess and her Aleutian friend, almost alone in the lobby of The Caprice.

'I advise you not to stay on the Isthmus,' said Conrad, having raised the issue of the Sigurtians' plans. 'In fact, better if you leave Balas, as soon as D''fydd can pass the transit medical.'

'Are we in such danger?' asked D''fydd.

They'd reported a version of their adventure to the authorities, as soon as they were safely back in the city. The Tourist Office had located the party they'd left behind: still camped beside that clearing. Apparently they'd been getting anxious, but they'd believed Ch'ro and D''fydd, Ifraa''k and Keelian were at the lagoons, watching air-fish, all this time. Detta'aan police had questioned the Sigurtians politely, at their hotel, avoiding awkward answers with the ease of long practice. And that was all.

'Better safe than sorry,' said Conrad.

'You are not in danger,' said the Princess. 'But Conrad is right, you should move on. Go to Speranza, you will be free of the Myots there.'

The *pangolin* was creeping on the tabletop. It found D''fydd's elbow, and scrambled, confidingly, to his shoulder. 'See, it likes me!' crowed the prince. He had established friendly relations with the little beast at the Aleutian's camp: it completely ignored Ch'ro and Conrad.

'*He* likes you,' agreed the Aleutian, with a curious, intent look.

'Affectionate, *not* edible,' said Ch'ro. 'Questionable intelligence.'

The Princess rose, and reclaimed her pet. 'Conrad, I believe we agreed to walk in the Diaspora Gardens. Shall we leave the young people?'

'By all means.'

She looked back; she smiled at them; she was swallowed by the permeable glass of The Caprice's rainbow façade.

'I don't understand how he can smuggle mud,' remarked D"fydd, when their elders had departed. 'I know we're not talking tonnes of the stuff, we're talking samples, rare particles, but I thought it was impossible to add anything to a Buonarotti lading. If the equations are wrong by a qbit, the ship founders with all hands—'

'He doesn't smuggle the silicates, he smuggles the *information*, in his mind. The old, incorruptible way.' Ch'ro tapped his friend's bowl of mélange. 'D'you know why people come to The Caprice for coffee?'

'Fashion.'

'I suppose: but also the coffee they serve is different. It's ground from a variety of beans they grow here: brought from the Blue – I mean, the molecular algorithm for the plant – as pure information, in a transiter's numinal consciousness. Before there was such a thing as Buonarotti freight.'

'So how come it's more expensive, if it grows here?'

'Fashion,' said Ch'ro. 'But it makes you think, doesn't it? If we transited awake, instead of in the dreamtime, if we could get onto the "Active Complement" of a ship, would we be more real on the other side?'

'I'd prefer not to go mad, thanks. Not just yet.'

'I'm going to try it, though. Sometime.'

'Insanity, or the Active Complement ...?' D"fydd sighed. 'I bet *she* never transits any other way. Her powers are limitless. Inexplicable!'

'No, just better left discreetly veiled. Obviously she angled you out of Tsunami's clutches by using a password that the gangster had to respect. She got it from Conrad, who is up to his ears in shady business here—'

'That *does not* explain what I saw.'

'Peace. I'm not trying to detract from her glory. We were strangers, and she saved our lives. We are forever in her debt.'

They fell silent, idly watching the coloured shadows of passers-by on Lateral. They felt at home in Detta'aan now. The holy city had a criminal heart, Isthmus aristocrats were implicated in organised crime, these things were never mentioned, but everybody understood. It was all very familiar. They could live here ... but maybe they'd better not try.

'We should have gone straight to Speranza,' murmured the prince. 'Why didn't we? We've been holding ourselves back. We've been *afraid* to escape. Don't you feel that now, Ch'ro?'

'I wouldn't have missed the air-fish.'

'I wouldn't have missed the Princess! I wonder how old she is—'

'Maybe a hundred, a hundred and fifty standard?' suggested Ch'ro, a little maliciously. 'She can't have made first landfall on Bois Dormant, she'd be three hundred years old. Blues don't live that long, however Senior they are. But she could easily be the heir of the original Prospector.'

Good taste – if not fear – had kept them from questioning the Princess's servants, and Conrad was not very approachable. But they'd consulted the Interstellar Visitors Register, and knew everything that was public. Bois Dormant was a virgin planet, original landfall very old, newly registered for development; in which the Princess held a Prospector's share. Her title was impeccable, no further details. She was unimaginably rich, in short. But her wealth, and her likely age, were mere prosaic facts—

The prince made the gesture for *it doesn't matter*. 'I don't care, really. Age in years doesn't mean anything. I wonder if she and Conrad have become lovers. A travellers' romance.'

'Could be,' decided Ch'ro. 'He's an immortal, and she's a Blue, but he's very *interested*. He's forever watching her, have you noticed? And he follows her around, since we've been back.'

'She doesn't seem over keen.'

'She's with him now.'

D"fydd had a sudden realisation. *She's* gone, he thought. *She looked back, she smiled: that was goodbye. We won't see her here again.* Yet he was not dismayed. Life coursed through him, a future of jewelled moments, tastes and smells, risk and endeavour, and yes, pain and fear; everything. He felt as if he'd just been born. *She told us to go to Speranza. We'll meet her there.*

'I propose a toast, Bloodman. Raise your bowl! To Speranza!'

'To Speranza!'

LVII

The Diaspora Memorial Park was a place to avoid in the festival: a crowded, garish playground for the Balas masses, seething with the worst kind of Speranza-isation. Off-season the park was less offensive, but a little dreary. The games arenas remained, but the outdoor rides had gone, and the facsimile alien monuments. Trees and flowers and animals had vanished from the Diaspora Dioramas: frugally reduced to their algorithms, and saved off by the City Council. An enclave of nature was laid bare, in the middle of the city: speckled mudflats, a wandering lipid stream, ragged vegetation.

'I miss the fog,' remarked the Princess, looking up at the cloudless sky, and a soft arc of moonshine (the separate moons indistinguishable in daylight). 'This is the Isthmus shorn of all romance.'

'Shame we couldn't have stayed in the marsh,' grumbled Conrad. 'The humid season will linger out there for another thousand *term*.'

'I'm afraid you don't love your Sigurtians any more.'

'I don't! From what I gather, they've been in similar danger all their lives. What made them think Detta'aan would be different?'

They had reached the inevitable, gigantic municipal sculpture. The Diaspora planets circled each other solemnly: Balas and Shet represented, with an unusual stab at accuracy, by a rotating pair of globes. The planets and their mechanism were solid glass. Virtual numbers, in Balas notation, shone in the air: numinal biped population statistics, the unbelievable distances (standard) between the inhabited planets ...

'Those vast spaces between the stars terrify me—'

'There are no stars,' murmured the Princess. 'They are not things, only knots in the fabric. There is vast space, and us, whoever we are. I'm surprised you know Pascal—'

'I don't.' The Aleutian sat on the plinth, where a busy pattern of virtual tic-tac-toe was supposed to represent the ocean of information.

'But I knew someone who did. Blue-lovers, renegades, we pick up each other's tags—'

She sat beside him, brows raised: politely aware that he had something particular to say—

'Princess, when all I knew of the Princess was what everybody knows I was intrigued by the pet you carried around with you, do you remember? A creature that closely resembles an Aleutian commensal.'

'An ingenious fake, I believe we agreed.'

'No. I don't think so,' said the Aleutian. 'Something *like* a commensal,' he continued. 'But our commensals are not conscious. They are tools. Gene-identical bio-prosthetics, in Blue terms. Your "pangolin", however, has a small but real mind of his own.'

'He's a toy,' breathed the Princess.

'I have watched him carefully. And, forgive me, I have watched his mistress: the fabulously wealthy and powerful Princess of Bois Dormant, whose past is wrapped in mystery, whose flawless youth is more than an appearance: yet she is evidently a Senior. Who is fluent, among her many accomplishments, in at least one language only spoken on Sigurt's World. A world the Princess never seems to have visited, as far as the record goes.'

'Conrad, you're the last person to comment on anyone's clandestine movements, in normal space or out of it—'

'The last person. Of course fluency in an obscure language can be acquired at a whim, in a heartbeat, by a Blue Senior of sufficient rank, anywhere with systems access ... I wondered, I guessed, but I was uncertain. Then, when D''fydd of the Myots was in my camp, I saw how the so-called "pangolin" reacted. I saw that it recognised the prince's chemistry—'

The Princess had been listening with a smile of mild interest. Suddenly her manner changed, her power armed itself. The air seemed to Conrad to freeze around him, like a vice.

<I am in your hands,> he said. <I am just a rogue, you could easily destroy me. May I say that I would never, in speech or silence, under any persuasion, reveal anything I may have guessed or surmised, about the Princess of Bois Dormant? But promises are nothing. I wish to tell you something; you will decide how to act on the information. Shall I speak?>

'Speak.'

The 'pangolin' had retreated to the Princess's throat. It clung there, trembling, peering out from the folds of her neckcloth.

'As I have remarked, a compatriot of mine, another *alien-lover*, was a member of the doomed Mission to Sigurt's World. Maybe you've heard of him, he used the name 'Francois'. He was travelling with his lover, a Blue woman, great Lady … His death is immaterial, he will live again. But he died alone. I believe that when he knew he must die, he may have tried to preserve the memories of that life, the love of someone who meant a great deal to him; the person he had become, who would otherwise be lost for ever—'

'What do you mean?' whispered the Princess.

'May I see if your familiar will come to me? I know he's been "listening" to the biochemical flux I shed into the air as I speak of these things. He hardly has a mind, but there's something going on. I believe he understands, in some sense, what I am offering—'

She took the phage from its roost, and set it on her lap. Conrad extended his clawed hand. The thing twined itself in circles, it shivered, it hesitated: as if struggling to make a choice. It moved, it flowed, and wrapped itself around the Aleutian's wrist.

The Princess sighed, and half-smiled.

'So be it.'

Then Conrad explained to her what Francois had done. It was a terrible few minutes for the Princess. She was plunged again into that last night, in the room with the ugly carpet, their last redoubt. That atmosphere, so long buried under other terrible memories. The numbing confusion, the screaming, the blood, the air thick with dust, so that you couldn't tell, from moment to moment, who had fallen, who was still fighting—

If her control was not as perfect as usual, Conrad gave no sign of having noticed her distress. He left the park, taking the familiar with him. The Princess stayed for a while, on the glassy shore of the sea of information, thinking of many things. Then she went to join her officers, who were making preparations for departure. As D"fydd had surmised, the Sigurtians wouldn't be seeing her again, in the lobby of The Caprice. Her curiosity on a certain matter was satisfied: now she had work to do.

The small army would travel in the Princess's customary splendour to the Twin Planets Port, and there they would leave the world – miraculously, astonishingly expanded since Bibi's day – of scheduled Buonarotti transits. *The Spirit of Eighty-Nine* was waiting for them.

INTERMISSION
THE NIGHTINGALE'S CHILD

O

There was a grey-area settlement nearby, who knows why or how it had been founded. A rash of new housing crept towards the Special Ankang, breaching the mandatory exclusion zone: but the monolith still stood alone, wrapped in a veil of Enclosure, facing the Urals across the desert of the Turgajskoje. Bibi looked out, from a high window band, and thought of Kirgiz. The Great House, the green and golden plain, a market where they sold fried grasshoppers.

'Your neighbours are getting closer.'

'It doesn't matter,' said the Superintendent. 'None of the new building is official, it might yet be pulled down, but there's nobody classified as dangerous in here now. Yeying was the last.'

Yeying—

The Myot prince had been easy to find. It had been far more difficult, even for the Princess of Bois Dormant, to trace a People's Army star cadet who had simply vanished, one fine day, from the Blue's cradle-to-grave surveillance. No reason given, nothing but silence. Yet she hadn't travelled far, she who had taken flight so brilliantly, while Honesty stayed at home, and Bibi made her sober way through Social Services College. Just a few hundred kilometres—

'Yeying, Yeying, ah, sad story. Allow me to pass her to you, ma'am.'

The Superintendent (First Class) was a Khazakh, medium height, square-built but gaunt, no meat on him; narrow, deep-set eyes, a tired smile. His name was Lung, a dragon. He did not look like the governor of a torture house. Evidently a blocked career, given those faded stripes, and the fact that he'd reached the age where longevity treatments come too late: but he seemed to have made his peace with life. The Ankang's creaky synapses delivered the file, across the breadth of the office, and Bibi saw her friend's face: confirming the worst possible outcome. Yeying, Yeying. It was unmistakably Nightingale, looking no older than when Bibi had seen her last; but not beautiful at all. Beauty does not survive the fate Yeying had suffered.

'It seems that her troubles started after the death of Caspian Konoe.'

'That's right. The investigation had been brief, out of respect for the family. She petitioned for it to be reopened. Her demands became noisy, her behaviour irrational. She was examined under medication: her response gave cause for the gravest concern.'

'It all happened very quickly. I see that she was committed here less than six months after his alleged suicide.'

'That's the military for you. They can take no chances.'

'And was Yeying really so very ill?'

'By the time I saw her?' said the Superintendent. 'Yes. I'm afraid so.'

His visitor, the tall, sombre-eyed woman in her long grey coat, white braid at the collar and cuffs, had given him no explanation for her questions, but convincing proof of her authority: not least her very Senior level of access to his confidential files. He spoke frankly, and hoped for the best.

'It's a textbook case, ma'am. Severe stress, acute or prolonged, reveals the underlying disease. She might have lived and died without any sign of her terrible flaw if she had not defied the authorities; but the illness was genuine. Yeying was suffering from untreatable criminal insanity.'

'She had the nanosurgery *before* she was committed.'

'The military again. Surgery failed to alleviate her symptoms, and the cortical lesions swiftly reappeared. It's the classic sign.'

'May I see her?'

'Let me take you to the projection room.'

Once, when she was in college in Hanoi, Bibi and her classmates had been taken on a tour of a Special Ankang. They'd visited the cell of a criminal insanity patient – a man who'd survived a Buonarotti transit disaster, many years before. He was the most terrifying thing to be near. How could the staff go about their business, every day? Knowing that, if this patient's medication ever failed, they would all be plunged into his agonising nightmare world, *and never escape?* Bibi had left that virtual hospital determined to have nothing to do with psychiatric care: and never, ever to travel to the stars.

The visit to Yeying's cell was virtual too, but not so terrifying. Bibi and the Superintendent sat together in a dark room, and observed the patient through a veil (like the glitter of Enclosure) that signalled very serious firewalls, and was there to remind them of their danger. If this had been ordinary madness they would have been able to share Yeying's perceptions, her hallucinations, her voices, her distorted reasoning. Here they could only watch the cognitive and endocrine scanning that testified to unrelieved mental agony. The soft-restraint cell was small, but not punitive. Yeying liked the corners. She crouched in them, shivering. Immediately you knew that greater freedom would have been insupportable.

'Here she is at her best,' murmured the Superintendent. 'We would attempt to reduce the medication dosage, but we never succeeded.'

'And in the end?'

'She starved herself. These cases are invariably suicidal. We can't hasten death, once a prisoner has been sent to us. But we don't force-feed.'

'Good of you.'

The prisoner, features locked in a mask of pain, was panting in terror, like a thirsty dog. *If she were living,* thought Bibi, *there would be nothing I could do.* 'Yeying was pregnant when Konoe died: I see from the medical scans that your patient has borne a child. What happened there—?'

'Ah, yes. The birth was normal; it was the calmest we ever saw her. A strong, healthy girl, and thankfully she tested free of her mother's disease.'

'What happened to the baby?'

The Superintendent didn't reply.

'Let's go back to your office,' said Bibi. 'If there are original documents related to this birth, I would like to see them.'

O

'Old Tai Bai' had not proved to be a reforming monarch. This region of the Blue, in particular, had become a rather sinister backwater, where ugly secrets could be buried in neglect: where paper records could moulder, never copied to the datasphere. Lung went to fetch the documents. Bibi stared at the characters on the plaque behind his desk. *The Good of Others Is All We Know of Heaven.* He didn't keep her waiting long. A withered card folder, almost empty. A slip of dull pink paper, greyed with age. Not a birth certificate, but a Social Practice form recording a birth at the Special Ankang. Three characters, scrawled faintly in the margin, drew her attention. Lung waited, rubbing at the grey stubble of his skull.

'What became of the child?' she asked again.

'In the nature of things, ah, sometimes children are born here, but we have no provision for raising them. I acted for the best.'

'She was "spilled water",' said Bibi. 'You sold her, for a little cash.'

The man nodded, hanging his head. 'One's salary is often delayed. Supplies are needed. Things are always tight.'

'Will you affirm my copy of this session, Superintendent Lung?'

Lung could hardly refuse. But he could choose how to accept, and how to acknowledge everything unsaid. He stood, as his nemesis rose to her feet; his eyes met hers for a fraction of a second, as she handed the folder back.

'I will be happy to give my affirmation, ma'am.' He bowed. 'A sad story. Yeying was very ill ... by the time she came here.'

O

Bibi's small army bivouacked in the open, braving the chill of early winter on the steppe, just to rest their bones on the Blue again. *The Spirit of Eighty-Nine* lay alongside, looking like a shabby small plane until you touched him. They all felt a little eerie, held in a bubble of unreality: a transit-capable pod, on the surface of the Blue, such things shouldn't be. But it was an adventure. They were glad to be here, under the frosty sweep of remembered stars. Sergeant Aswad had a brazier of Dettan charcoal going (there was no fuel wood handy, nothing but dead grass). They squatted around it, wrapped in unsealed bivvy cocoons, sucking on pouches of hot, sour Aleutian soup.

'Criminal insanity . . .' Col shook her head. 'I don't like it, Bibi. It's a horrible, horrible disease, worse than anything. Suppose we find this kid, and she's got it, and she takes us all with her to hell dimension?'

Drez and the Sergeant looked as if they agreed.

'Criminal insanity is a story I believed when I was a child,' said Bibi. 'I'm older now. I can believe a failed transit might leave someone untreatably insane: but if there *were* people able to enter non-duration at will, and edit the software of reality, they'd be recruited, not committed. I don't know if they exist, but I'm sure of that. The charge of criminal insanity is a brutal fiction.'

'But you said you saw a really sick woman. Was that faked?'

'The Army made her sick, Col. She was interrogated under a drug that triggers psychotic fugue. Just in case she recovered from that, they drilled tiny holes in her brain, scanned her head and backdated the scans, proving the holes had "reappeared" after reconstructive surgery—'

'What the funx did she *do* to them?' muttered Drez.

'Protested when her lover's death was called suicide.'

'So the People's Army got word to destroy her,' growled Col, 'and they obeyed orders, no reason why. Typical.'

'Nightingale knew something,' murmured Bibi. 'Our enemies were afraid she'd be interrogated if she went on making a fuss about Konoe, and they couldn't afford that. They couldn't send her to another planet, so they sent her straight to hell. These criminals are not afraid of overkill.'

Col stared at the glowing charcoal. 'So what now?'

'We'll start with the town. Once, I remember, you three decided to save my life by enrolling me in a brothel—'

The small army shifted, uneasily, at the touch of steel in Bibi's voice.

'I know you meant well, I know you were ready to spend your savings to give me a decent start ... Lung followed the same reasoning, and he saved her life; but I believe he sold the baby for cash. Even grey-area brothels keep accounts. We should be able to spot her, given the dates.'

'It's all for the best,' announced Sergeant Aswad. 'The Great Systems passed beyond human control a long time ago. The AIs see all. Anything they allow to happen, it's for a good purpose that's beyond our grasp.'

Col and Drez groaned. 'Oh, funx it, Aswad. Give that a rest.'

The religious discussion drifted off into habitual bickering. Bibi studied her iface. Her mission of revenge was growing, and becoming more complex. Three characters scrawled on faded pink paper: was that Nightingale's own handwriting? She thought so. Someone let you name your baby. And the record was kept. What does that mean?

The nostalgia of this cold night was powerful, but she would be glad to get away. The Earth she had known no longer existed. Her work was not here. She rolled herself in the cocoon and fell towards sleep: remembering that fateful night, hearing again Caspian Konoe's voice, urgent, exasperated, frightened, as he tried to save Bibi's life.

O

Ye swung herself into the Vlab frame. Her body danced, it came apart before the punters' eyes. She made herself into a landscape, under a faint golden dawn. She gave herself a river, silver and meandering, and lined the banks with birches and poplars, mist caught in bright, flecked leaves. She filled the picture with all that she was allowed – the Vlab had preset limits for direct cortical emotional stimulus – of longing, loss and need and hope of salvation. Some of the punters sighed, wet-eyed (they were all fairly drunk); some became restive. They liked her decorative trim, but not too much of it.

She began to strip, slowly, to an orgiastic beat: her body and her mind laid out, oh *uh*, oh *uh*, oh *uh*, no privacies left, it was a *vicious* rape but she was *enjoying* it, the Ultimate Degradation. Through disembodied eyes (she could do this routine on autopilot) she watched the crowd as they giggled and swayed in the knocked-down gravity. The Bloody Sickle was an expensive, fashionable venue, and the Coral Island a *select* orbital resort. Only the finest type of overstuffed bureaucrat or raddled and braided People's Army officer would be found in here. Eyes glinted in the stiff faces of Remote Presence dolls, a craze that was sweeping the orbitals, so you hardly saw a digital mask or a virtual self any more. Some of them were really nasty-looking things, scary to think of what a punter might want to *do* with a body like that—

But there was an extravagantly stylish Han courtesan, also a *famous* Vlab painter. A concubine, singer from liberal Europe, whose name was known on Speranza. If only someone had told Ye when she was ten, fifteen, that you can't be an independent artist. You can earn a fortune on your back, you can be a household name on the side, but *you have to have a sponsor.*

She flayed herself, at length, several different ways, to raw psyche dressed in butchered flesh; and finished with another image of her own.

A ragged boy on a path through fields. Dew on young wheat, woods in the distance. Unearthly joy, love without limit, love for the universe—

'Why are you always a *boy*?' asked Car, in the break. He was cheerful, he had made enough for another neoteny: he'd be a louche, charming ten-year-old again for a while. He was her friend, her only critic.

'It frees my imagination, somehow,' admitted Ye. 'There's a yin/yang about it, animus, anima. A displacement. It makes me whole.'

'Now you've lost me.'

The boy tossed back his beautiful blond hair and scanned the singles. Couples only want to play. He was like Ye, a whore who had not found a patron. Was he too beautiful, too fragile? At least he was still working, he still had a chance. But there was a new dressing on his left forearm: she knew what was under it, and she was afraid. Car liked very bad drugs.

She touched the gel. 'You're an idiot. You'll die.'

He showed his pearly little white teeth. Reformers like androgynes. Men like young boys. Women like the *details*, and he believed a rich woman would be his best ticket out. 'How can I die, Night? I'm a bot.'

'You *are not*.'

'Yes I am. All whores are bots. A bot can't die, or suffer, or feel bad emotions. I wish you would believe. I want everyone to be happy.'

'I can't talk to you when you're like this.'

She was supposed to stay on after her set, but she decided to go home. Madam Olena, unfashionably virtual, sat at a table near the door, gimlet-eyed for misbehaviour. She beckoned Ye over. 'Too sullen tonight! The Vlab shows us the artist's being, mind and body: stripped bare. The people want beauty and pain, they don't want your bad temper, like gristle in the meat.'

Ye bowed. 'Thank you for your constructive criticism.'

<See inside my head, you fat, stupid, pretentious bitch. You're getting kicked to death, right now—>

Ye's unspoken thoughts had to be shaped into words before they could be delivered to Madam's eye soc'; even at this close range. Ye knew this, but ever since she'd known it was too late, the stupid addiction had grown. She would pay for her insolence. How? What horrible little surprise?

Madam wouldn't allow them to use the mass transit. Ye had the limo put her down at the archway, so she could walk the alley that led to the Red Tractor Spa. Late at 'night' there was condensation in the air, between the blue-black walls. She could imagine it was rain, a drizzle of chilly rain, and that there was open sky above. If Madam fired her what would she do? She had run away often, when she was a child, but outside this house of confinement there was no air. The fare back to Earth, or even another orbital paradise, was utterly out of reach. Sometimes the terror of being trapped almost stopped her breath.

Car has the right idea, she thought, tramping through the once-in-a-lifetime space tourists (the Red Tractor was for the 'select' masses), past a shoal of lovely, squirming bodies in the freefall Marketplace Window. *I ought to be trying to kill myself, too.* In the lift with her, out to the Penthouse floor, incredibly beautiful bots went into sleep-mode. They were counting Ye as one of themselves: and she was flattered, she was touched, but in sleep-mode they scared her. The absence of presence.

She bunked alone, except when Car remembered to take a night off. Bots don't need accommodation. The corner unit was huge; it had fancy extruded furniture, it was a survival of the days when Ye had been rare and valuable contraband. Another Madam, not Olena, had told her the secret. *We have to disguise you, and offer you discreetly, but the truth is almost every customer wants human flesh. They don't want to screw a bot, they want you. Because screwing you is dirty, because you can feel bad emotions, because you can suffer.* Pity Ye had sort of taken that as a licence to sulk—

An old woman of twenty-three returned to her prison.

The door of the unit obeyed her biometrics, and anybody else Madam Olena thought should be able to walk in. She opened it with a kick, as was her custom, and saw three large figures looming. Unsure, for a moment. Sick at the thought of having to go through *that* again, and with three of the bastards at once, oh joy. Sudden hope: *Madam has put me back on the active list!* Maybe someone has bought my contract. For a night, for a week, for a month.

Swift calculation, *How much cred for me*—

Two men and one woman, all in the same green uniform, the cut and fabric oozing wealth; and criminal wealth, of course. The woman had tats, prison tats, all over her face. But there was something wrong. The younger of the two men strode past Ye to the door, which had sealed itself, and stood there with a snub-nosed shock pistol at the ready.

'What are you doing? Who *are* you people?'

'Robbers,' said the tattooed lady. She held a slim white case; it had a medical look that made Ye very scared.

She shrugged. 'Take what you can find, we're insured. None of it's mine. I'm a bot, we don't own things—'

'You're a Vlab artist,' remarked the man by the door. 'Isn't that an exploded concept? The software does it all now, you just plug in?'

'No! You should damn well try it, brainless goon—'

The older man took Ye by the shoulders, moved her over to a nasty, curlicued imitation of an antique dressing table, and sat her down.

'What are you *doing*? You're crazy, our guards will take you apart—!'

He shifted out of the way. The woman with the tats stood behind Ye, smiling: crinkling those brave inked lines in the dressing table mirror. 'Red Tractor's security just watched us walk in here, kid. They know who we work for. They won't touch us, and they can't call the cops, as what I'm about to do is not a felony.' She began to run her fingers through Ye's abundant black hair, as if planning to change the style.

'I'm a bot! You have no right!'

'You don't talk like a bot. Keep looking in the mirror. If you can't hold still we'll give you a sniff of something, but you don't want that.'

'Leave me alone!' shouted Ye, but she dared not struggle.

A surgical blade, invisibly fine, lifted a circle of Ye's scalp, sealing as it cut, releasing scarcely a drop of blood. The tattooed lady whipped out the first subdermal electrode. She repeated this performance until she'd got the whole pattern, crushing them between finger and thumb and flipping them into a compartment in her medical case. There was a hiss of anaesthetic spray, then the faintest whine, the faintest scent of burning, as she tackled the tougher job of detaching the arachnoid, which lay under bone, clinging to the meninges. Ye stared at the mirror, eyes fixed wide in terror and despair. The subdermals controlled her. The arachnoid gave her the neuro-profile of an embodied AI, a legal sex-worker, for the resort's censorship. Without it she was just an illegal human whore: a worn-out drab, the lowest of the low.

O

They took her to an empty cabin and let her sleep off the brain surgery for a few hours. She woke in low-g restraint, with disjointed memories of being wrapped in a musty quilt and bundled out of the Red Tractor: but she didn't know if that was real, or a pastiche of something that had happened a long time ago. The goons brought her breakfast, new clothes; they showed her to a minuscule bathroom. Then they escorted her through a part of the resort she'd never seen, the reality behind the décor. Bare walls, bare floors. Gravity was so low that walking was like keeping your footing in deep water.

'Now you meet the Princess,' said the younger male goon, opening a bulkhead. 'We'll wait outside.' The heavy lock sealing behind her.

The unit she entered was naked as a freight hold and cold as outer space. A baggage handler crossed the floor to another heavy-duty lock. The woman sitting on the belt was dark-haired, pale-skinned, beautiful: and so young-looking, with such years of power in her eyes, that she must be very, very rich. Ye had started to be afraid she'd been kidnapped by the Social Services, and was about to be returned to Earth for rehabilitation. This fate receded but the fear grew, flaring through every nerve and muscle. She could feel the raw vacuum and the dark, very close—

'Have you bought me?'

The euphemism, *bought my contract*, had no place here.

'I have not. Anything resembling a sales transaction would make legal difficulties. That's why we stole you, and we're keeping out of sight. When we get to Speranza you will be free, automatically.'

'To *Speranza*—'

'Here is an iface. A sum has been credited to you. It should be sufficient for the moment, but I know that a good Vlab, for instance, is an expensive item. Apply to my secretary for further funds, as you need them.'

The iface came gliding through the cold air. Ye caught it, and resisted a grovelling urge to check the credit line. She thought of the Bloody Sickle, and knew she was in the presence of real power for the first time in her life.

'I suppose you want something.'

'Indeed I do. I want you to help me to redress a wrong. In the meantime, as a first step, I desire you to continue your work as an artist.'

'Do they have strip-joints on Speranza?'

'All numinal biped life is there,' said the beautiful Senior, with a mordant smile. 'You, however, will be taking up a residency at a respectable small gallery. You must try to make your name.'

Ye looked at the iface. She still had the pride not to check the credit, but she read the ID of its owner. 'This Chinese writing, is this my name, now?'

'It is. Do you read Chinese?'

'No,' said Ye. 'Once I learned the character for *Ye*. It means night.'

'Night is correct, though *Ye* character can mean other things. Your full name is is *Yelaixiang*—'

Ye had a flashover: a side effect of working with the Vlab. A word she'd never heard could become a perception, though she had no idea what it meant. It was moonless night in a garden; the air was full of sweet, wordless song, falling on her like sprays of snow, like white flowers—

'One thing you should know: you must wear a mask.'

'Oh, I do,' said Ye. 'This isn't me, I'm ravishingly beautiful inside.'

'I believe you. Do you accept my terms?'

Speranza, she thought. *I would be more trapped than ever*—

'Yes.'

'Is there any wish I can fulfil, before we leave?'

My best friend is going to kill himself, thought Ye, *because he's convinced he can't die. If you are so generous, take him out, too. Please.* But Car was too far gone, his brain and body ruined. Shipping him to another space station, billions of kilometres away, would not change anything. And for all Ye knew, this woman was a worse monster than Madam Olena.

She set guilt aside, and shook her head.

'Then we will be on our way.'

PART FOUR

LVIII

Ch'ro and D"fydd had made the transit to Speranza, when they'd both been pronounced fit to travel, in a mood of trepidation. The mighty Princess of Bois Dormant had passed through their lives like a lightning flash, and vanished. They'd sent a (frightfully expensive) couriered message to D"fydd's guardian, telling him they were on their way, but there'd been no response. Would they be pulled over by the *taikos* in the Arrivals Hall, interrogated and shipped straight back to Sigurt's World? Would they be peculiar-looking outcasts? Would they have enough money to live, in the Diaspora capital?

Their fears proved groundless. They were met by an agent of the Mallorn Estate – a *facet* of Speranza System, taking the appearance of a grave, elderly Blue – and their path opened smoothly before them. The capital funds Tsunami had been after were not worthless (as Ch'ro had darkly feared). The ex-prince was a wealthy young man, while his noble companion had a comfortable settlement. The contact language of Speranza, after the revolution, was *money*. High-grade society embraced the romantic exiles, prick-ears, clicks and all. They were air-kissed by Hegemony Ambassadors – an affectation that alarmed them (especially, whisper it, when H.E. Bilis Müysteelid, the furtive-looking little Ki, aimed her teeth at your neck). They 'shook hands' with Domremy Li, Speranza's Head of State – the fact that Li's government had backed the Myot Oligarchs didn't seem to matter at all. They tried new pleasures, ate new delicacies; they met Permanent Secretaries at dinner parties; they attended a session of the Diaspora Parliament in person (very dull): just to say they'd been there.

Finally D"fydd remembered that he must *do something* with his life, so they enrolled at Kongzi, oldest and most highly regarded of Speranza's universities. Ch'ro chose language and history courses. D"fydd studied Virtual Engineering, Navigation Mathematics and pod-pilot preparatory classes. The different tracks brought a separation that was bewildering at first – they'd spent every waking hour together for so long. But it was a good change: they'd at last begun to live.

Fashionable Speranza, always 'homesick' (in theory!), observed the seasons of the Blue temperate zones. Spring came around with its flowers; summer followed, with heatwaves and soft fruit. The leaves on the trees, both virtual and real, turned colour and began to fall, and the Sigurtians were astonished to realise that they'd been on Speranza – or *in* Speranza, but nobody thought like that, the illusion was complete – for a whole year.

Halfway through the Kongzi Autumn Term there was a garden party at the General's, in the Dostoevsky Prospect, prettiest and most exclusive of the new residential domains. Tall burners breathed incensed heat over the leaf-strewn grasses, under Pepper's famous cherry trees. Shawls were worn, to offset the fashionable chill in the air. The elder statesman himself wasn't present. He avoided his Consort's social affairs, and she refused to be fobbed off with a software agent. Pepper Lily shone in glory – the queen of Blue Speranza, no longer in her first youth, a long way from her last. Her clever, caustic daughter, Vale Scolari, was in attendance, along with Vale's best friend, the stunning, impossibly well-connected Grove Lukoil. Kongzi uniforms, maroon and gold, were liberally scattered among the guests, the Sigurtian prince and his noble Neuendan companion included. Pepper encouraged young people, especially *interesting* young males.

Ch'ro strolled with Vale, who was telling him she wanted to do something with her life, but she didn't know *what* … Muscular shoulders, sheathed in green livery, excellent tailoring, snagged his attention. The rolling, low-energy gait of a spacer. A glimpse of a smooth, bland stranger's face. He seized his friend's arm.

'Whose Bloodman is that?'

'Whose *servant*,' corrected the young woman, cross at being interrupted. 'How should I know? Give me an eyeline, bat-boy.'

Vale had been ordered by her father – whose name was not Scolari, and the Scolaris didn't visit this house – to cultivate the Sigurtian princelings. She had obeyed, and grown genuinely fond of the pair (D''fydd perhaps more than Ch'ro). But they could be frustrating company—

Ch'ro scanned the cherry orchard as if his life depended on it, but the apparition had vanished. 'Dressed in green, with white braid. I can't see them any more. Vale, *please*. I have to know who that was—'

'Oh, all right.' She scanned her working record. 'Sorry, I have your person in green, but sans name tag. Not attached to anybody I know, or any drear adult I'm supposed to know. Don't panic, Dostoe doesn't have gatecrashers: I'll check Mama's guest list.'

'No, no, it doesn't matter—'

'Except now you've lost your beautiful footman and you're plunged into gloom. Why don't you get your own eye soc', and save yourself from these little disappointments?'

'I have plans. I might need, er, never to have had one.'

Vale tucked his wiry arm closer to her side. 'You don't *need* to be a virgin, noble Neuendan. You just like it that way.'

'I forgot to ask, will your brother be here?'

'The Permanent Secretary? Of course not! This is women's work.'

The Permanent Secretaries were Speranza's decision-makers; Domremy Li had the same official title, first among equals. Amal Yu, technically Vale's elder brother, was held to be the least effectual of them, a *guanxi* appointment, no doubt (a term the Sigurtians understood very well: on their world such arrangements were called *bloodsuck*). The capital of the Diaspora was disappointingly ordinary in this respect: politics were corrupt, big business had everything its own way, people were cynical. However, you had to admit the net result was something splendid.

'Please don't say you want him to get you a job. I shall disown you at once. Amal is *such* a bore.'

'Nothing further from my thoughts!'

Grove Lukoil, black-haired, blue-eyed, exquisite Grove, was trying to tease Prince D"fydd into arranging a private tryst.

'You like hooking up with me in a playsphere *envie*, don't you?'

D"fydd might have said, ungallantly, that he couldn't be sure if he ever had. The virtual environments known as 'sensual' or 'relaxing' were deplored by parents, much frequented by the young; and strictly anonymous. He stepped lightly: this was dangerous ground. The clasping manners of Blue Traditionalists were difficult to follow—

'I'm afraid of your papa. Don't tell me he doesn't keep an eye on you.'

'Papa respects my privacies.'

D"ffyd made the Blue gesture – a slow head-shake – for *I'm sorry, but that's not remotely plausible*. He liked Grove, although he liked her friend, Vale Scolari, a little more. Vale's vigorous, burnished chestnut hair and fierce green eyes made him think of some rare Blue animal, not as rare or delightful as a pangolin, of course: perhaps a caracal. He didn't blame them for their scheming parents, but he wished they wouldn't play the same game.

Someone tapped him on the shoulder. He reached for his iface, then realised that this was not a virtual prompt, and turned, *knowing already*, with an enormous lift of the heart. The face was wrong, but that didn't put him off for a second. Secretary Col stood grinning at him, in the same green uniform as when he'd first met her, a little richer than before. He took the slip of chaste white card, proffered in a white-gloved hand.

'The *Princess*! Is she here?'

'She's in town. She couldn't come to the party, still unpacking. She'd like to see you, and Scrappy. Soon.' Col winked broadly, and strolled away.

Grove seized the business card, before D"fydd could gather his wits. '*The Princess of Bois Dormant* ... What a lovely card.' She rapidly consulted her eye soc', and was able to exclaim, with reasonable truth, 'Oh, the *Princess*! I knew she was "due to board the station", as the old folks say. I didn't know she'd arrived! How bold of Pepper to invite her. Do you *know* the Princess?'

'We met on Balas.'

D"ffyd recovered his property, and hid the treasure inside his tunic. It was a year since they'd met; Seniority, mystery and the unbelievable distances stood between, but he was filled with bubbling joy. He grabbed the ends of his fine wool shawl, a genuine Blue kashmere, and spread it wide. 'What a *beautiful* day! I'm sure I could fly! Don't you think, Grove, Speranza is a *wonderful* place! Everything anyone could possibly want is here!'

'I think Sigurtians can be very annoying.'

LIX

The Princess of Bois Dormant, far-travelled, fabulously wealthy, rumoured to be one of *those* Blues, had acquired a property in Speranza some eighteen standard months previously. Her mansion unit, in Left Speranza's Old Diplomatic Quarter, had been furnished and decorated according to precise instructions; but never occupied until now.

The Old Dip, on the Diameter Horizontal along with Parliament Concourse and the theatres, was close to the *streets*, where the Prospectors lived: and still redolent of ancient democracy. Anyone could stroll around here, though the walls were high, the wide thoroughfares undecorated and there wasn't much to see. The visitor who approached the Princess's unit, one cold autumnal morning – very sharp in his body-mods, his vertical-striped, wide-shouldered jacket and yellow peg-top trousers – seemed confident, until he reached her gate. He prowled up and down, shivering in the perverse high-grade chill, waiting for a voice in his ear, a message blossoming in the air, but nothing happened. At last, brandishing the white card that was his passport, he braved the blank golden shimmer, and passed through.

On the other side he was in parkland. Mature trees rose from smooth grass; autumn-tinted shrubberies were hung with silver spiderwebs, under a sky of crystalline blue. Everything was virtual, from the vistas to the sensation of firm turf underfoot. The visitor checked this out by poking the bole of a massive oak: whistled silently and shook his fingers, in the universal gesture for *loads of money*. Old money. Speranza's nouveau riche believed that a virtual garden was a shabby, tasteless option. They were wrong.

There were no birds, no flying insects, but was that an animal, a large animal, slipping through foliage? A *hunting* animal? The sharp-suited visitor felt himself in danger, and he'd lived by his wits for too long to mistrust that instinct. He advanced with caution, peering behind him often, thinking of alien monsters, things of nightmare with diplomatic immunity, that could tear you apart and Speranza System would do nothing: and suddenly discovered, almost leaping out of his skin, that somebody was walking beside him. A slim figure in baggy brown overalls: lank black hair, young-old black eyes in a smooth young face, dark at the centre—

'What the devil! Where the funx did *you* spring from!'

<I am the Princess's ward. I shall take you to her.>

Covered in confusion, very scared, the visitor followed the Aleutian, whose 'Silent' speech, whose form and presence, woke buried memories and the most intense unease. The mistress of the domain was taking breakfast, in an austere but pleasant room decorated in the Blue 'First Empire' style.

The Aleutian left them. 'You are Dyke Blazer?' said the Princess. 'Please, take coffee, a croissant; whatever you choose. Sit down.'

Her visitor took nothing from the buffet. He sat on the edge of a throne-like chair not designed for human comfort.

'Congratulations. You have prospered, since the days when you were "Looty Loo", plying your trade as an illegal human whore in the alleys around the Church of Self. I see you no longer present as feminine?'

Dyke Blazer didn't blink: he'd known this must be about the past. He flipped up his tail with a practised gesture, and played at arranging it over his knees. 'I came to Speranza,' he explained, disarmingly, 'on the Prospector quota, long ago. Never made it to the Transit Lounge: I like it here, I can be myself. Don't get the wrong idea, I didn't convert. I'm not a Reformer, no way ... *Let a woman be a woman, and a man be a man.*' He raised his arms, displaying his pert bosom to advantage, and gave a little shimmy in place. 'I'm *this* kind of guy. But I know I'm a man and so's Lola ... You dig?'

'I'm delighted you find Speranza so agreeable,' said the Princess.

Dyke Blazer trembled, twisting his tail in clawed, lightly furred, human hands. 'What do you want from me, ma'am?'

'Relax, I mean you no harm. The Starry Arrow's file on your past activities is long closed. I am interested in a child.'

'A *child*—?'

'More precisely, her parentage. Shall I go on?'

The former 'Looty Loo' ducked his chin, the cautious Aleutian gesture meaning *yes*, or *maybe*; or *that's your story*—

'This child was born in a Special Ankang, in the Turgajskoje, some twenty-three or twenty-four standard years ago; her mother was committed there on a charge of criminal insanity. The birth was recorded, and the record kept. The baby was sold to a brothel in the nearby grey-area settlement. Some three years thereafter she was purchased from that brothel by a broker from the city. And there the child vanishes: probably she died. As you and I know, surplus infants die easily in the Enclosed Cities.'

Dyke ducked his chin again.

'But there are mysteries. The child's mother, a former star cadet of the People's Army, had been condemned for the worst of crimes. Why was she allowed to carry the baby to term? Why was the record of the birth preserved? And why was the baby taken alive from the Ankang?'

'I don't know—'

The Princess sipped her bowl of creamy mélange, watching, waiting.

'You, you want me to try and find this child—?'

'On Speranza? Hardly. My interest, as I said, is in her parentage. Please examine this document.' A faded Social Care form appeared in Dyke Blazer's field of view. He stared at it, his breath quickening. 'Observe the handwritten characters in the margin. Look closely, they're rather faint—'

'I don't read, er, Chinese.'

'Then I'll read it for you: *Yelaixiang*. A sweet-scented flower, native to the Blue, in English known as 'tuberose'. Literally, the Chinese name means *night comes fragrance*. Did I mention, the star cadet was called Nightingale? Her lover, and in all likelihood the father of the child, was Caspian Konoe-Hosokawa: Japanese royalty, and heir to the great Konoe-Olofact consortium. He committed suicide, you may recall. His Japanese given name was Kaoru, which means *Fragrant*. Now, let us analyse this last testament. What does *Yelaixiang* imply?'

'I don't know.'

'It's a subtle point, but the mother, a proud and sensitive woman, gave her baby a name that claims connection with the prince's clan. I believe the child was Konoe's natural, legitimate daughter: a rare treasure, and a considerable heiress. That is why she was allowed to live.'

The Princess sipped her coffee.

'People keep things,' she said at last. 'Trophies, souvenirs, insurance, who can say? I think someone kept the proof of a marriage. There is no such record to be found in the datasphere, but it may still exist. Given the circles in which you once moved, given the old contacts you may have maintained, perhaps you can find out something.'

'You want to hire me as a Private Investigator?'

'I want you to trust me. Help me to redress a wrong.'

'Do you *know* this proof is on Speranza?'

'I know what I have told you. Your fee has been delivered to your account. It will be doubled if you can provide useful information.'

'What if I can't?'

'Then you keep the first payment.'

The doors of the breakfast room opened. The Princess's ward appeared, silently bowed the visitor out, and returned.

<I'd like to chase him, mistress. Shall I—?>

'No need. He will run, without further encouragement.'

The Aleutian settled himself in the chair Dyke Blazer had vacated, 'reversed' the joints of his hind limbs, and became a large, toothy animal, a hairless dog or maybe a baboon, dressed in overalls.

'Long ago,' said the Princess, 'in another life, I blundered into something I didn't understand. It began with an obscure murder.'

<I know what that is. It means permanent death.>

'The victim was a half-caste—'

<I know what *that* means too. Poor devil.>

'—and an agent of the Republic. He died because he was close to penetrating a high-level conspiracy. The killer, who posed as a dear friend of the deceased at the time, just left this room—'

<Are you going to punish him?>

'There was wrong on both sides; I'm not here to judge Dyke Blazer. Under some unknown person's orders he later bought a child, and hid her so that she could never be found: but he spared her life.'

<So you're giving him another chance?>

'Maybe.'

LX

The Princess's second visitor that morning was the Vlab artist Ye. She passed through the gate in a tiny vehicle, no larger than a sedan chair from Ancient Europe; the bodywork blush-gold as a ripe peach. Her ride was deflated, deftly folded and handed back to her by a bland human servant in green livery: who showed her into a drawing room and requested her to wait. The Princess was with her agent, and begged to be excused for a few minutes.

She could not decide where to sit. A pool of light followed her, as she looked into false vistas of rooms and rooms beyond this one, and checked her appearance in reflective surfaces. Pistachio tunic over a purple grosgrain skirt, chocolate stockings and raspberry half-boots: a vivid ensemble, the not-uniform of the artists' quarter. The mask today was a doll-like black lacquer oval, with a rosebud mouth and white stippling around the eyes. She touched her satchel, to make sure of the contents, and felt the crimped outline of her little ride. On Earth inflatable cars were still whacking things you had to drag along like a cabin-bag. She'd longed for years to own one.

Now I find out what it all costs—

The Aleutian took her by surprise. He was crouched on a rug in an alcove, gazing at what seemed to be a silent black and white movie on an antique boxed screen. She had met a few aliens, Balas and Shet mainly, but it was the first time she'd seen an immortal in the flesh.

'Oh, I'm sorry.'

He shrugged, and continued to gaze: yet she felt herself welcomed. She sat down beside him, cross-legged. She couldn't decipher the 2D moving images very well. Maybe they were scrambled, unless you had an Aleutian brain. Minutes passed, and then she felt herself invited to speak.

'Are you one of the Silent Aleutians?'

'No. But I speak rarely, as I have not yet woken.'

'What does that mean?'

'It means I don't recognise myself. I study my records, this is one: but the moment doesn't come. My parent of this life believes that living here with the Princess will help me. The person I am loves the Blue, I have spent lives there: and Speranza, we say, is just the Blue with added civilisation.'

'You can say that again.'

The Aleutian said nothing; he watched his movie. Ye was fascinated by the way she felt: as if the immortal were a lifelong friend, as if they'd already talked for years. Or maybe a very calm, wise, super-intelligent animal—

'What's your name?'

'His name is René le Champi.'

The Princess touched the immortal's sloping shoulder; he turned his face, briefly, to rest his cheek against her hand. 'Come with me, Ye. Let me hear your report. And be warned, my ward is a subtle hypnotist. He will conquer you, without a shot fired: the way his people once conquered Earth.'

In another part of the room stood a handsome antique desk. It could have been freighted six billion miles from Paris or London: but Ye was sure it was a simple block of ceramic, covered in décor. A figure rose, courteously, as they approached – another first. Where Ye lived, Speranza system's 'facets', software entities, rarely took visible form.

'My agent,' said the Princess.

The bot bowed, and winked out of existence. Ye felt light-headed, assailed by the void. In the streets she could have been living in any liberal Enclosed City, where by chance she never happened to see an open sky. In the presence of this mysterious Senior she could not escape the awesome reality behind the décor: cold rock, airless dark, and the naked *information* that made the world. Another human servant, different from the one at the front doors, brought canapés and a carafe of aromatic yellow wine. The Princess surveyed Ye, approving the new clothes with a nod.

'Tell me, Yelaixiang. What do you think of Speranza?'

'Dreamlike,' said Ye, warily. 'Pleasure-seeking, rich, easy-going. No one is really poor, no one is really brutalized. One hears of political corruption, but one never sees police aggression, or, or *zombie* prostitutes.' She glanced at the Princess, with a flicker of conditional gratitude—

'A slightly inimical fairyland?'

'Yes ... I brought some cells, would you like to see them?'

She'd wondered about the cells, because surely the Princess could keep track of her every breath. It seemed she'd made the right gesture. The Princess studied the portfolio; Ye examined the desk furniture. She wanted to touch things, to test the depth of illusion. A piece of Balas crystal. A fragment of calligraphy, in a silver light-box. A table snifter case, the lid a shallow curve of sutured ivory or fine white ceramic, set in a matrix of grass-green emerald. She bent closer: the 'ivory' was the brain-pan of a baby-sized human skull—

The Princess of Bois Dormant watched her with sombre eyes.

'I was, er, admiring the calligraphy ... It's beautiful. Is that a *Di*? The Nebula Permanent Collection has just acquired one of her works, they're very rare, hardly ever come on the market. Do you know why that is?'

'She died young. These cells are good ... I'm going to enrol you in some masterclasses. Evidently your coding is excellent: but there are other technical skills, and you need to extend your general education.'

'I'll never be able to pay you back.'

'You owe me nothing. You'll begin your classes soon. I may also ask you to undertake, discreetly, certain small commissions.'

'Is that how I can earn my freedom?'

The works she showed at the gallery were not on sale; they had been reserved by an anonymous bidder: the Princess, of course. Ye's patron had made an investment and hoped eventually to make a profit. That's the way of the world, but *discreet small commissions* had a different sound—

'You are free now,' said the Princess. 'In spite of everything that has changed, this is still Speranza.'

But Ye was not free. On the orbital resort she'd been angry and innocent. Now she was corrupt, more trapped than ever, a rich Senior's toy artist, six billion kilometres from the open sky. *I am lost*, she thought. She heard cheerful voices. The servant who'd brought the wine approached again.

'The prince and my Lord Ch'ro are here, Princess. May I show them in?'

'By all means.'

Two young high-grades came bounding through the room, as if on springs. They were aliens, Sigurtians, with black velvet heads and pricked ears. They wore Kongzi uniform (of course!). The smaller one had sharp dark eyes and shiny, pointed white teeth; the tall one was just a blur of privilege, arrogance, gilded self-assurance. Ye stood, and bowed, and was introduced. She babbled excuses, grabbed her satchel and fled.

LXI

'Where have you *been*?' cried D"fydd. 'We knew we'd meet you here, but we've been waiting for *winters*, for aeons!'

'Please excuse his rudeness.' Ch'ro spread his hands, the Blue gesture for *helpless apology*. 'He's badly brought up and easily excited.'

The Princess was not offended. 'Where have I been? Several places. I was on the Blue, I went to Home, where I met our friend Conrad again—'

This was exciting news. The Princess's transits were ex-directory: her name never appeared on the Buonarotti lists, which D"fydd had kept under constant surveillance. But nobody *ever* visited the Aleutian planet.

A stranger came soft-footed out of the shadows, nodded to them and settled in an armchair. He seemed young, almost a child, as far as you could tell with Aleutians.

'Ah, here he is. Let me introduce my ward. This is René le Champi, who is to live with me for a while.'

Ch'ro and D"fydd declared themselves honoured. René said nothing, and preserved a bright-eyed silence as the Princess made polite small talk. She hoped they'd suffered no lasting ill effects after their adventure in the marshes, and that the wait for transit clearance had not been too tedious.

'Are you happily settled on Speranza? I'm sure the prince's guardian has been looking after you.'

Ch'ro and D"fydd looked at each other. 'Liam Mallorn is dead!' cried D"fydd. 'He's been dead for years. It's so strange. It wasn't a virtual self who "came to see us", bi-locating to the Manor, on Sigurt's World. It was an avatar. An agent from the Mallorn Estate was in the arrivals hall to meet us, and broke the news—'

'He was a real person to us,' added Ch'ro, with emotion. 'He was our protector, our teacher, our true friend. The Myots believed it. He'd fixed it all up to deceive them. You're right, he's still looking after us, through Agent Mallorn. But we'll never be able to thank him, there isn't even a tomb. I *wish* we could have thanked him—'

'How sad. Do you know how he died?' asked the Princess, coolly.

Ch'ro made the gesture for *it's not our business.* 'Not the details. It seems he was like D''fydd's mother: survived the massacre of the Baykonur Mission then died later on, from the effects of his injuries.'

'*Much* later,' said D''fydd. 'They say it was really the Mallorn disaster that killed him. His will to live was damaged, way back then; that's why the second tragedy he lived through killed him in the end.'

'Obituaries can be very touching.'

D''fydd looked around. He had realised that something was missing. 'I don't see the pangolin. Where is he?'

'Ah, my pet. I'm afraid you won't see him again. Conrad persuaded me to trade him in for a more developed model.'

'Oh ... That's a shame,' said D''fydd, childishly bereft. 'I wanted to see if he'd creep up my arm again.'

'I think not.' The Princess glanced at her ward. 'The pangolin's fate was the occasion of my visit to Home, in fact. Conrad wanted to introduce me to him: much changed. One might almost say, released from an enchantment.'

The young Aleutian's eyes brimmed with amusement. He stretched, he curled, like a supple, sinuous animal.

'My Grace!' exclaimed D''fydd, with a flash of intuition. 'Young sir, I almost think I know you. Were you *the pangolin?*'

<I was,> answered René, black eyes sparkling. <And somewhere in my back brain I remember you both; with affection.>

'I acquired my pet in strange and perilous circumstances, some years ago,' explained the Princess. 'I knew nothing of the remarkable truth until Conrad recognised him for what he was: an "encysted self", shed by an adventurer doomed to die far from his own kind. He was treated for arrested development; the result is as you see.' She smiled, as if such transformations, in her world, were uncommon but not extraordinary—

Ch'ro and D''fydd gazed, fascinated. Not a sign of crude acceleration, in the physical body that could hardly be two years old. It was wonderful, it was better than anything Sigurtian medicine could do. Unconsciously they leaned forward, yearning towards the immortal—

The Princess coughed behind her hand. 'My ward is perfectly capable of speech. He should learn to restrict himself to that form of communication, in the company of mortals, or we may have to wrap him in quarantine film – as was the cautious custom on the Blue, when I was young.'

'I'm coming round to the idea,' conceded René.

'Let us return to your successes. Am I to rely on the reports of matrimonial plans, involving Miss Vale Scolari and Miss Grove Lukoil?'

'Good Grace, no!' gasped D"fydd, horrified. 'Not at all!'

'But we are courted,' admitted Ch'ro, flushing. 'It's difficult.'

'Dear me. Your intentions are dishonourable?'

'We have no intentions!' D"fydd clutched his ears in despair. 'We tried telling them that we can't become aroused except in a Sigurtian winter—'

'*That* was so stupid,' said Ch'ro, bitterly. 'As it turns out, there are several thrilling nature-identical "Sigurtian Winter" *envies* in the catalogue.'

'Actually, if it was about clasping, I mean sex, we'd understand. But it's not. It's purely business. We're supposed to be friends, and they keep trying to trick us into betrothal situations. It's just unpleasant.'

'Could you advise us, Princess?' Ch'ro made the gesture for *I'm serious*. 'We have no experience, we'd be scared of this kind of thing on our own world, we're even more helpless here. These are two people we meet constantly, and count as our closest friends: it's a real problem.'

René looked from face to face, entertained by this mortal coil.

'All I can tell you,' said the Princess, after a brief pause, and with the same detachment she'd shown toward Liam Mallorn's death, 'is that they have no choice. Grove Lukoil and Vale Scolari are Traditionalist young ladies, a special breed of Blue womanhood. They are not free citizens, whatever the law says. They've been given orders: which they must obey. If you don't intend to marry, do not compromise them. If you do, they will suffer.'

Ch'ro and D"fydd sobered, and made gestures of assent: glimpsing lives as outwardly gilded, inwardly curtailed as their own had been.

The servant who'd shown them in brought snacks and wine. D"fydd wanted to ask why Sergeant Aswad, and Col, and presumably Drez Doyle, whom they hadn't seen, were masked. Ch'ro struggled with the knowledge that his illusory happiness was over—

'Do you remember,' asked the Princess, 'when we were on Balas, you offered me your service? I would like to collect. Would you do me a favour?'

'Of course,' said Ch'ro. 'We owe you our lives.'

'Yes!' exclaimed D''fydd, eyes shining. 'Ask us anything!'

'Then cultivate the young woman who left as you arrived. She's a Vlab artist, her name is *Night*. She has a residency at the Blue Dog Gallery: I'd like you to take your exalted friends there. Make her fashionable. Befriend her.'

'That doesn't sound like much,' complained D''fydd, crestfallen.

'You may be surprised. She is clad in armour.'

Sergeant Aswad presented the snacks, arranged with guardroom precision: the bland mask gave the prince a reproving look. 'Don't you worry, chum. There'll be trouble enough.'

LXII

There was a game deplored by the young that adult Speranzans played with avidity. Even Dyke Blazer and his kind were devotees. For the rich, this game had a physical location: a thick-waisted, domed and columned edifice – on the lines of the Pantheon of Ancient Rome – which had been shoehorned, rather roughly, into the majesty of Parliament Square. High-rolling players (mostly Blue males, like the majority of Speranza's leading figures) gathered there daily and stayed for hours, strolling the wide spaces of the 'floor': watching their luck on the boards, watching each other, picking up gossip.

There was mineral wealth to be scooped from airless lumps of rock; there were sunless, wandering, giant balls of gases to be mined for precious elements. There were the marginal colonies, where death by slow torture and appalling financial loss could be turned, by the alchemy of the game, into staggering profit for someone. But the queen of the commodities traded on this floor, the market that ruled all others, was planetary futures. The single "Earth perfect" virgin world opened for development, since the game began, had been the disastrous Mallorn: but this was not a problem. The Lottery was still running, coordinates were still bought and sold: speculation required nothing more.

The debut of Bois Dormant had naturally caused a stir. But the Bois Dormant Consortium were wise old trading agents, deep-rooted in the system: releasing stock, and information, in very modest instalments. They'd done nothing to shake the markets. The net result, so far, had been a spike in the numbers applying for the privilege of hurling themselves into the void – and a secret, hesitant, unspoken swell of excitement. A virgin world! Was this the start of the long-dreamed-of numinal biped inflation?

And what would that mean to Speranza?

Early one morning three prominent citizens met on the floor: the

Permanent Secretaries Ehsan Lukoil and Amal Yu, and Councillor Scolari – the same State Councillor Scolari who had once deployed Pepper Lily as his 'favourite weapon'. The 'Old Men from Earth', as they were known, were not often seen together. Perhaps, like all *arrivistes*, they found each other's company demeaning, an unwelcome reminder of the less-exalted past. Physically, a gulf had opened between Scolari and Amal, scarcely changed since the old days, and Ehsan Lukoil – who had become the ideal of Blue Speranzan masculinity: toned, tanned, muscular, a qualified conventional space pilot, a splendid rider.

Amal, still the ageing roué for whom Senior rank had come too late, toyed with a restorative bowl of 'Balas', scattered with live *koulis*. Ehsan downed an espresso, Scolari drew on an early snifter: they watched the Princess of Bois Dormant. She was talking to another habitual player, a disappointed-looking individual in a long, shabby blue coat.

'I *wonder* where she sprang from—' remarked Amal.

'Parvenue,' said Councillor Scolari. 'A spacer who attached herself to some mad old Prospector, and inherited a fantastic fortune. You won't find out more than that, I've tried. But her claim's rock solid.'

'Jacob,' said Ehsan to his secretary, who was in dutiful attendance. 'Get your arse over there, but be funxing discreet about it. Find out what the diamond-dripping bitch has been saying to Haku. I'm curious.'

Ehsan had preserved his oafish manners, very useful for intimidation; though the harsh, brilliant mind behind them was no longer in hiding.

The General often spent the whole day at the Exchange: alternating bursts of mental and physical activity with 'conferences' in his support chair. Yu was hardly in his dotage, but he knew the value of rest. He'd seen the 'Old Men' and avoided them; he was wondering how to approach the Princess. He was supposed to get an introduction: it was the kind of chore he detested. He'd pursued his usual routine – breakfast alone, a vigorous stroll, a ruminative, open-eyed doze – for a couple of hours, before he noticed that he was under attack. Nobody else had seen it, far as he could tell – except the bots, presumably, the 'croupiers' of this gambling den, and they didn't matter.

The General's mind was as sharp as ever. He gave no sign of concern, and did not consult his agent: people keep tabs on things like that. An acquaintance commiserated on the poor morning he was having.

'Win some, lose some,' rumbled the General, shrugging.

He wondered who the raider could be, and his thoughts jumped, unaccountably, to Pepper Lily's gatecrasher. *Somebody*, or rather some-body's servant, had invaded his consort's garden party (Vale had the evidence, on her eye soc'). Entered the Dostoevsky grounds uninvited and left a card: not with the mistress of the house but with one of her guests. A prank, a puzzling prank. A piece of insolence, probably one of those Kongzi brats.

He should return to his chair. A Senior preoccupied, calling on internal resources, can look doddery. The General thrust out his chin, ran a hand, with pardonable pride, over his still vigorous, still chestnut hair – and noticed the Princess of Bois Dormant again. *Who* was it she'd been talking to, before? He reviewed the floor's working record on his eye soc' – and recognised the odd fellow in the shabby blue coat, without recourse to a name tag. Not a word of the conversation, because of the damn privacy protocols, but he didn't like the conjunction. Why should those two meet?

One of *those* Blues – how did rumours like that get about?

In the fractional, multifarious ebb and flow of the boards, undeclared duels had to be dramatic before they attracted attention. By lunchtime the General was out by quite a sum, but he remained, as far as he could tell, the only person aware of what was going on. Except for his unknown enemy. He sat down, alone, to his sandwich, his sherry, and the discreet ministrations of his chair: signalling that he was in con-ference. He disliked making conversation at meals. The Princess of Bois Dormant moved through the crowd with the magnetic effect that winners have; it took her a little while to reach the General. He stayed where he was. By now he was very curious.

Call it curious.

'General Yu.'

'Princess,' said the General. 'Excuse me if I don't get up.'

'By all means. I don't want to interrupt your lunch.'

She was a tall woman, in beautifully cut grey morning dress: dark hair, regular features, a pale, glowing complexion. A collar of diamonds, pouring out light, shone at her throat, her shawl was dull gold, shot with exquisite and expensive supple-glass fibre. He'd hazard her true age as well the wrong side of a hundred and fifty; maybe two hundred. There's something in the eyes of Seniors of that vintage that they can't disguise. The thought that she was closer to the drop cheered him.

But it meant she'd been around a *long* time.

'I don't believe we've met. *Princess*, eh? I know about the real estate –

how'd you pick up the fancy title, if you don't mind me asking?'

'Not at all. I awarded it to myself, General.' She smiled, cheerfully frank. 'I am a nobody who made it rich, a self-made woman. I needed a little glamour to wrap around me.'

'Ha. I like that. Good for you.'

The Aleutian who followed her like a pageboy (more 'glamour') was already part of her legend. That sprig of immortality was with her now, surveying the mortals at play with invincible cool cheek. An air of covert mischief, eyes like black acid—

'Are you going to introduce your friend?'

'René? I think not. He doesn't speak.'

'One of the Silent, eh? One doesn't often find them away from Home. Has he been with you long? Funny, he seems familiar, somehow.'

René gazed into space, maliciously affecting to be deaf as well as Silent. The Princess looked for any sign of the *moment of recognition*, but there was none. She wondered, with hope and disquiet, if it would ever come.

'Perhaps you met in another life.'

The General shook his leonine head. 'Unlikely, and yet I've had several, in a manner of speaking. What about you? You must have tales. You're the heir of the original Prospector, I understand. The sixth planet, a new *uninhabited* habitable world, that must be quite a story—'

'My count is seven.'

'No, no, it's six.' Yu counted his fingers, laying on the brusque charm. 'The Blue, the Aleutian Home, Bala/Shet, Ki/An and Sigurt's. Or *Pendong*, as we're supposed to call it now, but I don't kowtow to the Myots ... Bois Dormant will be our sixth. You can't split Balas and Shet, you know, it's politically impossible. They count as one around here, or there's hell to pay. Or were you thinking of Speranza?'

'I was thinking of Mallorn,' explained the Princess, mildly.

The General took a moment, and sipped his sherry.

'Unfortunately, Mallorn no longer exists.'

'In normal space,' she agreed, 'it does not. But General—' she raised a hand, gracefully indicating the quivering boards '—neither does all our money.' She had bowed and moved away before he could respond.

At the Dostoe mansion Pepper Lily was agonising over her calendar – the battalions of dates and events that closed around her every winter, until they had a stranglehold on every living hour. Yu had never managed to work out whether she enjoyed herself; or was it self-inflicted torture? The new artist, Ye, that Daughter talked about. Should Pepper engage her for a soirée? Or wait and see, and risk being the *second* hostess to do so—?

Pepper Lily called Vale 'Daughter' to remind Yu that the girl was *not* his daughter. Legally she was Scolari's daughter, because Pepper was not married to General Yu. *Legally*, Pepper Lily was still Scolari's runaway concubine, a fallen woman. It was all in Pepper's addled head, all nonsense, but she refused to let it go. Her attitude infuriated the Scolaris, making them look ridiculous; an enmity Yu could ill afford.

He didn't know why he'd held out. He'd brought her to Speranza, he'd paid for her longevity treatments, and everything else. She was his consort, the mistress of his household. He'd given her a child, a daughter to play with – a ruinously expensive present, with the bribes on top of the labwork: Speranza had laws about artificial reproduction. But he had never married her. He wouldn't marry her.

'Did you meet the Princess on the floor? Did you speak to her? I must be able to invite her here, Yu. I absolutely *must*.'

'I met her.' Yu looked around the room, feeling a heaviness on his chest, a bewilderment. 'She attacked me. No one noticed, it's all right. The floor just saw me having a rough day. But I know who it was.'

'My God.' Pepper stared at him, blood-drained.

'I *said*, it's all right. I'll easily make up the losses, it was an afternoon's bad play. I don't know what I've done to offend her, that's what worries me.'

The fittings, the colours, all this luxury that he didn't recognise: his tastes had been formed too long ago. How Pepper kept up. Kept on keeping up. On, and on, and on, changing her face, her clothes, her furniture, her food. Didn't she ever want to stop? Fold her hand, grow middle-aged?

Pepper threw down her diary tablet, which went flying around the boudoir, ricocheting and ringing among the supple-glass hangings as it sought an uncluttered place to rest. 'You *stupid* old man. I don't care about *money*! My God, how can we repair this? What can I do for her? I'll have to think of something—'

'*Don't*—' Yu shuddered. 'Don't you try to charm her. Keep your famous charm to yourself when the Princess is around. She'll tear you apart. The way she smiled, something *monstrous* there, I can't explain it ...'

Horror shook him, and over what? A wicked, petty game that a rich woman had played with his holdings, for no reason. The dread he felt was out of all proportion to the damage, and yet he couldn't calm himself.

LXIII

Dyke Blazer thought long and hard about the Princess's offer, but he decided not to accept it. He told himself he was scared: that she was the police, that she had some nasty game going on. The truth was that his pride was offended. Strange as it might seem, the mighty Princess of Bois Dormant had the smell of an SP, a snotty yellowjacket. The cool way they looked at you, like they're sorry for you all right, but they're not going to turn their back—

He took his problem to the devils he knew.

As Ye had observed, Speranza lacked the teeming, dank lower levels of an Enclosed City on Earth. Out here in the Kuiper Belt, the idle poor were perfectly indistinguishable from the idle rich – allowing for differences in scale. Their material needs were bountifully provided for, they had no work; they spent their days in an endless round of pleasure, excess and discontent. Naturally there were problems, and this was recognised. There was no such institution as Social Care: but there were places one could go.

Dyke made an in-person visit to an office of the Compassionate Assistance Foundation. He sat in a waiting room, confidentiality protocols making him the only client – under the benignant gaze of Zubindah Scolari, Founder of the Assistance: flanked by her sponsors, Permanent Secretary Ehsan Lukoil and Permanent Secretary Amal Yu. Something behind the eyes of the cartouche portraits woke and watched him carefully; soothing music played. Persuasive messages whispered, moving images filled his view, wafted on an ambience meant to relax his defences (which it did not)—

Unlicensed Body-Mods: What They Can Do To You.
Bone Mass: The Cold Equations.
The Forgotten Plague: Alcohol Is Still Dangerous.
Protect Yourself: **Don't** *Exchange Neurons.*

369

All the notices were in English, as Dyke was a Blue, like most inhabitants of the streets. If he'd been another kind of numinal biped, there'd have been a different menu. At last he was prompted to a booth. He slipped the agreed exchanges into a preformed dialogue; and left with the massage tokens on his iface. Crawl in there with your eyes gouged out after a fight; oozing fluids, hideously deformed by a bad mod: you'd get massage tokens.

He'd never asked for a meeting before: *they'd* always made the running. He didn't know what would happen. He deciphered the code in the massage-token string, and found instructions to go into the Plant – an industrial level where Speranza manufactured limitless energy, using an age-old process involving ground-up rock, trace elements, organic waste and sunlight.

Same as in Baykonur, it wasn't the surveillance you worried about, it was your own kind. Dyke kept himself to himself but he knew what was going on: he was able to pick out a devious route that avoided territorial disputes and other trouble. Unmolested, he reached a cavern where vulture shapes pored over troughs of nauseating sludge, picking out resistant fragments: skulls, teeth. Images from the photo-system chambers played on the distant walls, a ballet relayed here by Speranza system for no obvious reason: as nobody had any business to be looking.

'Anybody here?'

It was the kind of dark corner where gangs came to settle their quarrels, undisturbed by the robocops. Did they mean to kill him? He peered into the shadows, and was suddenly swept off his feet. 'You're not dreaming,' roared a monstrous voice. One of the mechanoids held him in its claws. He could not see where the voice came from, or anything like eyes, but somebody was using it as a remote presence doll. Another one woke, and another. They passed him between them, a rag of disputed flesh. He was drowning in the stench, in the menace of their size, the boom of their distorted voices.

When they'd finished, the carrion-pickers became dumb machines again. Dyke stumbled back to street level: emerging in the scrubbed delivery bay of a nice little supermarket, not far from his partition. The scents of freshly baked bread, roast chicken and coffee filled his mouth with bile. He fell to his knees, bouncing a little as he crumpled, and emptied his stomach. A cleaner zoomed over to suck up the effluvia of his fear, and return it to the endless round. 'I don't want to know,' muttered Dyke. 'Leave me alone.'

The terror tactics revolted him. He huddled like a sick cat, combing his tail with shaking fingers, repeating inwardly, *There was no need for that, there was no need for that*, with outrage and finally with defiance.

He'd told the Princess he'd come to Speranza as a Prospector, and he hadn't lied. There'd been a little rat-pack of them from old Baykonur, pasted into the quota, all *on the same ticket*. For a few heady days they'd ruled the streets ... He didn't know what had happened to the rest, probably all gone under by now. Dyke was different, he'd been wise and he'd been careful. Modified his bod, reverted to an old name; and accepted the shackle that he couldn't remove. He'd never tried to hide from *them*, always been ready to do another dirty little errand—

Something told him it was change-or-die time.

He could still hear the not-so-veiled threat: *I'm delighted that you find Speranza agreeable* ... The Princess was right, Speranza was paradise: but a paradise with scope for villains. One wrong move and he'd be dead in an alley. He hesitated over the next few days: sketching plans and rejecting them, convincing himself that he dared to act. To use what he knew.

Trusted minor operatives in a big scam always end up knowing more than they should: if they have any sense, they act dumb for ever. But he'd kept a few forbidden tricks 'on file' – and he wasn't afraid to use them. *I will get myself some* power, he thought. *I'll find that proof she wants, and take it to the Princess. And then we'll see.*

LXIV

The Princess had asked them to make Ye fashionable. D"fydd and Ch'ro obeyed. They decided the best course was to explain their mission, frankly, to Grove and Vale; and it worked: the young ladies understood perfectly. The Sigurtians were determined this would mark a new beginning. There'd be honest friendship from now on, no more entanglement. The four of them followed the Blue Dogs, whirling in their gilded hamster wheel, into the streets. They surrendered their rides – semi-AIs, not cheap inflatables – at the door of the gallery. The cursor-Dogs merged with their original, in a vivid clamour of signs, 4D anime, little free-style hack-works dancing overhead. Speranza high-grades lived in a wonderland that pretended to be ancient Earth; the streets were different.

'It's always an adventure,' murmured Vale.

'An art show in itself,' agreed Grove.

The Sigurtians had never ventured so far into this *quartier* before. They were amazed at the pungent, toxic ambience, the visual assault, the multifarious forms in the crowd: as if the ungraded Blues were practising to become the next explosion of Diaspora variants.

'Everyone here is planning to "ship out"?' D"fydd stared frankly back at the passers-by, who were staring at a rare, prized kind of alien. 'They're all *Prospectors*? That's humbling. They have my respect.'

'Our colony class,' said Grove, shameless: this was a politically impossible expression. 'Originally, yes. That was the idea.'

'Not any more,' countered Vale. 'Blues lose bone mass horribly, as you must have heard, and the free treatments only stabilise it. We're terminally adapted to living in an asteroid. Then there's the mods, to which they're addicted. Most of them are medically unfit. If they wanted to leap into the void they wouldn't be allowed.'

'What about you? What if *you* wanted to transit?' Ch'ro covered himself in confusion. 'Oh, excuse me, I didn't, I mean—'

Vale laughed, and tucked her arm in his. 'Calm yourself, bat-boy. This is the centre of the universe, why would we want to leave? Anyway, it'll all be done in software soon.'

D"fydd clutched his ears. 'I've had a *terrible* thought! The Princess's pet artist, you can't tell from a trailer. What if she's no good!'

Miss Lukoil and Miss Scolari spluttered, and leant on each other's shoulders. '*D"fydd*, you are so sweet!' cried Grove.

My Lord Ch'ro patted the prince's shoulder. 'Bless you, child, you know nothing about the art world. She'll be superb.'

She was superb. Grove and Vale told their friends. The Kongzi students joined Ye's bohemian following. Their parents, eager for novelty, arrived as virtual visitors for the daytime viewing. Invitations from society hostesses began to come in, and Ye's name was made: it could happen very fast, in the tiny world of Speranza. On the last night of her residency she looked out with disembodied eyes, secure in the knowledge that she had several offers to consider; including an extension at the Blue Dog. She wanted to go to the foyer of the Nebula Immersion Theatre, because the Nebula was famous even on Earth. But the Princess would decide.

Yet how is this different from the Coral Island? she wondered. *What do I see out there? Tourists, lowlifes. Fat-cat bureaucrats, slavishly admiring what they don't even like. Corrupt apparatchiks, courtesans. Slumming high-grades, here because I've been made fashionable. The difference is that I have the vital ingredient: an owner.* She thought of Car, as she went to join her new, gilded friends, and felt that she'd put her foot on the first rung of a ladder made of corpses. Everybody began to talk at once. There was an ancient Blue picture, that Prince D"fydd recalled but could not name, a figure with a pale, bulb-shaped head, an open mouth. On a bridge, shades of darkness, a blazing winter sky. It had meant a lot to him, in his childhood.

'It made me think that Blues had no hair, and no ears, but I *loved* it.'

Vale checked her soc'. 'That would be Munch's *The Scream*.'

'Some childhood—' remarked Grove.

'It had its moments,' admitted the prince.

Names flew. Misha Connolly, not the hateful, nasty sex ones: a series about stones, ancient stones and sad people, rooted in each other, can't explain … Sigurtian art, very rich, very doomy. 'The Lar'z tomb

sculptures,' said Grove. 'That incredible *stillness*, non-duration in stone.'
How pretty Vale looked, in an impish gold mask; how adroitly Grove
positioned herself, so that the prince was clearly her partner. They were
babbling because Ye had moved them, and this was the only coin in
which she ever wanted to be paid, but she couldn't respond. Thank
funx, René was there with his silence, firmly tucking a beaker of fortified
wine into her hand.

<Drink. The world will look better.>

'I'll never be able to pay her back. She took me out of a Ukrainian
orbital, you don't know what that means, but it was bad. I was an
overaged sex-worker, an illegal human whore on the scrapheap.'

<That is nothing,> said René solemnly, <to what she did for me.>

'I worship her,' muttered Ye. 'But she frightens me. I'm serious.
There's something *terrible* inside her, and it's getting stronger. Don't you
feel that?'

The princelings had taken themselves off to the next table, to gossip
with the Princess's servants, Miss Night's discreet bodyguards. Grove
and Vale moved closer together, and indulged in girl-talk.

'How do you think it's going?' Grove offered her snifter case, the
question betraying a failure of professional nerve—

'You could have him.' Vale smiled as if she were saying nothing in
particular: the etiquette of privacy protocols. 'He's a babe in arms.'

It had been agreed between them that Grove, whose home life was
more unpleasant, would hunt the prize catch, while Vale would 'pursue'
the lesser attraction, Lord Ch'ro. There were risks, but Vale didn't care
if she *did* get caught out. Ch'ro might be quite an agreeable husband.

'You mean D"fydd is wise to my game and must be trapped: he's
not going to fall in love. Yes, I know. Damn, what a waste of effort.'

'Is your papa acting up?'

Ehsan had a violent temper, a 'weakness' he employed skilfully in
Parliament, where physical intimidation could be useful. It was less fun
for those who faced his tantrums in private.

'Nothing unusual,' said Grove, stoically. 'Domremy's in a snit about
something, a Debate went badly: I catch the fallout, that's all. But Jacob
said something. He said if I don't land the prince, he's *frightened* for me,
and I know he was told to say that.'

Jacob Mungea was her father's lover, never publicly acknowledged
because Ehsan was supposed to be a manly Traditionalist heterosexual.

As if anyone was fooled, as if anyone on Speranza could care less! He was kind to Grove: but she found his loyalty to her father inexplicable.

'That's funny.' Vale inhaled sniff, and looked dreamily at the jewels on her delicate wrist. 'My old dad muttered the same kind of thing to me, the other day. Out of Mama's hearing, of course: she'd have a fit. He said, *Marry your queer little vampire bat, you could do worse—*'

In a year or two they'd have to take such hints very seriously: but not yet. They knew their worth. It did not occur to either of them that the warnings might be connected; or presages of imminent disaster.

The Princess's Bloodmen were drinking tea, with vodka chasers and a dish of raspberry jam. 'Why the masks?' Col Ben Phu touched her disguised cheek. 'It was my idea. The tats, you know? The Princess is impenetrably disguised, because everyone in this dump is convinced she's two hundred years old. We're prettier to look at than when she found us. Drez had one eye at that time, and we were show'ng our age. But to my m'nd we're still s"p'c"s. Soldiers three, and one of them a tattooed lady. Could've started someone thinking. I didn't like it.'

'She's rat-arsed.' Drez licked his jam spoon, and rapped Col on the knuckles with it. 'Pay no attention ... She's talented, isn't she, our girl Night. That river in a landscape. That's profound, that is: nearly made me cry.'

D"fydd siezed on the point that had leapt out at him. 'The Princess *isn't* two hundred years old? Then how old *is* she–?'

'He's drunk too,' explained Ch'ro. 'He knows one *never* asks that.'

'Good, cos we're not going to tell you.'

'Luck'ly I've nothing between chin and collarbone or below the cuff, so as long as I keep my k't on, wh'ch I do, the face is enough.'

'Sometimes,' began the prince, struggling with the Blue courage he had imbibed, and ridiculous, atavistic horror at what he was suggesting. 'Sometimes a Bloodman ... I know you're a lady, Col, I say Bloodman because on Sigurt's that term is, er, unisex. A Bloodman's absolute loyaltyness may be truly served by, er, by divulgerating, to a proven ally, things—'

'We think you have secret, dangerous business on Speranza,' said Ch'ro, losing patience. 'Everything points that way. Won't you *please* tell us what it's all about?'

Drez and Col set down their spoons and stared blankly, without a word. Still without a word they got up, left the table and headed for an exit.

LXV

As sometimes happens on the Blue itself, winter had come in an hour to the Dostoe Prospect: though a housekeeping routine had stripped the boughs and cleared the leaves away, rather than a sudden frost or a storm. Parkland trees stood dark and bare above freshly ordered grasses, under the appearance of a cloudy, moonlit sky. No lights showed in the General's mansion. The family were not at home, and the servants' quarters lay below ground level.

'Funny name, Dyke Blazer,' murmured Col. 'Why would a Trad bloke, no matter if he's a bloke with tits, call himself *dyke*?'

'Ignorance,' suggested Drez, turning up his tunic's insulation. Dostoe felt cold as the steppes in November, after the warmth of the streets.

They'd been summoned from the Blue Dog because something had come up. They'd left the Sigurtians in a tiz, but no harm in that. With any luck the kids thought they'd given terrible offence, and would lay off the impertinent questions for a while.

'The original Dyke Blazer was a male musician,' came Bibi's voice. She and Sergeant Aswad were at the other vantage, on the front-entrance side. 'Murdered long ago, in the Ancient USA. The Starry Arrow file on our friend has "Looty Loo" as a suspected closet half-caste. Our hepcat may believe he *was* a soul icon called Dyke Blazer, in a previous life—'

They'd had Mr Blazer under surveillance since his visit to the Old Dip. He'd gone straight to the bad guys, as expected: nothing if not predictable. From their trace on his movements, Bibi and her small army now knew a great deal more about the enemy. But Dyke had been given no instructions to invade the General's home, at the meeting in the Plant. The expedition seemed to be his own idea.

Some might say that breaking and entering, in a 4-Spaced environment where nothing went unrecorded, in an exclusive residential domain with

376

invincible security, was an impossible crime. The hepcat, however, had a secret weapon. Bibi and Sergeant Aswad had set out in person, summoning Col and Drez, as soon as they knew where Dyke was heading. They'd had him in view, on their nightsight screens, as he entered the grounds of the Yu mansion: whereupon he had completely disappeared.

'He came over here first, and *then* he got invisible?' muttered Drez. 'Where's the sense in that?'

'I don't know,' said Bibi. 'But this isn't ordinary cloaking tech. Maybe he's on a timer, or maybe it's too fragile to use for extended periods.'

It was *always* possible to detect a cloaked soldier: by heat, by motion, by e/m signature, by a hundred inferences. Dyke Blazer had vanished utterly. He had entered a private domain without setting off any alarms, at any level. Had someone inside let him in? Not according to their data ... Something strange was going on. They felt the aura of it as they lay in ambush, heads wrapped in tech from the soldiers' space-outlaw years – as if this exclusive parkland had become a lump of rock in the Balas/Shet asteroid belt. All they could do was wait: like the servants, the ladies' maids and the valet in there, sitting up quietly until they were wanted.

Col watched Pepper's orchard. The mansion's perimeter field was sleeved in décor, so's nobody could peek: but looking over the fence, so to speak, wasn't an act of criminal trespass. (They were trying to keep on the right side of the law. Their trace on Dyke was perfectly legal.) Methodically she scanned the field of view, the boles of the cherry trees slipping from gleam to charcoal under the wavering moonlight.

What was that?

Nothing.

What was that?

Nothing—?

She screwed up her eyes, switched to naked visual (which of course showed her only the sleeve): switched back, and stared at *nothing*, a nothing that moved, though there was not a ghost of movement.

'I think he's out,' she reported, dubiously. 'Think I've got him.'

'Clarify that,' ordered Sergeant Aswad. 'We don't *think* in this outfit.'

'Can't, Sarge. Come and take a look yourself.'

The four of them regrouped at Col and Drez's position, a tangle of evergreens close to the Yu perimeter. 'Are we in cover, or are these bushes touch-proofed Vlab?' grumbled Sergeant Aswad. 'If they're virtual, we're naked from the pov of the house security—'

'Everything's bio on Dostoe,' Col assured him. 'Nothing but the highest tarty nouveau riche quality around here. Passing you the targ now.'

Col's crosswire appeared on each head-up screen. It was uncanny. There was nothing: but they *knew* something was there. The brain reports a presence for which there is no sensory evidence: very spooky.

Drez muttered, cleared the wire, recalled it. 'He's there all right, but not in the data. What is he, dead or something? What the hell's he done?'

Frustrated senses set the adrenalin going; they could *feel* the targ's dejected, halting progress, yet they saw nothing, nothing—

—and then, viscerally, a spike of terror.

'Funx!' Col hissed. 'Pepper's funxing menagerie!'

Four huge four-legged beasts had come leaping, silent and fluid, around the corner of the building. It was immediately clear that *they* had no trouble spotting the intruder. Dyke started to run. The dogs bounded after him. The small army knew, intensely, how enormous the orchard had become, how appalling the distance between their man and safety—

When they 'saw' the target fall, Bibi came to a swift decision. They breached the field together, which stung like ethereal barbed-wire coils and alerted the police, but didn't slow them down. The dogs fled—

'Where'd Dyke go?'

'Where'd the bastard go—?'

'He was right here—!'

'Funx, don't tell me we were imagining the—'

Drez stumbled over something in the grass, and simultaneously realised he was still seeing the orchard through his head-up.

'Come back to the real world, soldiers. He's here.'

Dyke Blazer's visible form emerged, from wherever it had been hiding. He lay staring upward, clad in a face mask, dark tunic, padded gilet, dark leggings, the informal burglar's stylish attire. His eyes caught moonlight; his clawed hands clutched, agonized, at his chest. Drez swiftly took a mediscan and shook his head. No external injury, but the man was dying – caught out, like a mind too open to illusion in a violent game *envie*.

'Heart's gone, he's finished.'

'All right, lad.' Drez applied a last-aid tag and gripped the hepcat's paw, the same as he'd done for many. 'I won't lie, it's over. You religious, yeah? Thought so. Stop me when I get there, Atheist, Buddhist, Christian—'

He thought he detected a faint nod: good enough.

'Repeat after me. *I love you, Jesus, my love above all things. I repent with my whole heart of having offended thee—*'

'*I repent*—' breathed Dyke, conscious of little, happy because someone was holding his hand: and in that momentary hope and certainty, he died.

'Good one,' said Sergeant Aswad. 'Well done, Doyle.'

The soldiers had seen plenty of the other kind – enough that they wouldn't refuse last-aid to their worst enemy. They hunkered down by the body, thinking of their mates on Sigurt's World, left to rot and slaughtered in the barracks. The Mission staff, non-combatants, falling in the last fire-fight, trusting to the last gasp in the bastard who owned this mansion. The best of mistresses, buried alive. Konoe dishonoured, Nightingale's terrible fate.

The small but crucial part 'Looty Loo', aka Dyke Blazer, had played in all that dirty business ... Including his top achievement, the nasty little job in the Turgajskoje that seemed to have been his undoing. Now here he lay, struck down: one of those universal soldiers, who really is to blame—

The first instalment.

'Search him,' said Bibi. 'The cops are on their way.'

LXVI

One cop arrived, mounted on a sleek, skeletal semi-AI: Speranza's evolution of the motorcycle. In embodiment he looked like the robocops of Baykonur, but a mind of a different order inhabited this shell. He took their affirmed statements, accepted Bibi's explanation for their invasion of the General's grounds; turned a blind eye to items of outlaw tech, examined the body *in situ* and arranged for its removal. He'd spoken to General Yu's steward. He talked to the man again, and asked the Princess if she'd like to accompany him to the house – since this mystery touched on her affairs.

The General had been paged, but had yet to respond. Col, Drez and Sergeant Aswad stayed with Dyke, to await the Violent Death Team.

The steward met them in the mansion's spacious entrance hall, a Blue male, medium height, chronological age perhaps forty or fifty. Crisp dark hair receded, greying at the temples; kindly, defeated lines were etched around his mouth and eyes. Unusually, he wore Grade Four uniform – well cut and in perfect trim – rather than the Yu livery.

He bowed, straightened, and looked into Bibi's eyes.

'This is very shocking, Officer, Madam Princess. Thank you for coming so quickly. We had no idea ... I'll show you to the General's study.'

'First things first, Mr MacBride,' the cop corrected him. 'I have a violent death. I need to see those dogs.'

'The dogs are pets,' said the steward, unhappily. One could imagine Pepper's wrath, if her insanely expensive living toys were doomed. 'They're natural bios, conventional-space-freighted from the Blue. They're not attack trained. They have the run of the grounds at night, but it's for the romance of it: they're harmless.'

'Yet they killed someone.'

'They're back in their pen.'

The steward led the way, down to the servants' quarters and through silent, brightly lit basement halls.

'How many mortal servants indoors?'

'Twelve,' MacBride answered, with deliberate calm. Never resist when a cop asks questions to which he knows the answers: the diagnostics are running. 'Plus the Family's resident physician. My wife, myself, the General's valet; the two ladies' maids, our cook and her assistants, the footmen, the housemaids. It's not a large staff.'

'Where's everybody now? On the premises?'

'Yes, everyone. In their rooms. I've checked that.'

The pen was in a yard reached by a flight of steps from the domestic offices. The dogs were smooth-haired, tall at the shoulder and rangy, with liquid, intelligent eyes. They rushed to greet MacBride, but cowered away from the cop's forensic gaze. They knew they were in trouble.

'This is Trixie,' said the steward. 'Tyler, Lopez and Hetty.'

'Fine animals,' said the cop. 'I think it's a shame to keep such big dogs cooped up on a space station, but the rich have their whims. They're subdermally controlled?'

'Of course.'

'Let's look at the study now.'

The General's sanctum told a curious story. No intrusion had been detected, none was recorded on the mansion's CCTV, and the feeds were not accessible to tampering on site. Yet there was clear evidence of a search, at first cautious, then reckless: paper documents spilled, upholstery ripped, hangings torn. Dedicated image screens, in antique frames, lay on the floor, the pictures shattered into a haze of pixels. The cop's head turned, taking snapshots.

'Tell me what happened, Mr MacBride, in your own words.'

'My wife and I were in our apartment, waiting up for the General, Miss Vale and Madame, as we always do. The first thing we knew was a call from the police, your call, Officer. We'd heard nothing, there had been no alarm. I confirmed the whereabouts of my staff and the doctor, locked their doors and came through to the main house—'

'You could have been endangering your life.'

'There was no intruder on my screens, and no sign of systems failure. The thing seemed impossible. I wanted to check our gateway, which is in here. I found the room as you see. Everything was in order just before I retired downstairs, which was after the Family left: I can affirm that.'

'Have you touched anything?'

'I stood in the doorway.'

'Anyone else been in here?'

'There has been no opportunity, since your call. So, no.'

'Is there similar unrecorded disturbance elsewhere?'

'I don't know yet, I haven't searched the house.'

The cop's serene gaze moved around the study again. 'Have you any idea what the lowlife could have been looking for, Mr MacBride?'

'Not specifically. There were some objects of value: I've taken a brief glance at the house inventory, apparently nothing's missing, but—'

'But whoever did this could easily have hacked the file.'

MacBride nodded. 'Officer, the General and my mistress will return soon. I'd like to wait for them in the foyer – would that be all right?'

'I've no more questions for the moment: you may go.'

The steward beat a dignified retreat. The cop looked at the Princess, as to a colleague and an equal. 'He's got something on his mind.'

'I believe he's been interrogated in the past.'

'Yeah, by the Starry Arrow bastards. Which would excuse the paranoia, but still. He was very prompt to protect his own people—'

'He's not stupid, he knows this is serious. Do you think the intruder had inside assistance?'

'Not so far. Have to see what the post-mort questioning turns up.'

If Dyke Blazer had been a different kind of citizen he'd have been in intensive care now, instead of on his way to a VDT séance – although with the mods and the deceased's age (Dyke was easily forty-five standard, a respectable lifespan for a Blue 'Prospector') the prognosis would have been poor. Neither the Princess nor the cop was going to cry about the social injustice, but Dyke's living testimony was a loss. The dead never refused to talk: unfortunately what they had to say was rarely to the point.

'I'm going to strip back a few layers, see how deep this goes,' said the cop. 'Will you wait?'

'Yes.'

A child's toy from a bad dream, he settled his bulk in front of the mansion's Speranza gateway, which was housed in a pretty repro escritoire; out of place in this masculine room, maybe a present from Pepper Lily. 'Do *you* know what the lowlife was looking for, Princess?'

'Possibly. My own interest in Mr "Dyke Blazer" concerned a civil suit I'm pursuing for a third party, that's all I can say at the moment. I don't think he carried anything away, but if it was data of course I can't be sure.'

'VDT should at least tell us that.'

Then the minatory shell was empty: the cop had returned to the system of which 'he' was a facet – an absence that could be corrected very swiftly should need arise. Bibi sat in one of the General's vandalised armchairs, looking around at the scattered trophies, the shattered pictures. She thought of the Great House in Kirgiz, and the virgin in the roof-beam: a world so long ago, so far away, so lost, she could hardly think of it as real.

For life is a dream, but a little less inconstant.

Sometimes, and now was one of those times, she felt the presence of her mistress like another person in her mind – as if in bequeathing all she possessed, Lady Nef had installed a copy of *herself.* It was Nef, this Nef self, who calmly accepted the testimony of the dishevelled room. In Fenmu, Lady Nef had insisted that her husband was innocent, as innocent as one could expect the Swimmer to be: guilty only of snatching at a chance of survival, when his wife was already doomed. Bibi had known better (or worse) but she'd almost been convinced.

Reborn on Balas, in the City of Lilies, she had searched for proof of Yu's premeditated villainy. She'd found nothing in the data as clear as this silent answer to the question she had asked Dyke Blazer.

Where is the evidence of the Konoe marriage?

Which it seemed Dyke had not found, but—

'Best I can do,' announced the cop. 'Want to have a look?'

She stood behind him. On the escritoire screen the study appeared, timed some minutes after midnight. The hardwood door, which was really an electrochemical gate, let *something* pass. A disturbance like dropped stitches crossed the ordered room. At first there was nothing more, then objects began to shift. A ghost, a poltergeist, dragged the pictures from the walls, threw papers about—

'There was no failure,' said the cop, impassively. 'Speranza security does not fail. There could have been a secret operation going on, given whose house this is. The spooks don't *tell* me things, know what I mean? But the answer's simpler, and very, very interesting. There is no data because as data he wasn't here. I've uncovered the 4-Space hole where he ought to be, but there'd be no chance of getting an ID, if we needed one—'

'I think I see.'

'Yeah, he wrote himself out of Speranza. I wonder who taught him how? It's not a trick that would tempt your average criminal. You can walk through gates, the way he walked into the mansion, and through the door to this room. You can be sure you won't be nailed by security. But any mortal creature looking at you, unmediated, has no problem – and any material barrier is still there, obviously. Plus, a space station that doesn't know you exist is a hell of a dangerous place for a soft body that needs air to breathe.'

The big action doll meditated, serenely. 'I've seen this once before, a while ago: we never did pin that on anyone. Who gave him the cheat? That's the question, and it won't be easy to get an answer.' Even a Speranza cop can be frustrated by the blank wall of privilege. 'Whoever it was won't be pleased at the stupid use he made of it tonight. I'm wondering about those dogs—'

'They could have been directed to attack?'

'It's a possibility—' The cop touched the spot where an ear might have been located: politely mimicking the mortal gesture for *excuse me, taking a call.*

'The General and Madame's ride just entered Dostoe.'

'Then I should leave,' said the Princess.

'May I say, your company tonight has been a pleasure.'

'You're very kind.'

'I am a bot,' said the robocop, 'and a police officer. Not many mortals can sit so quietly when they're alone with me. I appreciated that.'

The Princess, whose soul felt like a cracked shell full of roiling gases, unbearable memories, smiled and bowed. 'Thank you. I hope we meet again.'

'I'm never far away, Princess.'

Outside the study she didn't know which way to turn. But the General's steward was there, having anticipated her difficulty, like a good servant. He stepped up with a slight cough, and no repetition of the direct glance that had met her when she arrived.

'Perhaps you'd like to leave by the conservatory and the orchard, Princess. I can key you through the perimeter field.'

'Yes, I would ... You are working in the enemy camp, Mr MacBride.'

'Ah, I see what you mean. I'm a Reformer, yes. But I'm steward only for ceremonial purposes – Ogul's the driving force. She would hold the post officially, if it weren't that Pepper Lily prefers a male head of staff.'

'Ogul?'

'My wife, Ogul Merdov.'

He led the way, without lights this time, to a sunroom, cluttered with greenery, that faced the orchard. The air was moist and warm; fake moonlight shone fitfully through the glass. He opened a French door, they exchanged 'goodnights'. MacBride watched until she had passed through the perimeter, then he secured it again and returned to his duties.

LXVII

The General had slept badly. He was too old for cops and questions in the middle of the night, especially on top of Pepper's frenetic socialising, and a thoroughly indigestible midnight supper. Pepper said he should get treatment for the insomnia, but he refused. He wasn't ill. He could sleep like a baby, like an old soldier, if they'd ever leave him in peace. No chance of that for a while. It would come to nothing, but there would be endless fuss and aggravation over this, and no doubt Amal would be round in person—

He hated dealing with his son.

After breakfast – for which he had no appetite, his stomach was queasy, and everything tasted of ash – he retired to his study. The room was tidy, damaged furniture replaced: it didn't look bad. The pictures were gone, but they'd been Pepper's choice, so that was no loss. He felt better sitting at his desk. The police required, as a formality, that he review his financial and personal files, the material to which they couldn't have access without a warrant.

Everything seemed in order. The Princess's depredations had been more serious than he'd admitted to Pepper, but what nagged at him was the pattern in it. He'd been robbed by someone who played in just the same style as a dead woman. His Nef, his Beauty: lost so long ago. One or two little girls, now and then. How could he have known she'd take it so badly? A man, no, damn it, a *person* has to have his freedom. He noticed that a new fund had appeared on the boards – and guessed instantly, intuitively, where his losses had ended up. Nef's signature again: if she made a killing she'd always spend it on one of her charities. But how had the Princess known that?

One of *those* Blues?

He had never feared exposure. There's no crime in being one of the movers and shakers behind a successful political coup, and who could accuse him of anything else? No one. What's more, unlike his high-flying son he'd taken the back seat he was offered and lived quietly, no risks. He would bet it was Amal himself behind the stupid break-in, or one of the other dirty dogs; but whatever they'd thought they could find, they couldn't touch Yu. And Dyke Blazer was dead, which was a bonus. The last of the Baykonur crew, and good riddance.

He was in no danger, so why was he afraid? In sleepless nights, with the taste of ash in his mouth, he knew the truth. The Princess of Bois Dormant was a rich woman who played the game a little spitefully, nothing more. He wasn't being haunted by his dead wife, he wasn't being pursued by one of those terminally elusive Blue 'immortals'. No, it was stranger than that. After so many years, he'd suddenly started to be afraid of *what he had done*. Couldn't stop thinking about the past, wishing things had been different, et cetera and so forth. It was a mild bout of mania, and he couldn't get treatment because he didn't care for the idea of a cog. scan, no matter how confidential. He'd just have to put up with the discomfort, until it went away.

He had 3D mail. It would be from the police.

He accepted the delivery swiftly: never keep the cops waiting. There was nothing in the envelope but a small, dark, fibrous disk. What was he supposed to do with that? Swallow it? Stick it in his ear? The disk stirred, broke open and a tiny root emerged. Within moments a little flower was growing, right there on the polished mahogany. It was Vlab art, an exquisite piece of work, and probably the newest, most fashionable kind of invitation card. *Now Pepper's going to be mad*, he thought. *Well, I can't help it if people address things to the master of the house* ... He knew the flower. His wife used to have it in her 'English Garden', at the Great House in Kirgiz. Attractive little thing, sturdy, bold yet unassuming. What was the name? It was on the tip of his tongue.

Honesty.

She stood there, in his mind's perception. He could hear her voice, he could see her girlish rosy face all grimed and haggard, tunic torn and smoke-stained, the big weapon gripped in her small hands. Courage in the face of death, a gallant young life cut off ... The General tried to stand, but he couldn't. As the purple flowers transformed into a shower of silver coins, and the sprig of honesty vanished, he fell—

—a great thunder, bursting silently inside him.

LXVIII

Details of the 'Dyke Blazer' incident did not reach the public, but all Speranza soon knew that General Yu had suffered a massive stroke. The Sigurtians, isolated in their mansion (as the best-loved visitors are suddenly isolated, by a family crisis), were surprised to learn how important Yu had been: this old soldier who had held no official post, who had seemed like a relic, a relict, the tomb-wife of events that no longer mattered. There was newsfeed from his bedside, hourly bulletins popping up everywhere you looked. They sent messages of concern to Pepper Lily and Miss Vale, with their best wishes for the General's speedy recovery, and were shocked to learn from the incessant bulletins that recovery was not expected. The General, despite his splendid appearance, had 'reached the stage of artificial survival'. Brain damage was too extensive even for the last resort of a mind-transplant. Blue longevity had its limits: it seemed the old man's time was up.

But he did not succumb. After forty-eight hours he was 'stable' and the bulletins slowed.

The sad event cast a pall over the New Year, traditionally such a festive occasion on 'Blue Speranza'. Naturally there were no celebrations at the Yu mansion. Other parties and receptions were quietly cancelled, either out of respect, or in response to a feeling of unease, scarcely rational, that had gripped the fashionable world – as if one of the pillars of the universe had crumbled. Miss Night's opening, in the Nebula Theatre foyer, was among the few fixtures that survived. The crowd was dazzling. Perhaps the society figures and political notables were attracted by the patronage of the Princess of Bois Dormant – but Miss Night's exhibition was equal to the challenge. She convinced them. She silenced them, she made them feel the closeness of the cold dark. Their own mortality, their pain, their fragile grip on the beautiful, terrible illusion of *being—*

The artist had made her entrance masked. When she stepped down from the Vlab frame, after her closing image – a shower of snowy, scented blossom and wordless song, falling into the dark – there was a murmur of gratified astonishment. A rumour about the Konoe-Olofact connection, which the Princess was pursuing, had begun to circulate. Those Speranzans who were in the know believed they saw a striking resemblance—

'Curses,' murmured Jacob Mungea, gently mischievous. 'I had my heart set on the new genius being a cute boy in disguise ...'

Ehsan Lukoil was not present. His daughter, pale but surpassingly lovely in cream silk and black ribbons, with a black half-mask, clung to Mungea's arm. She tried to smile. She was here under orders, and a little for Ye's sake, but it was damned hard work.

Miss Night, a stylish dressing gown over her close-fitting Vlab jumper, came to join her sponsor, and to endure the congratulations.

'You did well,' said the Princess, quietly. 'Thank you.'

They were surrounded by well-wishers. Domremy even came over and paid her a compliment. Kongzi youths, who would have scraped a Vlab artist off their shoe, made gallant remarks about masks behind masks, hinting that they'd known all along she was *one of them*.

She didn't stay long. Col and Drez took her away, and she walked between them with a frisson: aware that the Princess believed she was in real danger, in this high-grade company. If the danger was real it was a relief, it steadied her. *My father is supposed to have killed himself, my mother died insane. And you're* congratulating *me on my parentage? And this* excites *you?* If the story was true, it spoke to her of what she'd always known, the horror in the heart of things—

Councillor and Zubindah Scolari, who had yet to be introduced to the famous Princess, had gravitated too late towards the centre of attention. Scolari stared after the beautiful Miss Night, transfixed, his heavy lips moving, unable to contain the revelation—

Nightingale—

'The likeness is unmistakable, isn't it?'

The Princess of Bois Dormant was beside him, with that Aleutian pageboy. 'Yes,' she continued smoothly, smiling. 'That was indeed the song of a nightingale, in the closing frame. I had no idea you were such a nature-lover, Councillor. But you do see the *other* likeness? I think you must have known Caspian Konoe, in, ah, your previous life?'

'The face,' said Scolari stiffly, 'is familiar.'

'I expect you recall my ward, too – René le Champi?'

'I can't say that I do.'

The Aleutian bowed, insolently Silent.

'I don't approve of Vlab art,' announced Zubindah, uncompromising in her moral views. 'It's meddling with the forbidden. I may be old-fashioned, but I won't have anything to do with neurophysical technology.'

'Then I'm sure I don't know how you got here, Miss Scolari.'

'Hmph. It's dangerous, whatever you say.'

The Princess smiled again. 'You may be right about the danger. I'm glad we've had this chat: I hope we'll meet again soon.'

LXIX

A few days after this event, at the end of the 'New Year' season, the Sigurtians were in their breakfast room, with Agent Mallorn. Couriered news from Myot and Neuendan had just been hand-delivered – a Speranza tradition – in the form of printed text on large sheets of paper, which were spreading untidily over the breakfast table. The Oligarchs had finally fallen.

Stirring, amazing things were happening far away at home: but Ch'ro and D"fydd were forlorn. Speranza was still comatose under a pall of shock; or waiting to mourn a death postponed. They had not heard from the Princess since Ye's opening, and their closest friends in 'Blue Speranza' society, Vale and Grove, seemed to have deserted them.

D"fydd had had an uncomfortable experience at the Nebula Theatre. He'd seen Grove Lukoil in the crowd, with her father's secretary, the self-effacing Jacob Mungea. Naturally he'd gone up to greet her. The young lady, her blue eyes framed in a black half-mask that made her beauty perfectly Sigurtian, had looked straight through him, expressionless, and immediately guided her escort in the opposite direction – cut him dead, as the Blues say.

At the time he'd been in the middle of an argument with Ye, in his head. *The world is not what you think it is. Not what your art says it is. Terrible things happen, but life is wonderful, love is stronger than death* ... Looking back, he felt very sore. It was just business, never friendship. *The novelty has worn off, I suppose another rich prize of a suitor has appeared—*

Agent Mallorn, as usual appearing as a keen-eyed, elderly Blue gentleman of a bygone age, expressed himself highly satisfied by the developments on Sigurt's World.

'Academic treatises do not dictate policy, but there is no doubt that the "History of Fenmu" sowed the seed of a reversal of feeling: from whence sprang a realisation, in the hearts of the minor Crater-States, that they were many, and alliance with Neuendan was *not* a futile, quixotic gesture. A change of government is by no means always good news, young sirs, but in this case we may confidently join the rejoicing. You need have no fears – you are poised to make substantial gains, thanks to the estimable Liam Mallorn, and the forward planning of your remarkable paternal grandfather, Prince D''fydd. An enlightened capitalist and a most astute investor. How I wish I could have met him—'

'They say he made one bad decision in his whole career,' agreed the prince, glumly. 'The one that cost him his life—'

'Ah, the marriage to your royal grandmother. A mistake I cannot bring myself to regret, my dear D''fydd.'

Ch'ro and D''fydd exchanged rueful glances: the facet's idea of a compliment was strange to mortal ears—

A tap on D''fydd's shoulder. 'Come in,' he called.

It was one of the Blue servants, bearing a small packet on a salver. D''fydd and Ch'ro had learned to pronounce their domestics' names, paid them well, and left them to their own devices: a strategy that seemed successful. The prince took the packet, and looked it over.

'What's this, Drea?'

'It's a "letter bomb", sir,' declared the young woman, proudly. 'It's a Blue art form, from before First Contact. All the Vlab artists in town (she meant the streets) are mad about them. It's kind of a recorded message.'

Blues have two ruling passions, Ch'ro had decided. Animals, and *anything* that's new to them. 'You'd better deal with it for us. And, er, stay to interpret. Or does D''fydd have to open it?'

'It'll open now.' Drea looked to Agent Mallorn, whose approval she regarded as pre-eminent: the Sigurtians were just boys. The facet nodded. She set the packet on a small table, and read aloud, as an air message blossomed.

'Pull the blue touchpaper and retire.'

'I suggest you obey,' said Agent Mallorn.

Drea pulled, and backed off. Two small girls sprang into existence. One was forthright and pretty, the other notably lovely, despite her bare face and straight nose. Both were dressed in blue-green tunics and trousers, in a slightly archaic style. Ch'ro and D''fydd were immediately reminded of how rarely they had seen a child on Speranza: because the little girls brimmed with childhood, a joy and a nostalgia for joy, for unsullied childish hearts—

The girls bowed, turned to each other and opened the air between them, as if they were pulling on a pair of curtains. From this figurative concealment the Princess of Bois Dormant stepped forward, in her long grey morning coat with the white braid, grey trousers of exquisite cut, a snowy neckcloth at her throat. Clad in sombre majesty, in the mystery that had always been her signature, she seemed to gaze at them:

'My Lord Ch'ro. Prince D''fydd. If you wish to pay your respects to the prince's guardian, and to join me in an adventure, here is your passport to the rendezvous. Make arrangements to cover an absence of some days.'

The little girls and the tall woman vanished. Nothing remained of the 'letter bomb' but a slip of white card.

INTERMISSION
THE SIXTH PLANET

O

The passport took them to a raw cavern, on a Horizontal RT line not open to the public, where older passages and units had been stripped out, and new development just begun. Infralines, growing almost visibly, looped across the distant walls: like blood vessels, like balloons of gut. The RT network ended here. A bridge led to another platform, where the trains departed for Right Speranza. No sign of the Princess on the empty station, but Ye was there: a small kitbag slung over her shoulder.

Ch'ro looked into depths, where big machines hung idle, reminding him of the defunct refinery on Balas. He'd have liked to try a glide, but the difficulty is always getting back up again ... D"fydd had been in a strange mood since the 'letter bomb': irritable, unlike himself. Was the enchantment breaking at last? Ch'ro wanted to hope, and knew he must despair.

D"fydd stalked the artist, feeling shy because of that argument in his head. Her unhappy genius nagged at him, half-confused with that beautiful message (he knew it had been Ye's work), which had seemed to D"fydd a promise, a warning – that the adventure was over, the mystery soon to be ended, the last word spoken. The love of his life was about to disappear, the way she'd walked out of The Caprice, but this time for ever.

'Thinking of buying a unit?'

'Actually, I was thinking about "shipping out".'

D"fydd made the gesture for *you're poorly informed*. 'That doesn't happen here. The Prospector Transit Lounge is right in the old centre.'

'I know. I was making a joke.'

'But you've considered it.'

'Why not? It's what Speranza was built for. The rest is just—'

'Accumulated crap. So you take a chance on nothing, lie down and vanish, if you can fight your way through all the helpful bureaucracy, medical tests and psych questionnaires. And that's the end of you.'

'Or you join the deluded losers in the streets, endlessly playing the numbers, trying to get hold of a good one. At least I can find my stake now. I don't have to apply for a random portfolio.'

The prince and the artist simultaneously realised that they'd given away too damn much. Everyone played the Lottery. Nobody who had a life seriously contemplated lying down in a Buonarotti couch, naked to the void.

Then a private train arrived on the other side, bodywork in sleek grey, with a trim of thorns and flowers. They went to join the Princess, her Bloodmen and the Aleutian: to cross over to Right Speranza.

'The first time I made this trip,' remarked the Princess, 'it was very different. We crossed on foot, by the old Umbilical.'

'Were you with the Princess then?' Ch'ro asked Col Ben Phu.

'Nah. We were locked up as foreign military.' Col jerked her chin at the Aleutian. '*He* was, though.'

When was that? wondered Ch'ro. *When he was the pangolin?*

O

Right Speranza Terminal was a suit store. Air messages warned, in all the Diaspora languages, that there was NO UNAUTHORISED ACCESS beyond this point, and listed the prohibitive dangers. Décor walls showed images of the city in space from the outside, as it was rarely depicted in Left Speranza: the grossly lopsided dumb-bell, suspended in blackness and brilliant stars. The suit that Drez picked out for Ye altered itself instantly to a perfect fit, supple and warm: the helmet smelled of nothing. She thought of the stinking, decrepit 'emergency' hard suits on Coral Island orbital, pity the tourists who would be scrabbling to get hold of one. Better to drown at once in the airless dark; they say it's not such a bad death.

René helped Ch'ro with his gauntlet seals. 'Have you *grown*, René?'

The immortal seemed taller, older, more substantial—

'I was "held back", like your prince, remember. I've had some catching up to do. I'm as grown up as you are, my lord. Possibly more.'

'How are we getting out to the Ring?' asked D''fydd.

Speranza's dead notables were enshrined in tiny satellites, called the Ring of Great Souls. They'd been told that Liam wasn't there: his body had been, by his own choice, 'returned to the system' – which had distressed them, though it was the normal fate of Speranza's dead. Maybe there'd been some mistake. Maybe he was an ex-directory Great Soul.

'That's not where we're heading,' said Drez.

O

Gecko bootsoles creaked on greenish ceramic alloy, in passages decorated only with vivid orientation arrows. The subliminal hum of the Buonarotti Torus roared in their minds. Helmeted, tethered together, they crossed an icy, black space, armament bays and missile silos 'below' them, prepared for the unthinkable: war in conventional space. When they reached the red and green lights of a row of private moorings there was one more lock, and then, floating in a veil of its own light, a classic, thoroughbred, transit-capable Aleutian pod.

'What a *beauty*,' breathed D''fydd. 'So this is why your name never turns up on the passenger lists! He must be yours, Princess?'

'No,' said René. 'He's mine.'

O

Eight was a crowd in the crew habitat. The Princess faced them, suited-up, her helmet under her arm, radiating the same sombre allure as her 'letter bomb' image. 'Thank you for your patience, D"fydd and Ch'ro, and Ye. You'll have realised that we are about to make a transit, and that we didn't want to discuss our flight plan with the *taikos*. I have promised D"fydd and Ch'ro that they will see their guardian again. To you, Miss Night, I promise that you will hear the true story of your father's and your mother's fate: a story that may perhaps *never* be told, except this once.

'My Bloodmen, my ward and I would welcome your company – it's not for nothing that the active complement on a "starship" is never less than eight persons. But it may be a turbulent passage: we're opening a way that has been shut for a long time and our destination is perilous. You're free to refuse: in which case I shall trust you to return to Left Speranza, and say nothing about this mission, not even to each other.'

'But can't you tell us anything more?' blurted Ch'ro.

Col, Drez and the Sarge glared at him, outraged.

'Better not,' said the Princess. 'Not until we make landfall. Well?'

'Of course,' said D"ffyd, for both of them. '*Of course!*'

'Of course,' said Ye. She was walking into the trap of all traps, and this was the answer. Stop fighting: let the dark have you.

O

The suits were stowed. Col and René were in the cockpit. Col was their navigator, René her pilot. In the crew habitat, still cramped for six, they waited for the moment of insertion; when they would live or die.

'What's he called?' asked Ch'ro. 'This racer, I mean.'

'He's *The Spirit of Eighty-Nine*,' said Drez. 'Don't ask me what it means, it's something the noseless dreamed up.'

The Princess and Ye talked in low tones. The Princess was telling the artist about her parents. Ye was drinking it in, like a desert drinking water. *We used to meet for breakfast, by the Syr Darya, the Great Pearl River. In the winter we went dancing . . .*

Drez dispensed ration packs, which bore the ident of a Shet conventional space freighter line, and explained it to the Sigurtians. 'The funxer stole her from a decent little house.' He paused to take a suck of nourishing goo. 'In the Turgajskoje, grey-area, where she'd've been safe. Could've been free before she was twenty-five. She was three years old. He took her to the city, had her turned into a zombie, know what that means? An illegal whore, made out to be a robot. All so she'd disappear for ever.

'The bastard who *did* it is dead,' he added. 'We're going after the bastards who made it all happen, that's what this trip's about. You're with us? Of course you are.'

Ch'ro worked at the intricate puzzle, a ball of light and shade, which had to be solved according to rules, profoundly satisfying rules, that he seemed to draw into his head from the thoughts of the others. He nodded, concentrating on his task. Ye is a lost heiress. The carved ball was actually a city, with millions of people living inside. Or something bigger, far too big.

'I must leave this.' He put the universe into Ye's hands.

'I've been thinking about death,' announced Sergeant Aswad.

'I know it's unlucky, but I can't help it. There was Dyke Blazer, and if he was a sinner what are we? We were poor and oppressed, like he was: we had a choice, we chose to kill for pay. He took a little child and did horrors, but we gave him the last rites, and do you know why? Because your sense of time can go before you do, and you die in non-duration. We had no last-aid on Sigurt's, it's against regulations: that's the Blue for you, that's what they think of soldiers. D'you get it? *Hell is real.* Hell dimension is real. Nobody deserves that. Don't you? I mean, don't you?'

'I'm losing my temper with this,' remarked Ye. 'Will you take over, Sarge?'

Good girl, she'd stripped the machine down like a pro, but it's never finished: the closer you look, the more work you see. Sergeant Aswad set his magnification high and relaxed, absorbed in the pursuit of perfection.

'When one is in transit,' said the Aleutian—

He paced the floor, hyper-alert. 'One seems to recover fond memories from the narratives of other transits: the details that are lost, and rightly so, as a dream is lost in waking. I remember, for instance, a salt cellar and a pepper mill. They stood on the table, in another saloon like this one. Self only knows what that meant, or why I should suddenly recall—'

'They were from the Great House,' said the Princess.

Sergeant Aswad counted ration packs. *Too many, we're too many, air and water's okay but we'll starve, who's going to take a walk? It'd better be me, I'm the oldest here.* Cold sweat ran down under his space-crew undress; *The Spirit of Eighty-Nine* had begun to shake like a demented leaf.

'Why is Ye with us?' whispered D"fydd. 'Shouldn't we send her back?' His motives were obscure, even to himself. Maybe he felt she was a rival for the Princess's affections.

'I don't see why.' René leaned back, stretching a skein of coloured wool between his clawed hands: yawned and gave the cat's cradle another twist.

'But she's so fragile. She's suffered so much.'

403

'Not at all. The Vlab work is wireless, and the arachnoid Col removed from inside her skull had done no lasting damage. She transits well. Don't be taken in by her bleak outlook, she is as strong as any of us. We ask ourselves: why do artists, especially the greatest, see so much dark, feel so much pain? Maybe we should reverse the polarity. The way I just reversed the grid, *vois-tu*? Why do we, we others, refuse to embrace the world as it really is? Ye is one of those who has trouble keeping her soul inside her breast, *and yet she lives*. We have such people at Home, but not me, never me, I was always too wise ... *Self*, how I detest this stage, the transition. Boredom sets in.'

He tossed the skein at the extra member of the crew—

'You'd better take this.'

The subliminal hum of the Torus ceased. Everything stopped and everyone knew that the Aleutian had just tossed their fate into the hands of—

Whenever D"fydd lay down for his 'watch below' in one of the four couches they shared, turnabout, he tried to count up how many watches there had been; and never succeeded. Everything happens in the closing phase of a Buonarotti calculation. There is *no way of knowing* if the navigator has made a deadly mistake until the quantum equations won't solve. He was afraid. People were avoiding each other best they could in here. That must be a bad sign – and now René had reversed the 4-Space polarity. Tragic passions clawed at the closure of his bed, dreams that could turn to murder. *I cannot give my friend what he wants. The Princess will never be mine.* But it was all settled, long ago, and our fate on this voyage too: so why worry? Why not hope? He listened for Ch'ro's breathing in the dark, and smiled in his sleep.

O

The Princess released a long, slow breath. 'Well done, everyone.'

Drez grabbed D''fydd's hand and pumped it. 'We'll keep you for a mascot, kid.'

'What did I do?' spluttered D''fydd, glowing modestly.

He would never know. The next moment it was all gone.

Col's head appeared on the cockpit intercom. 'Live contact, ma'am. You want to come and make yourself known?'

René came through to the habitat. The Princess and the Aleutian passed each other, exchanging one swift glance: for everything that had changed and would have to wait—

'Where *are* we?' breathed Ch'ro.

The outside cams showed violet-tinged sunlight, filtered through fronds of vegetation. The *Spirit* appeared to have landed in a forest clearing, as if on the Blue, but those weren't the Blue's vital statistics on the sensor displays. Was this Ki/An, could it be Bois Dormant? He didn't think so.

'We are on Mallorn,' said René.

'Mallorn,' repeated D''fydd, making the gesture for *I knew it.* 'I see, I see. The Lost World: so this is where Liam is buried. But how was it done, and how can we be here ourselves? Mallorn doesn't exist in normal space.'

'We're not in normal space,' said Drez. 'Simple.'

The soldiers were packing up. Water, rations, battlefield first aid. No weapons, it was tempting, but better not—

'The true fate of the sixth planet is *taboo*,' said the Aleutian. 'A Blue term, curiously appropriate, and quite absurd. We cannot invite the doom that fell on Mallorn by speaking of it, but you'll understand why we had to be discreet. There would have been a nanny-panic. The Torus knew, knows, our flight plan, and that is sufficient. Where is Mallorn, if it is not in normal space? The answer should be obvious. As you should know, *mes enfants*, when first landfall was made here, Aleutians ruled the Blue, and instantaneous transits were being made secretly from games *envies*. That model was swiftly abandoned, the dangers having been recognised. Mallorn must have already been tainted. But no one knew ... A group of Old Earth romantics claimed the world as their personal fief: which seems extraordinary now, but in those days we believed Earth Perfect planets were everywhere. For a while they prospered, but then—'

'No need to go *on and on*,' muttered Drez. 'The gag's for a reason ... *Sir*,' he added, wincing as René glared.

I knew there was something different, thought Ch'ro. *René's* talking!

'I know a ship foundered,' said D''fydd, 'catastrophically, taking the planet with it. Liam was on Speranza: that's how he survived. Some of them winked out of existence, wherever they happened to be, er, but Liam said that was a myth. I think you're saying Mallorn became a virtual world, like a game *envie*, but I don't know what it *means*.'

'Unreal.' Ye stared at the purple forest on the screens. 'But to us it will seem real, because we are here, we are in Mallorn space—'

'It won't seem *real*, miss,' corrected the Sarge. 'More like inside out. Like an imaginary place, where dreams come true.' He shuddered.

'But we're leaving the ship?'

'Yes.' The Princess stepped over the sill from the cockpit, brisk and matter-of-fact. 'I've delivered some couriered news, and the Mallorns have opened a path for us, to the old Ground Station.' She picked up one of the packs Drez and Aswad had prepared. 'Let's go. It's a short trek, but the path is temporary. The advice I've been given is *do not interact*.'

Before they disembarked, Sergeant Aswad produced a withered sachet from the locker where he kept plundered condiments. They must all *take salt*, an ancient Blue protection against evil. The Princess and the Aleutian submitted, without argument.

Ch'ro was dubious. 'I'm afraid I don't believe in magic.'

Drez rolled his eyes. 'What did we just say? I *knew* you weren't listening. We're not in the *modern* version of Buonarotti, we're back the way it was when it started. You're in this world in hell dimension, with all your demons. We need any ritual we can get. Stick yer tongue out, Scrappy.'

O

The first thing they noticed was the vividness. Mallorn shone from within, every detail a jewel. The air smelled of pitch and pine; the tree-things grew close, massive as far as the eye could reach. The ground was covered in needle-like fallen leaves, shading from black indigo to a bright turquoise where plunging spears of light struck. The second thing they noticed was the fear. They walked two by two along a narrow strip of red, beaten earth, not meeting each other's eyes: Col and René in the lead, Drez and the Sarge, Ch'ro and Ye. The Princess and D''fydd took the rear. As she looked up, marvelling, inexplicable anxiety rising like a cloud, the back of Ye's bare hand grazed scaly, fissured rind.

She walked on, but the tree became an eyeless, groping, crawling bear, a hundred metres long, a thousand groping arms. It followed them. It liked Ye, it wanted to have her. It found it liked the Sigurtians too. It buried the soldiers neck-deep in soft mould, and stuffed their mouths with leaf debris and crawling things; it thrust a lance-like air-root through René's body. Luckily Ch'ro remembered a lullaby. He clicked and crooned until the great beast fell comatose in front of them.

They had to make a long, scary diversion to regain the path.

'I'm sorry,' gasped Ye, 'I'm very sorry!'

'*Now* d'you get it?' Drez groaned, and tugged out a thing like a giant yellow louse that was fighting to crawl through his cheek. 'You're scared, aren't you? We all are. It's called virtuality paranoia, it's what drives you crazy. The place is haunted, possessed by demons, *that's* what's wrong with Mallorn being virtual.'

They were so big, thought Ye. *I was so small—*

'We should have suited-up,' grumbled the Aleutian.

'Better not,' said the Princess. 'Armour implies an arms race.'

'Still, I should prefer *not* to be raped by another conifer,' snapped René, but Ye knew he had heard her unspoken thought, and he understood.

'That was child's play, it could be much worse next time. Don't interact, Miss Night: don't *any* of us interact.'

Their path crossed a shallow stream. The soldiers, gripped by unease, insisted on testing the clear liquid that barely covered a bed of round, rosy stones and dark water weed, to make sure it was harmless. On the further side, D"fydd looked back. The red stones were rising, thrust upward by furry, fleshy lips. The stream-bed gave birth, graphically and painfully, to countless numinal biped babies, male babies that seemed to have been partially flayed. They screamed and screamed, they clung with frantic little hands, they sucked at flesh. Nothing would comfort them. The only answer was to slap them off, like biting insects, and run like funx.

'I'll claim that one,' said D"fydd, ruefully. 'I don't remember being that baby, but *Fall*, I surely knew him when I saw him.'

But it was the Princess, strangely, who was most shaken.

The spears of light declined. In passionate, entrancing twilight they reached a boulder field, the trees circling at a distance, and agreed to bivouac: eat and rest, and set a guard. D"fydd watched the sky. No stars, no true darkness, a strange uniform glow around the horizon. *Say this is summer, in a high latitude. But where are we*, really? he wondered. *In plain neurophysics, if we are virtual then we haven't left the Torus.* So that was Mallorn's doom: it became a transit fugue artefact. He tried to imagine the appalling, impossibly vast calculation, which had happened all by itself, and his brain staggered ... He felt himself clinging to the thoughts of others, the active complement, as to the warmth of their bodies in a bitter blizzard.

Someone was coming.

'Wake up!' hissed D"fydd.

A figure in a hard suit of antique design emerged from the gloom, and took off his helmet. They saw the Mallorn body-mods, silvery-blue hair in flattened 'Aleutian' locks, golden eyes with vertical pupils, pale gold skin—

'I couldn't wait. D"fydd ... ? Ch'ro ... ? Don't you know me?'

'Go to him,' urged the Princess.

It was Liam, not dead but alive. D"fydd and Ch'ro embraced their guardian, bewildered. They had never met Liam Mallorn in the flesh. Were they touching him now? A funerary portrait in a cold and rigid shell looked over Ch'ro's shoulder: but it was Liam who exclaimed, in his well-remembered voice.

'Good God! *Francois—?*'

'The same,' said René bowing. 'Calm yourself. I am not a ghost, merely a somewhat unorthodox revenant—'

But Liam had turned to the Princess of Bois Dormant. In disbelief and wonder he touched her dark hair, her face; he traced her features—

'*Bibi—!*'

O

Liam, Bibi, Francois – they sat on the boulders and gripped each other's
hands, they spoke in disjointed sentences of Black Wing Castle, that
terrible winter. The Flirtatious Hairy Serpent. Meagre blood tea and
pollen wafer rations, shared like feasts. Nikty, the gentle envoy who had
chosen to share their fate. Dunblane, Rashit, Lady Nef, Honesty ...
The painful, treasured centre of their lives, restored to them by this
reunion.

'Tell me what happened, Bibi. How did you survive? How did you
become the woman of wealth and mystery and power, who features so
splendidly in the couriered news you brought to us?'

'You know that I was taken alive,' said Bibi, 'because the Myots knew
I was pregnant. You know that I bore a child. The king kept me until
her grandson could live without my blood: it was years, but I didn't
know it. Then I was buried in Fenmu, alone for a long time. But Lady
Nef was there too. In the end I found her and she saved me. In the
end she gave me, she bequeathed to me, everything she possessed.'

'Everything,' murmured Liam, cat-eyes wide. '*Ah—!*' He turned to
his other friend. 'But *you*, Francois ... I saw you fall, I saw your head
burst like a melon smashed with a hammer. You were alone. How can
you be alive again, and knowing all, remembering all?'

'The details, maybe another time, Liam ... Suffice it to say, I was
with Bibi in Fenmu. When Lady Nef died, we escaped together.'

'These soldiers, do I recognise them?'

'Perhaps. They're veterans of General Yu's army, Orange Company,
they were with us on Sigurt's. I'd ordered Col to take the *Spirit* and
run—'

'The boy-racer! I remember our differences of opinion over that pod.'

'Indeed ... With peerless devotion to duty, Col Ben Phu, Drez Doyle,
private soldiers, and Sergeant Rohan Aswad remained in the Sigurtian

system for more than twenty years. They picked us up, when we left Fenmu.'

The soldiers grinned and muttered, reddening.

'Twenty years of mugging traffic, sir,' Col temporised. 'Not as if we had anywhere to go. Couldn't exactly head for Speranza—'

'No,' said Liam. 'You could not ...' He looked at Ye, and at his wards, considering each young face. 'This begins to sound like a deposition.'

'Yes,' said Bibi. 'And it continues. We made landfall on Balas, the soldiers, Francois and I. At the public library, in the City of Lilies, I used the level of access that Lady Nef had bequeathed to me, and studied the affair known as the Baykonur Conspiracy. I knew who: I wanted to know *why* my lady and I had been so cruelly betrayed. Now I am here, to tell my side of the story to the only Speranza agent I can trust.'

'*Ah!*' said Liam again. 'How did you know I was still alive?'

'I knew you'd been made the guardian of my son, and lived at peace with the new regime on Speranza, before dying of natural causes. I counted you as one of the enemy, unfortunately beyond my reach. Then I met Ch'ro and D''fydd. I found out that you had named the prince *Dafydd*, I found out his ... your ward's qualities.'

'Not my doing, Bibi. He is himself. He's a good boy, isn't he?'

'He is ... So, after that I took a closer look at your demise. I learned that the obituaries covered a supposed suicide, and Speranza had no record of a body returned to the system. I decided that I was looking at a disappearance, not a death. A disappearance that had closely followed the "Mallorn Vote" – when Domremy Li's government voted to abandon the research that might have restored Mallorn.'

'Domremy! He and his cronies pay lip service to the concept of "free worlds" sometime or never. In reality they prefer to expand the captive world where they are secure in power—' Liam stopped himself, abruptly raising a gauntleted hand, as if to ward off a blow. 'Alis is dead, you know. My partner on Sigurt's World.'

'I know.'

'She resigned and returned to the Blue. It was slow suicide: she knew she was too old to adapt. I thought I wasn't the suicidal kind. I had secured guardianship of your child, I had Dafydd to think of; Ch'ro too. But the Mallorn Vote was too much.'

'The obits imply you died of a broken heart,' said the Aleutian, softly. 'Ironic, eh?'

'My heart was broken when I knew what lay behind the siege of Black Wing ... Perhaps the truth is that I died insane. I put my affairs in order, I set up an agency to look after my wards. I cleared myself for transit with a false ID, and went to the Prospector Lounge in a bodymask, which is permitted. I couldn't use Mallorn coordinates, I'd have been hauled out of there. I lay down and committed myself to the Torus, making the transit of desire. I thought I would die. I landed close to the dome – our refuge, where we live: it detected my presence and someone came out to fetch me.'

'I left Fenmu the same way,' said Bibi. 'Into the deep.'

'What's the "transit of desire"?' whispered Ch'ro to Col.

'Suicide.'

'Wash your mouth,' growled the Sarge. 'It's when you don't have the coordinates, or nowhere to enter them, kid. You get in a couch, wish to be where you belong, and commit yourself to the terrible energies—'

'Wow.'

'I thought your name was René,' muttered D''fydd to the Aleutian, a trifle accusingly. 'I thought you used to be the pangolin.'

'I was. René-Francois, Francois-René ... René means *reborn*, D''fydd.'

The Princess had resumed her deposition.

'In the City of Lilies I found a story that I knew by heart, told from a perspective that I could never have imagined. I realised that the plot to bring the Young Emperor back to Earth had been a feint. The conspirators never intended to set "Prisoner Haku" on the Imperial Throne. They were working for a Speranza Blue faction that favoured a different restoration, through which they would gain control of the Diaspora Parliament. The *real* conspiracy was an outstanding success. The Republic fell and the Third Empire was established. Domremy Li emerged as the saviour of Speranza, with a mandate to rule as something previously unknown, the Head of State. Javed Scolari, Ehsan Lukoil, Amal Yu and his father were cleared of any wrongdoing, and ascended to glory. But there was still the matter of the smuggled couches – the breach of Buonarotti security, discovered in the nick of time, a capital crime that needed a criminal: and that was my mistress, Lady Nef.'

'Go on,' said Liam, calm as a judge now.

'Lady Nef had pulled strings to get her husband away from Earth, to save him from being implicated in a futile adventure that was about to become a public scandal. She didn't know that he had already denounced her, in a secret statement he'd handed over to Javed Scolari, affirming that *she* was the receiver of the clandestine couriered material, and responsible for the murder of Jing, the courier. Perhaps he didn't want to do it: but his wife was the price the gangsters were asking, and he paid up.'

'Go on,' said Liam again.

'I think Yu was glad of the Baykonur Mission post. He didn't want to be around for the coup itself. He didn't know that the Royal Myots were so dangerous: no more than you did, Liam. When Speranza closed the Port and we were trapped he must have guessed what was going on, but he kept his head. He refused to say die, and he survived to reap the benefits.'

'Ah, the Swimmer,' murmured Francois. 'That loveable rogue.'

'He must have been scared when the rescue ship arrived, and he waited to see the face of the Speranza envoy. But he was safe. Nef had been condemned. Trusted officers who might have defended her were dead. Caspian Konoe, who tried to start an inquiry into the fate of a young servant called Bibi, had unaccountably killed himself. His wife, a star cadet of the People's Army, was accused of criminal insanity, and died in torment. Meanwhile, Yu had dealt with the single witness who might have been a danger to him: by telling one more lie, and sentencing me to death in life.'

Liam nodded, slowly. '*Are* you a danger to them, Bibi? Do you have evidence? Hard evidence, not the secret truth only you can decode?'

Bibi shrugged. 'Against General Yu? Very little, unless I can get hold of a document that so far eludes me. But I can place Amal Yu in the crypt under the Church of Self, where the couches were discovered, at the fatal time.'

'Good God. Under involuntary interrogation?'

'I'm not afraid of Starry Arrow tactics.'

'No use, no use. It sounds spectacular, but recovered memory can be thrown out of court. Nobody will care. They'll have an answer—'

'And I've been seen talking to Haku.'

'*Haku—!*'

'The Young Emperor, yes. Not so young now. A touchy old man in a shabby coat, who plays the stock exchange on a shoestring and sees the fat cats, who were once his ardent supporters, passing him by without a glance. He's back on Speranza at his own request, he hates Blue gravity, but he hasn't been very well treated. He's the one person who couldn't be paid off. A modest pension and immunity from prosecution were supposed to be enough. I'm very, very rich. I believe he would support my testimony.'

'*Haku!* What a stroke of genius ... Ah, but it can't happen, Bibi. There's something you've missed. There was nothing mystical about "Speranza System's" acceptance of the coup, you must know that. It doesn't matter if Nef was innocent. If Lukoil and Scolari and Yu are villains, that's just too bad. The time of naive infancy was over, Speranza had to change. Domremy's regime is legal, and I affirmed the validation myself. You cannot roll back history.'

'I don't want to,' said Bibi, smiling. 'I promised Lady Nef that I wouldn't waste my life on revenge, and I won't. I've nothing special against Domremy Li: show me a politician who doesn't use dirty tools. I don't intend to put my ancient "evidence" to the test, Liam ... I've let it be known that I'm looking for proof of the marriage between my friend Nightingale and Caspian Konoe-Hosokawa. If such a thing were found, in the possession of one of the villains, it would be highly incriminating. But really it's immaterial, a Traditionalist fantasy. Nightingale was a citizen. Any child of hers is legitimate, and – I have made inquiries – the Konoe-Olofact estate is very willing to recognise Caspian's daughter, who is like a daughter to me, on tissue identity. I said I'd been "seen talking" to Haku: we were just talking. I have no further plans. I'm not going to denounce anyone. If the criminals choose to denounce themselves, that's their affair.'

Liam stared at her. 'Then why are you here?' he breathed.

'To speak the truth, *once*,' said Bibi. 'And to redress a wrong. I want to offer the Mallorns a way back to normal space. Will you help me?'

The Speranza agent scrambled to his feet.

'I must get back. I'll help you if I can, but really I came to warn you. In a virtual world it's everyone for himself. *There are rats in this trap* ...'

He replaced the helmet. The spaceman hurried away, diminishing strangely. It was some kind of hopping biped animal, with little front feet tucked up, that vanished from their sight.

'Ah, *l'ésperance*,' said Francois softly. 'She's a harsh mistress. The poor devil, all these years, suffering such guilt for the greater good—'

'That was an incredible story,' ventured D''fydd. 'Was it true?'

'Every word.' Francois-René looked at the prince curiously. 'Except that I was more guilty than the Princess makes out. Did you understand?'

'Some of it, I *think*.'

'Let's walk on,' said Bibi. 'No point in waiting for daybreak.'

O

The dome appeared in section, at the end of the long vista of their path, like the limb of a planet seen through a telescope. There was no sign of the Ground Station, no ruins. As they approached they saw silver skin, rising until it vanished between branches. It was featureless, but it sensed them.

'*What do you know?*' it asked, in English.

'*There is a flower in our woods,*' said the Princess, '*that buds continually, but never blooms. Its name is hope.*'

The outline of a gate took shape. They passed into a sort of vestibule where two life-sized figures, a man and a woman, stood in columns of light. 'This is a decontamination chamber,' said the woman. 'Anyone who has interacted with Mallorn, step forward now.'

The crew of the *Spirit* stepped forward, together.

Whatever the decontamination process was, they felt nothing.

They climbed a curving ramp, hung with singing, ringing curtains of small clear stones, through which exquisite, magical distances could be glimpsed; surely illusion. The Mallorns were waiting on a mezzanine platform furnished with museum exhibits: couches, cushions, chairs; hand-crafted, patinaed with age. They seemed like beautiful puppets, because they all had the same body-mods, and the same eerily calm expression. There were around thirty of them, men and women with the fine-honed look of Blue Seniors, wearing open robes over image-patterned one-piece suits of a bygone age. One of them rose and came slowly forward, one foot dragging, leaning on a cane. It was Liam.

'Madam Princess, you are most welcome. We are forever in your debt for this brave attempt—' and then he added, as if he'd forgotten the boulder field, 'D"fydd, Ch'ro, don't you know me?'

Renewed embraces, the strange feeling that Blues call déjà vu.

Beakers of wine and water, platters of small dry cakes were offered.

The visitors sat facing the Mallorns, as if before a tribunal.

'My name is Celebrian,' announced a woman in a silver-green robe, her 'Space Age' one-piece patterned with sky and moving clouds. 'This is Aengus.' The Mallorn beside her bowed from the waist. 'We are the joint captains. I can't express how astonished and grateful we are to see you here.'

They realised she meant the apology literally. Not a flicker of emotion disturbed her ineffable, calm serenity.

'We suppress strong feelings,' explained Aengus. 'It isn't safe, not even inside the dome. Please try to do the same.'

'We have studied your news, Princess,' said Celebrian. 'General Yu has fallen: we see the implications for our nemesis, Domremy Li.'

'We may be ghosts,' said Aengus, 'trapped here outside time, but we can read a pattern in the data, oh yes. We know what you've started.'

Drez looked behind him: sure he'd heard someone muttering in his ear. There was nobody there, only a strong impression of menace—

'Liam tells us you do not intend violence,' continued Celebrian. 'We are glad of that. But he says you promise us a way to return. How can that be, without violence?'

'I'm here, with my crew,' said the Princess, 'because the Torus accepted our flight plan. The quarantine has been breached, with permission. If you believe in Speranza System, that should be good news.'

'But you are one of *those* Blues,' countered Aengus. 'Above the law.'

Celebrian said nothing; the Mallorns' expressions didn't change. A silent whispering went around the platform, like angry, fearful thoughts—

'Also, I've launched something I call the Mallorn Fund. So far I am the sole investor, but here with me is Yelaixiang Konoe-Hosokawa, who intends to join me. And my household officers: partners in the Bois Dormant claim.'

'Money attracts money,' murmured Aengus. 'Money is value. I see where this is heading. It might work, it might shift the balance.'

'Free worlds,' Col spoke up. 'That's our style. We're in.'

'It's what we fought for, all those campaigns with Yu,' said Drez. 'It's what the Young Emperor promised us, free worlds.'

'He didn't mean a word of it,' added the Sarge. 'But we did.'

The whispering grew spiteful and insistent. Shadows without origin flickered around the circle, something ran up and down, sobbing—

'So that's my offer,' said the Princess, steadily. 'Mallorn may be restored.

But there will be investors, it will no longer be your private fief.'

'Time would begin again,' muttered one of the Mallorns. 'Some of us in this circle have been dead for a long time. What would happen to them? And the rest of us, we'd start getting old—'

'We knew we must lose control,' Celebrian answered the Princess. 'We were always going to lose control. That is not the problem, and if you think it is, you insult us. But there are complications. We have indigenes.'

'*Aliens!*' cried Ch'ro, embarrassing himself.

'Indigenous sentients, here?' Even the Princess was taken by surprise. 'Are you *sure*?'

'Sure? There is no such word. You shall judge for yourselves.'

O

The visitors were not confined, but they were avoided. They slept and ate in the entrance cave of a tunnel system, a route that led from inside the dome to the indigenes' principal settlement. A message had to be sent to their guardian, so she could call a gathering of the tribes. D"fydd watched the Mallorn who looked after the little messengers.

'Is that a real bat, from the Blue? May I touch her?'

'She's labwork. Infertile, we'll never let alien animals breed on Mallorn, but yes, this is a bat. How did you know she was female?'

That won't last, thought D"fydd, recalling the sparrows on Balas. He said nothing; he didn't want to break the shell of Mallorn calm. They had an awful, nightmarish look in the back of their eyes.

'She has a furry face.'

The little creature had a pretty, curly snout, bright, intelligent dark eyes. Tossed from the keeper's hands it darted away: D"fydd followed its progress, into the dark. *The Old Men from Earth are monsters, the Princess survived the Baykonur Massacre, she bore a child.*

I will think about what it all means later. Later, not here.

'Are those body-mods of yours intended to be batlike, young man?'

'Not really ... Isn't it strange that the indigenes have their, er, capital so conveniently linked to your dome?'

The bat-keeper gave him that Mallorn look: shining calm over plumbless depths of panic. 'A misconception. We have no idea where the indigenes live. We have no idea what dimensions our planet has now. The passages lead to the indigenes' settlement, on the shore of a great lake ... usually. Sometimes they don't.'

An embassy was prepared: gifts of necklaces, supplies of food, pieces of handwoven cloth. 'If we don't bring presents, they won't come near us,' said Liam. 'Big presents, big business, it's a simple language.'

When it was time for them to set out, Celebrian reappeared. She and Liam led the way, along a wide, dry passage. The crew of the *Spirit* followed, two by two. Lights sprang up ahead, and faded into darkness behind.

'I don't believe in the Olofact money,' said Ye to Ch'ro. 'If it exists, the Mallorn Fund can have it, for free. I want the worlds to stay virgin. I climbed the ladder of corpses and I want to pull it up after me: but I know I can't do that. Do you think Celebrian can read our minds?'

'Probably, but the Princess is stopping her.'

D''fydd and the Princess held hands. 'I set out to redress a wrong,' she said. 'It was something to do before dying. But the work keeps growing, and growing: it's so big, it's frightening me.' They were walking through a beautiful building: soaring, endless, awe-inspiring, ancient. Columns, crusted with greenery, vanished into space. Narrow windows, tall as trees, glittered. Beneath their feet crypts opened, banks of worked stone covered in rich tapestries of moss. 'Far to the north of here,' said D''fydd, 'there is a huge sinkhole. It goes right through the planet, it's full of wind-blown monsters, whirling round and round, and that's true, I read it somewhere. Imagine jumping in. Let's go and jump in.'

Her hand was warm and strong. He felt so safe, so happy.

'Is that a memento of Sigurt's World, that limp?' Francois asked the Speranza agent.

'Brain damage.' Liam pushed back his hair, to show the dent in his skull. 'The Myots put me back together, but they weren't too careful. By the time I got home, the bots advised it was safer not to meddle.'

Their path emerged from the depths and ran along a stone ledge above a sheet of dark water. They stared at pictographs, at shrivelled bodies and one-eyed skulls laid on glittering, calcified bones, on shelves that sloped into blackness. 'They're not skulls,' whispered Ye. 'They're *helmets.*'

'The "bodies" are the remains of hard suits.' D''fydd felt a shiver of Mallorn panic. 'But the bones are ancient. What d'you think it means?'

The indigenes' guardian met them, holding one of the little messengers in her cupped hands. She kissed its furry head, and released it. 'That's to tell the dome that you made it here safely. I'm Habonde. Come to the village.'

O

Habonde's cabin was on a terraced slope above the lake, where the forest seemed to have been cleared, long ago. D"fydd walked out by himself, under the sunless sky, peering at the shaggy huts, the remains of cultivated fields, the stumps of a palisade. Everything was so beautiful, so intense. The indigenes were not at home, they were gathering on their meeting ground. On the edge of the settlement stood a construct of a different order: very large indeed, open to the sky, the massive tree-things growing through it. The curved fragments of the walls were slick; no vegetation had taken root there. *This is a starship*, he thought: *an ancient starship. Why is it still here? The weird things that* we *saw didn't last, and they were obviously psychic artefacts—*

The Shet say that hell is the absence of the void. How can a void be absent? Out of nowhere, a brutal exhaustion struck him. His thoughts yammered and rattled, finding no matrix to rise from, no place to rest. The inconceivable weight of his own existence fell on him. His bones buckled, his shoulders drew together, his shrunken skull thrust forward, language gone—

'D"FYDD!'

Ye and Ch'ro were shaking him. 'D"fydd, D"fydd, snap out of it! You're going into analeptic shock! You can *die* in a game, you know.'

They had to haul him to his feet and drag him back to safety.

O

D"fydd slept. Habonde said he would be all right. She avoided looking them in the eye, but she seemed friendly. She set a meal out on the balcony of her cabin: boiled wheat berries, vegetables and yellow strips that tasted like egg. The wine, which she mixed for them with water (the Princess took her water neat) had a tarry flavour. The food grounded them, it normalized Mallorn.

'You can eat crops grown outside the dome?' asked Ch'ro, tactless. 'Oh, I'm sorry. It's delicious, I just wondered—'

'The dome is larger than you've seen: all my supplies come from there. It covers hectares. We grow wheat, vegetables, fruit, we make wine: and we keep "yellows" – you'll have met the little wild variety in the forest. The egg-masses are very good. We had domesticated some larger animals, beautiful creatures, I cannot think what to compare them to, no Blue equivalent, but we had to cull them. Mallorn drove them crazy, after the change.'

Drez examined the second half of a strip of louse-egg omelette, poised on his chopsticks: sighed, and shovelled it in. It's all one, in the state of all states, virtual or material. Protein's protein, carbs are carbs.

'Mallorns are childless,' said Habonde. 'We recruit by adoption. When we realised that we'd been quarantined.' She nodded. 'Oh yes, we knew what had happened, it was unmistakable ... A group decided to become settlers. They said the Ground Station offered no protection: which is true, it's all ritual, and self-control. For a while they succeeded, in a strange way. Expeditions would suit-up and come out (I don't bother any more, I rely on magic), and find people they'd *known*, transformed into the descendants of the survivors of a crashed starship. There was a difficult patch, when they were a civilising colony, they had guns, and a fort, and we were the savages.'

'Noble savages, I hope,' suggested Francois.

'Naturally ... We became converts to a gentle religion, and worked in their fields: that was good for a while. And now, well, as you see.'

In the centre of the meeting ground there was a tall mound with a flattened top. Some indigenes were going to and fro, heaping the sides of the mound with turquoise-needled boughs. The masses crouched in ranks. The shamans – wearing stiff pale skirts of peeled twigs, tall headdresses – were painting each other in red and white clay. Were they numinal bipeds? They were covered in dark hair. They had long, powerful legs, small hands and arms kept tucked against their breasts at rest; awkward in use. Large eyes, in circles of bare, whitish skin. A creeping, hopping gait.

'What about the rest of you?' asked Col. 'Surely there must have been more of a population, before the disaster? Are there other "domes"?'

Habonde gave her a look. 'No such concept. This is it, soldier.'

'Ground Station was our major settlement,' explained Liam. 'We were a "planetary nation" of a few hundreds. Speranza sent a relief expedition, to try and form a consensus reality: it had to be top secret. By the time I returned they had gone completely native. As you can see, time has run differently for them. They have lost function, lost the most basic skills. I'd say their consciousness is borderline. But—'

'They *are* the natives now.' Celebrian sighed. 'We have no choice, they are the people of Mallorn. *They* must decide.'

'It's a point of view,' muttered Drez. But he was afraid of Celebrian, so he didn't start an argument.

The ceremonies lasted all the next day. Habonde, Liam and Celebrian went to join the indigenes. They could be seen up on the mound: making speeches full of gesture and mime. Sometimes the masses hopped to their feet and began to lope around, dancing to a mouth-music that sounded like clacking stones. Sometimes they sat like rocks. When it was dusk, fires and torches were lit.

'What's going on?' Col pleaded. 'Liam's better than the others, but even he's screwy as a fruitcake. Give me a version that *adds up*.'

'Mallorn is reaching a decision,' said the Princess, 'that's all we can know. The minds trapped in this virtual world are divided, and whatever comes of this gathering is their resolution.'

'They kind of half-want to *stay* in hell dimension?' Drez whistled.

Francois shrugged gloomily. 'They are addicts. Mallorn is a drug.'

*

Habonde came back to the cabin alone. 'They want you to come down,' she said. 'They've made up their minds.'

The crew of the *Spirit* climbed the mound, by earth steps cut into the side. Acrid smoke stung their eyes and blurred the figures of the shamans. The Mallorns were hardly distinguishable from the indigene elders, their hollowed faces, their bowed shoulders, their pale-circled dark eyes.

The chosen shaman spoke; Habonde translated:

We do not remember what we were.

We know that our world will end if we join the scattering.

We don't want to be alone. Let us join the scattering.

LXX

Pepper Lily had invited the young ladies into her boudoir. Wrapped in a peach lace negligee, she sat at her dressing table: fidgeting with mirror angles and wardrobe choices. The starship green, with the piratical ruffles? The antique 'Chinese' robe? This dinner party would be her first social event since the 'crisis' that had wrecked her winter season. Everything must be perfect.

General Yu was not dead. He was in the house, a profoundly disturbing presence: Pepper kept him in his study, where she knew he would want to be. 'While there's life, there's hope,' she insisted. To those vile people who murmured that even her title to the Yu mansion would be in doubt, if the poor old man were allowed to die (no valid will had been found) – she had nothing to say!

'Men can fall in love at any time in their lives—' Pepper touched a maquillage wand to her reflection, making a minute adjustment that was immediately copied to her exquisite, poreless complexion. '*We* grow out of that phase. *We* love the permanent, abstract things. Like making a home, and, er, truth, and true beauty—'

She paused to gaze in reverence at her own etiolated form, the tiny 'bee-stung' breasts that peeped through lacy froth, the proud little head with its floating crown of red-gold curls. Pepper liked to tell people she had decided, *oh, when I was thirty-five or so*, that she was happy in her own skin, and she would never change her body-style again. Perhaps she really saw, in the virtual glass, the young woman she had been: the face and figure that had raised a ravenous child of the lower levels to greatness—

'We'll have the ceremony in the spring, it'll be just what you always wanted, no expense spared. But an affirmation, permanently filed: it makes all the difference, believe me. Now come here, I have something for you. Poor Yu used to buy me the *loveliest* things, that's how I knew I could trust him—'

'I expect Nef arranged that. She handled all his affairs.'

Pepper controlled herself, and ignored her daughter. She reached for one of the feather-light globes – called *bijouteries* – that danced around her, broke it with a deft touch and scooped out a handful of bright blue stones.

'Genuine *freighted* sapphires, for your eyes, Grove: and the setting is real, twenty-two carat, Chinese gold. The great man is too timid, so he commissioned me. Isn't that touching!'

'Mama,' snapped Vale, a young lioness at bay, in the cushiony clouds of her mother's bed. 'This is ridiculous. Just stop it, *stop it.*'

'It's not ridiculous. Why shouldn't your brother fall in love? He's a human being, isn't he? Grove's Sigurtian has gone off with the Princess, a boy that age and a bedizened two-hundred-year-old harridan, it's disgusting. He's left her in a terrible position. You're very lucky somebody is longing to take his place, aren't you, dear?'

Grove Lukoil stood by the dressing table, like a stunned animal.

Pepper's parties were adventurous and varied. Her dinner invitations were normally reserved for 'our own kind', by which she meant the select circle of Blue Traditionalists who had mansions on the Dostoe; or else old-money establishments on the Old Dip. Since it was 'our kind' who were spreading the vile rumours, she'd been obliged to cast her nets wide, for this evening's debut. A Shetian financier, and his life-partner – a Blue newswoman who had disgraced herself (in Pepper's opinion) by converting to the Void. The former An Ambassador: an aged monster who was quite senile and had to be watched around the mortal servants. A minor Balas aristocrat, with two shall-we-say 'artistes', God knows where he'd picked them up; unmistakable in their vocation. That ingratiating young man with the vulgar body-mods, the son of a former 'Prospector', and a *desperate* social climber—

It didn't matter, since Pepper could boast not one but two Permanent Secretaries. *Two* Permanent Secretaries, and one of them Ehsan Lukoil! Let any hostess on Dostoe beat that. The society pages were *not* getting a feed from this room, certainly not: but Pepper knew how to do things, there would be plenty of the right sort of notices. Soup was served – hot liquid in shallow bowls, Pepper's latest innovation. The social-climbing gangster stared at Grove Lukoil, and made up his mind to marry her, take her away from bitches like Pepper, guard that sorrowful loveliness with his life . . .

The wealthy Shetian asked Ehsan what he thought of the taboo-breaking 'Mallorn Fund'.

'What does Domremy think about thap, aah?' That rare creature, a speculator devoid of superstition, he was simply curious.

'He thinks the same as you, Haag'oon. The Princess is putting out a piece of fantasy ass, funx knows why, it means bugger all. If he likes the way she shakes it, Dom will grab a piece.'

'I might take a punt myself,' remarked Amal, out of bravado (his financial affairs, as everyone knew, were somewhat embarrassed).

'A *punt*? What is thap?'

'A harmless venture that might be successful, an uncalculated risk.'

Haag'oon opened his throat in a wide, blueish smile.

'Well, *of course* it's true, dear Feodosia,' whispered Pepper. The journalist was a reliable society gossip. 'And as soon as he knew of our interest, you can believe me, Ehsan sent the Sigurtian Pretender packing! So awful, what people are saying about that boy and the Princess. I suppose she thinks her money excuses any kind of behaviour.'

'What a pity the General didn't live to see this change of heart,' murmured Feodosia. 'How Amal must miss his father now—'

'My husband is *alive*.' Pepper's pretty lower lip trembled. 'As we sit here, my dearest Yu is next door, *hovering* between life and death—'

'I'm sorry,' said the journalist, tenderly. 'So sorry, Pepper.'

Pepper heard the yammering of jackals: and almost wished she'd invited *nobody* outside the family to this significant feast. *It doesn't matter,* she thought. *You won't bring me down. I have a trick or two left.*

Vale made distracted conversation with the Zeldi and his cheerful courtesans. The world seemed to have gone mad, since her father's stroke. Why was Pepper behaving so wildly? How could Amal possibly want to marry Grove? Why would Lukoil agree? It was several courses into the interminable meal before she realised that her friend, blue-eyed, exquisite Grove, was wearing the sapphires.

Ehsan Lukoil ate and drank with gusto, he pestered the human servants, he made the coarse jokes, as always. The marriage was entirely Pepper's idea, but Ehsan had allowed her to convince him. Anything to keep the silly tart harmlessly occupied, at this juncture: and Amal hadn't taken much persuading, despite his treasured 'confirmed bachelor' stance . . . Only one moment gave Ehsan pause. The dinner party had broken up early, a little too early for success. Grove was to spend the night with her friend; the Permanent Secretaries stood in the entrance hall together.

'Tell me one thing,' muttered Amal. 'Is she virgin?'

'Of course.' Ehsan raised his brows. 'What d'you take me for?'

A flicker of revulsion crossed his soul. *My pretty Grove! But you won't have her, you piece of shit. Nor shall any man.*

Vale sent her maid to bed, took off her dress and jewels and paced in a dressing gown, thinking furiously. Grove lay on a sofa, Amal's gift still clasped around her throat: eyes closed, like a worn-out child.

'This can't happen. I won't let this happen.'

The gossip was that Amal Yu was one of those ageing bastards who hung around the playsphere in disguise, in the violent, secret rooms that nobody with any sense explored. He liked real girls: bots made him feel inferior, no doubt. They said he'd been in trouble – hushed up – over his tastes, before he came to Speranza; before Vale was born. She was afraid it was all true, and supposedly it didn't matter, as long as it was only virtual. But Amal was *old*. Old, ugly and heartless—

'It'll be fine, Vale,' said Grove, without opening her eyes. 'It's a marriage of convenience. He won't touch me, and we'll be sisters.'

'*Won't* he, though? He's a dirty old man, that's what he is. I'm going to get you out of this, Grove.'

'How?'

That street-punk at the dinner table? He was invited everywhere ... No good, he was bound to be a creature of Ehsan's. One of their Kongzi male friends? No use, they would not begin to understand—

'The Sigurtians!'

'It was the Sigurtians who got me into this. Anyway, they're gone. They've gone off with the powerful and mighty Princess—'

Ch'ro and D''fydd didn't desert us, thought Vale. We *dropped* them. *Don't you even remember?* She was used to Pepper's constant rewriting of history, but this wasn't like Grove. Grove the stoic, Grove the realist had suddenly become Grove the pliant flower, who became hysterical if you asked her why ...

'No, no, they're back. I met Drea, the girl who works for them, at the Comsat yesterday: she says they're back, looking shattered—'

Grove opened her eyes. 'Vale. I was warned, and I didn't pay attention. Now I'm getting married to your brother, because I have to.

It's a little sudden, but it can't be helped. *Promise* you won't share my boring troubles with a servant girl you meet in a virtual supermarket.'

'Of course not: Mama would know at once. I'll go to their house, by myself. I'll talk to Ch'ro and D''fydd in person.'

'Oh yeah, and how will you manage that?'

Vale had never left the Yu mansion unattended in her life. *The world's gone mad ...* 'I'll think of something. I swear I will.'

LXXI

Ch'ro had tried to make a direct cortical record of the Mallorn trip: the new, gadget-free alternative to eye soc'. He wasn't surprised to find the results weren't worth keeping. His iface hub suggested he try again in twenty-four hours, but he didn't think he'd bother. Inchoate fragments, haunting and banal, bound together by the false causality of a remembered dream ...

He dressed with care in a wide-sleeved robe, tailored leggings, half-boots and a shirt that left his neckfrills on display. Quite the Sigurtian dandy, except that the open-collared shirt was supposed to prove that you *didn't* have a frilled neck. He burnished his ears and head with a soft brush until his pelt shone. The face in the mirror stared at him, blood-drained, hollow-eyed, an incipient suicide. It was early; D"fydd would still be sleeping like the dead.

Soon he was waiting in the Princess's drawing room, with no conscious memory of the journey, of having crossed her park; of being shown into the beautiful house. He walked around, recalling his feelings the day they'd met the former pangolin, and the Princess had asked them to cultivate an artist. *My life is over, my happiness is over. She sends out these lures—*

'Ch'ro? You wanted to see me?'

'It's about D"fydd.'

'Is he all right?'

Now that she was standing before him, the Princess seemed less daunting. She was dressed, immaculately, in spite of the early hour, but there was something distracted in her manner, which he'd never seen before.

He drew himself up, wishing he was taller.

'He's fine. I have something formal to say. To you alone.'

She made the *off the record* gesture. 'Agreed. Well, go on—?'

'I won't spread my claws in your way, that's all. I admit I had my doubts, er, for a long time, but I see how it is between you. I s-see that the age difference doesn't matter. I saw how close you were on Mallorn, I know that you, you c-care deeply for each other—'

The Princess groped for an armchair and sat down, pressing a hand to her brow. He waited, nonplussed, feeling he'd possibly made a complete fool of himself, yet still passionately sure he'd done what had to be done—

'Ch'ro—' She made a gesture of *helpless consternation*. Her eyes glowed, was she daring to *laugh* at him? No, please, not that.

'My Lord Ch'ro, you are a noble soul, I am in your debt, and, and I know how much this means. But I am not your rival! There is a very strong, ah, reason why I could never be your rival ... I'm sorry, but could you please leave? I'm expecting visitors, whom you should not meet.'

Her Bloodmen were outside the door, with their bland, masked faces, their intimidating livery. They took him by the shoulders, and he welcomed the indignity. This was the way it should end. Ch'ro the reject, humiliated, dragged to the servants' back door and thrown out on his ears. They hustled him down to the basement, to a kitchen, and sat him at a table.

'No offence, Scrappy,' said Drez. 'You don't want your face soc'ed around here by the bastards who just passed our gate. Trust us.'

Col set out vodka, open beakers and a kettle that breathed the fumes of blood tea. 'Strengthening mixture, can't beat it. We get the tea from the Diaspora Parliament Comsat, it's the real thing. D'you take sugar?'

Speranza-isation, thought Ch'ro. *Crass barbarity.*

'Listen.' Col leaned her elbows confidentially on the tabletop. 'There's nothing wrong with you: he's pointing the opposite way, that's all. It's natural numinal biped behaviour, fancying your own kind. I've been like it all my life, the military's full of us. It's nonsense, what they say about the People's Army. I've never had any trouble. Never.'

Ch'ro sipped the steaming, potent cocktail she pushed in front of him, purely to stop himself from passing out: and looked for the exit. *That's more than I needed to know, Bloodman. May I go now—?*

'It's just a phase you're going through.' Drez took a long swig, smacked his lips and spoke from wise experience. 'True love, I mean ... You don't want to believe me, but it's a temporary hormone problem. I stick to plain old-fashioned sex, me. It feels good and it does you good.

The Sarge is celibate, which is his choice, but Col and I, we've cuddled up occasionally, and taken comfort, despite our different sexual orientations.'

'He's right, kid.'

'I know a very decent little house, in the streets: boys, girls, bats, rats, cats, hippos, golden monkeys, all sorts. I could take you there today—'

Ch'ro leapt up and rushed madly around the room, the big Blues crying out and trying to catch him. He blundered into a door that opened before him, but the Princess's garden was no escape, those austere unreal trees, casting their unreal shadows. There was no comfort, no welcome, no place to hide. All he wanted was to be home, to be home ...

His flight took him to the Old Centre, that antique enclave of the *streets* right beside the majesty of Parliament. He wandered, lacerated and fuming, noise levels he'd forgotten to filter hammering at his brain. Intolerable, intolerable, insolent brutes, how dare they ... Clasping, *sex*: what is that? Scratching an itch. A negligible part of life. What Ch'ro had lost was nothing so petty as sex. He had lost *D"fydd*, his dear companion. To wake up knowing he was near. To have breakfast and discuss the day with him. To protect each other, to see him smile, to set off on our travels together. To play endless rounds of *c"tl'z*, on a boring winter retreat. To come home in the evening, and ... no more. No more Ch'ro and D"fydd. It's over.

Something brought him up against the Orion ob.bay, and there he came to rest. The street behind was busy with foot traffic, little sedans and smart-paced AI rides, but the bay was quiet. He stared at the jewelled vision, which seemed to hang so close. The claws of shame relaxed, and the pain of loss became simple, irrefutable: permanent. Ideas that had been waiting in abeyance rose into his mind. *The Oligarchs are defeated: I could go home. I am not a throwback, I am a forerunner, a true native, made by Fallen Planet for itself ...* A theory probably as absurd, as temporary as the last fashion in 'science', but it told of a change of heart—

I have a future, all of my own. What shall I do with it?

I want to be a navigator. He wondered if it was possible. He had no idea. Were there Sigurtian navigators? Could he handle the training? Someone sat down beside him: he was not surprised when he turned and found Ye there. 'Mind if I join you?' She rubbed her hollow eyes. 'Augh, what a monster hangover. Are you all right? You look the way I feel.'

'Like dirty little gamers after an evil binge.'

'Which is something like the truth! But we won, I think.'

Ch'ro gestured assent. 'What d'you think will happen now?'

'I have no idea,' said Ye. 'The government of Speranza will fall. The simultaneity will give itself a shake, and Mallorn will appear on the Buonarotti schedules tomorrow, as if it had never been away. I'm a bit terrified, under the hangover. Thank funx the Princess is in control—'

Not when I saw her this morning, thought Ch'ro. But the powerful and mighty Princess was entitled to his discretion, so he said nothing. They watched the great constellation, in companionable silence.

'I'm *sorry*, Ch'ro,' said Ye, at last.

'I know. It's all right.'

He sighed, lost in contemplation, lost in dreams.

LXXII

Zubindah Scolari had a remarkably mature presence – hard to believe this massive, stern-jowled woman was only a few standard years older than her vivid notional 'sister', Vale. But Scolari's daughter was nothing so frivolous as a young lady. She was the natural clone of her father's dead wife, grown from a tissue deposit Zubindah the elder had banked long ago. Indeed, there'd once been a rumour that *the copy was too close* – that the baby's brain had been forced into the neuronal pathways forged in the old woman: a cruel and thoroughly illegal procedure. Nobody would say that now. Zubindah was a moral paragon, the founder of the Assistance, Benefactor of the Streets.

Scolari made leaden small talk. Zubindah occupied a First Empire armchair and stared with distaste at the Princess's décor: the picture of a forbidding, old-style Traditionalist matriarch. The Princess of Bois Dormant thought of Councillor Scolari's Old Wife in the Country, pitied and secretly championed by servant girls, in Baykonur long ago—

The past is a kaleidoscope, different every time you look.

It was a morning for interrupted business. She hoped Ch'ro would forgive her, for sending him away so abruptly ... It seemed the Scolaris had intended to make this call of ceremony days ago, and had been frustrated by the Princess's sudden absence. She was reasonably sure that they hadn't managed to trace her movements, but they were full of dark suspicions—

'You've been talking to Haku, Princess,' said Javed, 'or so I understand. He's a strange old fellow: I wonder what you found to say?'

The Princess tried to recall. 'Have I really? Councillor, you'll have to excuse me. I'm a savage, a mere adventurer: I have no social graces, and I don't use an eye soc'. I recall *meeting* the famous "Haku", on the floor one day, but what was said, I have no idea.'

Smiling, she offered the Councillor an emerald and ivory snifter case, and directed her servant to refresh Zubindah's beaker with Sigurtian tea.

Javed took a vial, broke the cap and inhaled reflectively. 'Twin Planets: very good ... I wondered if he'd inspired a trip down to the Blue?'

'Nothing like that. I'm surprised he's not better known, and let me see, I may have told him so. We can surely admire the former "Young Emperor" as a figure of romance, now that the whole thing is history.'

Scolari digested this opinion. He turned on the Aleutian, the erstwhile pageboy, who was now claiming to be the same immortal Scolari had once known in Baykonur. Eyes like black acid, disturbingly familiar.

'I should have recognised you,' he announced. 'I met Francois le Champi often, when he was Nef's secretary. Her *intimate* secretary.'

'No offence taken,' said the Aleutian, showing a hint of teeth.

'I *would* have recognised you, but you're not that person, are you? You may be the same genetic mix in a young body, but the Aleutian who used to call himself "Francois" was a renegade. He died alone, *isolate*, as they say, with no means to pass his memories on. Isn't that the way it works?'

'That's the way it works.'

<You haven't a shred of evidence, in other words. D'you think I don't know that the only true immortals, in Aleutian law, are the ones who stay at Home? Your so-called former self was the degraded lover of a condemned criminal, and you're trying to make something of it, I don't know how. You could end up in trouble yourself, if you don't watch out.>

<Evidence of what?> enquired Francois, politely responding in Silence to the Councillor's shifty glare. <I'm afraid I don't follow.>

Zubindah rose and arranged the stately folds of her shawl, frowning: perhaps at her father's incontinence. She was letting nothing slip.

'Father, I'm sure the Princess has many calls on her time.'

A formal call, in person, should last no longer than fifteen minutes.

Francois jumped up and chased the visitors into the hall. <Scolari. You Blues believe that death is permanent, don't you?>

Sergeant Aswad suppressed a groan, and opened the front doors.

<You'd better hope it's true. For if it is not, and you and I meet again, you are going to pay for what you did to my Lady, and to Bibi—>

435

<What was that?> asked the Princess.

<My own business.> 'Well, now, this will be interesting. I assume he'll make immediate plans to have us murdered.'

'You're mistaken,' said the Princess. 'Scolari's uneasy and suspicious, that's all. Blues don't know what they're saying when they speak in Silence.'

'Depends on the Blue ... Ehsan, meanwhile, won't come near us. He's the brains of the outfit, by a very long stretch.' Francois took sniff, inhaled once and abandoned the vial. 'That was a strange way to reveal your true relationship to the Myot prince, Bibi.'

The Princess stood, and crossed the room. She cleared a window space with a gesture, and looked out into her parkland. 'By telling Liam my story and letting D''fydd listen? I know. I couldn't help it ... I *will* tell him. I just wanted him to know before I told him, do you see? So it wouldn't be such a shock.'

'Hm. Did you mean him harm, when you sought him out on Balas?'

'*No ... !* All right, yes. He was a pampered, rich young man, and my little girl was dead. I hated him for that, I wanted to ... Well: then I met him, and he was *D''fydd*, and it seems so long ago. I was a different person.' She governed herself, and turned to face him. 'How much do you remember?'

'Everything.'

'You mean until you were killed? Until the end of the siege?'

'No, I mean everything. I remember what I did to you, for which I have no excuse except ... I have no excuse. I remember being with you in Fenmu. The creature I was then had no ability, very little ability to reflect on its experiences, but it stored them. Those experiences are with me now, on the other side of the moment of recognition, and I do ... have that power.'

He looked at his own clawed hands, loose in his lap.

'Oh God,' whispered Bibi. 'This is unbearable.'

'I remember Nef, in her perfected life, our guardian, our saviour. I remember little Di, how she grew, how her soul shone. I remember lying with you on that hard bed, in the filthy reddish dark of that miserable cell. You and I falling asleep, and in my embrace, our ... our child.'

She came to sit beside him, fingertips pressed to her mouth, tears spilling. Francois returned her gaze, his nasal contracted in grief, in complex emotion that only Silence could hold: his own eyes shining with the Aleutian tears that brim and never fall. Finally, he drew her close. <Bibi, my dear, my dear.> He kissed her brow, and held her against his breast, the soft darkness in the centre of his face pressed to her dark hair.

LXXIII

Never seeing yourself as a prisoner is a good strategy – until you need to escape, and there doesn't seem to be much time. Then all you can do is be bold, be bold. Vale walked into her father's study and there he was, in his support chair, heavy-lidded, half-open yellow eyes seeming to look straight at her. It was grim. He was breathing because the chair inflated and deflated his lungs. Nanotech fibres, reaching in through his back, through the material of his handsome dressing gown, were pumping the old heart muscle. Other chair-functions supplied nutrients, sluiced the digestive tract, drew off toxins. And so it would continue, until massive tissue collapse intervened.

His valet was sitting with him. As Vale entered the man leaned forward, and gently wiped a dribble of excess saliva from the General's chin.

'I'll take over for a while, Rocket.'

'This can't go on, Miss. It's against nature.'

The Yu household had always been divided: inevitably. Drama was Pepper's lifeblood. The General's camp, ironically, now wanted him dead, but Pepper decreed otherwise and everyone was helpless.

Rocket left the room, shaking his head.

Vale remembered running in here, sobbing, one day when she was a little child: 'Papa, papa, is it true I'm not your real little girl? That you had me *made up*, like a story—?'

The General had swept her up onto his lap. He'd told her that she was his jewel, his unique treasure. That there was hardly any such thing as a 'natural' high-grade child; and he would lay odds that the kids who teased her most were the ones with most illegal labwork in them. She hadn't understood a word, but she could still hear his rumbling voice, still feel the strength of his arms, surrounding her with love. '*I had three "natural" children. It doesn't mean a thing ... You're the pick of the bunch, my little Vale.'*

He had always defended her.

Dad, she thought, applying another sterile wipe to the flaccid lips, *I need you to give me the key to my chaperones. You know, the lovely secret key you were going to give to my husband, on my wedding day?*

She slid her hand inside his dressing gown, fumbled the catch of a fine gold chain and worked the charm free, into the palm of her hand. Nobody had really told her what had *happened* in here, the night before her father had his stroke: but if there was extra police surveillance watching her now, she wasn't afraid of it. She wasn't afraid of the mansion's internal cameras, either. Neither Pepper, nor the MacBrides, were likely to open a window on the dead man's tomb: and nobody else had access.

She took the key to her bathroom and moved swiftly, laying out her cosmetic laserblade, the wipes. Pepper was behaving like a lunatic, but you could bet she still had a page to tell her if Daughter was stealing time behind the only gate she could lock. *Vale, what are you doing in there?* But the feed from this room was pixelated to protect the young lady's modesty, so she was safe enough. The key was an heirloom from the Gender Wars, more than three hundred years old. How many treasured young ladies had it held prisoner? Yet it was so dainty, so easily destroyed ...

Vale and Grove had never spent any time with the 'young ladies' of Speranza, daughters of rabid Traditionalists who'd moved out here after the revolution. Pampered grubs who hardly left their rooms, who were forbidden the games *envies*; who lived in dread of the day they'd be sent back to Earth, to marry into the tiny Orthodox community. Miss Scolari and Miss Lukoil were not that kind. They would not be shipped home. They were purely status symbols, not the icons of an obsolete cult. *They* would make show-off marriages to princes of the Diaspora, and meantime they studied at Kongzi, they went to parties and shows, they had male friends—

The little blade shook in her hand. She was about to break with her family for ever, to betray tradition, to lay bare things that should never be revealed to outsiders. There would be no possibility of forgiveness—

Ch'ro had arrived home in trepidation, but D''fydd hadn't asked him where he'd been, and he'd realised, guiltily, that he could trust the Princess.

She would never mention his mad escapade. They both felt dreadful. She'd warned them there'd be after-effects: it had been a common problem, in the old days. They'd declared a winter retreat, and taken roost in the small drawing room, the only room in the house where they'd installed Sigurtian furnishings. Everything that must be said, everything that must change, could wait. The shutters were closed, the stove was warm, a ten-day storm raged outdoors, such as they'd loved in childhood winters.

They were bickering over a game of *c"tl'z* when Drea announced 'a young gentleman'. They'd diverted all messages, they were accepting no callers.

'Who is it, Drea?'

'He didn't give a name, but Agent Mallorn has let him in.'

'Oh well then,' said the prince. 'We'd better see what it's about.'

The caller proved to be a slightly built Blue in student dress, with a feminine streak of pelt above his lip: he seemed very agitated. As soon as they were alone he pulled off his Kongzi cap, chestnut hair tumbled and the mask vanished. It was Vale Scolari.

'Please,' she cried. 'Excuse me for intruding.' There were speckles of blood in her hair, blood on her hands. She didn't seem to know what she looked like. She didn't seem to care. She stared, wild-eyed, despairing, like someone who has just committed a terrible crime.

'Marry me, Ch'ro! You have to marry me! We've been partnered in public, it's all I can think of. Marry me, take me back to Sigurt's. We can take Grove on our wedding journey, and then you can divorce me. It's *Grove*. They're killing her, destroying her. She's not Grove any more, she's just some witless *young lady*. I have to get her away—'

'There's blood in your hair, Vale,' said D"fydd, slowly. 'What's happened? Has there been an accident? I'll get Drea back—'

'No, *no*! Not Drea. I promised Grove. Nobody must know: I can't be here. The blood's nothing. I cut out my chaperones, same as Col and Drez did for Ye. I smashed the key, but I had to take the subderms out as well, or Pepper could have found me. It doesn't hurt, it doesn't matter, I'm not real. I'm just a piece of labwork—' She staggered, fell to her knees with her fists to her mouth repeating, in a frantic whine, muffled by knuckles, *Just a piece of labwork, just a piece of labwork, just a piece of labwork—*

Ch'ro lunged forward and slapped her across the face.

'*Ch'ro!*' exclaimed D"fydd, horrified.

Vale put her hand to the stinging mark, and looked at them in bewilderment. 'I'm sorry. I'm so sorry. I had to come to you.'

They gave her a beaker of hot blood tea to sip, and she told her story. Lukoil's anger because his daughter had failed to snare the Sigurtian prince. The sudden wedding plans. The dead man in the study, the monster that Amal was, Grove's terrible passivity. The melodramatic step Vale had been forced to take, to get out of the house without the prisoner's tag she'd been wearing, all this time, and her friends had never suspected—

'Everything's gone crazy since my father had his stroke. Nobody tells me anything and I don't care. I don't want to know: except for Grove. The state she's in now, she'll affirm anything they put in front of her, and Pepper's *obsessed* with getting this marriage filed—'

'Excuse us,' said Ch'ro.

They took a turn around the room, into privacy. 'This is what the Princess warned us about,' muttered D''fydd. 'We compromised them.'

'With the added complication that Vale's father is the wicked General Yu, Amal Yu is another villain, and she doesn't know a thing about it.'

'The characters are Blue, the situation is pure Myot. Vale is like the two of us, when we were kids: fighting in the dark with our noses cut off, while our enemies played their games. She knows nothing and we can't tell her, but we have to help ... A forced marriage: so this is either dynastic, or it's about money. Most likely money, am I right?'

'Let's see what we can find out.'

They returned to their visitor.

'Does Grove have any money?' asked D''fydd, bluntly.

Vale looked at the blood under her fingernails, wondering how it had got there. She heaved a shuddering sigh. 'Yes and no. She has a marriage settlement, a generous one, which Ehsan can't touch. But my brother doesn't need money! He's a Permanent Secretary, he runs up debts, but his credit is always good—!'

That may not last, thought Ch'ro.

'Does the dowry go straight to Amal, when the contract is signed?'

'It goes to the head of the family, my father, which means Pepper right now. She has power of attorney, as long as the General is living.' Vale started, suddenly electrified. 'Oh, God, *Pepper*. She's the one who needs money. I'm such an idiot. At least, she thinks she does, because there's no will. She's a fool, the law will protect her. But why would Lukoil agree? He *hates* mama.'

'Myoter and Myoter.' D''fydd tugged his ears, and found this did not enlighten him. 'I think we'll have to call the Princess—'

The effect on Vale was dramatic. She recoiled, teeth bared in terror, the blood fled from her face. 'You can't do that! The Princess of Bois Dormant is my father's worst enemy!'

'She's our friend. Don't be afraid, she'll help you.'

'No, no! *Don't don't don't—!*'

'Then we'll come back to Dostoe with you,' said Ch'ro, to ward off another panic attack. 'Right now. We'll tell Pepper that you and I are getting married, that should provide a diversion.'

'Ch'ro, you can't *marry* me. I was raving!'

Vale looked down at herself. She had ordered her wardrobe to make her a suit of boy's clothes; she had left the house dressed like this. She felt light-headed. The masquerade was a final touch of madness: this could not be serious. They must be on their way to a fancy-dress ball.

Ch'ro offered his arm, in the courtly Blue style. 'I'm not much of a catch, Miss Scolari, but I don't see why we shouldn't marry, if it's the simple solution. What are friends for?'

LXXIV

There was a garden on the lower level of the Yu mansion. It was nothing like so opulent as the grounds above, in fact it was quite small; made more extensive by false vistas. On special occasions all the mortal servants enjoyed this amenity. Mainly it was reserved for the steward and his wife. MacBride was walking there, when a neat mechanoid showed the Princess of Bois Dormant to the garden gate. Mrs MacBride was 'not at home'. The Princess had glimpsed a woman's profile – a sharp eye, shrewish with anxiety – peeping from an inner doorway: and that was all she saw of Ogul Merdov.

Down below, as up above, winter was coming to an end. Buds were swelling; spears of green pierced the dark earth. The blue sky was vaguely oppressive, tainted by the closeness of the actual ceiling (all the Dostoe basements were rather low); but the air was fresh and moist, and smelled of growing things. She saw MacBride at the end of a gravelled path, and walked slowly towards him.

'Thank you for this,' he said. 'You're very good.'

'Thank you for not giving me away, Mahmood.'

He bowed his head. He could not yet bring himself to speak her name. The young, beautiful Princess and the middle-aged upper servant walked together, to the turn of the path and around a tiny loop, onto the same path again, but with a different vista.

'Bois Dormant, isn't that from a fairy tale? The one about a princess who can't touch a distaff or a needle, because a wicked fairy has doomed her to sleep for a hundred years if she pricks her finger? I always thought that was a strange kind of curse. Does it have a deeper meaning—?'

'It means that the Princess Aurora cannot become a woman.'

'Until she's woken by a kiss.'

Far away and long ago, in a modest love hotel in Baykonur, under a fragile blue sky, a young girl called Bibi had offered herself to her lover. But it was not to be, and they had parted in tears. Now he had a wife, and she, she had become someone utterly beyond his reach—

'I put my name to a false accusation, long ago. I didn't know that it would harm *you*. I did it out of craven fear. I have regretted it for ever: as the most despicable act of my life.'

'Mahmood,' said the Princess, gently, 'you fell into the hands of the Starry Arrow. I know what that means, and I've forgiven you: long ago.'

She understood, with the clairvoyance of old love, lost love, that he'd made his affirmation in thrall to Ogul Merdov. *Ogul* . . . What a bitter sting that would have added to her despair, in Fenmu! It didn't matter any more, but still, but still. *Oh, Mahmood. She made a servant of you. The wild geese, at Kushan, the vows we made. What happened to your pride?*

They looked at each other. 'I see you have,' said MacBride, softly.

'Are you happy, Mahmood?'

'We rub along.'

They stopped to admire a group of the delicate flowers called 'snowdrops', breaking through a crust of snow in the roots of a leafless tree.

'I think "Bois Dormant" was for Honesty's sake,' said the Princess. 'When we were on Speranza, on our way out to Sigurt's, we had such a good time. We had first-class tickets for the Tchaikovsky ballet, *The Sleeping Beauty*, in the Nebula Theatre. Honesty's favourite character was Carabosse, the wicked fairy, who gets her revenge on everyone who has injured her—'

'I must look out for it . . . I couldn't come to you, or send a message of any significance—'

'So I came to you. You have something new to tell me?'

'It's not about the police matter, not exactly. It's about a young lady, Grove Lukoil. I think her life is in danger.'

'Ehsan Lukoil's daughter?'

'Yes. Her name had been linked with that of the Sigurtian prince.' Mahmood reddened and looked away. Prince D"fydd was said to be the Princess's lover; it wasn't his business. 'She had a disappointment. At least, her father was disappointed. I don't think there was anything but friendship on Miss Grove's side. Now the plan is that she should marry Amal Yu. It's very sudden, and I'm suspicious. She's staying in this house, and she is not herself . . . I can't put it more clearly.'

'Try.'

444

'I'm afraid she's being influenced, drugged, I'm not sure what means they're using, into signing over her fortune. Which is hers alone: which is the price the high grades pay for making artificial children. The law doesn't trust them to treat their vanity-creations decently. I don't believe Amal wants a wife, not even in name. I believe he and Pepper may be planning to do away with the girl, and split her marriage settlement between them.'

'But why would Lukoil have agreed to this?'

'I don't know.'

'Have you considered talking to the police?'

The whole Yu household had been under *probable cause* observation since the night of the break-in. The Princess was being kept informed, and knew nothing of any suspicious treatment of a young lady. But a 'probable cause' order, especially when applied to persons of the Yus' rank, was selective: it only pertained to matters directly related to the investigation.

'That's something I could not do,' said Mahmood, with dignity. 'I cling to scraps of my independence—' he glanced at the sleeve of his Grade Four Reformer uniform '—but I've worked for this Family for more than twenty years. And I have a wife, whose whole life has been with the Yus.'

The Princess found his declaration surprisingly painful. She came near to leaping the gulf, to insisting that he *must* still be Mahmood, he could not be this diminished, mediocre *old retainer*. A tap on her shoulder saved her—

'Excuse me, I have to take a call.'

The police officer in charge of the 'Dostoe' case stood in her perception: the robocop helmet that served as the head of the facet's avatar somehow expressing grim satisfaction. 'Sorry to interrupt, Princess: but I thought you'd like to know. We've had a breakthrough.'

'Oh yes?'

'Yeah, just now. We have a bit-match on the cheat we found in Blazer's intellectual possession. Can't tell you the name of the mortal coder yet, but I *can* tell you, beyond reasonable doubt, who handled that dirty piece of string immediately before our hepcat. You'll find it interesting news.'

'You have a name?'

'We do. Make sure this goes no further, not yet. It's Javed Scolari.'

MacBride had taken a step away from the Princess, although there was no need. He saw nothing, heard nothing: he waited, deferentially. The cop winked out of existence. The Princess of Bois Dormant stared at the place where he had seemed to stand. She felt that she saw there, imprinted on the winter garden, the closing phase of an intricate equation. An adjustment that she had initiated but had never controlled: the strings of os and 1s, inevitably, mercilessly, falling into place.

LXXV

The General in his support chair was a silent witness to the preparations for his son's marriage. The bride, of course, would not appear until the climactic moment. The bridegroom, somewhat eccentrically, had not been invited. Amal's presence wasn't strictly necessary, until that 'no expense spared' wedding party in the spring. Nothing was going to happen, this winter afternoon, except a formal exchange of contracts between two families.

Lukoil watched old Yu while Pepper scampered about, arranging her accessories. The tablet on which the affirmations would be recorded. The document, three copies on nature-identical vellum – which Traditionalist custom insisted must be signed, witnessed by human agency, and vaulted. The witnesses would be Pepper's maid and Grove's: but they didn't need to be present for the act, in fact, better not. The flowers: one must have flowers. Arrangements of stephanotis and tuberose to flank the vellum documents. A bouquet of white roses and ivy for Grove, an orchid corsage for Pepper, a manly version of the same for Lukoil. The air of the room had a faint whiff of unpleasant odours masked, disagreeing with the flower scents.

She's a hard little nut, thought Ehsan. *I give her that. Don't know if I could live with a six-week-old corpse in the house myself.*

Pepper had dressed for the occasion, in the new Sigurtian look (*tactless, in the circumstances*, thought Ehsan) and as always there was no doubt who, or *what*, Pepper was dressed for ... The open-necked shirt was crossed by bandolier sashes that negated those fashionable tiny tits: finished at the hips with a pair of cute toy pistols. Boyish half-boots, and the tail of the shirt *curtailed* to the extent that every scampering move offered a glimpse of pert buttocks, nicely cupped by very tight 'Sigurtian' leggings. Oh my, an errant petal has fallen onto the rug.

Pepper has to pick it up, bending over with her backside to the prospective father-in-law.

Pepper's tricks, seen with a cold eye, were like a cartoon show, a cultural history exhibit: this was the way of a certain, long-gone, whorish little world—

'You never fail to get a rise out of me, Pepper.'

Pepper bridled, glanced at herself in her eye soc', and perched herself on the edge of Yu's desk.

'This is how it goes, Ehsan. Grove affirms the marriage contract. We two both affirm it. Her settlement is immediately transferred to the Yu family, and I put it in a fund nobody knows about but me: for safe keeping. She's so lucky! Poor Vale has hardly anything, you know. Then you and I take a trip to Balas/Shet. The City of Lilies, the name itself conjures up such romance. And there you *marry* me, Ehsan.' She peeked at him, coquettishly, through a mist of red-gold. Her hair was treated to make it 'weightless'; the squirming curls gave her the look of some lively, poisonous sea-creature. 'We'll honeymoon on the Shet orbital archipelago. The climate is delightful, the gravity is a dream, and they cater specially for human, I mean, Blue visitors. You *promise* you'll marry me, don't you?'

'Your beauty has me by the balls, Pepper.'

Pepper didn't need his 'promise'. She knew he had to please her. She had seen them start to panic, after the General's stroke, and had soon figured out what it was about. Secrets, long buried, that would be exposed when Yu died ... That would be so like the General! To booby-trap his own death!

It was Pepper who'd spotted the significance of Grove's marriage settlement. A man on the run needs *cash*, anonymous funds, he can't use his own credit. She didn't give a damn about Scolari and felt no compunction about double-crossing Amal. Amal, besides other *detestable* qualities, could not marry his father's concubine. Or maybe he could, she wasn't sure, but it would look indecent. Anyway, he was ugly, and had let himself go. Ehsan was presentable.

'You don't have to *do* anything, you know. We can be chaste.'

She skipped down from the desk and pretended to examine the documents again, wiggling her butt. Ehsan accepted the invitation: came over and groped her soundly, until she giggled and squealed.

'Funx that. I bet your arse is as tight as a virgin boy's.'

'Let go of me, bad boy. I must fetch Grove.'

Pepper trotted off, high as a kite on the thrill of her own scheming. She was terrifying. At any moment she might decide to sell the story to a tabloid agent, or confide in a sexy robocop ... Lukoil, trapped by circumstance, resumed his sardonic communion with the dead. *She really is the stupidest, meddling little tart alive, Yu. What the funx did you ever see in her?*

LXXVI

Pepper had Grove brought to the study, and dismissed the footman. The bride, robed in white, a white lace shawl around her shoulders, lay on the daybed where General Yu had been accustomed to take a nap after lunch; if he was at home. She looked the very ideal of a delicate young lady: Amal Yu's child bride, who would never leave the house again, whose frail health was proof of her perfection. Pepper fidgeted around. Lukoil dealt with his daughter, who was displaying a degree of passive resistance.

'Where is Amal? Shouldn't he be here?'

'You don't need to see your bridegroom until the wedding day, Grove. This is just an exchange of contracts.'

'I don't know if I want to do it, Papa.'

She looked up at him, the blue of her eyes seeming blotted into the whites. She hadn't been eating, she was having breathing difficulties, which partly explained her extreme lassitude – but from somewhere she'd found the stubbornness of a creature that knows it has one little scrap of power.

'You were warned, Grove,' said Ehsan, sternly. 'Your reputation is tarnished, you must marry, and Amal's willing. Will you have him, or would you prefer to go down the gravity well? That's your choice.'

'I wonder where *Vale* is—' remarked Pepper suddenly, brightly.

'Grove does not need a maid of honour, Pepper. Forget Vale.'

'No, but I wonder where she *is*? She was around this morning, she spent some time with her poor papa, but now I can't seem to *locate* her. She can't have left the house, of course. She must be on the lower level, visiting the MacBrides or, er, seeing to something in the kitchen—'

Ehsan looked to his daughter. Grove had closed her eyes; she seemed to have suddenly fallen asleep. 'Lock that gate—' he snapped.

'Why should I lock the gate, won't that look suspicious?'

'Do as I say.'

Ehsan sprang across the room. He had instantly jumped to the right conclusion: he knew what it was to be the father of a wilful young lady. Pepper gave a little scream of horror as he attacked the dead man. Ehsan pulled out the fine chain that was still clasped around the General's throat.

No chaperone key.

'What's going on?' squeaked Pepper.

'Where's the key to Vale's chaperones?'

'Oh—! Oh, I never touch that. Legally Vale is *not* my daughter, you know – in law I'm only the concubine. It's not my fault if I have no rights—'

Ehsan felt the mindless red-gold tentacles closing around him. He had an impulse, sharp as the realisation that Vale had escaped, to grab his daughter and remove her bodily from the scene. It came too late. Pepper, who had a passionate aversion to taking orders, had not locked the study gate. Vale Scolari emerged through the appearance of antique hardwood, closely followed by the Sigurtian princelings.

'*Vale!*' exclaimed Pepper. 'Why are you dressed like that, for heaven's sake? Where have you been? I've been looking for you all over the place.'

'I don't know what you think you're doing here,' said Ehsan, brutally, to the Sigurtians, 'but you're interrupting a private ceremony. I'll have to ask you to leave. Before I throw you out.'

'You won't throw anybody out.' Vale dropped to her knees by the couch, and took her friend's lax hand. 'Grove? Grove? Has he done it? Oh God, has he? He can't force you. Tell him you don't consent.'

'Maybe it's for the best,' whispered Grove, opening drowsy eyes. 'I don't know what else to do ... I must marry ... I feel so faint.'

'You see!' cried Vale, frantically. 'Listen to her, she isn't Grove! He's destroyed her, he's driven her out of her mind—!'

'You know,' said D"fydd, affably, 'I don't think we *will* leave, Lukoil. Grove's obviously not herself, and I have a feeling a change of air might help. No offence meant, sir, but you'd better let your daughter come with us. If she convinces us she's a happy bride you can resume the ceremony at a later date. Right now, this does not look—'

The prince made his little speech while advancing, as if casually, on the bridal couch. Lukoil did not wait for him to finish. He floored the young man with a ferocious roundhouse punch—

'Have you gone mad?' shrieked Pepper, running at him, waving her arms. Lukoil swept the tentacled bitch aside, but the other Sigurtian was upon him. Ch'ro leapt, Ehsan swatted him, but the bat-boy came back for more. Permanent Secretary Lukoil was gripped by a vicious, four-legged whipcord *thing*, inhuman limbs like pincers around his ribs, an inexorable clawed grip pulling back his head: razor-edged incisors bared.

'What are you *doing?*' shouted Ch'ro: unable, as always, to bring himself to use teeth in a ruckus. '*Why* did you attack D"fydd—?'

Lukoil threw the Sigurtian across the room, and stooped to pick up his daughter. Pepper was fainting in an armchair. 'Stop it! Stop it!' yelled Vale, fighting Lukoil's hard hands. 'Leave her alone!'

The study gate opened once more. The Princess of Bois Dormant stepped through, accompanied by the Yus' steward, MacBride. MacBride immediately locked the gate. D"fydd sat up, shaking his ears. Ch'ro peeled himself off the piece of furniture that had blocked his involuntary flight. The Princess surveyed the scene.

'My Lord Prince, noble Neuendan ... How unexpected. Is this your idea of resting quietly at home?'

'I brought them,' cried Vale. 'I *needed* them—'

Ehsan Lukoil stared at the Princess for a moment, breathing hard, dismissed her presence as something he couldn't deal with, and turned on MacBride. 'Let me pass,' he ordered, savagely.

'Excuse me, sir. With all respect, I was paged by a security alert to attend a disturbance in this room. I'm afraid I'll have to ask you to—'

'MacBride,' said the Princess. 'Consider. We have no reason to detain the Permanent Secretary. '

Lukoil's departure froze them all, as if they expected his instant return, his renewed violence. Then Grove roused herself. She struggled to rise from the daybed. 'Where is the marriage contract? I must sign. Oh, my heart is beating so fast, I can't get my breath. I must sign!'

Vale laughed, in passionate relief. 'They *didn't* get her to affirm! Grove, it's over! Relax, girl! You held out, you've *beaten* them, he's gone—'

'I can't breathe,' gasped the bride, seeming unaware that Vale had spoken. She tried to stand and failed, which increased her distress. 'Where is the contract? I would be better if I affirmed it. This weight on my chest would go away. I must, I must do my duty. Let me affirm it—'

'Maybe we should let her do it?' suggested D"fydd, very disturbed at this sight, and feeling himself to blame ... 'Just to calm her? It won't be binding. We're all here to witness it was under duress—'

The Princess and MacBride looked at each other.

'No,' said the Princess, with a fearful presentiment – *they're not afraid of overkill, these criminals.* 'I think that would be most unwise.'

She knelt by the couch, looked into Grove's face and took her wrist, against the girl's fretful resistance. 'How long has this been going on?'

'I don't know,' whispered Vale. 'She hasn't been herself since New Year. But this is worse, much worse—'

'I think we need a doctor.'

The Yus' physician, a dignified, sixty-something Blue Rus named Raisa Hossein, was swiftly summoned. Astonished to find that it was not to attend the General's final crisis, she examined the patient perfunctorily and glared around, especially scandalized by the presence of *male* strangers.

'What has been happening here? What has happened to Madame?' Pepper was still collapsed, eyes closed. Grove continued to struggle, repeating her senseless mantra, gasping for breath, feebly and horribly intent on getting to the desk, where the white flowers flanked that fateful tablet—

'All will be explained,' said the Princess. 'Let's concentrate on Miss Lukoil. There's something strange in this sudden collapse.'

'Nothing strange at all. The young lady is a little overexcited, and no wonder. Please clear the room. I'll administer a mild sedative.'

'I suggest you check her subderms for malfunction.'

Dr Hossein stared, greatly affronted. Some things must *never* be mentioned, especially not in mixed company. 'Miss Lukoil's *chaperones* are none of my business, nor yours, madam. I'll scan her for the source of these breathing difficulties, although I'm sure the cause is purely nervous – young ladies are prone to hysterical symptoms. These stereotyped phrases, the behaviour we call *overcompensating docility*, it's typical of her kind—'

'Shut up!' shouted Vale. 'If you can't treat Grove like a human being, get out of here. Oh, God, I should have called the Dostoe emergency service!'

'*Miss Vale!* The emergency doctor is *a bot*! Its records may be viewed by male eyes, I could not possibly allow the Permanent Secretary's daughter to be attended by a *bot*!'

Grove had fallen back, panting and half-unconscious. Vale bit back a furious riposte. The doctor, fuming with indignation, applied a mild sedative and an oxygen mask; and passed a scanner over the patient's torso, studying the results on her 'black bag' screen. Abruptly, her expression changed. She rose, moved away from the couch and beckoned MacBride and the Princess.

'This young woman is dying of acute heart failure, and I cannot ascertain the cause. It may, after all, be a fault in the chaperones. I'd like to give her a heart and lung bypass: but the problem is CNS, and the CV bypass is electrical. An electrical field stronger than ambient, when we do not know the cause of the brain damage, might do irreparable harm. We must contact the Permanent Secretary at once—'

'We must save her life!' snapped MacBride. 'Remove those damned subderms!'

'Impossible. You forget yourself. I cannot act without her father's authority.'

The Princess and MacBride stared at each other in consternation. Vale was intent on Grove; Pepper was still fainting. Ch'ro and D"fydd stood back, shocked and helpless. Something moved, like a rock shifting. They all heard a sound, unlike anything produced from a numinal biped throat—

'Hi-hoc. H'iye– S'oc—'

General Yu had spoken. He was leaning out of his chair, despite the net of fibres feeding into every vein. He had raised one arm. He hit the dead hand against the side of his temple, once, twice: and plummeted forward, his body hitting the floor as a dead weight.

'Eye soc'—!' cried Vale. 'Oh, my God—'

The doctor, moving with all speed, took a pair of nano-tweezers: the tips snaked, invisibly, behind Grove's left eyeball, and she withdrew a tiny bead of ceramic alloy. Almost immediately, Hossein gave a sigh of intense relief. 'Her vital signs are recovering. My God, what a horror averted, and on her wedding day ... In my opinion, a young lady should be forbidden to use those things, they're a menace!'

The Princess had taken possession of the tweezers. She dropped the soc' into a sterile vial: sealed it and tagged it, with her own and MacBride's affirmation. The doctor wisely decided to make no comment on this move, and busied herself – having checked that the dead man had no further need for medical attention – making Grove comfortable.

'That explains why Lukoil went crazy!' exclaimed D"fydd. 'He'd turned her eye soc' into a murder weapon. That's why he tried to carry her off, he had to get her away, once he knew the game was up—!'

'With respect, Prince D''fydd,' said MacBride, 'let's not speculate.'

The study was oddly quiet, as if a storm had passed through it, leaving silence and debris. The Princess went to look down at General Yu's body. His rugged old face in profile was calm, as if relaxed in sleep. '*Between the stirrup and the ground, he mercy sought and mercy found*—'

'What's that?' asked D''fydd, who had joined her.

'Something my Sergeant would say. He says we shouldn't refuse last-aid to our worst enemies, and I've come to believe he's right.'

'Of course he's right.'

Pepper Lily had decided it was safe to regain consciousness. She stumbled across the room, and fell on her knees beside her General.

'What shall I do? What shall I do!'

'I think you should send for Amal,' suggested the Princess, straight-faced. 'It would be proper. His father is dead. He ought to be told.'

'Amal! That bastard! *He killed his father!* He and Lukoil together. They plotted this, it was all their idea, oh, I can prove it, don't you worry. This is murder! My poor Yu, struck down, when I always said he could recover—'

'Calm yourself, Pepper. The Violent Death Team is on its way.'

LXXVII

Ehsan found himself struggling – as he rode, hard and fast, through the fashionable traffic – to put it all together. Was it Yu's stroke, was it the break-in, was it the Princess of Bois Dormant, and her inexplicable interest in a shifty old sponger? It must have been the break-in: a disproportionate police response, and he, a Permanent Secretary, unable to get an explanation. So the alarm bells had started ringing, although there was no material reason ... He remembered deciding he'd have to murder his daughter and take her money, a last-resort plan he'd hatched long ago. Not much of a murder: young ladies – synthetic 'human beings' – were never long-lived, and he'd be saving her from Amal. But how in hell had he let himself get snared in Pepper Lily's ludicrous scheming? She'd presented herself as an indispensable ally. He had seen an incontinent babbler who must be silenced, and without adding to the suspicious deaths that were beginning to accumulate—

If she imagined she could force him into marriage, if she didn't realise she was signing her death warrant, then he'd be a fool not to take advantage. She's lost her meal-ticket, she leaves Speranza, she's never heard of again, what could be more likely?

It all looked so damned unnecessary now, a flailing at nothing, a fit of needless panic that had brought him to the brink of catastrophe.

By the time he reached his mansion on the Old Dip he'd reviewed the damage, forgiven himself and moved on. A footman took his ride. In his rooms he briskly wrote himself out of the system, destroyed the cheat (with an entanglement bomb that would take out every copy) and broke out the concealed weapons. A note for Jacob? *Whatever there was between us, it was over long ago* ... No. Words are for women, actions speak for men. His rooms were like a suite in an expensive spa: austere, anonymous, empty. *I never lived here. I am someone else. I am always someone else*. He chose a closed sedan, a neutral bodymask, and left the mansion by a private exit.

The address he wanted was also on the Old Dip, in a slightly run-down apartment block mostly occupied by lower-rank officials. He put the car in his pocket and walked up the stairs: in the dark because the living-presence-activated lights did not perceive him. Strange how Speranza immediately seemed more real, when it didn't know you existed. He emerged onto a well-lit cul-de-sac, and saw the guard outside Haku's front door. Who had ordered *that*? Lukoil stepped back, instinctively, although he had nothing to fear.

Why was he here? He'd made up his mind – after the break-in, when he knew Yu was likely to be subject to a Post-Mort interrogation – that if he was forced out, he'd kill 'Prisoner Haku' on his way to the exit. Fixed ideas, the enemy of all Seniors, be flexible, be flexible. But since when had Haku merited protection? The guard stretched his arms, and yawned. Ehsan saw that what he'd mistaken for a robocop shell was a Green Belt in body armour.

Deeply shocked, not so much that Haku had a human minder, but at his mistake (he had *seen* a robocop: failure to interpret sense perceptions, another of those traps), he retreated. Back down the stairs. He felt himself moving, smoothly, into the alert calm of emergency mode. Before he reached the street he'd dumped the sedan in a recycle bin and changed his bodymask. Perfectly at ease again, he took the RT: moving with the populace like a ghost. He stayed on the train, beyond the public network. At the last intersection on the Horizontal he crossed over to the Right Speranza platform. Gates did not exist for him, and physical barriers on the rapid-transport network, such as the carriage doors, were automatic. Why have the RT running out to Right Speranza at all? In case of what impossible emergency? The RT system was wildly over-determined, something he'd protested against in his time. The answer was always why not, better safe than sorry, Speranza can afford it—

That man MacBride. Damn his insolence. I shall *destroy* him.

He fully expected to return, after a few months, maybe a year. All a political leader asks is that you show some discretion. When it came down to it, he was guilty of nothing more than *gently* coercing his daughter into a very suitable marriage; and an outburst of temper. Grove's death would probably never be seen as suspicious. If it were, he'd like to see them prove he'd been responsible. A defective eye soc', for funx's sake. He hardly knew why he was taking such extreme precautions, but it felt right. Obey your instincts. Every wise rabbit has more than one exit from his burrow. He smiled, sourly, as he remembered the source of that aphorism. The old Swimmer had loved his aphorisms ...

Let Amal and Pepper tear each other to pieces. Let Javed and the monster Zubindah sit tight, and see if they could survive. Lukoil's position was secure. He was *necessary* to Domremy. Drop out of sight, admit nothing, and all things will pass. My God, compared with the screw-ups that had plagued the so-called Baykonur Conspiracy, this was hardly a wrinkle.

Suited-up, he headed for the conventional-space docking bays. Of course, he'd never had the slightest intention of letting Pepper drag him off to some crap Shet tourist habitat, clumsily adapted for Blue idiots. Unlike the rest, Lukoil had never forgotten that Speranza was a space station. It was not some nowhere, only accessible by transit. It sat within reach of the Blue, the original and enduring power base. He'd always kept a pod fuelled, supplied and ready for adventure, a resource he'd trained the populace, and his colleagues, to see as natural: part of Lukoil's superb lifestyle. He would take the long trek, the slingshot route back to Earth Orbit, and dock with one of the orbitals. Six billion kilometres of interminable boredom, since he'd be solo, but he was confident that he would be welcomed. He knew his way around.

On foot. Right Speranza was anti-technology, another example of the mania for Space Age austerity, surviving under the veneer of 'Domremy's build'. Suggest any change over here, and you get a barrage of, *Let us never forget the cold dark. Let us never be trapped by our sophistication.* So much for being invisible to the system. At each bulkhead, and there seemed a fantastic number, he had to stop. Enter a manual code. Wait for the pressure and air to equalize, step over the sill. The sill seemed damned unnecessary. It had been a long day and he was tired.

Something about a break-in, and then Yu had a stroke. An utterly disproportionate police response ... Lukoil hated to catch himself repeating himself, but he wasn't having a Senior episode: he was rehearsing the facts. He wanted to get them fixed in his head. He stumbled over the final sill, beyond which he was 'on the docks', in the space between the inner and outer skins: and dropped his helmet. It bounced away, leisurely, back into the airlock. He lunged after it, fell awkwardly, and the bulkhead closed on him.

It did not withdraw, because it didn't know he was there. It reported a problem: the smart material switched to nanomode, sealed itself around the unidentified object, and went on trying to close. The suit, though unaware of a living presence inside, maintained integrity as a first priority: but the pressure was inexorable, appalling. Before long the soft body inside the unbreached shell was crushed, organs bursting, blood exploding from eyes and mouth: but time had no meaning where Ehsan was. For him, the dying seemed to last for ever.

LXXVIII

The preliminary hearing in the complex case known as the 'Dostoe Break-In' was held in one of the smaller courts of the Halls of Justice, an octagonal chamber clad in time-hallowed grey-green ceramic. Raked seats looked inward, as in a theatre, toward the judge's bench, the witness stands, the court officers' desks. All those mortal persons who were liable to be called as witnesses, by the prosecutor or the counsel for the accused, were physically present. Javed Scolari and Amal Yu, who were being held under house arrest, chose not to appear; Scolari's daughter likewise stayed away. Pepper Lily, who had made contradictory but extremely damaging statements against her stepson, the Scolaris and the deceased Ehsan Lukoil, had been permitted to attend the hearing 'in virtual form'. She wore black, a hat with veils; she wept, she did not seem aware that she was herself likely to be on trial.

Ehsan's body had been found by a police search party, and was still with the Violent Death Team.

The judge, His Honour Cyprian Lalian, a severely beautiful Balas Senior generally known by his 'Blue' name, explained the nature of 'bit-cop' evidence, using a development in Speranza's current affairs as his example ... A few days before this, Domremy Li had launched the Mallorn Recovery Project – employing the tactic anciently known as a 'U-turn', as a pre-emptive defence against the Dostoe scandal. 'We have all been hearing a great deal about "virtual worlds",' said Cyprian. 'Perhaps most of us, most of the time, forget that Speranza itself is a "virtual world". Every individual "on board", every last molecule of Speranza's air, is coded. Those who fear that their every move is scrutinised are mistaken, but this great mass of code can be searched by what is vulgarly known as "number-crunching", and associations between different "software objects" may be established to varying degrees of certainty – within a short or an excessively long period of time, depending on the "cribs" available. The fact that the "Dostoe cheat" was found in Dyke Blazer's possession provided a very strong "crib", a known element – reducing the volume, so to speak, of information that must be searched, bit by bit, for the previous possessor. When the police tell us that there is "probable cause", we know that investigation is in order. When the police tell us there is "mathematical proof" that a mortal individual was in possession of a certain intellectual property, and transferred a copy of this property to another mortal, we may regard the transaction as proven. Thus, in this case, we may state beyond refutation that a crime against the system has been committed, which attracts a severe penalty. If found guilty, the defendants will be stripped of Speranza citizenship, and denied access to the Buonarotti network for the rest of their mortal lives.'

Javed Scolari and Amal Yu would stand trial. Zubindah Scolari, and Pepper Lily, charged with the offences of 'providing a venue for serious crime against the system' and 'withholding knowledge of serious crime', would likewise stand trial. The prosecutor let it be known that the police intended to reopen a case of the same crime against the system, dating from the time of civil unrest, and there might be further charges. This was noted. Pepper Lily's counsel reported that the Yu family, resident on the Blue, had declined to cover the charges of her defence out of the Yu estate: and hereby applied for legal aid. This was granted.

(The General's will had been found. Vale's marriage settlement was protected; the residue of the estate would return to the General's still-living daughter on the Blue. Pepper had been left her jewels, her wardrobe, and a small amount of credit.)

His Honour Cyprian found that the evidence against the late Ehsan Lukoil, victim of misadventure, as the mortal creator of the code, was insufficient. Another, unrelated charge of tampering with his daughter's eye soc' was uncontested, but strong doubt as to his intention must remain. As a 'Traditionalist' he had a duty to his daughter, and perhaps her long-term welfare was the thought uppermost in his mind when he took steps to ensure her acceptance of what must have seemed a very suitable match—

Having exhausted the break-in, His Honour Cyprian moved to the late General Yu's Post-Mortem testimony; and the shielded data storage that had been discovered in his skull. The documents contained therein included the General's will, and an affirmed contract of marriage between

People's Army star cadet Yeying and Caspian Konoe-Hosokawa, dated some twenty-four standard years ago ... The judge apologised to 'Miss Konoe-Hosokawa' and her grandmother (who was attending the hearing in virtual presence, bi-locating from Japan), for the painful intrusion. The prosecutor then enlarged on the significance of the latter document, as new evidence in case of the 'Baykonur Conspiracy'. He called 'Miss Konoe-Hosokawa' to the witness stand. Ye testified that she'd had no knowledge of her parentage, but she had been surgically rendered a so-called '*zombie whore*', in childhood: a fate from which she'd been rescued by the Princess of Bois Dormant. The Prosecutor then called the Princess herself. When she rose to take the stand, the court officers (who were bots, of course, like the prosecutor and the defence counsel) rose and bowed; in deference to one of *those* Blues.

She was questioned on the Konoe-Hosokawa case, which had come to her attention by means not relevant to this hearing. Her session with the Superintendent of the Special Ankang was accepted as material evidence, to be forwarded to the Blue authorities.

'It seems,' said the judge, 'that General Yu believed that the proof of this marriage, and the survival of the Konoe-Hosokawa heiress, served as a form of insurance, should past crimes come to light. Ironically he has furnished the police, here and on the Blue, with reason to reconsider the whole Baykonur case, and his own supposed "innocence" in that affair.'

There was no mention of a Yu servant girl named Bibi, who had died long ago: but the judge found that the Third Empire's request for extradition, in the case of Amal Yu, and Zubindah and Javed Scolari, was well supported.

The Princess slipped away, alone, before the end of the hearing. She sat by a 'dry fountain' of coloured light, in an empty courtyard of the Halls of Justice complex, thinking of many things. A figure, familiar and unfamiliar, came smiling towards her, through the veils of memory.

'Mahmood,' said Bibi. 'Is it over?'

'All but the summing up.' He looked well. He had been praised from the bench for the determined and prompt action that had saved Grove Lukoil's life. 'Princess, something tells me won't meet again. I want you to know, your return has been an inspiration to me.'

'On the contrary, I'm afraid I've destroyed your livelihood. What will happen to the Dostoe household now?'

'Most of the staff will return to the Blue. Speranza will pay for their gravity rehabilitation if they need it. Lady Nef's surviving daughter lives in the Great House in Kirgiz: your childhood home. They'll join that household. I'm going to try and make sure the dogs go home too … Ogul and I intend to stay on Speranza. We'll keep house for Miss Vale as long as she needs us. Beyond that, all I know is that I shall live a better life.'

'I believe you will,' said Bibi.

'And Ogul too. Well, I must be off. Goodbye, Princess.'

'And Ogul too. Goodbye, Mahmood, I'm very glad we met again.'

La Tartine, where she and Honesty had met Francois and his Aleutian friends, was now intolerably big and busy, a favourite with the tourists. She spotted Francois at another kiosk, a modest venue with only five or six tables, at the foot of the Nebula Facade, and went to join him. 'Is it over yet?'

'I have no idea. I was no longer required, and I find that form of numinal biped ritual excruciating. What happened to you?'

'I met Mahmood. He's gone back to Dostoe now.'

'What a charade. Self, I'm glad Ehsan isn't alive to stand trial, he'd have walked away. He didn't leave himself vulnerable to the bit-cops, and naturally, he is to be protected—'

'Be reasonable. You cannot expect Domremy to do without Jacob Mungea, therefore Lukoil must rest in peace—'

They were interrupted by a frankly elderly individual, lean and spry in his characteristic blue greatcoat. Haku had been required to attend the hearing, but neither the prosecution nor the defence had called him to the stand. He was looking mightily relieved.

'Princess! I won't stay, I just wanted to offer my congratulations. How good of you to take an interest in Miss Konoe-Hosokawa's case, what a detective you'd make, and how you are vindicated! And by the way, many thanks for the hot tip. Mallorn: I'm going to make a bit on that. Francois! Good to see you looking so well. Old days, eh?' The old man winked, patted the Aleutian's shoulder and trotted off.

'If you're looking for something to grumble about,' said the Princess, 'there he goes: the false prophet you and Lady Nef and the General served, to your destruction. The excuse for the Baykonur Conspiracy, the cause of all our woes. Living happily ever after.'

'Ah no.' Francois shook his head, shrugging warmly. 'No, no, you've got to love Haku. He has *charm*, the old sinner. Always did.' He picked a wandering cell from his throat and offered it: a tiny snapshot of everything he was, right here, right now. Bibi took the bolus between her lips, and felt – as near as any mortal can – what it is to be an Aleutian. To be *this* Aleutian.

'Well, anyway: I wish Honesty could have seen that. The Young Emperor, actually stopping to talk to me! What a coup.'

Francois recalled *The Thoughts of Youth*. The girl in the blue dress, gazing at sea and sky, dreaming of the undiscovered country of her own life. <I remember you when you were a little girl.>

<Then we are quits,> said the Princess, following him into Silence. <Because I remember you when you were a little boy, so to speak; quite recently. With a horrible taste for playing with mortals.>

<If I may play with you, the rest of them have nothing to fear.>

<Then I must accept.>

LXXIX

Ye and the Sigurtians stayed to the bitter end, in solidarity with Grove and Vale. The Princess's household officers stuck it out too. They left the Halls of Justice after dark, feeling drained and obscurely sanctified. 'We are fools,' announced D"fydd, laying his head on a café table and rubbing his weary ears. 'Do you realise, we'll have to endure all that *again*, at the trial?'

'Nah,' said Drez. 'You only have to turn up for your own little bit, and you can prob'ly get away with doing it in b-loc.'

'You two won't even be called,' added Grove, 'since it looks as if my dear departed parent didn't do anything wrong.'

'Do you *mind* him getting off?' asked Ch'ro, seriously.

'I don't care if the squashed corpse was a fake and he's starting a new life on Ki/An, as long as I never see or hear from him again.'

'Poor old Pepper,' remarked Vale, viciously. 'She's going to be deported, at the least – if her counsel manages to shut her up before they send her to Fenmu. Down the gravity well, and no more treatments, it must be her worst nightmare.' She looked at Ye. 'I don't know what to say about my father, and what he did to you. I knew he had a dirty side, I didn't know how bad it was. But I loved him.'

'He was supposed to have me killed, and here I am,' said Ye. 'Set that down on the clean side of the balance sheet. And he saved Grove's life: when it could do him no good at all. Set that down too.'

'We're all in the hands of the Systems,' said Sergeant Aswad. 'The best of us can fall, the worst of us can do a good deed. The Halls of Justice may punish, but it's not for us to judge.'

The young people were silent. Col and Drez rolled their eyes. D"fydd warded off a sombre mood by demanding if anyone knew how His Honour Cyprian managed to get through those mind-numbing, serpent-length sentences – without *once* visibly drawing breath. Finally, the soldiers, the Sigurtians and Ye left for the streets, to make a night of it. Grove pleaded tiredness, and Vale stayed with her.

'Alone at last,' said Vale.

Grove ran her hands over her cropped head. *Alone*, no chaperones buried in her scalp. No guardian. Jacob Mungea had been relieved of that role: the judge had declared the appointment null and void. She was a free woman, a free citizen of Speranza. It was hard to believe.

'Perhaps I should get my ears fixed to match my Sigurtian crop. And a black fur domino, of course. What do you think?'

'I love you just the way you are.'

Blue-eyed, exquisite Grove looked startled, but only for a moment. 'You know,' she said, 'I've a feeling you and I may have more in common than we ever realised.' She took Vale's hand, kissed the palm, and closed Vale's fingers over the kiss. 'My lioness. Your place or mine?'

LXXX

It was dawn, standard time. On the floor of the Exchange the gamblers who'd played all night were meeting the early risers. The Open University pages were running small-audience studies on the Mallorn Project: the fantastical feat of building a Torus big enough to reverse what had happened to the Sixth Planet. D"fydd wandered through the mansion, flipping channels, wondering why he was awake. What had woken him? He wasn't sure. *So we get a sixth planet, so the Inflation begins ... But what's left,* he wondered, *in this teeming, prosperous, amoral asteroid, of the hope Ch'ro and I came to find, of the flower that buds continually but never blooms?*

Speranza—

He wandered into the breakfast room, made a low window with a sweep of his hand and sat looking out. He imagined he could feel something uncanny: some hint of the nearness of the Torus, a hangover from the trip to Mallorn. That's numinal biped nature, the weirdness and the marketplace, entangled together ... The Princess was gone, she'd left the station. He wondered if he would ever see her again. His view of the mansion lawns shook itself and reformed. He screwed his eyes shut, and opened them again. There was a transit-capable pod, *not* the *Spirit*: a new model, not all that beautiful, sitting there suspended, a hand's breadth above the turf.

He paged Ch'ro, insistently, half-convinced he was dreaming.

He wasn't. The pod belonged to Col Ben Phu, Drez Doyle and Sergeant Aswad. They were setting up in business together (what kind of business was yet to be decided). They'd come to offer the Sigurtians one last adventure, trying the paces of the new acquisition.

'But where's the Princess?' demanded D"fydd.

Col shook her head. 'Haven't a clue.'

'I think you have,' said Ch'ro. 'Speranza System wouldn't have let you park a pod here, if you weren't still running errands for one of *those* Blues.'

Drez grinned. 'You're too sharp for us, Scrappy. How will you lads travel, eh? Awake or asleep?'

D"fydd chose the dreamtime. He didn't have the heart for a fugue narrative without the Princess, in a ship that was not the *Spirit*.

When he woke she was looking down at him. 'Welcome,' she said.

He sat up in the couch, and took her hand. They twined their fingers together, Sigurtian claws, flat Blue nails. The unnaturally clean and tidy habitat was deserted, no sign of the soldiers, or Ch'ro. They disembarked together, without having spoken another word.

The sky was clear aquamarine: a small sun, almost as white as the sun of Sigurt's World, burned brightly, a little beyond the zenith. The pod had made landfall on a raised shelf of sandy stone above a seashore. Behind it, an endless backdrop, rose the trees: not in massive monoculture like the forest of Mallorn, but immensely varied, green of every shade, leaves and branches and boles in every form of growth. A thorny creeper, with white, four-petalled flowers, filled the understorey and sent tendrils across the greenish sand. 'Where are we?' breathed D"fydd.

'Can you guess?'

'This is Bois Dormant.'

'Yes.'

He turned to the silver-flickering blue expanse that stretched limitless as the trees. 'I've never seen a water ocean before. Is it salt, can I taste it?'

'Go ahead.'

They walked along the shore, hand in hand. D"fydd licked salt water from his claws, fascinated.

'Once upon a time—' she began.

'What does that mean?'

'It's a Blue expression: it means, let me tell you a story. Once upon a time there was a little girl who lived in the White Rock caves. Her name was *Gwibiwr*, which means traveller, but she was called Bibi—'

She told him the story of her childhood, and how it had ended. The choice she had been given by the General's wife, her life at the Great House. Her short career as a cadet, under the tutelage of Francois le

Champi; her college education, her first love, how she and her friends had fallen foul of the Baykonur Conspiracy – and a thousand other things.

'I was younger than you are, and engaged to be married, when I was taken away, for the third time in my life, from everything I knew, and everything I thought lay ahead of me. You've heard that there was a young Blue woman, betrothed to the Myot prince, who survived the massacre and bore a hybrid child, and that she died later. That was Bibi, that was me. I did not die. As soon as my son could live without my blood they sent me to Fenmu, to join my mistress, so I couldn't testify against the criminals who had betrayed us. I never saw him, not once. Not until many years later, when I tracked him down to the coffee shop of The Caprice, on the Lateral Canal in Detta'aan—'

They sat on a heap of boulders, above the tide. D''ffyd gazed out to sea. Lines of little white clouds were drifting along the horizon. He had already known the truth. He had heard it on Mallorn, without grasping it: it had been working through him, unconscious memory—

'You must have hated me.'

'You saved my life,' said Bibi. 'Once at the time of the massacre, and then a second time, when I found you again. Lady Nef had given me everything she possessed, and tried to convince me not to waste my life on revenge. But when I left Fenmu, I was thinking of nothing else. I was eaten alive by hatred, half-mad with grief and loneliness. Col and Drez and Rohan couldn't help me, nor could Francois, the way he was then. But I met you, I began to love you, and I got better.'

Bibi wiped her eyes. 'Now you'll be thinking that I've had a miserable, horrible life, but it isn't true, D''fydd. Happiness is beyond good or evil fortune; joy belongs to non-duration ... I was very happy in the Great House, I was happy in Baykonur. I remember happy times when we were facing certain death in Black Wing Castle. I remember being happy even in Fenmu. When Lady Nef first taught me that I must learn to *rule myself*, I thought "ruling yourself" meant doing what you had to do to survive, but always staying the same, like a rock inside, no matter what. Now I know that if you want to rule yourself you can be as hard as you like on the outside: hard as a rock in matters of loyalty, honour, obligation. But inside you must be soft, yielding, always ready to accept change, to embrace life in whatever form it takes. That would be my advice, D''fydd, if I were giving advice: but you don't need it. I'm not religious, I don't understand what Sigurtians mean by "Grace", but I know what the term means in English, and that's the quality you have, it's what people love in you. I'm proud to know you.'

'I think you may be partial,' said D"fydd, trying to grin.

'I think you may be right,' agreed Bibi. She touched his face, tracing the outline of his cheek, which had lost the last baby down in the time she'd known him: and smiled. 'Let's find the others.'

They found *The Spirit of Eighty-Nine* parked under the eaves of the forest, on the shore of a lake; just beyond the shallow cliffs. The white sun was near to setting, the air was cool. Ch'ro and Miss Night competed at skimming pebbles over the water. Francois, joints reversed, sat and watched them, giving worthless advice. The soldiers had lit a fire, which sent up a companionable stream of smoke. The party had attracted the curiosity of one of the blue heron-deer creatures. It snorted and ambled away as Bibi and D"fydd came to join the party.

At nightfall, Sergeant Aswad laid out a cold collation, with dewy bottles of champagne, and bread from the best baker in Speranza. They ate and talked, sharing a sweet valedictory feeling. How long would it take to build the Mallorn Torus? Would Grove and Vale be happy together? What lay beyond those hills that stood in the west? Mountains, and more forest—

'I wonder, will every virgin world be forested?' said Ye. 'It seems to be a pattern. Every untouched habitable planet a dreaming wood, waiting to be woken by the rough kiss of numinal biped expansion—'

'A pattern of two,' corrected the noble Neuendan. 'First people thought there'd be a billion virgin worlds, then there were none, now we have two, and you want to say they're all going to be alike. Why should they be? The Fallen, I mean Sigurt's World, was never forested. Forests would burn like hell, every winter. And they'd have died in impact storms.'

'One could say the same for Home,' said Francois. 'Which is, by definition, the ideal world, since it is the birthplace of the immortals. We have nothing like forest, nothing you could call a tree, nor ever did.'

'With respect,' said Ye, grinning, 'if Home and Sigurt's weren't supporting numinal biped life already, nobody would be rushing to colonise. Whereas Bois Dormant will be an overnight success. Look your last, the beauty that we see will not remain unpolluted for long—'

D"fydd set a claw across her lips.

'What's this? I'm to speak no evil?'

'You're to look on the bright side,' said D"fydd, firmly. 'I *insist* that you look on the bright side, at least most of the time.'

'Will you look on the bleak side, sometimes?'

'Only when it's funny.'

The stars came out. The young people, the Princess and the Aleutian stood up for Evening Dance. Col, Drez and the Sarge sat shoulder to shoulder, watching the figures form and break, and thinking of the future. They'd taken warning on Mallorn: they knew they'd lost their officer.

'Funny how things turn out,' remarked Drez. 'Yelaixiang and D"fydd, Nightingale's child and Bibi's son. Shame our Lady didn't live to see it, she'd've liked that. Poor old Scrappy, left on the shelf.'

'May look like *the shelf* to you,' corrected Sergeant Aswad, in a superior tone. 'I say he has his mind on higher things, he's a deep one ... What d'you think about our Bibi and the Noseless, then? Doing it yet, or not?'

'If not,' said Col, judiciously, 'then very soon. Look at the way he looks at her. He's convinced she's his *trueself*, his soulmate, and he is hers.'

'I thought Francois didn't believe in any of that guff,' protested Drez.

'Tuh. So he *says*. I say there's no such bugger as a lapsed Aleutian.'

They opened another bottle, split it between them, and toasted the future in finest nature-identical Veuve Clicquot.

'Free worlds!'

When D"fydd woke again he was lying on grass, dappled shadow playing on his eyelids. He remembered that they'd left the shingle for a smoother bed, under the trees. He sat up, and Ye roused from the turf beside him: Ch'ro was still fast asleep. Filled with calm presentiment, telling each other things, in Silence, that they weren't yet ready to speak aloud, they went to the lakeside, holding hands. The boy-racer had gone. Drez, Col and Sergeant Aswad were standing on the shore, looking up.

'Where is she?'

Col handed him a tablet. He opened it and read a message, written in the Myot script: *Live, dear young people, and be happy. We'll see you again.*

Drez pointed to the sky. Several of the brightest lanterns of the night before were still shining: Bois Dormant had daystars, like Ki/An. But one white, glittering point, as he watched, twinkled and vanished. The *Spirit* had flown.